# Praise for John Barlow and the DS Romano series

'A striking debut. John Barlow's *Right to Kill* offers an intriguing plot and a gritty sense of place. I hope we'll be seeing a lot more of DS Joe Romano in the future.'
**Peter Robinson, *Sunday Times* bestselling author of the DCI Banks series**

'Yorkshire Noir at its most authentic. A gritty, uncompromising thriller, but written from the heart.'
**Paul Finch, *Sunday Times* bestselling author of the DS Mark Heckenburg series**

'Joe Romano is a modern take on the classic police procedural detective... I can't wait to read more. Welcome to the mean streets of Leeds... the best and worst that Yorkshire has to offer.'
**Russ Thomas, *Sunday Times* bestselling author of *Firewatching***

'Breakneck pace, terrific protagonist and a kick-ass sidekick... The sense of place just leaps off the page.'
**Neil Lancaster, author of *Dead Man's Grave***

'The twisted big brother to *Happy Valley*. Joe Romano is a wonderful creation... Dark, chilling, deeply psychological and utterly gripping.'
**Michael Wood, author of the DCI Matilda Darke series**

'A strong start to a new series, a smart and lively read packed with ideas about justice and vigilantism and loss.'
**Dominic Nolan, author of *Vine Street***

'An excellent, pacy story that's full of heart. It also poses some big questions about society. It's funny, dark and set in Yorkshire! DS Joe Romano is a new favourite.'
**Chris McDonald, author of the DI Erika Piper series**

'Yorkshire's got a new hero in DS Romano. Fast-paced and full of heart, *Right to Kill* is the start of a thrilling new crime series.'
**Nick Quantrill, author of the Joe Geraghty series**

## About John Barlow

John Barlow was born in the village of Gomersal, West Yorkshire, in 1967. He worked as a cabaret musician before reading English Literature at the University of Cambridge, followed by a doctorate in Language Acquisition at the University of Hull. He held teaching posts in a number of universities, before moving to Spain in 2004. He currently works as a writer, ghost writer, translator, and occasional food journalist, and lives in the Galician city of A Coruna with his partner and two sons.

## Also by John Barlow

*Eating Mammals*
*Intoxicated*
*Everything but the Squeal*
*What Ever Happened to Jerry Picco?*
*Islanders*
*Hope Road*
*Father and Son*
*The Communion of Saints*

### The DS Joe Romano Series
*Right to Kill*

# TO THE GRAVE

## JOHN BARLOW

ONE PLACE. MANY STORIES

HQ
An imprint of HarperCollins*Publishers* Ltd
1 London Bridge Street
London SE1 9GF

www.harpercollins.co.uk

HarperCollins*Publishers*
1st Floor, Watermarque Building, Ringsend Road
Dublin 4, Ireland

This edition 2022

1

First published in Great Britain by
HQ, an imprint of HarperCollins*Publishers* Ltd 2022

ISBN: HB: 978-0-00-840890-9
TPB: 978-0-00-840891-6

**MIX**
Paper from
responsible sources
**FSC** **FSC™ C007454**
www.fsc.org

This book is produced from independently certified FSC™ paper
to ensure responsible forest management.

For more information visit: www.harpercollins.co.uk/green

This book is set in 10.8/15.5 pt. Sabon

Printed and Bound in the UK using 100% Renewable Electricity at
CPI Group (UK) Ltd, Croydon, CR0 4YY

*For Merce*

# TUESDAY

# 1

Big man. Tall. Plenty of heft to his shoulders.

He's in an old grey sweatshirt and joggers. Hair cropped close, thick neck, solid, like the rest of him. He runs a hand over his scalp, fingertips following a long, thin scar behind the ear on the left side.

He sits alone at the bar, a pint of lager in front of him. Half of it left, the head long gone. When no one's looking he takes a quarter bottle of vodka from his pocket and pours a bit into his glass. For the last hour he's been nipping to the gents' for a swig. But now? *La naiba cu asta, Stefan!* Screw it. Not much left, anyway. Is good, as he likes to say. Is all good tonight. Everything's good. Only a few more weeks of this.

Then noise. Men burst through the doors, loud, mouthy. He's seen them in here before. In their late thirties. A bit older than him.

He sighs, eyes down, takes a drink.

'Now then, white boy!' one of 'em shouts across to the young man serving behind the bar. 'Stella, if you please! Four pints, in four pots.'

The barman says nothing as he takes a glass. He has dark

skin. Indian? Stef can't tell. There's so many 'round here. Indians, Kurds, Pakistanis, Poles … Difficult to tell. The people, though, they seem to know who you are, where you're from. Instantly.

Stef looks to his right. The guy ordering is average height. No excess fat on him. Taut. A worker's build, or a soldier. Dark floral shirt, expensive faded black jeans. He's up to the bar now, arms out, balled fists resting on the counter. There's a jumpiness to him, his whole body wound up tight.

The first of the lagers is set down. Then another. They all watch as the beer rises silently in the next glass. The barman doesn't even look at him.

'Come on,' says the guy. 'Joke, innit?'

'You know my name.'

The man in the shirt turns, looks at Stef, but points across the bar.

'He went to school with our lass. You ever do her, Rash?'

'No,' says Rashid as he sets another pint down on the bar.

The guy pulls back, like he's offended.

'Yer sayin' she's ugly?' He waits for an answer. 'Come on, I'm just havin' a laugh, Rash. We're gaggin' here!'

'Pump, innit.'

'Excuses, yer lazy twat!'

At his side, Stef is listening. Hardly understands a word. But he's trying to glean what he can. He likes it here, the people, their liveliness, the constant chit-chat. It's a nice place, Batley. Even the name, as if it's a joke. *Batley*, where Batman lives. But he doesn't like the man next to him. He's seen him before. Rude man.

He looks down, cradles his pint. All day he's been washing

4

cars. Seven o'clock start in the dark. Hands freezing, slices of bread and a Mars bar for lunch. How many pounds does he get for eleven hours? He feels waves of dizziness now, the vodka and lager kicking in, can't calculate. He knows that it's enough for one pint a night, plus the vodka. Cheapest thing there is. Drinks it all day, a little sip of vodka now and then, helps him get through the shift. Better than the streets of Bucharest. That's all he knows. And it's going to get better still. Him and Ana are going to make it better. Make it all good. Just a few weeks more.

The lagers are lined up.

The guy pulls out a twenty, slaps it down on the bar.

'Here. Don't keep the change.'

His mates reach in and take their pints, move off. But he stays where he is, eyeing up the glass of headless lager to his left.

'Yer beer's flat, mate.'

Stef tries not to look up, but he does.

'Is beer.'

'Yeah. Flat beer. Yer drinkin' it or tryin' to cop off wi' it?'

'Is my beer, OK?'

'Keep yer hair on, gypo.'

Stef doesn't understand.

'Hair,' the guy in the floral shirt says, reaching across and gently patting Stef a couple of times on the back of the head. 'Y'know? Keep it on.'

He waits for a response, a sarcastic grin on his stubbly face, the tendrils of a tattoo running halfway up his neck on both sides, snakes perhaps, or flames.

Nothing. Stef stares at him, uncompromising. He stares with his shoulders, with his whole body.

The smaller man shakes his head in disgust.

'Not a word!' he says as he turns.

Then he stops.

'You're in my country, mate. My boozer. Learn a bit o' the fuckin' lingo, right?'

Stef finishes his pint in a single draught, wipes a cuff across his mouth, puts the glass down.

It's his boozer, too.

A few miles away Joe Romano stands outside a chip shop on the main road through Cleckheaton. The light's fading, and he's the only one there. Behind him the odd bus growls past, a few lorries, their brakes hissing as they come up to the lights.

He thinks about eating. A fish and some peas, perhaps, cut out the chips? He catches his reflection in the window. Definitely put on a few pounds. There's a heaviness in his stance, his frame drooping a little, a pallor of disappointment to his face.

He should be out celebrating tonight with his colleagues. The verdict came in mid-afternoon. Double murder: guilty, temporary insanity. And he'd solved it, sort of. Him and Rita. It doesn't seem important now.

The defence did a number on him. What exactly was his relationship with the accused? Why had he been out drinking with her during the investigation? Did he have romantic feelings for her? He'd stood in the witness stand and denied it all. And as he gave evidence, Christine Saunders sat there, the beginnings of a smile on her face, a fondness, he thought, as she waited patiently to be judged. Two young men dead, but she appeared to be unmoved by the fact that she'd killed them. The insanity didn't look temporary to Joe.

Did he have feelings for her? He barely knew the truth anymore. He'd sensed a mystery in her, something beguiling yet melancholy, to be unwrapped carefully, almost to protect her from herself. He'd felt something that he didn't understand. Attraction, yes. But it was more than that. He'd gone with his instincts. And he'd been bloody right.

Try telling that to the jury.

His phone buzzes. A message from Rita, who is definitely out celebrating: when yer comin???

'I'm not,' he says, staring at the phone.

He's taken a week off work, desperate to avoid as much of the trial as possible. He told Rita he'd see her for drinks after the verdict. But now he can't face it.

Another message from her: yer didnt get her nickers down, but we got her sent down! whre r you? we're in the Brodrick gettin tanked.

Tanked? No. Not tonight.

No fish and chips either, he decides. There's blues on at a pub in Dewsbury, starts at eight. He'll go and nurse a pint on his own, listen to songs of disappointment and loneliness. *Woke up this morning ...* That seems about right.

Turning away before the smell of hot beef dripping gets the better of him, he makes his way back to the car.

It's a noisy sort of calm in the pub. Music playing in the background, the rumble of the TV high up in the corner. But no one's listening. They're all holding their drinks, pretending not to look at the two blokes over by the bar, whose faces are about a foot apart.

'I go,' Stef says, but his arms hang down by his sides, feet set. He's not going.

'Aye, get yersen off, lad.'

'Not good the company now.'

'Cheeky fuckin' toerag! Remember whose country yer're in! You lot still comin' over here. Workin' for next to nowt. Wanna watch that mouth o' yours, pal. Watch who yer're talkin' to!'

'No problem, friend. All friend here.'

'I'm not yer friend, yer twat! I've seen you down't car wash. Illegals, all o' yers.'

'No problem.'

'One phone call, yer on yer way home. Wherever that is. Timbuk—'

'Get off from me,' Stef says, his body tense, his accent so thick it might be saying anything.

He places a hand on the other bloke's shoulder, pushes him slowly out of the way, eyeballing him as he moves past.

'Eh, manners, sunshine!'

Stef stops, his back to the bloke now, who's started singing.

'You are the sunshine of my life ...'

Stef stares at the floor, no idea what it means. Shakes his head.

'Off yer go, gypo. Heard of Brexit, mate? You shouldn't be here. None of yer. Piss off back to Poland, yer scag.'

'You go fuck you.'

Stef starts to walks towards the door.

The punch gets him on the back of the head, dead centre, just above the neck. So hard he's blinded momentarily, rocked on his feet, falling forwards. He steadies himself, spins around, catches another punch square in the jaw. His arms come up as he drops his weight to one side. With a massive hand he grabs the bloke's blue neck as hard as he can and lifts him clean off the floor.

Joe pulls out of the deserted car park in his second-hand Mondeo and makes his way through Cleckheaton's cluttered outskirts. New builds in sickly pale brick, crammed together like Lego between rows of old terraced houses and industrial units. He looks at the houses as he drives, the glow of light behind curtains, TVs on, dinners on laps, kids arguing … Too late for him now. Divorced, his son at college. Job done, after a fashion.

On he goes, down a brightly lit dual carriageway. There's a string of these old mill towns to the south of Leeds. Strange names. Cleckheaton, Heckmondwike, Batley … pizzas and kebabs and Indian, private cabs, tatty corner shops, carpet showrooms in old chapels. Joe's a city boy, grew up in Leeds, that's his patch. But he's got to know these local towns pretty well over the last year, driving around, going over the investigation, wondering what he could've done differently with Christine Saunders. He comes to a junction, the lights at red.

He indicates, takes a left as the lights change. BATLEY, the sign says. Still an hour to kill. Why not? It's on the way. He's done this route before, done 'em all, entire evenings alone, town after town, trying to work things through …

He became a copper to help people, to do good. But that's not the job, not really. The best officers in CID ignore all the moral stuff. Right and wrong hangs around them, but it's little more than a distraction, something they've learnt to keep at bay. Work the case, get it done, move on. But him? The biggest investigation of his career, and he'd got involved, almost messed the whole thing up.

For the best part of a year he's been thinking about leaving CID, and desperately searching for a reason to stay. A double murder conviction to his name? Not a bad way to check out of serious crime. Perhaps he should go now. Get a desk job, push papers around 'til he retires. Put an end to the fiction that he can make a difference, that he can help people.

The traffic into Batley is quiet. On both sides of the road he sees the familiar hotchpotch of small businesses: spruced-up Victorian buildings with sandwich shops on the ground floor, tyre places, bed showrooms, burgers, more Indian and pizza, bargain footwear … There's an enormous mill at the crossroads, glowering down, dwarfing the road, everything. But even that's been reborn as a shopping centre.

There's an edginess here, an air of survival, something raw and brassy that he likes. These towns still have character, they're still fighting, like boxers who keep getting up off the canvas, exhausted, moving automatically, until you stop fearing for their safety and marvel at their resilience.

He turns down a side street, drives along a bit, takes another turn. Dead end. What the hell is he going to do in Batley for the next hour? He needs to sit down with Andy Mills and tell him he's thinking about a transfer. But things have been nuts in CID. Andy's up to his eyeballs in a grooming investigation. Rita too. Day after day, week after week, hacking away at the coalface of human depravity. Plus tonight they'll already be shit-faced, drinking the pain away under the guise of celebrating a case from last year, and waiting for him to join them.

He pulls in. The street runs on for about a hundred yards; another, smaller mill at the bottom, its brick and stone almost black, windows boarded up. Not a soul about.

Halfway down there's a pub. It looks rough, the kind of place you wouldn't go without good cause. He's got a nose for pubs. Every copper has. Most of the street is made up of old, squat factory units with narrow alleyways between them. There's an exhaust fitters, shuttered, lights out, and next to it an MOT garage, also closed.

It was in a town like this that he'd met *her* last year. She'd killed those young lads just a few miles from here. It's been on a loop in his mind ever since. He's just been waiting for the trial, for it all to be over.

He checks his phone. **Where r u?** from Andy, his boss and best friend.

'Where are you, Joe?' he asks himself, slipping the phone back into his pocket.

A sound. Immediately he knows it's not right. The pub door has burst open. A large man in grey joggers comes out, moving quicky. There's more noise, shouting. The guy's panting. He pauses to get his breath back, hands on knees. A bloke in a flowery shirt appears, pint glass in his hand. He's bawling, the tendons on his neck standing out, his voice so loud that the wrongness of it is unnerving.

Joe reaches for his phone, feels the adrenalin flood through his body. Already dialling, he watches as the bloke smashes the glass against the wall, then, from a position right behind the other guy, swings his arm in an arc and slams the glass into his face.

'DS Romano, Leeds CID. Urgent assistance. My present location. Ambulance and back-up now. Assault. My location now! Now!'

He leaves the call on, phone back in his pocket, out of the car, running.

'Police!' he shouts as men pile out of the pub.

The big guy has dropped to his knees, hands up to his face, blood streaming through his fingers as he tries to defend himself. He falls onto his side, cradling his head as the other bloke kicks him in the kidneys. He twists on the ground, and the man above him begins stamping on his throat, fast and precise, his arms out like an acrobat to steady himself, bawling manically.

'Police!' Joe shouts as he runs.

There's a dull, cracking thud each time the foot makes contact with the guy's neck. He curls up into a ball, the collar of his grey sweatshirt turning red, his body utterly still.

Joe has his warrant card out. He's shouting. Everybody's shouting now, but no one else intervenes. The attacker's hand is covered in blood, and there's snot bubbling from his nose, saliva around his mouth as he snarls with rage, ranting incoherently as he kicks and kicks. Joe tries to pull him away, struggles to get hold of the silky shirt. He gets an arm and shoulder between the man and his victim. A few others now weigh in, helping Joe to pull him back. It takes three of them to drag him away.

Joe drops to his knees. The victim is silent, but he's breathing. His face is a mess, one eye open, the other closed, a gash right across it, the socket pooling with blood. On his cheek a shard of glass is lodged in the flesh, more blood oozing out. Joe decides to leave it there, checks that the bloke's tongue isn't blocking his throat, hauls him carefully onto his side.

'Ambulance on the way,' he says, pressing his mouth against his ear. 'My name's Joe. Help's coming. Stay calm. Breathe.'

He kneels there, feels himself shaking, beginning to

hyperventilate. He forces himself to breathe long and deep as he searches for the guy's pulse.

He takes stock. The bloke in the floral shirt has disappeared, and no one else seems particularly concerned. A handful of men are still there, hanging back, like they're watching a street performance but losing interest.

He gets a pulse. It's fast, but steady. The guy looks up at him with his undamaged eye. Not frightened. Grateful?

Joe sinks further to the ground, sitting in the blood and dirt, feeling the wet of a puddle soak into his trousers. He hears the sound of sirens in the distance. Getting a hand under the guy's head, he tries to ease it to a better angle so the blood in the eye socket can drain away. With his fingers he gently presses the guy's cheek to try and stem the bleeding there.

Then he turns back to the men watching.

'Where's he gone?'

No one says a word. The sirens get louder. He feels the blood on his fingers, cold and sticky in the air. He twists carefully, keeping the guy's head still with one hand, and gets his phone out. Immediately it's covered in blood, the touch screen useless. He rubs it on his jacket, selects the camera. Holding it up, he takes photo after photo, the auto flash lighting up the street and the pale, surprised faces of the men, who move off back into the pub.

'Evil bastards,' Joe shouts as the last of them disappears back inside. 'Not one of you gonna help?'

The pub doors close. The sirens are loud now. Then they stop.

'What's your name?' he asks.

Nothing.

'Help's coming. You'll be OK. Help's here. What're you called?'

He hears the vehicles spinning down through the gears as they round the corner.

The guy moves, tries to speak. His breathing is fluttery, and his one decent eye closes.

'Ana,' he whispers. 'Ana. Please. Ana.'

# 2

Dewsbury and District Hospital. Joe sat in the waiting room wearing thick light-blue jogging trousers and a T-shirt that they'd given him. On the floor next to his feet was his bloodied Burton's suit, rolled up in a plastic bag. He flicked through messages from Andy and Rita, who were both at the incoherent thumbs stage, still protesting his absence.

He'd made an initial statement at the scene, and they'd brought him here for a check-up. He'd told 'em he was fine, but without much conviction. The truth was he'd been glad to come. No point pretending you're not in shock. A few minutes in a cubicle with an overworked junior doctor had settled him down. That plus three Twixes and a few bags of crisps from the vending machine. He was ready for home. Yet here he was.

'DS Romano?'

A man walked towards him. Tall and heavy, thick mop of black hair, jeans and a brown leather jacket. DS Slater from the crime scene.

'Yes, I was just …'

'We can send your statement over to Leeds for signing tomorrow, if you want. We're wrapping up here.'

'OK. I was just wondering whether I might pop in and see the victim? Make sure he's all right?'

'No probs. They're keeping him in. Broken ribs, stitches to his face. He'll have some scarring. And he's doing a Mr Invisible on us.'

'Really?'

'Won't tell us owt.' He opened his notebook. 'Stefan's his name. That's the lot. Can't get another word out of him. No surname. No address, no place of work, no friends or family to call … Nothing.'

'Illegal?'

''Course he is. They're bloody everywhere. Factories, nail parlours, food processing, takeaways. You name it. We got houses full of 'em. It's the United Nations round here! I'll log it. Someone else can deal.'

'Got the bloke that did it?'

'That scumbag? The lad behind the bar ID'ed him straight off. Oh, and thanks for them photos. That's a dozen witnesses, once we pull 'em all in. We should be open and shut on this 'un. Fellas like that don't stay tight-lipped. This in't gangland, it's friggin' scuzland.'

Joe got up.

'What was it all about, then?'

'Bit o' bother in a pub? What's it always about? Nowt.' He gestured over his shoulder. 'Johnny Foreigner picks a fight in a place like that, what does he think's gonna happen? You know how many times these foreign workers get into shit like this?'

'His fault, then?'

Slater shrugged.

'When I was with him,' Joe added, 'he asked for someone called Ana. *Please. Ana.* Did he mention that?'

'Ana? Sure it wasn't Mamma? Wouldn't be the first time someone cries for their mammy.'

Joe couldn't tell whether it was a joke.

'I'll just show my face. Sort the statement out tomorrow, then? I'm at Elland Road, Leeds.'

'Yeah, you said. How's Rita doing over there?'

'Rita Scannon? You know her?'

'She's Batley born and bred. Fifteen years she were here. Then she pissed off to Leeds, haven't seen her since. Good copper. Tough bitch. Bit of a gob on her.'

'I worked a murder case with her last year, as it happens.'

Slater tucked his notebook in his jacket pocket, smirked like a dick.

'Aye, I know. Lot of media interest, if memory serves.'

'It happens.'

'Unusual methods, I heard.'

'We got a conviction.'

'That's the main thing, Sergeant! Rita's still in our CID WhatsApp group. She's out celebrating tonight, pissed photos, the lot! Can't spell for shit. Anyway, you should be buying 'em all a drink. It were your case, right? Double murder?'

Joe paused, tiring of Slater.

'I'll just say goodbye to Stefan.'

He turned, began walking towards the ward.

'By the way, DS Romano, just for the report, what were you doing outside the Feathers in Batley?'

Joe stopped.

'None of your business.'

Stefan was alone in an A&E cubicle, sitting up in bed. One of his eyes was covered with a large white patch that came halfway down his cheek. On the other side of his face were two narrow transparent strips, a series of tiny butterfly clips running along them. The rest of his face was red and swollen, his neck covered in bandages.

'Hello? Stefan?'

He looked at Joe with his good eye, had difficulty focusing.

'I'm Joe. Remember? I was there, earlier on?'

Stefan was cautious, as if he didn't recall. Then he nodded. It became more vigorous, before he winced, steadied his head, raised a huge hand.

'I just popped in to make sure you're OK,' Joe said, shaking his hand.

'Is good.'

Joe smiled. 'I wouldn't say that! Could've been worse, I suppose.'

Stefan didn't understand.

'Is good,' he said, his voice hoarse, 'what you do. Good man.'

Joe nodded. 'Glad to have helped.' He looked around. No drips, no machines. Not as bad as it might have been. 'They'll be keeping you in.' He sensed the man's incomprehension. 'In here? You, here, yes?' He pointed at the bed. 'Sleep here? Tonight, yes?'

He felt like an idiot, talking to an adult like this. He sat on the edge of the bed.

'Stefan? Who's Ana? You're gonna need someone to help you when you leave.'

'Not police!' Stef said, his good eye wide, imploring. 'Please, Sir! Please!'

18

Joe took a second, replayed the evening's events: by the time he got out of the car in Batley, Stefan had already been glassed. Joe had identified himself, but Stefan would have been in shock as he dropped to the ground, his defences going haywire. All he'd seen was someone coming to help him, someone in a suit and tie. Now the same person was in a T-shirt, talking to him after the coppers had left.

'Who's Ana? You need to ring somebody. Ring? Telephone?'

'No telephone. Not …' He held up his hands.

'You don't have a phone?'

'No.' He struggled to raise himself up in his bed, bringing his head close to Joe's. 'Ana Dobrescu. Leeds. Ana. Please.'

'Leeds? Right,' Joe said, standing. 'You have her telephone number?'

He shook his head.

'Like sister. Best. Best in the world. Best person.'

'Ana Dobrescu.'

'Yes, yes. Please. Ana! Everybody love Ana.'

'OK, I'll do my best to find her.'

Stef's whole body tensed.

'No …'

'Police?' Joe asked. 'Got it. No police.'

# 3

It was almost one in the morning when he got home. He parked up and considered the place: age-darkened bricks, sash windows, stone lintels. It was only a terraced house, but it was a *good* one, large and solid, proper attics, somewhere that looked as though contented lives might well be going on within.

He'd told everybody at work that he was taking time off to go walking in the Dales. That was bullshit. Apart from avoiding the trial, his plan was to do as little as possible. Morning paper, croissants, Radio 4 … Since moving in he'd never had the time to enjoy being here. And as his Crown Court appearance had loomed, he hadn't been enjoying the nights much either.

He walked up the small, semi-neglected garden. It appeared slightly less neglected in the blue-tinged light of the moon, the overgrown grass an eery turquoise. He slid the key into the lock, pushed the heavy black door open. The hinges complained just a touch, and the brass letter box clattered momentarily. There was a heaviness, a sturdy bulk to the whole house. From the first minute it had been home: somewhere that feels like you're meant to be there. All he needed was somebody to share it with. The last time he'd found someone, she'd turned out to be a double murderer. *Che sarà*, Joe.

He stopped.

Something wasn't right.

He looked at the staircase straight ahead. Then past it, down the hall.

What was it?

The lights were on downstairs, on their timers. But something wasn't right. A tickle of fear in his stomach. Somebody was in the house.

How did he know? Look ... Look ...

The kitchen door was wide open. He always closed it. In case of fire. He did it every morning, all internal doors, wherever he was. Now it was wide open.

He stood, held his breath, heart racing.

Think.

They've heard the door go. What are they doing now? Waiting, like you. Where? He listened.

Nothing.

He pushed the door wide open.

'Police!' he shouted. 'Police!'

He slammed his palm against the door, making as much noise as he could.

'Come on out. Police.'

He glanced up and down the street. Someone to phone 9-9-9 whilst he tried to make sure the intruder didn't get away. Not a soul.

He got his phone, fumbled to find the dial screen. Then he saw two bare feet on the stairs. Bare legs. Stomach. He watched as a young man came down, adjusting his red Paisley boxer shorts and scratching his downy belly.

'Sam?'

'Dad? What you doing?'

'Opening my own bloody front door!' he said, stomping through to the kitchen. 'Jesus Christ!'

He flicked the kettle on, let his nerves settle.

'Sam?'

His son was a second-year medical student. But today he was standing in the kitchen doorway in his boxers, sleepy and a little drunk.

'Lectures were cancelled,' he said. 'Just popped down. What're you wearing!'

Joe looked down at his light-blue joggers. 'Shit. Left my suit in the car. When did you get in?'

Sam dragged himself over to the sink, got himself a mug of water, downed it in one. Another.

'Got the Megabus. Arrived about seven. You weren't here, so I went out. We've only just got back.'

'We?'

Sam's eyes shot up towards the ceiling.

'Oh, right.'

'I'm off back to bed,' he said as he made slow progress across the kitchen. Then he stopped. 'Congrats, by the way. You got a conviction. It was on the news.'

'Yeah, they've all been out celebrating.'

'Not you?'

'I got caught up in something. Bloke got glassed in the face. I was a witness.'

'Bad 'un?'

'Hospital job. But he was pretty lucky, they said. Scarring, mainly.'

The kettle began to hiss. Joe thought better of it, switched it off, got a bottle of wine from the fridge.

'I was sitting there, in A&E, getting checked out …'

'You?'

'For shock. It's standard procedure. Young doctor, almost a kid. I was thinking, a few years and that could be you.'

Sam leant against the doorframe.

'What was it? A fight?'

'Aye. Outside a pub. It's … it's terrifying, violence like that. I know I'm a copper, but even so, it's … evil.'

He got a glass, poured himself some wine. His hand shook a fraction as he held the bottle. He let the glass fill to the brim, then used both hands to bring it to his mouth and took a drink.

'I'm having lunch with Grandma and Grandad tomorrow,' he shouted after Sam, who was already in the hall. 'Fancy coming?'

A grunt. Or not. Hard to say.

'I'll take that as a maybe,' he said as he listened to his son tramp back up the stairs of his new house.

House? Or was it just a knocking shop for students?

He took the glass and bottle into the living room. Kandinsky print above the fireplace, decent sound system, two mid-priced armchairs and a sofa that he'd rushed into buying. Just him and an occasional lodger-son. Not quite a home, not yet. He sat on the sofa, tried to relax.

He thumbed through the news on the *Guardian* app. An inflatable boat had sunk off the south coast. Three refugees dead. He looked at a photo of the covered bodies on a dockside, tried to imagine what drove people to risk their lives like that. And for what? To be an illegal alien? To get glassed outside a pub while blokes stand around and watch? Britain had become a country where immigrants were immediately resented, where their deaths weren't even the top story in the *Guardian*. What on earth had driven Stefan to come to Batley?

There was a pad and pencil on the floor beside the sofa. He grabbed them, set the pad on his lap, and stared at the empty page. Then he wrote, in the middle:

Stefan – Batley – pub – glassing – Ana Dobrescu – No police!

He googled her: Ana Dobrescu Leeds.

'Jesus, it's that easy!' he said, clicking on the first link.

He hated technology, how it had insinuated itself into every corner of our world. But you couldn't have it both ways. Would Stefan even be alive now if he hadn't been there, his GPS position beamed straight to a police switchboard?

REBUILD: GIVING FOR LIFE. He scrolled down the website. A Leeds-based charity, the name Ana Dobrescu at the bottom, listed as 'Translator'.

'Bingo. See you tomorrow, Ana,' he said, tossing the phone down and taking a long drink of wine. 'Your friend Stefan really wants to see you.'

The tremble in his hands had subsided. It wasn't a medical check-up he'd needed. It was alcohol. Back at the crime scene, one of the coppers had given him a fag. He'd smoked it without thinking, automatically. Your body just craves a bit of dulling down.

He closed his eyes, tried to forget what he'd seen. But it

came back to him, the arc of the arm … the eye socket filling with blood … the appalling stupidity of it. Ten seconds quicker across the road and he could've stopped the whole thing.

'My suit!' he said, opening his eyes, remembering that it was still in the car. 'Ah, sod it. The blood won't come out now, anyway.'

The face of a young girl caught his attention. She was staring at the camera, her expression wide-eyed, pleading, empty. He picked up the phone, scrolled up and down the website. There were more images. Kids in a hospital ward, its walls a faded, water-stained green, the fittings battered, flaking paint …

He brought the phone close to his face and read the text below, almost too tired to make out the words.

'Romania?'

A minute on Google was all it took. Dobrescu was a Romanian surname. He'd thought so. Ceauşescu, wasn't it? The president they'd put up against a wall and shot. He added the word *Romania* to the pad, then let it drop to the floor.

Even as he drained the last of the wine, his eyes were closing, behind them the image of Stefan curled up on the ground, bleeding, no one coming to help him.

# WEDNESDAY

# 4

There was no sign of life from Sam's bedroom as Joe showered and got dressed. His suit was still in the car, ruined now, probably. He got his other one, a slightly darker grey, the one that doubled for weddings, baptisms and funerals. Tie with his shirt? Yes. He was on leave, but today he didn't feel like dressing down. He rarely did. Being casual made him feel unprepared for life. He would occasionally take off his tie, but only in the right company.

Getting Ana Dobrescu's number was simple enough. He did it as he was making coffee, putting on his best speaking voice and pretending to be someone from the University of Leeds looking for a translator. The woman at the charity was pleasant enough, rather charming, in fact. And she found Ana's number in a matter of seconds. Stefan had said 'no police', so Joe decided that no one needed to know who he was. Anyway, he'd always liked the idea of being a university lecturer. If only he'd studied a bit harder.

He poured himself a coffee, sat at the kitchen table, and dialled the number he'd been given.

'Hello. Is that Ana? Ana Dobrescu?'

'Yes.'

'My name's Joe Romano. I'm ringing about a friend of yours. Stefan. He asked me to call you.'

'Hello?'

She'd heard what he'd said. He was pretty sure of it.

He waited, listened to the silence. Then:

'I was with Stefan yesterday evening, in Batley. He was attacked in the street. He's injured. In hospital.'

He heard a muffled sound, as if her hand was over the receiver.

'He's OK. He's going to be all right. But he asked me to let you know.'

'Where is he?' she asked. Either her English was terrible or she was having difficulty speaking. 'Please, where?'

'Dewsbury General. Do you know it?'

'I find,' she said, her voice breaking up.

'Good. He's—'

But she'd hung up.

'Short and sweet, Ms Dobrescu! Well, I've done my duty, I guess.'

He held the phone in his hand. The sight of Stefan's large, blood-soaked body on the pavement in Batley had barely left him all night. Simply phoning a friend didn't feel like he'd done his duty. Still, he was on leave. Lunch with Mum and Dad, leisurely morning first.

He considered reading the news. But the idea of seeing those dead bodies on the dockside again put him off. Then there was Stefan, lying in a hospital bed, waiting to be deported. 'No police,' he'd said. Of course he had. He'd been scared shitless, swaddled in bandages and wondering what was next for him.

30

His friend Ana was ten miles away in Leeds. The closest person he had? Or the only person?

He finished his coffee.

Perhaps Stefan needed another friend.

# 5

The atmosphere in the operations room at Leeds CID was subdued. Those officers who weren't out on calls sat motionless in front of their screens, a couple of them on the phone. No one noticed Joe arrive. Who'd miss him if he suddenly disappeared to another department?

He got settled at his desk, didn't bother to boot up the computer. He had half a dozen cases ongoing, nothing that wouldn't wait 'til next week. The good cases didn't come his way often. One had, last year, and he'd almost screwed it up. *What was your relationship with the accused?* He wasn't going to miss testifying in court, that was for sure. In fact, there were a lot of things he wouldn't miss about serious crime, he thought as he looked down at his desk.

As usual, it was a mess. Folders piled up, a mug crammed full of pens and pencils, more of them on the desk, along with a framed photo of Sam outside the Louvre, arms folded, one of those confident teenager smiles, as if the adult world was just waiting for him to make his glorious entrance.

He began to tidy up, ramming a few stray pencils back into the mug. Then gave up. He wondered who'd get all his humdrum cases if he went now. Fifteen years in CID, sitting at desks like this one. How much good had he really done? How many people had he helped? A few boxes ticked here and there, some crimes off the stats, folk sent down for nonsense they'd done through desperation or stupidity. And the only person he'd ever convicted of a double murder? He'd bloody fallen in love with her. Who's the stupid one now, Joe?

A voice from the door.

'What you doin' 'ere?'

Thick West Yorkshire accent, enough to make it sound affected. But it wasn't. It was DC Gwyn Merchant. That's all I need, Joe told himself, hunkering down. He wasn't in the mood for laddish chit-chat. He definitely wouldn't miss that.

Gwyn wandered over, tall and loose-limbed, his dark-blue suit way too good for a copper, especially one as young as him.

'Just popped in for a minute,' Joe said. 'Is Rita around?'

'Dunno. She'll be sufferin' if she is. Off her tits last night. What happened to you? You never showed up.'

'Long story. Got involved in an incident. Had to hang around, make a statement.'

'Owt interesting?'

'Glassing outside a pub in Batley. That's your old turf, isn't it?'

'Yeah. Rita an' all. Which pub?'

'The Feathers. Wilberforce Street.'

'Bloody hell! What were you doin' there?'

'Another long story.'

There was movement, the kind that forces you to look up, a wave of energy coursing through the air. Rita let out a massive huff-groan, loud enough to make everyone know she'd arrived.

She wasn't tall, but she was solid. Black leather jacket, crew cut, nose stud, Docs, bossing the entire room just by walking through it. You'd need a good reason to get in her way.

'Jesus Christ, I feel like shit!'

She shuddered as she got to Joe's desk, her ample bust shaking beneath a Buzzcocks T-shirt.

'Sick as a dog. Stand well back, fellas. My breath's friggin' rank.'

Rita had been on the double murder case with him last year, although she'd managed not to get onto the front page of the *Yorkshire Post* for socializing with the main suspect. She was currently on secondment from the neighbouring Kirklees district as a specialist CID interviewer, and making it quite clear to anybody that'd listen that she wanted to make her move permanent.

Her breath wafted across to Joe. It smelt like a kebab had died in her mouth.

'He's been getting into fights in Batley!' Gwyn said. 'Fancy a brew, anyone?'

'Coffee. Loads o' milk, two sugars,' she said, as she lowered herself onto a nearby chair, her legs wide apart, hands on her knees, thighs ready to burst out of grey jeans which were skin-tight but probably weren't meant to be. 'Fights? You?'

'The Feathers!' Gwyn shouted as he disappeared into what they called a kitchen, but was just a cupboard room with an old humming fridge and a coffee machine on top of it that sometimes got knocked off. If there weren't actually any coffee grounds underfoot, there was always a light dusting of sugar down there.

She closed her eyes, pressed both palms into her face, head

34

tipped right back as she let out another moan. Joe watched, amused at the high drama of her hangover, remembering to breathe through his mouth. They'd only been working together a year, and even that wasn't permanent. But she was the closest thing he had to a partner. DS Rita Hridi Scannon-Aktar. He'd miss her if he went. Couldn't deny that.

She opened her eyes, blinked, looked around, as if surprised to find herself there. Her complexion was mid-brown, but perhaps a shade lighter than normal today, a bilious hue to her soft, fleshy face.

'Batley? The Feathers down Wilberforce Street?'

'Yes. I witnessed an assault outside the pub. I was just driving past. They're sending my statement over. Ask 'em to leave it with Andy if I'm not here.'

'Aye, well you should've been out with us.'

'Look where that'd've got me.'

She hawked up a big phlegmy one, grimacing as she strained to wrestle it back down her throat.

'You weren't, though, were you? Driving past.'

'What?'

'Wilberforce Street. It's a dead end.'

He sighed, hands behind his head. It felt like he was back on the stand.

'I'd pulled off the main road to make a call. Some bloke comes out the pub, then another one comes out and glasses him.'

'God, I hate that. You fight wi' yer fists, not a bloody glass. The victim OK?'

'He'll live. I'm off to see him now.'

'You're all heart. Who attended?'

'Slater. Kirklees District. You know him?'

'Yeah. We were in CID together for ages. He's a dick.'

'Nah,' Gwyn said, returning with two mugs. 'He's a prick. He were my DS for a couple of years an' all.'

'Prick? You reckon?' she asked.

'Most def. A-1 prick.'

Joe smiled.

'Are these established policing terms over in Kirklees?'

'Like ranks,' she said, taking her coffee and inhaling the steam. She took a sip, slurping it loudly to cool it down. 'So, Joe, you're an arse, and he's a twat.'

'Rather be a twat than a prick,' Gwyn said, shrugging as he made his way across the room to his desk, no offence taken.

'And you?' Joe asked her.

She stared at him, serious-faced, her dark eyes wide open, warm but with just a hint of a threat.

'I'm a bitch.'

She held his stare, then finally let a smile creep onto her lips.

'It's someone else's case, Joe.'

'I know. Poor bloke was alone, though. Not a single person came to help him. It shook me up a bit, to be honest. I've never seen a glassing before.'

'Aye, well, it's not your problem now. 'Tis scary, though. I saw a young lass get glassed once. Horrible. Just don't—'

'Get involved. I know.' He paused, let the idea run a little. 'You busy?'

She huddled down over her mug, sighed.

'Doing an interview for Andy later this morning. That room's gonna reek.'

'Case getting bigger, right?'

She stretched, screwing up her face as she tried to squeeze the hangover from her body.

'More victims every week. Young lasses just turnin' up, wantin' to make statements. You should hear the bloody stuff they're sayin' ...'

She sniffed with disgust, looked down at the floor.

'Charges any time soon?' he asked.

She held up a hand even as he spoke.

Joe didn't need telling. Operational details of the grooming inquiry were not open for discussion. If you weren't part of it, you knew nothing. All he did know was that even folk like Rita and Andy Mills, the toughest and most resilient officers on the Force, would sometimes come out of interviews and case meetings ashen-faced, going for a quiet fag alone or just sloping off home.

'Actually,' she said, 'I'm free the rest of the day. Dunno why.'

'Do a bit of digging for me?'

He tore a page out of his notebook, handed it to her.

'Suppose. It'll take my mind off stuff. Why not get a data clerk to do it?'

'It's unofficial.'

She read the name on the page.

'Ana Dobrescu. Russian?'

'Romanian. Lives in Leeds. The bloke who was glassed asked for her. Anything of interest you can find. I'll be back in a while.'

She struggled to her feet, jiggling her hips as she yanked her jeans up, then turned to go, speaking up into the air as she went.

'Don't get involved.'

'I'm just curious.'

# 6

Curious? Here he was, a week off work in prospect, on his way to sniff around someone else's investigation. The traffic out of town was heavy, and it only got worse on the Dewsbury Road. But he preferred it to the motorway. A couple of miles out you hit the open countryside. It wasn't pristine, but it was reassuringly green, and it stretched out, left and right, to help you forget that you'd ever been in the city at all.

He kept glancing down at his bagged suit in the passenger footwell, covered in the dried blood of an immigrant. He repeated the phrase to himself. The blood of an immigrant. His own family had been immigrants. Perhaps that's why he was on his way to see Stefan now, some foreign bloke who'd got himself into trouble in a grotty backstreet pub, alone, hardly understanding a word. Compassion more than curiosity, then. But compassion had never been much of an asset for Joe in CID.

The car park at Dewsbury and District Hospital was full. Sticking his OFFICER ON DUTY card in the windscreen and parking anywhere he felt like was always an option. But he wasn't on duty, and he didn't feel like lying. After a while he saw an old couple making painfully slow progress back to their car. He waited as she guided her husband into the passenger seat of a Fiat Punto, easing him down gently, making sure he didn't bump his head, then hauling his legs in and shutting the door.

As the Fiat pulled slowly out, Joe noticed a triangle of fawn material hanging out of the bottom of the driver's door. He got out, waved his arms, started to walk after the car, then broke into a jog as it picked up speed. Twenty yards later it came to a stop. He heard the central locks click on as he approached the driver's side.

'Your coat,' he said, pointing at the bottom of the door.

She was a bit like his mum, same sort of age, the same make-up, hair silvery white. She stared straight ahead, hands on the steering wheel.

'Coat?' he said, still pointing.

She relaxed. The locks clicked off and she opened the door.

'Oh, thank you very much. It would've been ruined!'

'No problem.'

She turned to the man in the passenger seat.

'My coat was in the door,' she said in a slow, animated voice.

He looked at his wife, his eyes glossy, his face blank.

'Trapped?' she said, enunciating like a stern schoolteacher. 'My coat was trapped. In the door.'

She smiled at Joe, raised her eyebrows in frustration.

'Thank you. Nice to see that there are still some gentlemen in the world.'

'We're all over the place,' he said, glad that he'd worn his suit. 'Drive carefully.'

'Oh, I always do!'

He watched them move off. After his divorce, Mum had got into the habit of asking him whether he'd met anyone. Her concern seemed a little too urgent, a moment of seriousness between them whenever they met. Now he understood why. She wanted him to grow old with someone else.

He fed the ticket machine with pound coins, amazed at the cost of parking. He comforted himself in the knowledge that he was still reasonably fit and healthy. A good thing, too; he couldn't afford a chronic illness, the parking fees alone would cripple him.

The hospital building looked a lot bigger in daylight than it had last night. There were people milling about near the main entrance, a few souls in dressing gowns having a cig, one man hooked up to a drip on a portable stand as he smoked. What're the chances that he's got something wrong with his lungs? Joe asked himself as he walked through the cloud of tobacco smoke and into the main entrance. He'd spent the last twenty years willing himself not to smoke, trying to make sure that the odd one didn't become a habit, and hating himself whenever it did. But to see someone ill enough to be hospitalised, yet braving the cold in his jim-jams for a fag? It was almost life-affirming, a perfect picture of the unfathomable human mind.

After ten minutes of getting lost and asking directions from anyone in a uniform, he found the holding ward. A dozen beds crammed into a large L-shaped room, all occupied, and most of them with a visitor or two sitting close. Nurses came and went, and there was a genial, almost homely atmosphere. Patients were chatting, laughing, occasionally shouting across to one another, making light of the situation, while one or two others slept.

And there was Stefan, in the furthest bed, still in the bandages. He was sitting up, listening to a young woman who was perched close to him on the edge of the bed, dark hair, slight of build, in a cream summer dress with a brown leather jacket over it. Her body was rigid, but her head moved from side to side as she spoke. Then she hugged him, still shaking her head, still talking. For his part, Stefan shifted, his exact expression difficult to make out beneath the bandages, but it wasn't a happy one.

Joe approached, but hung back just short of them. The conversation was clearly in another language. It sounded serious, not the buoyant tone of the other visitors in the room. She ran a hand down Stefan's cheek as she spoke, leaning in and talking right into his face.

There was a leather bag on the bed. Sensing the presence of someone behind her, she reached for the bag, drew it towards her.

'Hi, Stefan,' Joe said. 'You're looking a lot better!'

Stefan raised a hand, but his eyes flicked towards the young woman.

'Hello,' Joe said to her. 'Ana? We spoke earlier. I'm Joe.'

She nodded, taking the bag in her hands as she stood. She had a pinched, elfin face. Red eyes drilling him with a bare energy. A painful half-smile etched in fine lines, the skin so thin and colourless it looked like it might flake away if you touched it.

'It's ...' she said, looking around. 'Thank you for calling.'

'Glad to help.'

A pause. She didn't want to speak. Didn't want him to be there at all.

41

'Is there anything I can get you, Stefan?' Joe asked. 'Do you need clothes, or something to eat? Anything?'

Stefan smiled, but it wasn't clear whether he understood. Joe turned to Ana.

'If there's anything I can do to help? Perhaps he needs somewhere to stay? Or just someone to take him home when he gets—'

'I can do that.'

'Right, right.' He looked at the man in the bed. 'You fancy something to eat, drink? There's a café, and a machine out on the corridor. Some food?'

Stefan grinned as best he could whilst trying not to move his face too much.

'Here the food, very good!'

'Really? Oh, have these.'

He got a small bag of grapes from his jacket pocket. They'd been in the fridge at home. He set them down on the end of the bed.

They both stared at the grapes, then at him, confused.

'In Britain, we take grapes, y'know, to people in hospital. I dunno why. A tradition, I suppose.'

'I like,' Stefan said. 'I think … ehm … you are a …' He gave up, spoke in what Joe assumed was Romanian.

'He says you are a kind man, and that he is very grateful.'

'Right. And the injuries are not too bad? Healing properly?'

Again, she spoke to Stefan in Romanian, who replied, then attempted a reply in English.

'Only skin bad. And …' He gestured to his bandaged neck, then raised both arms to demonstrate the extent of his bulk. 'Strong man.'

Joe got his notebook and wrote.

'Here's my number. Whatever you need, just call.'

He tore out the page, tucked it under the grapes, and made a telephone sign with his hand. 'Phone, OK?'

Stefan gave a thumbs up.

'Before I go,' Joe said, 'I was just curious. What was the attack about, if you don't mind me asking?'

Ana uttered a few words to Stefan, but she was looking at Joe.

'It was just an argument,' she said. 'It got violent. Was nothing.'

'Right, I see. Well ...'

Two nurses arrived, a young woman and an even younger man. They pulled curtain dividers around the bed and began to change Stefan's bandages, chatting to him amiably whilst making it clear that his visitors were getting in the way. The young woman's forearms were covered in tattoos. As she worked, Joe could see that even the undersides of her arms were inked almost solid, right up under her short-sleeved shirt; thick, dark images that swirled across her white skin like a horrifically disfiguring rash.

What's the world coming to, Joe? he thought, laughing at himself, there in his dull suit and tie, doing a passing impression of a tight-arsed prig from fifty years ago. I bet Sam's got a tattoo somewhere or other. Perhaps I should get one.

He smiled at Stefan, repeated the telephone sign, then waved goodbye.

'We're in the way,' he said. Then, to Ana: 'Can I have a quick word? I'll be waiting outside.'

Even as Joe turned to go, she began speaking to Stefan, her

43

voice loud and fast but utterly incomprehensible. Romanian and Italian are not that different, he'd always thought, but his fluent Italian was of no use to him now. Apart from the word telephone, and repeated mentions of someone called Marina or Maria, the conversation might as well have been in Greek.

He stopped at the nurses' station on the way out, leaning in as far as he could and briefly showing the young man sitting there his warrant card.

'Hi. A quick question. The big guy in the corner with the facial injuries. Have my colleagues been in to see him this morning?'

'Police? No. I've been on since seven. Just you and the girl.'

'OK. Have you managed to get a name yet?'

The man smiled, revealing a set of grey teeth that seemed older than the rest of his face.

'I had to drag it out of him! Stefan Nicolescu,' he said, reading from the patient log. 'Nothing else, though. No address. Nothing.'

'Will he be in long?'

'Doctors'll decide later. But he's only on this ward 'til tomorrow morning. Twenty-four-hour turnaround here. We'll know a bit later where he's going.'

'Great. Thanks.'

He waited outside the ward, close to the wall next to the vending machine, just out of sight. When Ana appeared, she looked around, didn't see him, and walked straight along the corridor, moving fast, head down. A second later she'd disappeared through a set of doors.

Joe followed as briskly as he could without drawing attention to himself. Through the doors, and he saw that she was already disappearing around the corner at the end of another corridor. He picked up the pace, trying to remember the way out, at a jog now, but sensing that he was losing ground. Another corridor, then another, and now she was out of sight. He felt his pulse quicken, and realized that he wasn't quite as fit and healthy as he'd imagined.

By the time he got to the main entrance there was a sharp pain running up his left side. He wondered whether he might just keep on going all the way to A&E before he collapsed. He staggered through the rotating doors, saw her outside.

'Ana!' he said, gasping for breath but managing to keep going.

She stopped, turned. Her breathing was also fast. She was defiant, angry even, as she considered the panting man who had followed her: suit and tie, average height, dark hair.

'I almost missed you?' he said between breaths. 'A quick word? Would you mind?'

She stood there, seemed to weigh him up. His expression was kind, but a little sad. Like a priest.

But he wasn't a priest. That much she knew.

'Why?' she asked.

'Look, we can sit over there. Please?'

She led the way, without a word.

They sat on a bench not far from the entrance, the wind coming and going in short, curling blasts, sending sprays of thin, dark hair across her face. The leather bag was on her lap, held close.

'So, I saw the attack yesterday, and I'd like to make sure

Stefan is going to be all right. If he needs help of any sort, I'd be—'

'Police, right?'

He smiled.

'How did you know?'

She let out a tiny hiss of amusement.

'Is quite obvious.'

'The suit and tie?'

'I say to myself, either a police, or he works in an office or a bank. But then, why isn't he there now?'

'Excellent. You could be a detective.'

She laughed a little, but she was keen to be away, looking around, fiddling with her hands.

He showed her his card.

'Detective Sergeant Romano,' she said. 'Is interesting, the name. Romano. Like you're from home.'

'Romania? Like Stefan?' he asked. 'I only know Bucharest. And that was only a weekend, I'm afraid.'

'I am from the outside of it, eh, the …'

'The outskirts?'

'Yes.'

'And you've been in the UK long?'

'A year.'

'First time here?'

She nodded.

'You like it?'

She thought for a moment.

'Here? It can be a very nice place. Sometimes. For some people.'

Joe smiled. He knew the feeling.

'Working?'

'Before, yes. Legal. I have a permit. Not working now, though.'

'I'm not working either, as it happens. I'm taking some time off. I'd like to ask you a few questions, if that's OK. Ana Dobrescu. Like that?'

He showed her his notebook, her name written neatly in pencil, below it her phone number.

She shifted on the bench, a hint of amusement in her voice.

'Nobody else gets the spell right!'

'Spell? Oh, the spelling.'

She frowned.

'How did you know my number? This morning?'

'I'm a detective, remember? Your name's on a charity website. Rebuild: Giving for Life. I gave them a ring.'

The frown darkened.

'I used to volunteer there, a little.'

'Not now?'

'No. Not now.'

She pulled her bag closer, twisting her fingers around the handles, pulling it into her midriff.

'And you live in Leeds?' he asked.

'Bilton.'

'Really? Nice part of the world!'

'Yes, it is very nice.'

'Nicer than the outskirts of Bucharest?'

'Many times nicer!'

'And do you live alone, Ana?'

A pause.

'With someone. We met at the charity.'

'Name?'

'Ben Churchill,' she whispered.

He made a note of the name. Didn't push for further information. And she didn't seem eager to provide any.

'OK. Let's be clear. I saw Stefan being attacked, and I want to make sure he has some support when he gets out of here. I'm off duty all week. I'd like to help. That's all.'

'It was just an argument in a pub,' she said.

'He hardly knows a word of English. How do you even get into an argument if you can't speak the—'

Her laugh was short and sarcastic. But it felt honest, uncontrived.

'We don't need to speak to be attacked. Some people, they hate us. To them we're just foreign workers. There's lots of attacks. Fights. Whatever. No one cares. We don't matter.'

He let her regain a little calm.

'Everyone matters,' he said. 'When someone gets assaulted like that, it matters. It matters to the police. To me.'

She pressed her thin lips together, pulled the bag a little closer.

'I'm concerned about what Stefan's going to do now,' he said. 'He isn't here legally, I assume. He told me not to call the police.'

She shook her head.

'He wouldn't have been illegal much longer. It was all planned.' She sighed, glanced back at the hospital building. 'But now?'

'What was planned?'

'Too late. He told the hospital his name. The police know now. *You* know. The plans have to change. It's …'

She closed her eyes, as if she'd already said too much.

When she opened them, she squirmed in her seat, avoiding his stare, but she didn't get up. She wasn't ready to go. Not quite.

'Why do you want to help?' she asked.

Joe took his time, watched as she brought a hand up to her throat and touched a gold cross on a fine chain around her neck.

'I saw someone in trouble. That's all.'

'*Bunul Samaritean*,' she said. 'Sorry, it's Romanian. I mean …'

'The Good Samaritan? Yes, St Luke's Gospel. I crossed the street to help someone who needed help. Who knew the Road to Jericho was in Batley!'

'Jericho!' she said, impressed by his knowledge.

Joe was also impressed.

'At last I can tell my mum that all those Bible study classes with Father Murtaugh up at St Hilda's had been worth it. St Hilda's, it's a …'

'Church. Yes, I know.'

Her small frame relaxed a little, her fingertips still touching the cross.

He let her sit there for a while. The nerves within her seemed to be held down, under control. But they were still there. She was like a little girl, the way her face registered fleeting waves of horror.

'Stefan is illegal, yes,' she said. 'But we were going to make it better. For all of us. Now? I dunno. Now I have to do things quickly. Too quickly. On my own. Is dangerous.'

Her voice was close to a monotone, as if she'd said the same thing to herself over and over again.

He didn't speak, his priest's face expressionless.

'Is all too soon, this. But no choice now.' She glanced at her watch, her speech slow, as if the very words frightened her. 'Is all dangerous now.'

He let the silence between them assume its presence.

'If you're in danger, Ana, I can help.'

'I will be.'

'Is somebody harming you?'

Her body tensed.

'Ana? I'm here to help.'

She lifted her head.

'The police. I go to the police. Yes. But not yet. I can't.'

He shifted on the bench, still watching her. There was a sense of resolve in her now, a determination to be strong. It was unnerving to see, in someone so frail, so physically unassuming.

'How bad is it, Ana?'

'Very bad. The worst thing.'

'What's that? Are you suggesting someone might try to kill you?'

'Is possible. I have no choice.'

'We all have choices. Sounds like you're walking into danger. That's suicide.'

'No! Not suicide! Never that!'

He paused, keeping things at his own pace. Gave it a moment.

'How does Ben Churchill fit into this?'

Her eyes widened until she looked like a child. He'd seen that stare before. Recently. Where was it? A vacant, pleading stare?

50

'I have to go,' she said.

He got a card from his wallet.

'My details.'

She took a piece of paper from her jacket pocket, the number he'd given Stefan.

'I already have it.'

'Ana,' he said, 'we can deal with this. Whatever it is. You'll be safe with me.'

'I can't. I have to see some people first. Help them. Then I ring.'

He sighed.

'Another Good Samaritan? Are you going back to Bilton now?'

'No.'

'OK. I definitely want to speak to you before you go home. Are we clear on that? I'll ring. We need to talk about this again. Soon.'

They stood. Joe struggled to make sense of the situation, but what could he do? Take her back to Elland Road? Gut said yes. But on what pretext? He smiled as gamely as he could as they shook hands. Hers was small and dry, no rings.

One last try.

'If someone is going to harm you, you need to tell me.'

Her face lit up. A smile full of wonder, like an angel.

'I will!' she said, holding up his number. 'Me and Stefan? We're going to do something good. Very good. I'll tell you everything. But not now. I can't. Not yet.'

He gave up.

'OK. But soon. Goodbye, Ana.'

And only then did he realize that he was still holding her

hand. As he let go he felt like a parent seeing a child move away into another life. Like the time he'd dropped Sam off on his first day at college, watching his only son turn and walk away from him.

'I'll ring,' he added. 'Before you go home, remember? Let me know what this is all about. And you have my number. If you need anything at all. OK?'

'Yes. Thank you, Sir.'

She moved quickly away towards the taxi rank, phone already pressed to her ear, the wind catching her hair, sending it everywhere. A young woman in a foreign country who was in danger, and needed help. But not now.

He got close enough to note down the details of the taxi. Checked his watch as it moved off. 10.45 a.m. Force of habit.

He stood there. What if she'd been his daughter, talking about being in danger, about being killed? He wouldn't have let her out of his sight 'til he'd sorted it. Not a chance. This young woman was someone's daughter, yet here he was, letting her go. Because that's all he could do.

He was definitely in the wrong job.

# 7

Cars, lorries, coaches. The motorways are always like this here. Always full. Everything going too fast.

The driver glances at her. She sees his eyes in the mirror, dark, unsure. But kind. He looks away, concentrates on the road. He's old. Not from here. She struggles to understand him when he speaks. Indian? He understands me, though, she tells herself. He was suspicious at first, but I managed to persuade him to come.

She tries to keep calm. Not a smile. Can't manage that. But something normal, as if this is all normal. It's not normal, though. There's a hard ball of nerves in her stomach. She wants to gulp the air, to open the window and scream. But she resists. Lose control now and none of this will work. Only one day to be brave, Ana.

She can see the roll of money in the driver's shirt pocket. There's more in her bag if needed. Twenties, lots of them. The driver said it was too far to come. But money always works. Money is everything.

They pass signs for Barnsley, Rotherham … She recognizes the names from when she used to come down here on the train, or with Miriana in the car. The towns are all the same. Houses stacked up against the valley sides, and next to them warehouses and workshops, old yards full of lorries and metal left there to rust. It reminds her of home.

But here, between the towns, are great expanses of open space, birds overhead, the grassland rising and falling, huge sweeping hills all held in place by those electricity towers, the cables criss-crossing the country like ribbons on a package.

England. A fresh start, they told her. New country, new job, all good. But it wasn't good. It wasn't good at all. Now this. Driving down a motorway, hoping there's still time, risking everything to make it better. She presses her nose to the window, tries to imagine a different life. Is this her home now? There's nothing for her in Romania. She can't go back, not now. They'd kill her, for sure. No, this is all she's got. One chance to make things right. She watches the green fields, the birds, tells herself it'll be worth it.

All of a sudden, she sees a shopping centre, as big as a cathedral. Bigger. A massive green dome covered in lights, surrounded by car parks that go on forever. What is it about the English? They love their shops more than their churches …

She turns on her phone, checks the time. He's rung again. The police. Can't risk telling him anything yet. All this has come too soon. The attack on Stef, everything. This is not how she'd planned it. Stef has to disappear. She told him. Gave him money. He knows what to do. There's no choice now.

Detective Joe Romano. She googles him. He speaks Italian and French. Plays in a band. The police with a kind face. Kind but serious. Someone you can trust. Romano. It has to be him. Destiny. Will he be enough to save her, though?

They're slowing down, pulling off the motorway. She knows that once she does this, it'll be too late to stop. Just stay calm, she tells herself. Soon there'll be a police to talk to. I can tell him everything. He'll help me. Sergeant Joe Romano. Like a priest. A confessor. She runs the crucifix through her fingers as she watches the motorway file away to her right.

Only a few minutes now. The roads are narrow, flat brown fields on both sides. She feels sick, the acid rising into her mouth. She swallows it down, forces the nerves away. Because this is better. For everybody.

Then she can see them: a series of enormous containers in the sky. And the buildings beneath them, long, endless, like a prison camp.

'Can we stop at the gate, please?' she asks. 'I have to see somebody. Just give them a message. Then we go.'

The driver pulls up. He says nothing, but he's staring at her in the mirror. He senses the kindness in her, sees the immense human goodness beneath a veil of fear and vulnerability. He wants to help her, to protect her. But he doesn't want any trouble.

'How long?' he asks.

'I don't know. I have to find someone. Please, you wait?'

She reaches into her bag, then places a hand on his shoulder, pressing down hard, a mess of twenty-pound notes in her fingers.

'Please. Please?'

The closest building is a hundred metres away, perhaps a little less. It looks deserted; all the buildings do. But they're not.

Inside they're noisy and hot, and the air is horrible, the smell of shit in your nose, in your lungs, so powerful that it stings your throat, sweet and bitter, like the stink of diarrhoea. New country, they said. New job, all good. But it's not all good. Not yet.

She gets out of the cab and walks, slowly at first, carefully, keeping close to the fence. She goes all the way to the near end of the first shed, holding the bag tight to her as she pulls open the door.

The driver watches her disappear inside. He looks down at the money in his hand. She's already paid him for the trip, way over the odds. This is extra. He counts it. Six twenties. *Extra?*

'What the f—'

He starts the engine, shakes his head, thinks about phoning his wife. But what will she say? Two hundred and seventy quid for half a morning's work? She'll tell him to stay. Help the young girl. She's in trouble. Don't drive away. Not now.

He switches off the motor.

Five minutes, less, and she's coming back. Running fast over the uneven ground, one arm out to steady herself. She glances behind her, legs pumping, never letting up.

'We go,' she says, getting in and slamming the door.

Her breathing is heavy, irregular. He has no idea what she's done, only that the desperation in her voice is so intense that instinctively he drives off. As they go, he looks across at the buildings, expecting someone to come out. But the door remains closed.

From the back seat, she stares at him.

'Thank you,' she gasps.

She huddles down, her body rocking with each massive breath. He watches her in the mirror as he drives. Her face is strained, contorted, like an animal that's escaped death. But her eyes are wide and alive.

'Is done now,' she says, looking straight ahead.

# 8

He took the A58, circling around the vertical sprawl of modern Leeds, which was forever changing, each year a little bolder, spiked with cranes that yanked more and more high-rises into the sky. The city centre had been casting off its old, soot-stained clothes for years, trying on new ones without ever being completely satisfied with the results. The latest additions, massive, otherworldly blocks covered in metal latticework, hardly seemed to be buildings at all. Not unappealing in themselves, but more like buildings for London or Shanghai. Up here they felt awkward and a bit uncalled for, like your grandad in cycling shorts.

Then he dropped down into Sheepscar, and the city switched back to the old Leeds that he knew best, full of tarnished red-brick buildings that had been reassigned and repurposed over the decades, not bulldozed. Caribbean cafés, mosques, Polish stores; a slightly tatty bazaar of difference and optimism, each influx of new arrivals leaving its trace. Even the chemists' had foreign names. All things considered, Leeds was not a bad place for a Romanian immigrant to find herself. Had to be better than the outskirts of Bucharest. He checked his phone as he headed north. Nothing from Ana.

Ten minutes further out and he was on a familiar tree-lined avenue. He parked, turned Classic FM off, and looked at the place where he'd grown up. A large pre-war villa, the garden at the back big enough to disappear into with a book or your guitar. The perfect place to be a child.

'Second visitor!' his mum said, pulling open the front door. 'We're honoured!'

'Really?'

He hugged her, feeling the lightness of her arms and shoulders, how he seemed to tower over her, although she wasn't that short.

'Sam's here.'

'Ah, good. He's home for a few days. Is that coffee I can smell?'

'Just made it. Congratulations, by the way. The verdict was in the *Post* this morning.'

'Right, yes. Dad around?'

'Just got back from Manchester. Can you imagine? He has to have his tailor in Manchester?'

'Mine's at Burton's. Mr Off the Peg, he's called.'

'Nothing wrong with that, love. You never had your dad's, ehm …'

'Elegance? Savoir faire?'

'Vanity, I was going to say. Clothes maketh not the man, Joseph! They're out the back.'

She left him to it, returned to the kitchen.

He wandered into the living room. It was neat and silent, with deep bay windows and three ancient sofas, all of them more comfortable than his new Swedish ones. Somewhere to snuggle. You can't snuggle on Swedish cushions. There was stuff everywhere, a whole family's worth of memories: two Sicilian majolica vases as tall as children, a wedding present for his parents from the old country; a brass fire set from his grandparents' house in Wortley; a heavy, carved oak dining table and chairs, made by a Polish carpenter that Grandma and Grandad had met during the war. On it went: an upright piano stacked with sheet music that his mum used to play before her hands started giving her gyp, graduation portraits, oriental fans, ornamental cruets, a pottery hedgehog he'd made at school when he was ten …

He poked his head into his dad's office. The room was full of the stuff from the Romano Theatrical Agency, long since closed: a bulky olive-green filing cabinet, a desk big enough to sleep on, a couple of Rolodexes, plus framed photos on every available surface, all of them signed: Tommy Cooper, Helen Shapiro, Frankie Vaughan, Les Dawson, a few bands that had shown promise in the eighties then faded … And, of course, there was Grandad.

He picked up the old framed photo. Its sepia tones were faded to a milky orange. Gustavo Romano was posing for the camera, head held high, a serious young man in a voluminous white suit and a pointed hat. A classical Italian clown. No hint of a smile. As Grandad had never tired of reminding his grandchildren later in life, clowning was no laughing matter.

Gustavo Romano emigrated to the UK just before the war and began working as a clown in Blackpool Tower Circus. By the 1950s he'd given up performing to establish the Romano Theatrical Agency, which Joe's dad had inherited and run all his working life.

'Wish I'd seen you at the circus!' he said, looking fondly at the photo.

But he'd only ever known his grandad as an old man. Now his dad was old. Before long it'd be his turn.

'We all get old,' he told himself, as if he'd thus discovered the most hallowed secret of the universe.

They were sitting around a large wrought iron table in the sun lounge at the back of the house, which overlooked a vast, immaculate garden. He saw his dad first. It didn't matter who else was with him, you always saw him first. Tweed jacket, a maroon waistcoat, striped tie, the air of someone who'd seen things, known people: Benito Romano, son of the circus, literally. In restaurants, waiters would automatically go to him first, drawn to the deep-sunk lines of his old Sicilian face, the thick silver hair, a touch of colour in his cheeks, half-nobleman, half-Mr Punch.

'Ciao, Papà!' he said, hugging him from behind, kissing the top of his head, then a smile for Sam, but getting it wrong, more like a silent wince.

His mum had followed him out, and took charge of the coffee. Born in Leeds, she'd done a pretty good job of absorbing her husband's ancestry. The coffee was absurdly thick and black. There was sugar on offer, but no milk. It hadn't been until Joe's first holiday in Italy as a kid that he'd realized that having milk in your coffee was allowed.

Sam's pasty face showed all the after-effects of last night, although he was halfway down a bottle of Birra Messina.

Joe sipped his coffee, decided it needed a good dose of sugar.

'Dad? Before I forget. You don't know a bloke called

Churchill, do you? Ben Churchill. Lives up in Bilton. You know all the rich folk up there.'

Benito frowned.

'I used to. Went to a party in Bilton once. Cilla Black was there. You've never seen a woman so drunk! It's young money up there now. The characters have all gone.'

'And that bloody golf club!' his mum said.

'Golf?' Sam asked.

Benito huffed.

'I put myself up for membership, years ago. I was invited for an interview. Informal, just a chat with the committee members. Some fella asked me about Mussolini. I tried to keep it light, bit of humour. I think I said, "At least he kept the trains running." Can't remember, really. Anyway, I didn't get in. Some Indian fella's bought it now.'

'Well, I damn well remember!' his mum said. 'After everything the Romanos went through during the war!' she added, pointing at her husband, as if it was somehow his fault. 'This country's always been racist.' She turned to Sam. 'They wouldn't let him join a rotten golf club. Because of the name. And look at us now! Look what we've done to Europe!'

'Yes,' Joe said with resignation. 'Let's talk about Brexit!'

'Funny,' Sam said, 'it's happened to me. Couple of times, the last year or two. Folk asking me where I'm from. The surname, y'know?'

No one said anything. And then Joe realized. They were still ashamed. The Romanos. After all this time, the memory of the war still hurt. There was a faint vulnerability, a sense of being very subtly marked out. Like a scar. It fades, but it never disappears.

Joe remembered explaining the internment to Sam when he was a kid. During the war, Gustavo Romano had been interred in a camp on the Isle of Man, along with his wife and son. They were there several years, prisoners of war, along with hundreds of other Italians, before his case was finally reassessed and he was allowed to return to the circus.

No one ever talked about it. As a boy, it had taken Joe years of sly questions, wheedling it out of his mum, the non-Sicilian, when they were alone. He'd visited the location of the camp a few years ago, but there was nothing left, just a modest display in the local museum.

'But you don't mean they were racist?' Joe asked. 'Because of your surname?'

'No,' said Sam. 'But it's new. There's this thing now; I dunno, it's kind of like you're allowed to be a wee bit xenophobic. The other day I was outside a club, and there was this group of lads. Eastern European. The bouncers were being picky, just didn't want 'em in. No reason. And people in the queue were shrugging, accepting it, like it was all right.'

'Blatant!' his grandmother said, raising her voice. 'The *Windrush*. Need I say more?'

'No,' Benito said, bringing the volume right down.

Joe smiled. It had always been a family of two halves. Dad with his *Daily Mail*, Mum with her *Guardian*. He watched his mum now as she brought the cup and saucer to her lips, which were heavy with bright pink lipstick. Her hand trembled a little as she held her saucer, the blue veins that snaked round her hands and fingers pronounced, wedding bands loose, held there by the knuckles. But there was an assuredness to her, the same as always, a firmness that had kept them all together. What would he have been like without her? Without Dad? These two people, with their strengths, weaknesses, their histories ... What if he'd had to face life without them, to make absolutely every decision on his own, every mistake, knowing that there'd be nowhere to come if it all went wrong? Where the hell would he be now?

'How long are you staying?' he asked Sam, just to change the topic.

His mum reached out and patted Sam's knee.

'As long as he wants.'

'I think it's a sign, Sam,' Benito said. 'Some things aren't meant to be.'

'Things?' Joe asked.

The old man shuffled, got himself comfy, as men of a certain age do before they impart wisdom.

'Every time Dr Stevens gives me a rectal examination, I say to myself, thank God I don't have his job. Can you imagine how many men's backsides his fingers've been up?'

'It's just the one finger, Grandad.'

'Hundreds, thousands of men's backsides!'

'Bennie, for goodness' ...'

'And then he goes home and caresses his dear wife's face!'

'Oh, please!'

His mum was laughing now, they all were, all three of them. Not Joe, though. He didn't understand a thing.

'Grown men!' Benito added.

'What's that supposed to mean!' Joe asked.

'All them arses aren't gonna be young 'uns.'

'Can't believe I'm hearing this!'

His dad cocked his head.

'They bleach 'em now!'

Sam nodded.

'You know,' Benito continued, the voice of authority, 'not that long ago people's arses were black from the *News of the World*. Now they're bleaching 'em white.'

'You heard about perineum sunning, Grandad?'

'I have! Sunbathing your bum?'

Sam was grinning, happy. Joe hadn't seen that for, how long?

'It was a fad a while back,' Sam explained. 'Total rubbish.'

Joe's jaw hung open.

'How do you know so much about this, Dad?'

'The internet! I'm on it all day. You can get anything. Watch anything. Then there's the memes. I'm …' He looked around at the faces of his family. 'Don't retire, Sam! Whatever you choose to do. Find a job you love and never stop. Theatrical agent to the stars, I was! You remember the time Shirley Bassey came for tea?'

'Yes!' they cried in unison.

'And now look at me! Bored out of my mind. I didn't want to retire. I went through the Rolodexes the other day, clients, producers, hardly anyone left. Tell you what, Sam, we'll start a new agency. Me and you. I'll show you the ropes. Eh? I still have some contacts.'

'No he doesn't,' said his wife. 'That's why he's on the computer all day, to see who else has *gone*. And to watch those old TV shows!'

'When can he join, Joe?' Benito asked.

'Join what?'

They all looked at him, expectantly.

'The police,' his mum said.

He took his cup, drank. His whole body felt heavy, numb, and he didn't know whether it was shock or sadness.

'You're thinking of joining the police?'

'Yeah,' Sam said. 'It's just an idea.'

Joe got his phone, hardly believing what he'd heard. He called Ana. She didn't answer. Three times, now. He looked up, saw that they were all waiting.

'It's ...' he said, finding it hard to muster the energy to speak. 'It's something to think about.'

Lunch was fine. By long-held tradition, nothing controversial was ever discussed at the Romano table. Even back when Joe was eighteen, the day he left The Romanos, the band that he and his brother had started, the family had talked about other things, about anything, rather than mention the record deal that their dad had managed to get them, and that he and Tony had managed to screw up.

After they'd eaten, he went into the garden, stared out across the lawns that led to the three enormous sycamores at the back.

He felt the presence of someone behind him.

'It's not the end of the world,' she said.

He laughed to himself.

'Does he remind you of anyone?'

His mum came closer, until he could smell her perfume, the same she'd been wearing forever.

'Nothing wrong with changing your mind, Joe.'

'You were so disappointed with me!'

'I'd only just got used to the idea of you being a teacher.

In Chapeltown, of all places! Then you gave it up and joined the police. Let Sam decide. You can't make decisions for him. We didn't with you.'

He looked at the lawn, tried to remember exactly where Dad had built that makeshift swimming pool from ladders and a tarpaulin. They'd had to drag him out of it in the evenings, wrinkled like a prune, exhausted, happy.

'The thing about the war,' he said. 'Dad was a baby, right, when they were interred?'

'Bennie? He'd just been born. Nineteen forty. Four thousand Italians, all sent to camps.'

'Funny, isn't it? So many Italians living in Britain back then. Immigrants, making ice cream, in circuses, whatever. All here to work.'

'What's brought this on?'

'Yesterday. I saw an immigrant get attacked in Batley. Glassed in the face.'

'Oh, God! That's awful. Was he badly injured?'

'Yeah. Tough guy, though. He'll be all right.'

'Terrible, terrible … Batley?'

'On my way to a blues night in a pub. I was meeting some-one,' he added, hoping the white lie would head off any talk about his love life.

'Ah, good.'

'Two immigrants, actually. A young woman in particular. She's in trouble. Needs help.'

He felt her hand rest gently on his arm.

'That's what you said, all those years back. Remember?'

'Not really.'

'It's why you joined the police. You said you wanted to help people.'

'I still do.'

She squeezed his arm.

'So help her, Joe.'

# 9

Gwyn Merchant was at his desk, reading through his note-book, jotting the odd thing down and cross-checking details against a couple of documents laid out in front of him. On his screen was the mugshot of a young man, fat in the face, dark under the eyes, an expression of pure boredom.

Rita made her way towards him, shoulders rolling, heavy-footed.

'Who's that?' she asked, ready to punch their lights out, whoever it was.

'Ryan Makin. Friggin' gobshite. He'll be going down for robbery in about …' he looked at the clock on the screen, 'an hour. I'm off to give evidence.'

Rita threw herself into her seat, which groaned in complaint but managed to stay in one piece.

'What's up wi' you?' he asked. 'Face like a slapped arse.'

'Andy Mills being a twat again.'

'Bosser-tosser,' Gwyn said.

'I'm now on leave. *Forced.*'

Gwyn looked at her.

'Aye, well. You were going at it pretty hard last night. Looked a bit stressed. Happen you need a break.'

'What? You an' all! I don't need a break. I want rapists and perverts in jail, is all.'

He shrugged, let it go. But he'd seen how the grooming inquiry was wearing people down, how they were hitting the bar harder, earlier; how their normal chit-chat had withered away, a heaviness in their movements, and a weary reliance on drink, taxis home at nine, already pissed.

She began leafing through some print-outs on her desk, suddenly disgusted at the world.

'What's that?'

'Background stuff for Joe,' she said. 'Some Romanian woman.'

'I thought he were off to the Dales, wherever that is.'

'You know where it is. It's where folk like him go walking.'

'Folk like what?'

'Educated folk.'

'Gotta have a degree?'

'You ever been?'

'Nope.'

She scanned a page.

'Ana Dobrescu. Only been in the country a year.'

'Another suspect he's trying to shag?'

'That stuff last year? I don't think he was, y'know.'

'Not what you were saying last night down the Brodrick.'

'Aye, well, I said a lot of shit last night. Main thing, we got the verdict.'

'You and the mighty Joe Romano. Double murder to his name, and it still looked like summat were up.'

'That's Joe all over!' She looked across to the doors as they opened. 'Ah, the man himself!'

Joe was in a particularly thoughtful mood as he arrived.

'The patient all right?' she asked.

'About as good as can be expected. Tough bloke. You get anything on Ana Dobrescu? I met her this morning. Something's not right. She's in some sort of danger, said that someone might kill her.'

She handed him the papers and he flicked through them.

'She lives in a flat in Chapeltown? She told me Bilton.'

'Lying about her address?' Gwyn said. 'Living in Bilton sounds like a foreigner bird's fantasy, shackin' up with the millionaires.'

'That guy who got glassed? He's here illegally. He wanted Ana. No one else. Some sort of plan.'

'What's she like?' Gwyn asked.

Joe found a copy of her passport photo among the print-outs.

'Old-looking, worried,' he said. 'Only twenty-nine, it says here. Knew her Bible, though!'

'Religious liar, then,' said Gwyn, returning to his screen.

Joe moved across to his own desk.

Rita got up and followed him, perching on the edge of the desk. Several files and a stapler disappeared beneath the spread of her buttocks.

'So, you go to the hospital to check up on a bloke who got glassed, and you pick up a damsel in distress for good measure?'

'Felt a bit like a cry for help. J-D-F-R.'

'Just doesn't feel right? That's not much to go on.'

71

'Illegal foreigners, eh?' Gwyn said from across the room. 'They've always got an angle, Joe. On the make. That's why they're 'ere. An' there's shitloads of 'em.'

'She's in danger. Dunno what. Said she lives with someone called Churchill.'

'First name?' Gwyn asked. 'In Chapeltown, right?'

'No, in Bilton. That's what she said. With someone called Ben Churchill.'

Gwyn typed, waited, stared at the screen. Typed a bit more. The whole thing couldn't have taken him more than half a minute.

'There's only one Ben Churchill in Bilton. He's got a gaff on the golf course. The bloke's minted. Clean record, an' all.'

'Bilton's the most expensive property in West Yorkshire, isn't it?' Rita asked.

'Too right, it is! Clever cow!' said Gwyn, flicking off his terminal. 'What a great catch for Little Miss Foreigner! Like I said, Joe, they've always got an angle. You just found hers. Money.'

Joe tried to ignore the casual prejudice, knowing that he couldn't really deny it, not a hundred per cent. Immigrants come for a reason. The Romanos certainly had, back in the day.

Meanwhile, Gwyn was getting ready to leave. He came across, squinted at the photo of Ana Dobrescu from the Passport Office.

'Not much of a looker, is she? I mean, if she's a millionaire's bimbo.'

'Thanks for the input,' said Joe. 'She's putting herself in danger. Might be killed.'

'Sounds like bullshit to me,' Gwyn said, patting down his

72

pockets, checking his phone. 'She's playing you, Joe. I can get her pensions record if you want. Unofficial. I know a lass down the DWP.'

'That'd be useful. I'll text you her passport number.'

Gwyn stopped.

'How does an immigrant lass meet some rich bloke in that neck of the woods?' he asked.

'She volunteered at a charity. Told me she met him there. Rebuild: Giving for Life, it's called.'

Gwyn was already on his phone.

'Got it. Rebuild. Based in Leeds. Bloody hell. Now that's the kind of woman millionaires shack up with!' He brandished the phone, having zoomed in on an attractive woman with a radiant smile. 'Sophie Benedict. Rich man's totty and a fancy name to match!'

'Once again, your input is greatly appreciated. God knows what we'd do without your expertise!'

'Don't mention it,' he said, slipping the phone into his pocket. 'Right. I'm off to court. Guilty as a bugger, this 'un. I'm on in an hour.' He straightened his tie, smoothed the creases from his Paul Smith suit. 'Good to go.'

He strode out across the room like it was his own private domain. Tall and slim, the suit a perfect fit. He'd been a DC half a dozen years, but it could've been thirty by the look of him.

'Break a leg!' Joe shouted.

'Twelve honest men and true,' Gwyn bellowed into the air above his head. 'Let's be 'avin' yer!'

'See that?' Joe said, after he'd gone. 'No nerves, nothing. I hate giving evidence. I was a bloody wreck last week.'

'You were fine. We got a conviction. End of.' She paused. 'By the way, sorry about that message on WhatsApp yesterday. I were a bit pissed.'

He smiled, slipped the print-outs into a folder. Then he rang Ana. She didn't pick up.

Rita hoisted her black Docs up onto the desk, got a Snickers out of her pocket.

'Sod it, Joe. Get yourself up to the Dales.'

'I was never going to the Dales.'

'Aye, I know. Just go home. Have a rest.' She took a bite. 'You and me both! Andy's just taken me off the grooming case.'

Joe nodded.

'It's about time. You look terrible.'

'None taken, dick.'

'Anyway, I might have a little job for you. Explain to our Sam that policing's not all it's cracked up to be. Describe your current workload, the kind of folk you've been interviewing. He's just jacked in his degree, says he wants to be a copper.'

'His degree? Road to riches, innit, medicine?'

'Failed his exams. It's more than that, though. He just hated it, I think. Imagine doing your job if you hated it?'

'You'd never stick it. There's gotta be something you like.'

'What is there to like, really? You've been on that grooming gang case for months. Dealing with rapists and their victims all day long. It's the worst of people, Reet. *I am the way into the city of woe … I am the way into eternal sorrow … Dante, by the way.*'

'Aye, I know. Leeds just signed him.' She filled her mouth with chocolate yet managed to keep on speaking. 'Happen I do need a break. Been going at it a bit hard. But them lasses need someone on their side. And they've got me. You sure you don't want him to join?'

'Sam? No. I'm not sure. I'm …' He paused. He wasn't even sure if he wanted to carry on in CID himself. He hadn't told anyone he was thinking of getting a transfer, though. It would be like admitting defeat, signing for a lower division club, opting for an easier life. 'I'm kind of unsure about it all, to be honest.'

He closed his eyes, tried to imagine Sam immersed in the City of Woe, the worst that humanity had to offer. The sheer banality of the evil would knock him sideways, fellas capable of glassing someone in the face for a misplaced word. And grooming gangs? Fellas capable of anything, full stop.

When he opened his eyes, Rita was most of the way down the Snickers, bits of chocolate on her T-shirt. And she was grinning at him.

'When I came to work here, some of the old lads warned me about you.'

'Warned?'

'Most irritating copper in Leeds, they said. Especially when you were young. Always thought you were right. Never gave up. Never had a laugh about stuff. Mopey, annoying Italian bastard.'

'Sicilian. It's different.'

'Yeah. Pedantic, an' all.'

Joe recognized himself completely. He was a bit too serious, too introverted. He'd never been one of the boys, easy banter over a pint, everyone getting along, keeping it light. He just couldn't do the social stuff, not for long, not a whole evening. It wasn't deliberate, and wasn't always how he wanted to be. But he was a bloody good detective. That much he knew.

'Look at ya!' she shrieked. 'On your hols, and you're sat behind your bloody desk!'

He smiled.

'She hasn't answered her phone. Said she was in danger, that someone might kill her. She looked frightened, Reet. What would you do?'

Rita slung her feet off the table, letting out a massive huff. Then she stopped.

'I'll tell you one thing. If she really is in danger, I know the first bloke I'd be looking at.'

'Fancy a trip to Bilton later on?'

She dropped the Snickers wrapper in the bin and turned to leave.

'Aye, but I'd run it past Andy.'

'What?'

'The golf club? Get the OK first. A lot of brass play their golf in Bilton. Plus, y'know ...' she said, jiggling a thumb in the air as she went.

'I need permission to investigate a crime now?'

'What crime? Just clear it with the boss. It's the high and mighty up there.'

'Screw the brass and screw Bilton Golf Club.'

'And *still* a DS at forty-five!' she cried out into the air above her head as she made her way towards the door.

'Yes,' Joe said to himself, sitting back, strangely pleased at the validation.

He looked around, most of the other desks empty. The calm helped to create the comforting fiction that nobody in Leeds was currently committing a crime. He considered the idea: an entire city behaving itself.

'But that's not how it goes,' he said to himself as he cleared what little room there was on his desk and spread the papers out. 'Someone's up to no good.'

He pressed fast dial.

'Andy, you got a minute?'

# 10

'You can piss right off.'

'I think it's justified,' Joe said, standing in front of Detective Chief Inspector Andy Mills' desk.

But Andy was in no mood to argue.

'What are you bloody investigating?'

Joe opened his hands wide.

'I've got reasonable cause to—'

'No you haven't. Not answering her phone? That's bad manners, nowt else.'

Best part of two decades he'd known Andy. Training college together. Good mates ever since. Best mates. But still.

DCI Mills pulled himself up in his chair, his white shirt straining, saucers of sweat in the armpits; a big man, whose size was normally an asset, the kind of bloke whose presence fills a room even when he sneaks in, trying to go unnoticed. But today his very bulk looked like something he could hardly bear.

'I'm running a grooming investigation here. It's spiralling. We're bloody stretched, Joe. Officers getting burnt out, going on the sick. I've had to send Rita home. Rita! We don't have time for one of your wild goose chases.'

'I know. I know. But it's …'

Andy was shaking his head.

'There's no crime, never mind a crime assessment. You're a copper, Joe, not a social worker.' He sank back in his chair, hunched his shoulders then let them drop, doing his resolute best to force the tension from his neck. 'Go on, then. Tell me. Make it quick.'

Joe explained the events since the attack in Batley. Andy's face registered no surprise. Very little moved him to surprise these days.

'By the way,' Andy said, tossing a thin file into his lap, 'this came from Kirklees. There's a statement to sign.'

'Right.'

'And if there's owt in this Ana stuff, it's not our district. Kirklees can sort it. You're a witness to an assault. That's all.'

'She lives in Leeds.'

'So tell her to report a friggin' crime!'

Joe waited, watched Andy's brain working, knew he'd got him.

'This Churchill fella,' Andy asked. 'What do we know about him?'

'He's rich.'

'Aye, an' he'll have lawyers to match. Does he have a past? Domestics? Assault?'

'No record. She's in danger, though. Frightened. She's registered as living in Chapeltown, but told me she lives with him. In his house.'

'In leafy Bilton? Bloody hell, Joe. You know how to pick 'em. Don't go poking 'round up there 'til you know what's what.'

'Can I at least open a file on her? Just to monitor the situation?'

Andy exhaled until it seemed impossible that there was any air left in him.

'Aye, but don't be getting anybody else involved. I can't …' He sagged in his seat, shook the tiredness from his head. 'I can't be doin' with any shit from rich blokes' lawyers, not now.'

'OK. Still on for that drink tonight?' Joe asked as he got to the door.

No reply.

He turned, saw his friend sitting there: British Army, active service, then a copper, all the way to DCI. And he looked exhausted, punched out, like a large, overweight ghost.

'You all right?'

Andy laid his hands on the desk.

'A drink's all I'm livin' for, my friend.'

Back at his desk he opened the file on yesterday's assault, read through his statement, and signed it. DS Slater's card was stapled to the file. Out of courtesy he gave him a ring.

'Hi, Joe Romano here. About the glassing in Batley yesterday?'

'Yeah. Suspect's been keeping us company. Picked the shithead up last night. Twattin' on about a car wash down Millard Road, said the victim worked there, illegal.'

'Really?'

'We called in just now. The bloke that runs it said his staff had buggered off. Anyway, we're busy interviewing witnesses. Plus we've got security footage from inside the pub.'

'What happened, inside?'

'This Stefan bloke was attacked first, retaliated, landed the other bloke on the floor. Twice, actually. Pretty funny. Anyway, our star witness is a serving police officer. That's all we need to seal it for GBH.' He paused. 'Hope that star witness gets his story straight about why he were there in the first place.'

'I've gone through the statement and signed. Nothing to add.'

'Send it over, then. Job done.'

'One thing,' Joe said. 'I was passing Dewsbury Hospital this morning so I popped in to see the victim.'

'Ha! Mr Nicolescu! I had someone up there to go over his statement again, interpreter waiting on the phone. He'd pissed off.'

'Discharged himself?'

'Not even. Went to the shitter, never came back.'

'Jeez, so now you'll have to find him as well.'

'What for? We've got a pile of witness statements and a medical report. We don't have the manpower to chase down folk like that. Anyroad, illegal workers disappear. They know the ropes. Vanish into thin air, back into the bloody rabbit warren. We've got no chance of finding 'em.'

'I spoke to a young woman when I was there …'

'Keep it to yerself, Sherlock. I'm sick of this 'un already.'


'Rude bastard,' he said, throwing the file on the desk after ending the call. 'Sod him.'

He took a couple of envelopes from his pocket. Yesterday's mail. He'd picked it up on the way out this morning, hadn't had time to read it. He carefully nudged his bronze letter opener into the corner of the first envelope and let it slide along the fold, cheering himself up with the thought that no one was asking him to confirm his password before he was allowed to read his own mail.

Is this becoming a bit of a fetish? he asked himself as he pulled the letter from the envelope, delighting in the crisp sound of the paper.

Then he realized that it wasn't for him. It was addressed to Sam, a statement of accounts from the University of Edinburgh. A final statement. He read down the page, slowly assimilating the information. Sam had settled his account and left the university. He was no longer a student.

His whole body sank, as if he'd been kicked square in the gut. Sam had come home for help because he didn't know what else to do. And his useless father hadn't even noticed, too busy trying to help people he'd only just met, folk he knew nothing about.

He grabbed his phone, dialled, racking his brain for the clues he'd missed, asking himself why the hell his own son hadn't as much as mentioned it before, how long this had been going on.

'Sam? Where are you?'

'Manchester.'

'Why is everybody in Manchester today?'

'What? I'm seeing a mate.'

'What time's your train back?'

'Gets in about seven, I think.'

'Right. I'm meeting Andy in town tonight. We could have a drink before that. Whitelock's all right for you? Have a chat.'

'OK,' said Sam, didn't argue. 'Whitelock's.'

Joe hung up, stared at his phone, wondering if Ana was ever going to ring him. Or whether it was already too late.

# 11

Stefan sits next to Ana, looking down at his hands. There's a patch on his left eye, butterfly clips still running along two cuts on his cheek. His neck is bruised, purple in places, and his large body engulfs the chair. This morning she told him to get away from the hospital as soon as he could. She gave him money and an address. And here he is. The new plan.

Across the desk from them is a middle-aged man with thin red hair. He's reading through the photocopied sheets of a rental contract, then another one. Ana turns to Stefan and smiles, just for a moment. Stefan manages a careful nod in return.

'So, we leave the rental on the flat as it is for the moment? And you want to pay a full year in advance on both houses?' the man asks.

'Yes,' she says. 'There will be more houses, I think. For now, just two.'

She turns and speaks to Stefan in Romanian. He listens, concentrates, makes no response other than to look at her with one wide-open, adoring eye.

'I have the money here,' she says.

The estate agent watches as she gets a brown envelope from her bag and slides it across the desk. He's mesmerized by her, by her small, unassuming face and the stiffness in her body, by the strange urgency in her politeness, the resolve in each word.

'Is all there.'

'OK. I'm going to have to count it all, I'm afraid,' he says, using his index finger to hold the envelope open as he peeps inside. He smiles. 'I don't often get payments like this.'

He tips the bundles of banknotes out onto the desk, removes the elastic band from the first one, and begins counting, placing the twenty-pound notes in a neat pile of ten, then another pile on top, at right angles, then another … They watch as the stack grows.

'And the IDs?' he asks as he counts.

'I have them all tomorrow. No problem.'

'Mr Nicolescu's, too?' he asks, without looking at Stefan. 'The original?'

'Passport tomorrow,' Stefan says, forcing the words out, slow and loud.

'Right. Right.'

He goes on counting. There's a lot of cash. Two large terraced houses, a full year's rent on each.


They emerge from the estate agent's into the afternoon sun. Stefan shakes his head in disbelief, like he's just walked into the bright lights of a different world, a different life. They stop, look at each other, and embrace.

'Quick,' she says, pushing him away bossily. 'I've got things to do. And you need food.'

There's a Tesco Express just down the street. She sets off,

looking around as she goes, making sure Stefan is close by her side, pulling at his arm, letting herself fall into his great bulk.

'What do I get?' he asks as they take a basket.

'Whatever you want. Just for you. We can do more shopping later.'

She watches him wander down the first aisle, his hand reaching out for something, then pulling back, unsure of himself. The same Stefan as always. Strong, dependable, indecisive. How long has she known him? Silly question. Since he was born. And now their lives are beginning again.

She exhales, feels the churn of dread in her stomach getting worse, the waves of tiredness pulling at her consciousness. She checks her phone. Another missed call from Sergeant Joe Romano. The phone's been switched off most of the day. She can't do this with interruptions, with police ringing her, checking up. She'll talk to him when everything's ready. Danger? The danger is now. But it has to be like this. It has to be now. There's still one person that she needs to talk to. And it's not going to be an easy conversation.

# 12

The drive up to Bilton was slow, the traffic dense as it chugged out of town, through bands of increasingly impressive housing, until swathes of green countryside took over, every old farm building converted into a luxury home. Not a farmer for miles. No immigrants either, probably. Apart from a young Romanian woman, so she said.

Dead asylum seekers on the radio. The news sounded like it was on a loop, recycled, the same stuff, year after year, the tone always a little crueller, a degree less concerned. Gentleness and compassion now felt like forms of weakness that no one dared to utter, not even the BBC. It wasn't the human suffering that ground him down, it was the ease with which we now accepted it. That's why he'd become a copper. Not to accept it. To fight to make a difference. And that's why he was going to Bilton.

He'd been warned to tread carefully at the Golf Club, which for Joe Romano was more or less an open invitation to go poking around. He found a spot at the back of the car park. Ahead of him a sea of Beemers, Audis, Mercs, even a Ferrari ... By contrast, his second-hand Mondeo was like the kid on free dinners who'd somehow managed to get into a fee-paying school.

A beat-up Land Rover arrived not long after him, raced into the car park, right past him, and lurched to a stop at the end of the row.

'Cavalry!'

The Landy was old, covered in dents, and the tarpaulin on the back was so badly stained it looked vaguely insanitary. Out jumped Rita, rolling a cig as she slammed the door closed with her arse.

Joe got out to meet her.

'You want one?' she said, as if they were already halfway through a conversation.

'Wouldn't say no. It's been a strange day.'

'Hey, look at you, Posh Boy, you took your tie off!'

'Max casual. I'm on leave, remember?'

She rolled another, lit them both, and handed him one.

'Fancy around here, isn't it?' he said. 'Your presence is certainly gonna get people's attention.'

'Fourteen stone, half-Bangladeshi copper with a crew cut and a pierced nose? Getting folk's attention's practically in my job description.'

'Pity you didn't throw a bit of lesbian chic into the mix, but you'll do.'

'Didn't have mi dyke kecks handy.'

'How's Ruth? It is Ruth, isn't it?'

'Yes. Sexy as hell. Great cook. Overworked.'

'Glad to hear it.'

He took little puffs on his cigarette to keep it alight in the breeze. Then a long draw: the momentary shudder of physical revulsion, the foolish thrill, looking around to make sure your mum can't see you.

'Any news on the glassing?' she asked.

'He's done a runner.'

'What a surprise!'

'He worked at a car wash in Millard Road, Batley. You know it?'

'Millard Road? Yeah.'

'Illegal workers?'

''Course they bloody are, Joe! A car wash? Do you live round here or what! Bloke who runs it, I know him. His son played league with our kid.'

'Well, his workers've disappeared.'

She took a long draw and exhaled with a sigh of satisfaction.

'That is interesting. I'll have a word.'

They looked across at the clubhouse as they smoked. The main section was an Edwardian mansion, beautifully proportioned, with an array of more modern additions, all stone-faced, impeccable, but not quite as convincing.

'This is the kind of place where Premiership footballers have their weddings,' he said.

'Been in the news, hasn't it? Indian billionaire?'

'Yeah, I read something about it.'

She sucked hard on her rollie, then blew out a massive cloud of smoke, enough to shroud them both for an instant.

'Nice, isn't it?'

'It's what money buys,' he said. 'And to think I could've been a member!'

'You?'

He smiled.

'Dad just told me. He applied to be a member, years ago. Got turned down.'

'Why?'

'No idea. Something about Grandad, perhaps? He was pretty well known back in the day. A circus clown. Not very *golf*, is it? Or the Sicilian thing? Whatever, Dad didn't get in.'

'But your dad's British, right?'

'He's still Sicilian, though. Perhaps the name didn't fit. Anyway, Ana Maria Dobrescu.'

'What's the state of play?'

'Ben Churchill's got a house on the course. She used to volunteer at a charity. Met Churchill there. Now she lives with him. She fears for her life, and is gonna tell me everything. Thoughts?'

'*Says* she lives with him.'

'Let's see.'

They began to walk down the car park towards the course.

'By the way,' she said. 'We're getting married.'

He stopped.

'You and Ruth?'

It was like a slap in the face. But the sting of the blow was warm, delightful.

'I'll … I'll get a new suit.'

'It's "congratulations", Joe!' she said, already laughing at him. 'The word's congratulations!'

Joe wasn't sure what he felt, only that he was happy for her, the most unconventional police detective he'd ever met.

'There's gotta be a better word than congratulations. Come here while I have a think.'

He gave her a Sicilian hug.

'Fantastic! Great news!'

A man in a dinner suit appeared at the doors of the club-house.

'Excuse me!' he said, half-shouting as he came nimbly down the stone steps towards them. 'Can I help you?'

'I'm getting married, love!' she called over to him, as if this explained everything, right down to the Docs and the Buzzcocks.

'She's just got engaged!' Joe added, as the man got up to them.

He was in his late fifties. Tall, well kept, with a flat, smudged face and a careful smile.

'Oh, I see. Congratulations. And to the groom!'

'Groomette,' Joe said, holding up a finger.

'Groom … oh, right, yes.'

Then he waited, a trace of amusement in his manner as he weighed them up.

'This is Detective Sergeant Scannon,' Joe said, 'and I'm DS Romano.'

'Charles Malthouse, club president,' he said, not bothering to look at the warrant cards as they held them out for him.

'I …' he said, 'we have a formal dinner tonight. Hence the outfit.'

'Penguin suits not the norm?' Joe asked.

'No. We're quite informal usually.'

Malthouse said nothing more, and managed to do so with an air of well-mannered patience. The silence ran on a little.

'OK,' Joe said. 'We're just going to take a quick walk down the fairway.'

'Nothing untoward, I hope?'

'Nothing at all.'

'Good. I'll ask someone from security to accompany you.'

'That won't be necessary. We'll keep out of everyone's way.'

'I'm afraid I'll have to insist.'

'I can insist a bit harder than you, Sir.'

Malthouse was unmoved.

'We could phone Jerry MacDonald?' he said. 'He'll be arriving for drinks in a little while anyway.'

'Five minutes, by the eighteenth green,' said Joe, reining it in.

Malthouse nodded, turned, and left.

'Prick, prick, prick, prick …' Joe said, one prick per step as he marched down the side of the fairway.

'Nah,' Rita said, struggling to keep up. 'He's just a knob.'

'Thinks he can intimidate me with the Assistant Chief Constable's name? Prick!'

'The eighteenth green's over there,' she said, pointing behind them.

But they weren't going to the eighteenth green.

They kept close to the trees as they walked down the course, away from the clubhouse, ignoring the president's offer of a security guard. Gradually Joe's pace slowed.

'What do you think when you see all this?' he asked. 'Acres of pristine land. Helipad. Clubhouse like a five-star hotel.'

'Paradise, innit.'

'Not real, though, is it?'

'Looks real to me.'

'Most of the members here'll work in Leeds. I mean, they'll see the beggars and *Big Issue* sellers, the blokes in tabards and work boots, gaunt women pushing prams. The grim slog of it all. But then they drive up here, leave it behind.'

She pulled her face into an expression of horror.

'Jesus Christ, you're right! The world's unfair. I never knew!'

'No, no. It's not that. Why do we allow it? The rest of us?'

''Cos we'd all be here if we could. Your dad fancied a bit of it.'

The grass was soft and thick beneath his feet. He saw how it mutated into freshly mown fairway across to the right, then dense woodland beyond that. A perfect realignment of nature. But it didn't seem natural to him. And Ana Dobrescu living here? That didn't seem quite right either.

'There. That's the one.'

In the mid-distance, down behind the eighteenth tee, was a large detached house. Modern, two storeys but rather low, with flat roofs and sliding glass doors on the ground floor.

'Ben Churchill. Forty-six. Single. Bought this place about ten years ago. He's got a cladding company.'

'Cladding?'

'Y'know, the stuff you put on buildings. Make 'em look new. That's about all I have on him at the moment.'

'And she worked for a charity?'

'Gwyn just sent her pension stuff through. She worked for an employment agency before that. First eight months after she arrived in the country.' He found the file on his phone, thumbed through it. 'She stopped paying tax and social security four months ago.'

'Aye, well, why pay your stamp when you've moved in with a millionaire up here? Sounds like she's quids in. Gwyn's right. Immigrants work fast.' She stretched out her arms. 'A garden like this, and somebody else cuts the grass. Give me a cool mill, I'd be up here like a shot.'

'She's still registered as living at a flat in Chapeltown, though. Then she moves up here. Quite a leap, isn't it?'

'Big change for Mr Churchill, an' all. Funny though, she's a bit plain-looking. I mean, not your typical gold digger, is she?'

'That's what Gwyn said.'

'The voice of reason. Wait, somebody's coming out.'

He squinted.

'That's Ana. And the bloke behind, in the jogging suit? It's gotta be Churchill.'

The man sat at a table on the terrace behind the house. Ana tended to some plants against the wall, then went inside, returning with a glass of something. She gave him the glass and he drank. Her movements were gentle, and she gestured with her hands as she spoke, stopping occasionally to emphasize something she'd said. Then she sat down next to him, squeezed his arm for a second.

'I'm not going any closer,' said Joe. 'I want her to trust me. Go on. You've lost your dog. See what's what.'

'Pug or Rottweiler?' she said as she headed off, shoulders rolling, boots thumping down onto the fairway like she was trying to give it a good kicking.

He got his phone and sent Ana a message:

Hello, Ana. I haven't been able to contact you. Please ring me as soon as possible. Best wishes, DS Joe Romano

A few minutes later Rita was stomping back towards him, cutting right across the fairway in front of four golfers. They waved their arms, shouted at her. She held out her warrant card, shouted back, carried on.

Joe watched her, the bounce in her movements, in her Buzzcocks-bosom. She always cut through the unimportant things in life, just brushed them aside. Who wouldn't want to marry someone like that?

'Sir, Madam? Excuse me …'

Joe looked around. A uniformed security officer was coming towards them.

'All right, love,' Rita called out. 'We're going.'

He might have been thirty. Not very tall, skinny, the epaulettes on his grey uniform verging on ridiculous.

'You can't walk here.'

'We're done, love.' She stopped, head back, hands on hips. 'Nick? Is that you?'

The young man continued towards her.

'Rita? Haven't got my lenses in. Eyes were itching like a bastard.'

'I didn't know you worked here!'

'Aye, about a month.'

'Cool! This is DS Joe Romano.'

The three of them stood for a moment, forming a triangle that was slightly too large for normal conversation.

'President's orders, you can't—'

'Charles Malthouse,' Rita asked. 'Prick or knob?'

Nick considered the options.

'Knob, probably?' he said, his tone suggesting there was some room for debate. 'He did tell me to escort you off the course, though.'

'We're going, officer!' She grinned. 'And what's that you're packing there, cowboy?'

'Erm … it's a torch. Heavy bugger, an' all,' he said, slightly

94

embarrassed as he ran a hand down the thick faux-truncheon hanging from his belt.

Nick and Rita chatted about mutual friends as they walked back up towards the car park. Meanwhile, Joe, a couple of paces behind, wondered whether he should explain that a CID officer cannot be legally ejected, that there was a hierarchy to these things, and that a security guard was at the bloody bottom, despite the size of his torch. But he said nothing; it'd only make him sound like a prick.

He checked his phone. No message from Ana.

'See you Sunday, then!' Rita said as they got to the cars, her grey-uniformed friend waving a hand behind him in the air as he left.

'How d'you know him?' Joe asked.

'Nick? He goes to the Triple-A meetings. Bit of a lost soul. We get a lot like that. He's OK, though.'

'Triple-A?'

'The Agnostics and Atheists Assembly. Ruth goes. I just tagged along to start with. But it's … I dunno, it's good. *Nice.* Fills a gap. Hard to explain. Fancy giving it a try?'

He thought about it.

'No. Not for me. Does that make me a judgemental prick?'

'Kind of does, yeah.'

'OK. Tell me about Ana and Churchill.'

'They looked serious,' she said. 'I'd obviously interrupted something. We had a quick chat. She's … how do you say, weird.'

'How so?'

Rita shook her head, frustrated at her inability to explain.

'To look at, she's not pretty. But she's … ahh, what is it?'

Joe knew exactly.

'There's a strange aura of goodness about her,' he said.

'Spot on, cock! See what a university education does for you?'

'Was there any affection between them?'

She blew out her cheeks.

'Listen, mate. I've interviewed lasses who swore they were in love with the bloke who were passing 'em around to his mates like a friggin' bag o' jelly babies.'

'So she could be a victim?'

''Course! He looked knackered, though, like he'd just come in from work.' She rolled a cigarette. 'They hadn't seen my friggin' dog, though. Are you sure she didn't say anything else this morning?'

'You know as much as I do. She's in danger, planning something, and she fears for her life. Did she look at her phone while you were there?'

'Didn't see a phone.'

'Right. I've gotta get off. I'll see what Andy says later. We can't just wait for a body, can we?'

# 13

She's got here early. Holding things together, focusing on breathing, trying not to shake. They ask her if she wants a drink while she waits. She orders a glass of wine.

She has to do this now. It's the last thing. Then she can go home. Home? Is it really home? None of this feels like home. Everything, since she came to England, has felt unreal. She remembers packing her few possessions, wondering what her future would be. Then the airport, saying goodbye to Stef, to the others. Always the clever one, Stef had said, grinning through his tears as they embraced. That's why they picked her to come here. The clever one. New country, new job, new life ...

But for this? No, not for this. The cruelty was too much. The suffering. The lies. So she'd decided to do something about it. Something good.

In front of her is a folder. She opens it, scans the first page, then the second. Rows of writing, in pencil, neat and ordered. A lot of information. Stef had given her some of it, but his writing was so bad she'd had to copy it all out. Now they have all the information they need. Everything the police need. Only one thing left to get. But that's the hardest part.

She looks towards the door. Still no sign of Miriana.

It's all happened too soon. She needed more time to persuade Miriana, to beg her, to show her how things could be. But now there's no choice, no time. Stef gave his name to the hospital. The police'll have it, and they'll trace him back to the agency. The people back in Romania won't be pleased. This has to be now.

She considers ringing Sergeant Romano, telling him who she's about to meet. No. Talk to Miriana first, try to convince her too. She's a victim. They all are. This is the only way that it's going to stop. For everyone. Miriana has to know. And she has to help. She must.

And when Ana looks up, there she is, at the door. Miriana Dalca.

Instinctively, Ana fumbles with the papers, pushes them into the folder, and stuffs it into her bag. A long, single breath. Then she gets up out of her seat. Smiles.

It has to be now.

# 14

Whitelock's was busy for a Wednesday evening. But it wasn't noisy. Pints were going down quickly, ties off, an air of quiet relief as another day was eased from memory. The pub, hidden along a crooked alleyway in the centre of town, couldn't have changed much in two centuries, part museum, part age-darkened refuge from modern life. He'd done his first serious drinking here. A bunch of fifteen-year-olds huddled together outside, all smoking, trying to look older, and all looking exactly fifteen, the tallest of 'em going in for the beers ... He'd been pissed in this alley plenty of times before he'd ever set foot inside the pub.

Sam still wasn't there, so Joe got himself a corner table and let his Tetley's settle. It wasn't brewed in Leeds anymore, but the name was the same. *Pint of Tetley's, please.* They could put that on his grave. He used to drop in after work when he was a young teacher, spark up a conversation with some bloke at the bar. Today the lone drinkers were all staring at their smartphones, heads down.

'Progress!' he said to himself, getting his own phone out and checking for messages.

Nothing.

He thought about texting Sam. There'd been a lot of messages between them when he first went off to college. Things were *awks* or *dope*, and *YOLO* was the justification for everything. Joe would pretend these words were a part of his everyday vocabulary, then deliberately misuse them. The texts had eventually stopped. Kids move away, grow up, become people you hardly know. A doctor, though? That would've been doing something good with his life, making a difference. Police?

He turned the phone in his hands, wondering whether to call Ana again. Six or seven calls he'd made over the course of the day. Was she wasting police time? Or perhaps he was wasting his own. Logic told him to forget her, to enjoy his days of freedom, think about his future. But logic only takes you so far. His instincts had been right before.

He laid the phone down and took a sip. No more than that. A difficult conversation with Sam in prospect, then a night out with Andy; the last thing he needed was a fast start.

Then his phone rang.

'Hello? Ana?'

'Yes. It's me.' She sounded serious. 'Sorry not to be answering the calls.'

'Are you OK?'

'My phone was off. I had to do some things. I'm sorry.'

'No problem.' The background noise sounded like a bar. 'You out and about?'

'About? Oh, yes. Spanish food. Is nice!'

'And you've been busy helping people?'

A pause.

'Did you see my message?' he asked. 'How about we meet tomorrow? In the morning?'

'Yes. I've been, had to getting … er, *been* getting …' she said, speaking quickly, her speech a little disjointed, 'somebody else.'

'Another person?'

'Yes, I think. To speak to you also. Is going to be bigger. More information. Something very good.'

'OK. Do you know Elland Road police headquarters? Nine o'clock tomorrow morning?'

'Yes, yes … I know it. The … eh … is best I explain tomorrow. I hope. Everything.'

'I'll look forward to it. Just ask for me when you arrive.'

'Thank you, Sir.'

He hung up.

*Another person?*


Sam was ordering a pint of lager at the bar. Joe waved to catch his attention. He nodded, waited for his change, took a sip before he came over.

'Now then,' Joe said as Sam took the stool across the table, eyes down, staring at his pint.

He looked like a kid who'd just been caught with his first cigarette and was now waiting to face the consequences.

'I was going to tell you,' he said.

'Don't worry about that. How long have you been thinking of leaving? I mean, it's all right to change direction. But this is a big one.'

'I failed some exams last year. Failed most of the resits the start of this term. Been working in a Café Nero in Edinburgh since then.'

'You've not even been going to lectures?'

'No point. I'm already too far behind. I'm … It's not just that. It's …'

He seemed lost, in an unfamiliar place, his words awkward, not his own.

Joe looked at the child he'd loved since the moment he was born. It had always been a proud, unwavering kind of love. Yet there'd also been an underlying sense – not fear, more of a subtle, clinging anxiety – that something would go wrong, that the world wouldn't be unfailingly kind to his son.

'Uprooted at sixteen, high school in France, then back here, straight to uni,' Joe said. 'Perhaps we pushed you into it? Medicine, all that?'

Sam had a drink, winced at the effort of swallowing, said nothing.

'I decided I wanted to work for Interpol,' Joe continued, 'so you got carted off to France. Can't have been easy.'

Sam managed a smile.

'I got a lot of cred for that. Dad working for Interpol!'

'Glorified translator, truth be told.'

'That why you gave it up?'

'Yeah, that and the fact your mother ditched me for a Frenchman! How is Philippe?'

'Still a bit of an arsehole. Well, he's all right, actually. Mum seems happy.'

'Good. Good. Y'know, when I jacked in teaching and joined the police, it was because I wanted a job that mattered, something that had more of an impact. With medicine, I always thought it would—'

'I can't do it, Dad. The work? I just can't. Failed so much stuff last year. I'm too far behind.'

'Andy Mills failed his sergeant exams the first time, did I ever mention that? Too cocky. Too much boozing. DCI now.'

Sam looked right at him.

'I tried. I mean, really, really hard. There's folk doing sport, theatre, messing about, parties, drinking ... they all did better than me.'

'You not been partying, then?'

He shrugged.

'Some. But it's not that. I can't hack it. It's ... it's ... I can't bloody remember it all. There's too much science. I'm sorry. It's just ... sorry, Dad.'

His voice gave out on him. His mouth began to twist, and he pressed his lips together, his face straining. He was a bag of emotions, pathetic, heartbreaking.

Joe wondered how long it was since he'd seen his son cry.

When they came, the tears were silent, part of a long, drawn-out crumpling of the body. The hopelessness on his young face was so complete that Joe had to look away.

He waited until Sam's breathing was somewhere close to normal.

'OK. That's that. No more regrets. You're stressed out and I'm on leave. Let's make a night of it, decent blow-out with Andy. Sound good?'

'The police,' Sam said. 'It's just an idea. I mean, you changed track. It matters, doesn't it, being in CID?'

Joe felt himself sink, just a little.

'Dante called it *the way into eternal sorrow*.'

'What, he was a copper?'

'Very funny.' He had a drink. The beer tasted watery. 'You see the worst of folk, Sam. It's not always about doing good. I dunno whether I actually make a difference. In fact, it's rarely about that. It's … I'll tell you what, let's forget it for tonight. Fresh start tomorrow. OK?'

Without thinking, he held out his hand. Sam stared at it, confused. Joe pulled his hand away, and the embarrassment was annulled by two long drafts of their pints.

When Sam put his glass down, it was almost empty.

'I don't think I can face an evening with Andy Mills. Do you mind?'

'No. Off you go. Don't drink too much. Speak later?'

They both stood up, an awkward semi-embrace across the table. But Sam was keen to be off, back to a life that Joe knew nothing about.

He sat down, alone. Took his phone and began thumbing through stuff. With the internet constantly at your fingertips you never have to fully confront your own feelings. And right now, although he hated to admit it, he was more than willing to put off thinking about his son's future, or anything else. He amused himself with random searches about music and musicians, moving quickly from one Wiki page to the next, until he arrived at Morrissey, which persuaded him to turn the bloody thing off.

He looked up, and there was the uncompromising figure of Andy Mills, arms resting on the bar, two pints of bitter lined up. Andy picked up the beer and turned.

The night had begun.

# 15

A couple of hours later DCI Andy Mills was leaning against the bar in another old city centre pub. He was irritable and defensive, and Joe was wilting badly. They were both half-pissed, saying stuff they'd already said, repeating whole chunks of conversations without noticing.

'Grooming gangs, incels on shooting sprees, trans-whatever it is?' Andy said. 'What's friggin' wrong wi' folk?'

He'd already asked the same question half a dozen times. It didn't matter. Nothing did. He was just saying shit, looking for an argument, grouchy, worn out. His shirt strained to hold an upper body that seemed to have been built from the remnants of a larger animal. He took a long pull on his pint. Joe watched the pronounced pulse of his throat, a man well into an evening of self-medication.

'I tell you what,' Andy said, holding his glass up and glowering at it as he spoke. 'In our previous lives, when you were teaching French to spotty school kids, and I were getting shot at by turban heads—'

'Glad all those race relations seminars have had an effect on you.'

'It were friggin' Helmand! They were shooting at me, and they had turbans on!'

'Fair enough.'

Andy inhaled, as if his next point would prove him entirely right.

'When I were in the Army, I'd never even heard of grooming. If you'd've told me, I wouldn't've believed you.'

Andy Mills was heading up the current sexual grooming investigation. There'd been a subtle but determined battle to avoid it. Ranking officers had grabbed other cases, cried off, any excuse. But Andy was ex-Yorkshire Regiment. Scared of nothing. He'd volunteered to take the case out of disgust for his colleagues, above and below.

'Now,' he said, hands set on the bar in front of him. 'Normally it's white blokes doin' it. National stats. Just look ...'

'I know ...'

'But none of that gets in the bloody papers. This one in't white blokes. It's not my fault, Joe. It's ... it's ...'

'There's no point in—'

'Givin' 'em booze, drugs, phones. Passin' 'em around like bloody sex dolls? Jesus Christ! Don't these blokes have families, wives, daughters?'

'It's complicated.'

'Is it? Men doing this to young women? I were in three different meetings today, being told—'

'Not just the crime. It's how we deal with the ... the bigger picture.'

'We got one bloke. Fat thirty-odd-year-old, shagging a young lass in the back of his car up in Bilton Woods. She were living rough, she's a user, and she's, er ...'

'Low IQ. I know, I've heard the odd thing.' He felt the effects of the beer. 'Where did you say?'

But Andy was in full flow now, speaking in a muscular half-whisper that was supposed to be private but which anyone within fifteen feet could have heard.

'… he's not even denying it.'

'So make the case.'

'There's so many cases! Plus she's eighteen! Eyes of the law, she's not a kid. None of 'em are. Meantime, there's a line of folk in and out of my office telling me to keep it on the QT until we've got a case against 'em all. And don't mention that the suspects are all the bloody same *ethnic group*.'

'There's a lot of respect for the way you're—'

'I don't care what friggin' ethnic group they're from! Neither should the police!' His whole body sagged. 'But it's me that's sounding like a bloody racist in every meeting.'

'You're not that,' said Joe, holding up his hand to attract the attention of the young woman behind the bar. 'You're …'

'I've seen some stuff. In the Army. Bloody hell. Bad stuff. I've …'

'I know.'

'You can understand it. Some of it, anyroad. Blokes fightin' for a cause, in their own land. But this shit?' he said, shaking his head as he spoke, his face grey and oily, like he'd got the flu. 'I just don't get it. You break the law for a shag? Why? There's dating sites, there's apps …' He looked at his watch. 'I get a taxi down Water Lane now, girls on the street, I can take mi pick.'

'It's about rape, not sex,' Joe said.

They both waited as their new pints arrived. The girl served them without a word. Not sullen. Just young, disengaged, keen to get back to her phone.

'See that?' Andy said as she wandered off. 'How old is she? Nineteen, twenty? Same as our Karen. Send 'em out into the world. Job done. It's not, though. It's not enough. Every lass that comes in, I'm thinking, how close is our Karen to being one of 'em? Would I even know if she was?'

Joe felt the room begin to move around him.

'Can't stop 'em living their lives,' he said.

But Andy wasn't listening.

'I've been ringing her every night, see what she's up to, who she's with.'

'More good than bad.'

'What?'

'There's more goodness than badness in the world. The Road to Jericho?'

'Yer what?'

'Crossing the road. That's what you're doing, Andy. Something good.'

'Dun't bloody feel like it. Our Karen told me to piss off, to leave her alone.'

Andy necked a third of his pint, stood back, wiped his mouth.

'This Ana?' he said, as if to lighten the mood.

'I'm meeting her tomorrow morning. She's bringing some-one else, she said.'

'Aye, well, just see what's what. Don't mess about. If it's abuse, bring that Churchill fella straight in. I'll have at him, no probs. But if not, if she's playing you, Joe, you arrest *her.*' He looked at the beer left in his glass. 'Jesus, I need a curry.'

'Nando's for a change?'

'Fifteen quid for chicken and chips? And shit beer in a bottle? On yer friggin' bike.'

# 16

The key took its time finding the lock. He pushed the door open, shouted upstairs. No reply. It wasn't the first time he'd been drunk in the new house, but it was the first time the walls had moved as he walked, the first time he'd banged into doorways, missing handles as he reached for them, like being in the house of mirrors at a fairground.

His phone rang. Rita.

'Joe? Summat's been bugging me. Ana and her rich boy-friend?'

'Yeah …' he said, feeling the sting of jalfrezi bile in his throat.

'When I spoke to 'em today, he moved in his seat a few times. Put his glass down, changed position. And she was watching, ready, like he might've needed help.'

'She was looking after him?' he asked.

'He seemed tired, uncomfortable. But there was something about 'em. The way they looked at each other. It was more than looking after him.'

'In love?'

'I've been thinking about it. They looked content with each

other, homely. Something special. Tender. Aye, that's the word. Exactly how you'd want to be with somebody.'

''Til death do us part. Or is it us do, part, us death do part, 'til …'

'What?'

'Death. Means to an end, sometimes. If she's playing … somebody's … me.'

'You tired and emotional?'

'Yep. Thanks for that, Reet. See you tomorrow.'

He got a glass of water from the kitchen, necked it, got another. Went through to the living room. He lowered himself down onto the sofa, but somehow got it wrong, ending up semi-sprawled on the cushions, the glass falling to the floor.

'Shit!'

The room was spinning good and proper now. Bloody stupid pints in the curry place. No one needs so much beer with a meal. No one wants to be the man who asks for a half. Pathetic.

He reached down for the glass. There was a pad there. He picked it up, water dripping from it. He read:

Stefan – Batley – pub – glassing – Ana Dobrescu – <u>No police!</u> – Romania

He wiped the pad on his trousers.

'Now Stefan's pissed off. What did she say?'

He tried to force the beer from his head.

'Something … to help people … It's … like, it's her … Remember?'

His head fell back, eyes closing.

*Remember what, you pissed twat?*

'She worked for a charity. Ana. Helping people.'

*What the hell're you on about?*

'The road to Jericho. More good than bad. We're … we're good. Most folk are good. Focus on the good.'

He dropped the pad, and his eyes closed.

*See you tomorrow, Ana.*

# THURSDAY

# 17

The traffic was at a standstill. A perfect sky, green fields rolling away into distant woodland on both sides. Seven-thirty on a Thursday morning, but no one was drawing inspiration from the majestic Yorkshire countryside now, not if they were on the Harrogate Road. Joe joined the back of the queue. The oncoming lane was empty, but some cars and vans were turning around, stop-starting, backwards and forwards, getting in each other's way as they manoeuvred themselves into the opposite direction. He pulled onto the verge, slapped a POLICE notice on the dash, and set off at a jog.

He rang Gwyn as he puffed his way past the long line of vehicles. As he got closer, more of them had switched off their engines. There was an eery quiet, drivers out of their cars, standing there, contemplating the silent tragedy ahead. Twenty, thirty seconds and it could have been them.

'Are you here?' he said, breathing heavily into his phone.

'Yeah. Bad 'un. It's Churchill.'

'Alive?'

'Just.'

The accident had been phoned in forty minutes ago. A black

Mazda sports car, wrapped around one of the concrete columns of a bridge about seven miles north of Leeds. No other vehicles involved. The car's registration had immediately flagged up Churchill's name, and with it the Ana Dobrescu file.

Joe quickened his pace. Ahead of him he could make out the scene more clearly now. Ambulance, police cars, three fire service units, all parked at odd angles near the bridge. Orange suits, green, yellow. People everywhere.

Gwyn was over by one of the patrol cars.

'You 'ad yer brekkie?' he asked Joe, glancing across at the mangled car, its front end collapsed almost to nothing, as if the concrete pillar had devoured half of it in a single bite. 'No airbag.'

'It didn't work?'

'Bloody thing'd been taken out.'

'Really? Was he alone?'

Gwyn nodded.

'Right,' Joe said. 'Let's get the car down to forensics as soon—'

'Flatback's on its way.'

'Good.'

Five paramedics crowded around a large space on one side of the car where its side panel had been cut out, along with part of the roof. They were passing things to a colleague who was kneeling on the passenger seat. Their movements were urgent but controlled, bodies leaning into one other until they touched, as if the intense human proximity of their work might have been enough to save a life.

'Shit,' said Joe. 'Ana's coming in at nine. Bringing somebody with her. You think she was gonna be talking about *him*?'

'You jokin'? This is her. Gotta be, one way or t'other. Screw talking. Drag her in on bloody suspicion.'

Joe paused, phone in his hand.

'She'll be coming in anyway. I'll ring to confirm. Won't mention the accident.' He searched for her number. 'You reckon this is about Churchill's money?'

'When's it not about money, Joseph?'

'When it's about sex.'

'Aye. Sex and money. Jesus! Poor bloke!' Gwyn said, looking towards the bridge.

Ben Churchill's body was now being lifted from the wreckage. Neck brace, oxygen, drip, full-body cradle beneath him. They watched as he was inched free of the car, so slowly that he seemed not to be moving. Yet out he came.

Joe studied his phone.

'Ana's number? Showing as unavailable.'

'Why does that not surprise me for one friggin' minute?' Gwyn said, before taking a deep breath and striding out towards the remains of the car.

# 18

Batley. She pulled off the main road, the Land Rover bumping across a large expanse of open ground. The morning sun hung above the horizon, blazing down on the M62, the rumble of traffic bouncing around the sky, familiar, constant. It never stopped, day and night.

She parked amid a pool of soapy suds next to a strip of tarmac that served as the washing area. There was a dark green Portakabin not far behind it. The rest of the area, perhaps the size of a football field, was a combination of concrete and bare earth, gouged up into muddy ridges by lorry tyres. Way off in the far corner was a truckers' café in an old bus, a white plastic table and chairs outside. All-day breakfasts, it announced.

She'd kickstarted the day in there a few times over the years. Full English and double fried bread, sweet tea, couple of fags for afters. She resisted the urge, swung herself down from the Landy, lighting up a tab end she'd found on the dash.

Two young men in orange tabards were clearing away hoses and buckets.

'It's here,' one of them said to her, pointing at the car wash area.

'Wash this?' she said. 'Yer must be joking. The muck's the only thing holding it together!'

He nodded, carried on working, no eye contact. He spoke to the other one, but not in English.

'Haven't seen you two here before,' she said.

'New,' he said.

'Today? What, both of yers?'

He nodded again.

'Right couple of chatterboxes, an' all. Mr Morgan about?'

She didn't wait for an answer, went over to the Portakabin, threw the door open. It smelt of damp, aftershave and farts. She dropped the rollie on the ground outside, didn't want to add to the sorry mix.

'Dale Morgan Esquire! How yer doin'?'

Fifties, thickset, flabby, in a mid-blue shirt with white collar and cuffs, like he was off to a fancy dress as Gordon Gekko. He was counting loose change, putting the coins in stacks in front of him.

'They've already been,' he said.

'Hey, pleased to see you an' all, Dale! Who's been?'

He stopped.

'Your lot. About the glassing. How is the lad?'

'He'll live.'

Dale got up, pulled a thin cardboard folder from a drawer and let it drop onto the table, then slumped back down into his chair.

'Bit quick with the paperwork there!' she said, leaving the folder where it was.

'The whole crew pissed off. I got back from dinner yesterday, they'd gone.'

119

'Stefan's lot?'

'Aye. Five Romanians. Don't bother trying to find 'em. The house they lived in's empty. I called round last night. They left in a rush, neighbours said.'

She took the folder, leafed through it. Five DWP records, all Romanian names.

'Did you show this to Slater's lot?'

'Yeah. They weren't that interested.'

'There's no record for Stefan Nicolescu in here.'

He shrugged.

'You know how it works.'

'Them two outside?'

He sighed.

'They've just started working today. Syrian. It's a few quid in their pockets. Helping me out. They're claiming asylum. Please?'

She looked around. The walls were covered in old matchday posters for the Batley Bulldogs, plus some older ones, from when they were called Batley Football Club, which she'd never understood, since they were a rugby league side. There was also a massive colour photo of the Mount Pleasant ground, a few faded team photos, plus a large glass frame full of old newspaper cuttings.

She'd known Dale Morgan since she was a kid. His family lived on the same estate as the Scannons. Rugby league mad, all the Morgans were. Dale signed for Batley as a young man. Never made it out of the reserves. Wasted his best years trying.

'Your Nick doin' all right?'

'On remand in Wakefield.'

'What! Prison? I thought he were playing somewhere. Featherstone, wasn't it?'

He blew out his cheeks.

'Nah. It fell through. He had a lock-up full o' plasmas as a friggin' back-up, though. You didn't know?'

'I've been working in Leeds. Has he got a decent lawyer?'

He patted the stacks of pound coins in front of him.

'Doin' what I can.'

She read a few of the headlines from the cuttings on the wall, looked at the dates, tried to remember if she'd been to any of the matches. Years ago her brother Carl had been in the juniors with Nick Morgan. Big lads, both of 'em. They were called juniors, but that just made 'em keener to prove they were men. The matches were brutal. She'd been to plenty, although her memories of Mount Pleasant were basically the balti pies and the fact that it was always raining. That, plus eighty minutes of absurd, unrelenting violence.

Carl never made pro. Then he went and got himself killed.

'Them Romanians? Been working here long?'

'Few months. Pretty reliable. *Were.*'

'Where did you get 'em? I mean, if I want illegal workers, where do I go?'

'Bloody houses full of 'em round here. Asylum seekers, refugees, illegals from Europe. Give one of 'em a job, they're all here asking. An agency's less hassle, though.'

'You pay the agency direct, and they sort you out with the paperwork?' she asked, opening the folder and spreading the contents out on the desk. 'If I ask them lads outside now, they're tell me they're Romanians, right?'

'Aye.'

'These IDs?' she asked, quickly taking a photo of each sheet. 'Get 'em from a Romanian agency, do you? Know anyone called Ana? Romanian girl?'

'No comment.'

'Come on, don't be a twat, Dale. Where d'you get 'em?'

She closed the file, tossed it back across the desk to him. Then she turned, looked at the cuttings on the wall again. Found a report of a juniors match, Nick Morgan in the line-up. Carl Scannon, too. She'd been there that day, sitting in the sparse crowd. Her brother was a winger. Bloody fast. Bit clumsy with the ball, if you had to be honest. Nick Morgan, though, he was class. He'd been in and around the professional ranks for years, without ever making it stick. Now he was awaiting trial.

'I've got a mate up at Wakefield prison. I'll ask him to make sure Nick's OK. Remand, right?'

'Aye. Bloody dickhead.' He let out a long, exhausted breath. 'Workout Agency, it's called. Romanians. They're in Leeds. They give you the paperwork, plus all the workers you need. They pay the workers direct. You just pay the agency. Cash business, no receipts, no nowt.'

'Right. Tell Nick I'll have a word. Oh,' she added, as she opened the door, 'this is between us. The attack? Not my investigation. I was never here.'

'Cheers, Reet,' he said, finding something on his phone and scribbling it on a scrap of paper. He got up, brought it to her. 'The agency? Woman called Miriana runs it. Her number.'

'Laters, big boy. And go see yer bloody son!'

# 19

Andy Mills was behind his desk, no worse for wear. He never was. Even when he claimed to have a hangover, it was more like he was just playing the part, in sympathy for less resilient souls.

'Ana's fancy man!' he said, sitting back, hands behind his head. 'And let me guess? She never showed up for her statement?'

Joe said nothing.

Andy picked up the phone. 'All right. I'll do the talking.'

He dialled, switched to speakerphone.

'Jerry MacDonald?'

The accent was southern. Educated. Self-assured.

'Good morning, Sir. It's Andy Mills, CID.'

'Hi, Andy. What can I do for you?'

'We need to search one of the houses that back onto Bilton Golf Course.'

'Anything serious?'

'Yes, we think so. I thought we should ask the club. Perhaps better if the request didn't come from me, though.'

'Ha! The club president's certainly not your greatest fan. Anyone up there now?'

'Officers on their way.'

'OK. I'll ring Charles, the president, make sure there's someone there.'

'Could you ask them not to enter the house, Sir?'

'Absolutely. Who's the SIO?'

'DS Joe Romano.'

'Romano? Ah, yes. Our very own media sensation from last year.'

'He did bring in a double murder.'

'Yes, yes. Make sure he does things by the book this time. See if he can stay out of the tabloids.'

'I'll make that very clear. Thanks for your help, Sir.'

'See?' Andy said, as he ended the call, a childish grin on his fat face. 'Brass think very highly of you!'

'Sod that. How come you know that prick at the golf club?'

'Senior officers' dinner a few months back. I got pissed. Spewed up in the fireplace. Just not done at a golf club, apparently. Anyway, off you go.'

'Can I borrow Rita? She's off the grooming case, right?'

'She's supposed to be resting.' He let out a breath. 'Go on, then. I've got no bugger else.'

'Great. I'll try not to ruffle any feathers.'

'Ruffle all the feathers you want. Find the girl, Joe.'

# 20

Half an hour later he drove slowly along a residential street that curved around the edge of Bilton Woods. Ana Dobrescu had certainly landed on her feet here. The houses were large, modern, and well spaced. When he'd been looking to buy somewhere, he'd done the odd million-plus property search, just to see what he couldn't afford. And most of the priciest houses were up here. He looked ahead, saw the huge 4x4s, a million in bricks and mortar behind each one.

He pulled up outside Churchill's address. Two garages, flat roofs, a sizeable house, but one of the less ostentatious ones. Not so much as a blade of grass out front. No need. There was a golf course at the back with acres of the stuff.

Rita was already there, sitting on the large concrete step outside the door, her chunky legs in front of her. Black jeans ripped at both knees, pink Hello Kitty T-shirt several sizes too small, a glittery roll of belly fat resting on her belt. Her battered black denim jacket added a touch of maturity, but only because Joe couldn't see the words HEAD FAIRY done in rhinestones on the back.

Sitting next to her was Nick Evans, the grey security officer's uniform still looking a couple of sizes too big for his narrow frame. They passed a rollie between them as they watched Joe approach.

'Right, I'm off,' Nick said, taking his cue and standing to leave. 'I'll leave the keys with you then, Reet?'

'Keys?' Joe asked.

'The club has a spare set.'

'I knocked,' Rita said, showing no signs of moving. 'Nobody home.'

'Actually,' said Joe to Nick, 'could I pick your brains? Bloke called Ben Churchill lives here. You see much of him?'

'Yeah, when I'm on earlies, doing the rounds.'

'Time?'

'Six-thirty start. He's normally up. Wanders around outside a bit with a cup o' tea. I'd do the same if I lived here. Listen to the birds, have a stroll.'

'It is nice,' Rita said, fag in her mouth. 'All this fresh air.'

'Has he had any sort of trouble with the club?'

'Trouble? Not that I know of. Always gives me a wave. Friendly, like.'

'This morning?'

'Nah. Not today.'

'You know his girlfriend?'

'No. Not really. Seen her, a bit.'

'Come on, make yourself useful!' Rita said, waving her arms.

Joe grabbed her hands and hoisted her up.

'See you later,' Nick said, phone in his hand as he went.

'Was he here when you arrived?' Joe asked, as the security guard disappeared around the side of the house.

'Yeah,' Rita said. 'The girl still a no-show?'

'Nothing. No calls. No messages. Phone's off.'

'How's the rich boyfriend?'

'Still alive. Gwyn's down at Jimmy's with him.'

She pulled a bunch of keys from her pocket and handed them to him.

'The club's turned off the alarm. It's on their central system.'

'That must be why they have a set of keys.'

'How are we doing this?' she asked.

'Properly.'

Once they were in full body suits, shoe protectors and latex gloves, he eased the door open and shouted, slamming his hand into the door and announcing his presence, just like he'd done outside his own house the other day.

They waited.

'Right,' he said. 'Let's make sure she's not here. Also, he might have left a suicide note.'

'Or, y'know, a recently amended will.'

They worked systematically through the ground floor. It was spacious and modern, its angles softened with thick carpets and rugs, several improbably large leather sofas, plus some eye-catching contemporary paintings. The overall impression was slick and declarative. But here and there were touches of something simpler: a plain white vase with coloured paper flowers, a small stack of paperbacks, George Orwell, Agatha Christie, Sophie Kinsella … And on the fridge in the kitchen, half a dozen postcards, all of Romanian churches.

'Another world!' she said, as they poked their noses into cupboards, drawers, behind furniture and curtains.

'Amazing what cladding buys. Gotta admire it, I suppose. Quite an effect.'

Back in the living room Rita picked up a CD from a pile on a large glass-and-steel coffee table.

'*The Best of Mădălina Manole*. Heard of her?'

'Nope. Romanian?'

'Looks like it. Our Ana's certainly been making herself at home. How's your place, by the way? Painted the front room yet?'

'No. But my bedroom's finished. Ironically.' He squeezed himself between a large potted plant and the curtains, making sure there was nothing unusual there. 'Right, what's left down here?'

They moved across to a short corridor, the last couple of rooms to look in before going upstairs. Joe pushed the first door open. It was a guestroom. Single bed. A polished wooden crucifix on the wall above it. Ana Dobrescu's body on white sheets.

'Ana? Ana?' he said, loud and clear. 'Ana ...'

His voice tapered off as his strength drained away.

Her eyes were closed, her skin grey but spotted with tiny red marks on the face. There was more colouration on her neck, red and purple blotches, faint in some places, the colour of ripe plums in others. She was laid out symmetrically, hands resting on her belly, one on top of the other.

Rita went into the room first, placed the back of her hand gently on the girl's cheek.

'Cold.'

'A dead body,' he said, as they came out of the house and struggled free of their white suits. 'Life's just an on-off switch, isn't it?'

128

'A murdered body, though?'

'Yeah, I know. It's—'

'Different.'

'She told me she was in danger,' he said, already dialling. 'Andy? I'm up at the house in Bilton. Ana Dobrescu. Dead. Murdered, looks like.'

'Jesus Christ! Right. We'll have a full response team up there in twenty-five.'

'Rita'll stick around. I've got to get back to Jimmy's. The bloke's not dead. We need to know where he fits in.'

'Fits in? Sounds straightforward to me.'

'I'm not so sure.'

'Aye, well you wouldn't be.' A pause. 'Fair enough. But, Joe? You've got a main suspect tucked up in a hospital bed. Sometimes it's simple, right?'

# 21

St James's University Hospital, Leeds. Gwyn Merchant was alone in the Intensive Care Unit waiting room, slumped on one of a dozen low-slung sofa chairs. Fuming. No attempt to hide it. No *ability* to hide it, which Joe considered a good quality, although it also meant that Gwyn could be a spectacular pain in the arse, along with his many other defects.

'Now then,' he mumbled as Joe appeared.

'If you're gonna punch somebody,' said Joe, sitting in the next-but-one seat, 'could it not be me, please?'

He leant all the way back, pushed the balls of his hands into his eyes, blanking everything out.

'You heard? About Ana?'

'Aye,' Gwyn said. 'She were telling the truth, then. Boyfriend did it? Affairs of the heart, eh?'

'I dunno.'

Gwyn grunted. He was wound up tight, like one of those blokes in the pub, just waiting for somebody to spill his pint, no one so much as getting close, never mind eye contact.

'So,' Joe said. 'Churchill?'

Gwyn gestured towards the door.

'In there. I heard him moaning. Tried going in, see if I could get owt out of him. Some arsehole kicked me out.'

'It is a hospital, I suppose.'

Gwyn got up. He'd had enough.

'I'll get back to the house. I'm no use here.'

'There's a response team, plus Rita. Go back to HQ, start uploading stuff to the system as it comes in. Meeting in an hour. And see what else you can find out about Ben Churchill.'

As Gwyn got to the door, a young man in green scrubs appeared. He was tall, about the same height as Gwyn, and they were blocking each other's way, both of them on the balls of their feet, like schoolboys working themselves up for a fight.

'Murder investigation,' Gwyn said, pointing to Joe. 'We're gonna need to talk to him.'

'When we're ready, *officer*.'

Joe sighed.

'Gents, please?'

The young man in green finally lost patience, barged past Gwyn, and slumped down on a seat, throwing his feet up onto the one opposite.

'We see death every day in this job. Gotta learn to keep your cool.'

Joe's spirits sank. He didn't need confrontation now. But when he looked, the doorway was empty.

'Knob'ead!' they heard from the corridor, and the sound of heavy footsteps receding.

The doctor was perhaps thirty, but the situation lent him the kind of hardened authority that Joe could only dream about.

'We need to speak to Mr Churchill as soon as possible. Do you have any idea how long we might have to wait?'

'Ruptured spleen. One of his kidneys is done for. Broken ribs and pelvis.' He let out the petulant sigh of a teenager who'd been given way too much homework. 'I mean, as soon as we can get him stable, he's yours.'

'Understood.'

'Oh, and there was alcohol and morphine in his blood. Way too much of both.' He swung his feet down and marched towards the door. 'You can see him if you want. But he's gonna be out of it, couple of days probably. After that, depends on how soon we can patch things up, how he responds. You can ring the ward for updates.'

As he bounded out of the room, Joe saw that a woman had been standing in the doorway, listening. She was in a white doctor's coat, about Joe's age, or a little older. Dark shoulder-length hair and a kind, full face.

'Hello?' she said. 'Police?'

'Yes. Are you treating Ben Churchill?' Joe asked.

'I'm Jill Wallace. Yes, I'm his physician,' she said, with a voice of well-practised concern, coming across and taking a seat opposite him before he had time to stand.

'Are all young doctors like that?' he asked, looking at the doorway.

'Quite a lot of them! It can be very stressful. Long, long hours.'

'Then a bolshy goon from CID barges in.'

'Well … yes. Here's the ward number, so you can ring for progress reports.'

She held out her phone. Paused. Then she looked at it, confused, tapping the screen again.

'Ah! There it is. I never quite got the hang of contacts.'

He got out his notebook and a pencil.

'I never got the hang of anything much after the turn of the millennium.'

'Please feel free to use me as a go-between,' she said, holding up her phone as Joe copied the number into his notebook. 'Dr Adams is extremely good at his job, but a bit of a nightmare to deal with.'

'Thanks. My son's studying medicine,' he said, not quite accurately. 'Should I be worried?'

She thought about it.

'You get to know your patients. For years, sometimes. Then, suddenly, you don't see them again. It's not for everyone.'

He put his notebook on the low table between them.

'We're the last generation, you know?' she said. 'That remembers a world before *devices*. People who grew up using pencil sharpeners, rubbers and paper clips.'

'Cheques. Postcards. Letters!' he said.

'Written by hand! When did you last get one of those through the post?'

'I … I have absolutely no idea!'

He did, though. It was last year, a handwritten letter from Jackie, after the divorce had gone through. *To leave everything the best way possible*. It had been full of compassion, yet distant, the goodness of a woman who'd cast you out of her heart but wanted you as a friend. Screw that, he'd told himself as he set fire to the bloody thing in the kitchen sink late one night after too much scotch. Set off the smoke alarm on the ceiling, had to smash it with a broom to get it to stop. Then he saw the ashes in the sink. No back-up, no cloud.

'I just saw a dead woman,' he said. 'She was twenty-nine. That's why I'm here.'

'Ben's a witness, I assume?'

'Has Mr Churchill's family been told about the accident?'

She shook her head.

'Issues of confidentiality. I can't reveal—'

'No one?' he asked, looking around at the otherwise deserted waiting room.

She smiled.

'He has a friend. A partner. I'm afraid we didn't have a number for her.'

Joe found Ana's passport photo, held his phone up.

'Her?'

She took her time, but finally confirmed that it was Ana.

Joe sat back.

'I need you to tell me everything you know about Ben Churchill. His character, his personality, whatever comes to mind. Here.' He held out his pencil. 'You can write it all down, old-style.'

A slight shake of her head.

'The ethical position isn't clear-cut. Anything I say would have to be very general. And I'd have to insist on it being anonymous.'

'OK.'

'Is he …?' she began.

'If I can also speak anonymously, he'd be in a cell right now, under caution, were it not for all this. The girl,' he continued, still holding out the pencil, 'she came to see me. She was in danger. I could have got her safe. But I didn't. Now she's dead.'

'But … *Ben*?'

He was still looking right at her.

'It's my fault. She was strangled, we think. Please.'

He left the pencil on the table between them, along with a card. As he got to his feet, his phone rang.

'Amazing it hasn't rung sooner,' he said, glad of the distraction. 'I'd better be going. I'll look forward to your notes. Thanks for the chat.'

With that, he was out of the door, phone pressed to his ear.

Ben Churchill's face was pale, waxy. His eyes were closed and his chest rose and fell gently. He seemed at peace, amid the tubes and flickering machines and the stomach-curdling stink of medical cleanliness.

'We've induced a light coma.' Dr Adams stood next to Joe and regarded his patient without much obvious concern. 'Touch and go, I'd say. He won't be playing twenty questions with you today, though.'

Joe looked at Churchill's thinning hair, his unremarkable features, the outline of his slight body beneath the sheets. Yesterday this man had been at home with Ana, the two of them out on the patio behind his millionaire's house. Tender, Rita had said. Then what?

'Can I see his hands?'

The young doctor pulled back the sheets. Churchill's hands were not large. The fingers were thin, smooth, nails short, well maintained. Not the hands of somebody used to physical work.

'OK,' Joe said quietly.

Back in the waiting room he checked his phone. Messages from the scene of crime team were coming in. A bag had been found at the crime scene. Ana's passport. A phone. A mug.

Mug?

He scrolled down the messages. Things were cranking up quickly.

He gave Sam a ring.

'Sam? Hi, it's me. You all right?'

His son's voice was a little croaky, that still-in-bed fuzziness as he answered.

'Look, there's been a murder, and I've someone else in intensive care. It's gonna be a long day.'

A pause.

'The way to eternal sorrow. That's what you said, right?'

'Dante knew the score. It all feels pretty eternal at the moment, son. I'll see you as soon as I can. Have a good day.'

# 22

When Joe got back, Andy Mills was in the ops room. Pantomime scowl. Everyone giving him a wide berth. On a notice board behind him were two enlarged images of Ana Dobrescu: a passport photo, her features dark and imprecise in the enlargement, and an image of her lying dead in Churchill's house, eyes closed, tiny gold cross around her neck.

'All right, cock,' he said as Joe approached. 'You were right. Don't friggin' gloat.'

'I wa—'

'Your team's ready and waiting.'

'Good. How long do I have 'em?'

'Got a main, haven't yer?'

'A bloke in intensive care's what I've got.'

'Background on him?'

Joe beckoned Gwyn over.

'Churchill? What've we got?'

'Cladding company. Sole owner. The company declared two hundred grand profit last year. Bloke's minted. House is worth a mill, an' all. Divorced, no kids, no record.'

'And now fighting for his life,' Joe added.

Andy Mills took a second, considered the information.

'Right. Couple of days, see where we're at.'

'You're joking?'

'Thought you'd say that.'

DCI Andy Mills let out a sigh, long and hard. The room fell silent.

'Right,' he said, so loud that it sounded like he was accusing someone of murder there and then. 'Twenty-nine-year-old woman, Romanian national, found dead this morning in her millionaire boyfriend's house. Strangled, looks like. Meanwhile, *he* drove his motor into a bridge. Airbag had been taken out.' He turned to the images behind him. 'Victim known to DS Romano, who will be Senior Investigating Officer, DS Scannon assisting. Quick wrap-up on this. Get cracking.'

A couple of seconds later he'd left the room.

'He didn't hang about!' somebody said.

Joe waited for the door to swing shut, then moved across to speak to Rita.

'Get everybody up to speed. Won't be a minute.'

He walked down the corridor, saw that Andy's office was empty. Went past it, to the very end, into the gents'.

Andy was leaning over a sink, the tap running. With cupped hands he threw water onto his face, although most of it went on his shirt and the floor around him. Then he straightened up, face dripping, hands pressed against the wall, his whole frame shaking.

'You all right?' said Joe.

When Andy opened his mouth to talk, nothing came out. His breathing was heavy, irregular.

'You know what this is.'

'Aye,' Andy whispered.

'Get yourself off home.'

'Clean missen up, first,' he said, still leaning over the sink.

'Get off home. I'll ring.'


In the ops room, Rita was organizing the teams, handing out information packs.

'Right,' Joe said. 'Andy's gone home. Bug or something. Everybody know what they're doing?'

They all nodded.

'Ring it all in, soon as,' he said as they prepared to go. 'However trivial. Get it on the system. If it's open and shut, let's make sure.'

'Romanian authorities?' Rita asked. 'We need details about her.'

'I can do that,' said Joe.

'Ooh, look at Mr Continental!' Gwyn said, big grin, just the right side of insubordination.

'I have my uses.'

No one could argue with that. How many sergeants in Leeds CID had contacts at Interpol? Joe had spent two years working in Lyon as an international liaison officer. The fact that his career move had been a flop served to temper any jealousy at Elland Road when he came back, tail between his legs, to take up where he'd left off.

'Right,' he said to Rita as the teams dispersed. 'We'll be looking at a charity called Rebuild. Ana used to volunteer there. Plus there's an employment agency where she worked when she first arrived in the country.'

Rita flicked through her info pack.

'Workout Employment Agency. Looks proper dodgy. That car wash in Batley, where Stefan worked? I called round first thing. They were using Romanian workers from the same agency. Stefan included. The agency gives 'em worker IDs, but they're not the ones for the workers they send.'

'Yeah, they all do that,' Gwyn said.

'Funny, though. The woman in charge of the agency is called Miriana Dalca. She's listed at Companies House as the managing director. But they had her ID at the car wash, like she were gonna be down there scrubbin' dirty mudflaps. Agency's owner, an' all. Omor Balan. They had his ID on file.'

'Ah, bollocks!' said Gwyn. 'They just need a few legit IDs for data protection, insurance, what-have-yer. Anybody with a social security number'll do. Then they send anyone they want. Workers sign in with false names. Unregistered, illegals, whatever. No one's bothered. Data protection laws are written on bog paper.'

'I've got this Miriana's number. She's not picking up.'

'Right,' Joe said. 'We'll pay her a visit. Let's make a start. This might be straightforward.'

'Here's hopin',' said Gwyn, on his way back to his desk.

'Oh, how was your evidence in court yesterday?' Joe asked as they prepared to leave.

'Played a blinder. Jury eatin' out mi hand. Guilty prick's goin' down, sure as.'

'Aye, well,' Joe said, 'let's see if you can use that charm of yours on a taxi company in Dewsbury. The details are on the system. Ana took a cab when she left the hospital. Where did she go?'

'One more blinder comin' up.'

'You have to admire his confidence,' Rita said, watching him go.

# 23

There was a dull, low-pitched noise as they both parked outside Ben Churchill's place; a second-hand Mondeo and a beat-up Land Rover to add to the various CSI vehicles crowding the street. Rita got out and wandered over to chat with a uniformed officer standing guard on the blue-and-white tape cordon in front of the house.

The sound came and went in waves, a distant thud in the air. Joe looked around. James Leonard, the crime scene manager, was there, plus a variety of others in body suits and shoe protectors, all coming and going, nobody rushing, nobody dawdling. The side of the house was also cordoned off, tape stretching out onto the golf course.

'Joe!'

Leonard was a little younger than Joe. He always had the manner of someone who was a bit interested in what he was doing, but not excessively so.

'Hi, James. What's that noise?'

'Helicopter. There's a helipad up at the golf club.'

'Right, right. So, developments?'

'We're going through the house now. Body's ready to move when you are.'

'What have we got out back?'

'A woman's bag. Looks like the victim's. Passport. Phone.'

'OK. We won't be long.'

They slipped into body suits, confirmed their IDs for the officer on the cordon, and went around the side of the house, following the trail of aluminium stepping plates that stretched around the edge of the golf course and into a small section of Bilton Woods, where his two best young constables were now standing.

'Lucky to get them two,' Rita said.

Joe nodded as he watched them. They made an odd couple. Gemma Pearson had worked her way into CID the old way. Her battered leather jacket, ginger hair pulled tight back, and a face like a ferocious but not unattractive bulldog all seemed designed to emphasize the fact. Mark Francis was black, stocky, with close-cropped hair and a demeanour way too peaceful for a copper. He had a degree in English Literature from Sheffield, then a couple of years in uniform before being fast-tracked into the unit. He was wearing the same dark-blue suit and tie he always wore. Gemma and Mark were often paired up. *Street and book*, people called 'em. *The two smarts*. You'd be hard pushed to find two DCs that worked better together.

Gemma saw them, beckoned them over. A CSI was on his knees close by, combing the ground close to the trunk of a tree.

'The body was probably here to start with,' she said. 'The ground's flattened. The bits of leaves and what-not on her clothes seem to match. Her bag were here an' all.'

'Looks like someone carried her back in,' Mark added. 'There are footprints in the grass, on the edge of the course. To and from the house. Just one set, we think. They're trying to narrow it down to shoe size.'

'Churchill?' asked Joe. 'No one else lives here. So he carries her in, lays her out on the bed.'

'Not the master bedroom, upstairs, though,' Gemma said. 'A downstairs guestroom.'

'Yeah, that's a bit strange. What's this about a mug?'

She twisted around, used her foot to point to an evidence marker in the ground about three yards to her right.

'Found there. Same as the ones in the kitchen. It's all gone to HQ.'

'Good. Let's get prints off it, and make sure the phone goes straight to Alex in IT. House-to-house as soon as you can.'

Joe turned, saw a well-dressed figure walking towards them.

'Oh, God, it's him.'

He held up his hand as he bobbed under the cordon and walked across to intercept Charles Malthouse. Rita stayed where she was, hands on hips, taking it all in.

'I'm afraid I'll have to ask you not to come any closer,' Joe said.

Malthouse pulled up abruptly, as if he'd only just noticed the plastic tape of the cordon, which was now right in front of him at waist height.

'I assume,' he said, 'this is related to your visit yesterday?'

'Afraid I can't say. But' – Joe glanced at the activity in and around the house – 'I'm sure you can appreciate the seriousness of the situation.'

'Mr Churchill?'

'Nothing official yet. What I need is a list of all current members of the club, and anyone who was out on the course last night or this morning. Plus all security footage for yesterday evening.'

Malthouse weighed up the request.

'Our security arrangements have become very tight. There are people here now who … well … I'd have to check.'

'Half an hour, or we get a warrant. I don't care who's dropped by in their helicopter. Half an hour, or we'll come in patrol cars, lots of us. We believe a serious crime has been committed on the club's premises.'

Malthouse stared at the house, said nothing.

'Right,' Joe said, cutting short the pensive moment. 'We'll be up to the clubhouse soon.'

'I'd better see what I can do, then,' said Malthouse, still looking at the house.

'While you're about it, why not mention it to the Assistant Chief Constable? He'll be backing us up on this one. At times like these, all the niceties just disappear.'

He spun around, phone in his hand.

'Better smooth that out with Andy.'

*Shit, I forgot …*

Rita caught up with him as he marched across to the house.

'It's your people skills I admire most, Joe.'

Clear plastic stepping mats formed walkways to and from all rooms and the front door. Officers trod on them carefully, heads down, taking it slow, making sure they didn't slip as they carried evidence boxes out.

They stood in the main living room, with its full-wall glass doors out onto the terrace and the swathes of manicured green beyond. Apart from the three immense dark-brown leather sofas, there was an array of modern floor lamps, each one heavy and metallic and probably costing more than a DS's weekly take-home. He couldn't even guess the value of the works of modern art on the walls, but they weren't Kandinsky posters in Ikea frames.

James Leonard came up behind him, clipboard in hand.

'Nice place. We're in the wrong job!'

'Are there any signs of packing?' Joe asked. 'Cardboard boxes in the garage? Suitcases? Does it look like stuff's been taken? Or stolen? Empty shelves, drawers, anything like that?'

Leonard flicked through the notes on his clipboard. 'Nah. There's still cash lying around. Nearly four grand in notes, stashed here and there. Nice watches, fancy stuff everywhere. Nobody's taken a thing.'

'Right. Shall we?' Joe said.

They went to the guestroom on the ground floor. The white doorframe was spotted with patches of dark grey dust, the same for many of the surfaces within. Three CSIs were working methodically on the wardrobe, the carpet, and the bedside table. Ana was still on the bed. Her body floated there, as if weightless, while around her work progressed in silence.

Joe stood in the doorway, Rita and Leonard behind.

'Duty pathologist?' Joe asked.

'Come and gone. Death about twelve hours ago. Strangulation. Slight bruising on the forearms, on the back of one hand, on both shins, just below the knees.'

'Anything stand out? Size of the handspan?'

'Not really, not at this stage.'

'Was she wearing a cross? I didn't think to look when we found her.'

'Yes. A small gold crucifix, very fine chain. It's been taken in as evidence. It was very precisely arranged around her neck. Someone had taken care when they laid her out.'

'Can you send us a photo of it?' Rita asked.

'You knew how this might end, didn't you?' Joe said, talking to the body on the bed, ignoring everyone else there. 'You were going to tell me everything, weren't you. Something good. Very good.'

The CSIs stopped work.

Rita's phone pinged. She held it up, showed him the image of a small gold crucifix.

'Jesus on the cross, eh?' Joe said. 'He knew as well, knew he was gonna die. Get behind me, Satan!'

He realized his voice was way too loud. The CSIs cast embarrassed glances at one another. Then they got back to work, none the wiser.

# 24

They stood in the main entrance to Bilton Golf Club, waiting for the president. Polished wood floor, small glass chandeliers, carved oak staircases that curled upwards left and right, not too big, not too boastful.

'Amazing, isn't it?' she whispered.

'Is it? I wonder,' he said, 'when people with absolutely nothing see my house, or where I grew up, do they hate it as much as I hate the idea of this place? Is it all relative?'

She huffed.

'Aye, well you could make eating a chip butty philosophical. It's nice, is all.'

They were shown into the president's office.

'The house,' Joe said as they sat down, 'plus the cordoned-off area, will be out of bounds for the rest of the day, at least.'

Malthouse sat on the other side of a large antique desk, listening patiently. The room was panelled in dark oak, a dozen gold-framed oil paintings taking up much of the wall space. There was a glazed Victorian plant stand over by the windows, large green leaves spilling from its rim like an explosion of nature elegantly frozen in time.

Joe's appetite for class confrontation had drained away. Aggression was pointless now. Ana Dobrescu was dead, and he'd done nothing to stop it. All he could do was clear up the mess.

'We'll let you know when those areas are released,' he added.

Malthouse seemed vague, distracted.

'Good. And, of course, you'll have unhindered access to club property.'

'Thank you. For the moment, we'll be focusing on Mr Churchill's house.'

'I'm afraid I'll have to correct you there, Sergeant. The club bought the house from Mr Churchill a month ago. We're planning to base a security team there. As soon as the property becomes available.'

'The house belongs to the club?'

'Yes, it does. But the owner wanted to carry on living there for a short time following the sale. Lock-stock, as it happens.'

'Lock-stock?'

'Indeed. The sale was rather unusual all round. Still ...'

'Is Mr Churchill a member of the club?'

'Associate member, by virtue of owning the house. He's occasionally dined in the restaurant, but he's never played a round, as far as I know.'

Joe considered the information as Rita took notes.

'How much did you pay for the house?' she asked.

'That's confidential, I'm not—'

'They go for about a million, don't they?'

'Like I said—'

'Call it a mill, then.'

Malthouse ignored her. He rose from his seat and handed Joe some papers. 'Current membership list, contacts, plus course bookings for yesterday and today.'

Joe took them, had a quick look, passed them to Rita.

'Right,' she said. 'We'll let you know if we need to contact anyone on the lists.'

'In the meantime,' said Joe, 'where were you yesterday evening?'

'For the purposes of elimination, I assume?'

'From early evening until this morning, please.'

'Of course, yes ... I was here. There was some legal business to deal with. I was with the club solicitor most of the evening. We had dinner here around ten. Then I stayed, as usual, until twelve, when we close. Drove home.'

'You locked up yourself?'

'A security guard helped me. We were the last two to leave.'

'Name?' Rita asked.

'Nick Evans.'

'Yeah, we saw him this morning.'

'Nick's been with us a month or so.'

'OK. It'll be on the security footage. We'll be needing that,' she added.

There was a knock at the door, which swung straight open.

'Ah, Tim, come in,' Malthouse said.

But Tim was already through the door, an air of fast-moving superiority, a thick file under his arm.

'Police?' he asked Joe. 'Tim Whitehead. I represent Mr Rajvansh.'

He didn't offer his hand.

'Mr Rajvansh,' said Malthouse, 'is the club's new owner.'

Whitehead stood there, opened his file, and read from the top sheet of paper.

'My client arrived by helicopter at ten minutes past twelve today. The helicopter came from Leeds and Bradford Airport, where Mr Rajvansh's private flight from Dubai landed some minutes before that. Here are copies of the flight logs, and his passport. Also his UK immigration documents, all in order.'

He passed various papers to Rita, who put them on her lap along with the rest.

'You'll be able to confirm the timings of my client's flight from Dubai with the Civil Aviation Authority, and his entry into the UK with the Borders Agency. Prior to this trip, he had been in Dubai for forty-eight hours. We can provide additional evidence of this if required.'

'And why are you giving us this information?' asked Joe.

'Because we believe Mr Rajvansh can be excluded from your current investigation.'

Joe let the suggestion settle.

Rita didn't.

'A criminal investigation on his newly acquired property? You don't even know what the crime is.'

'He was not in the country until midday. You have the timings.'

'He'll be needed for an interview, love.'

'I really think—'

'Helicopter?' she asked. 'The airport's, what, a ten-, fifteen-minute drive from here, isn't it?'

'He's dining in St Andrews this evening, hence the mode of transport.' He closed his file. 'In fact, he's heading off about now.'

Joe looked at Rita. They were both tempted. Stop the 'copter? Drag Golden Boy in for a chat?

'How long is the bossman going to be in the UK?' she asked.

'Until the weekend. He'll be back here on Saturday for a function.'

Whitehead gave Joe a card.

And with that, he was gone.

Charles Malthouse sat there, the edges of his mouth turning upwards a touch.

'And there we have it,' he said, as if a small but distasteful secret had just been divulged. 'The new regime. A genuine billionaire. He invested in the club last year. Wasn't content with that. Now he's buying the lot. Made us an offer we couldn't refuse.'

Joe was thinking.

'You said Ben Churchill has sometimes used the restaurant here?'

'Yes. Now and then. If I recall, the last time, he was with some people who run a charity. They're temporary members, on the waiting list, y'know. We allow them to use facilities to entertain donors.'

'Security footage of that evening?' Joe asked.

'No. We only keep copies for a fortnight. Although that's all about to change. Once the new system is up and running, the footage will be stored forever, I believe. It will be an extraordinarily secure location.'

'The new security centre's gonna be in Ben Churchill's old place?' Rita asked. 'The new owner must be keen to see the back of him.'

Even as she spoke, the low rumble of a helicopter rose from

behind the building. Meanwhile, Joe pulled out his phone, searched for the webpage of the Rebuild charity, got an image of the founders standing on a building site.

'Do you recognize these two people?'

Malthouse took a second, passed the phone straight back.

'Yes, that's them. The Benedicts. Michael and Sophie. In fact, they're doing a presentation here on Saturday. The new owner is attending.'

'Mr Billionaire?' Rita asked. 'Big fish for a local charity, isn't he?'

'That's none of my business.'

Malthouse sat back, seemed to relax.

'I found your father's application,' he said. 'Benito Romano. Nineteen eighty-one. Black-balled, as they used to say.'

Joe frowned.

'How on earth did you know?'

Malthouse smiled.

'Your surname is quite unusual. It also seemed vaguely familiar. So I googled you. Grandson of a circus clown! Then I remembered. I was here at the time, you see, working as the club secretary. I remember your father's application. In fact, I wrote the letter of rejection.'

'And to think all he wanted was to hit a ball around absurdly expensive grass!'

Malthouse laughed.

'It's about to become even more expensive!'

'Why was Dad rejected? Because he was the son of Gustavo Romano? Clowns not dignified enough?'

Malthouse shrugged.

'Because he was a theatrical agent, perhaps?' Joe added. 'Too vulgar? Or was it his surname, his Sicilian heritage?'

'That'll be the one.'

'You sound very sure.'

Malthouse took his time. 'My father was club president at the time. He was a racist, in a certain way.'

'There are *ways*?' Rita asked.

'He drove a tank in the war. He was shot at by the Italian Fascists. He saw a lot of death. Then he was transferred to the French border.'

'Where he was shot at by the Germans,' said Joe.

'Absolutely. It scarred him for life. Many men of that generation were the same. They refused to buy German cars. Or Italian, Japanese …'

'My grandparents were interred here,' Joe said. 'Dad too. He was only a baby.'

'People are a product of their experiences. I don't excuse my father's prejudices, but I saw how deeply he was affected by the war.'

'Has anything changed?' Joe asked.

'No. We see people through the filter of our own lives.'

'Indian billionaires, for example?'

'For example.'

'What about Romanians? There's been one living in Ben Churchill's house. Have you ever met her?'

Malthouse shifted in his seat, crossed his arms.

'I've seen her. The younger woman! People talk, gossip. It's only natural. Treat it like a soap opera. It's not, though, is it? Not now. It's a tragedy.'

'Quick sale, was it, the house?' Rita asked.

Malthouse ran a hand across the desk.

'Mr Churchill got the market price, not that he seemed particularly interested.'

'And the girl?' Joe asked.

'Immigrant. After his money, I assume. Now the poor man's dead, whatever it was.'

Joe shook his head.

'Churchill's in hospital. It's the girl who's dead.'

Back in the lobby, the three of them got to the main doors.

'Thanks for your help,' Joe said. 'We'll be in touch.'

'Here's the security footage for yesterday,' Malthouse said, handing him a DVD. 'Your surname would not be a problem these days. I suspect that golf's not your thing, though. And this club in particular seems to irritate you.'

'It's, I dunno, really ... I've got nothing against your club.'

'Several of your senior colleagues are members.'

'I know. I know.'

'And it is not *my* club anymore. I just got the sack.'

'Right,' Joe said, as they got back to their cars. 'I'm off to see those charity people.'

'Me?'

'The employment agency where she used to work. Why did she leave? What do they know about her? Speak in half an hour, see where we're at.'

# 25

The Beck. A muddy stream, almost hidden beneath the tangle of trees and brambles that lined its banks. It meandered along the valley bottom not far from his grandma's old house, down past the wine works and the fireclay company. Both long gone. His dad had played in the Beck when he was a boy. All the kids round here had. There were endless family stories about rope swings over the water, lads caked in mud, his uncle Frank shooting water rats with his air pistol ... a halcyon post-war version of Leeds, Grandad away every summer season in Blackpool, the rest of the family here. The Romanos doing well, trying to forget the war.

The Beck was now stranded between the ring road and a hotchpotch of warehouses and industrial units that had spread up the valley side. Nobody played here anymore. Yet something remained, something he didn't want to let go of, but which he hardly knew.

He pulled off the ring road and drove up past windscreen repair shops, car parts depots, delivery companies ... How many dodgy break-ins had he investigated in places like this over the years? *I have measured out my life with spurious insurance claims.*

156

He'd phoned ahead, made sure someone was going to be there. Rebuild: Giving for Life, was housed in what appeared to be the smallest and least remarkable building, two Portakabins jacked together and painted white. At the hospital, Ana said she'd met Ben Churchill here, but that she was no longer a volunteer. It was worth a quick poke around, at least.

He parked up and sat there, indulging in a few moments' silence, emptying his mind and floating gently away from himself. He looked down at the Mondeo, a middle-aged bloke at the wheel, Burton's suit, boring tie. Detective Sergeant. It felt like a bad joke, that he'd ended up here, chasing someone who was already dead, someone he could have saved, and that this might be his final case in serious crime.

'Hello. I'm Michael Benedict,' said the man at the door, a well-rounded southern accent, almost a drawl. 'We spoke just now.'

The small, sparsely furnished office smelt so strongly of old carpet that it made Joe's nose itch. Benedict wore impeccable cream chinos and a powder-yellow casual shirt with a small fleur-de-lis embroidered on the breast pocket. He was mildly handsome in a distant, faded sort of way, his face a little drawn, and his body slender, with well-groomed hair on the turn to silver.

A woman was sitting with her back to them, facing a screen.

'Hello,' she said, getting up quickly. 'Sophie. Sophie Benedict.'

Joe immediately recognized her from the charity's website. Her manner was friendly, buoyant, and her smile was disarmingly feminine. She was also tall, with shoulder-length blonde hair. Perhaps a decade younger than the man, she wore a plain white shirt and tight jeans, and she had a pronounced physical confidence, as if she'd walked straight out of a magazine.

'Rebuild: Giving for Life,' Joe said, pointedly keeping his eyes away from the woman's skin-tight jeans. 'I've read your website.'

'This place isn't much,' Michael Benedict said. 'But it does keep the costs down. Are you based at Elland Road, by any chance?'

'Yes.'

'So you must know Jerry. Jerry MacDonald?'

'Well,' Joe said, 'with an Assistant Chief Constable it's more a matter of knowing *of*. But yes, we're in the same building. You know him?'

'Just socially.'

'From Bilton Golf Club?'

'Yes, as it happens. Yes.'

Above a filing cabinet were two framed photos, one of Michael, the other of Sophie. The shots were professional, glamorous, especially hers, in stark contrast to the rest of the room, with its battered desk and filing cabinet, which looked like they'd been reclaimed from a skip.

'Sophie and I founded Rebuild a couple of years ago,' Michael Benedict said. 'I was working in finance, reckoned there must be more to life than making money. So we decided to put something back.'

'And you're full-time here?'

'We are.'

Benedict opened a door. It gave onto a storage area, empty apart from some wooden pallets stacked against the back wall and what looked like a strongbox in the corner.

'When this place is full there's enough to fill a container. You know, a lorry.'

'So you send things abroad?' Joe asked, sticking his head into the room.

'Originally, yes. NGOs would give us a shopping list, and we'd try to oblige. Clothes, bedding, soap and toiletries, non-prescription medical supplies.'

'Donations from the public?'

'Mainly companies. We've developed a solid network of business people in the region.'

Benedict closed the door and pointed to a framed photo on the walls: he and Sophie surrounded by a gaggle of Rotarians, men and women in suits and cocktail gowns, all smiling at the camera.

For a moment they stood in silence. The place was cold, and there was a dampness in the air that made the stale smell worse.

'Originally?' Joe asked.

'It's mostly financial donations now,' Benedict said, pointing to more photos. 'These are some of the projects we help to fund. In Eastern Europe.'

Benedict stopped, looked at his wife for support.

'Most companies prefer to give money,' she said. 'Less hassle. Tax deductible.'

She ran a finger across the photo of scrawny children in closely packed hospital beds.

'Getting funds into Eastern Europe is surprisingly simple. Electronic bank transfers. We're small enough to stay under the radar, but large enough to make a difference. It's all direct payments, so corrupt officials can't get their hands on it.'

'Why do you need this place, then?' Joe asked.

'We don't!' Michael said. 'We're moving out on Saturday. We've been offered free office space elsewhere.'

'Up at the golf club,' Sophie said.

Joe looked at the framed images on the walls, recognizing some of them from the website: Michael and Sophie Benedict standing in front of a dull concrete building, he a little drawn, showing his age, she as stunning as today; in another image there were children in a rudimentary playground, a single swing and a small metal climbing frame; several others showed kids in hospital wards, the walls a faded, water-stained green, the fittings battered, flaking paint …

'Romania?' he asked.

Benedict paused, just for a moment.

'That's a good guess!'

'Not a guess. I'm here about a young Romanian woman called Ana Dobrescu.'

Their eyes widened.

'Ana?' Sophie asked. 'Is she in any kind of trouble? She's here quite legally, as far as we know.'

'Legally?'

'In the country, I mean.'

'Her work here involves translation?'

'Not work, exactly,' Sophie said. 'She's helped out when we needed something translating, or a phone call to Romania. An occasional volunteer.'

'She told me she doesn't work here anymore. But her name's on your website.'

'Haven't got around to taking her name off.'

'I see … Is one of your donors called Ben Churchill?'

'Yes!' they said in union.

Sophie tapped one of the photos of a hospital ward.

'He's heavily involved in funding this project. One of our star donors.'

Michael moved close to his wife, put an arm on her shoulders. Together they looked at the image of the hospital.

'We're helping out with a couple of places. But this one, the children's orphanage and hospital,' he said, 'we're … well, we're quite proud of our work, to be honest, aren't we?'

There was a quizzical edge to his voice, as if the idea of being proud had only just occurred to him. Sophie smiled at her husband, let her head tilt a little way towards his.

'Yes, we are,' she said, her voice soft, her hair falling onto his shoulder.

It was a touching kind of modesty, Joe thought, played to perfection. Dozens of potential donors had probably heard exactly the same.

He thought about when to tell them. You only get one chance. The first reaction means everything. Not yet …

'So Ana didn't actually work for you. Do you know what kind of work she does? We're a bit hazy on that.'

Michael's eyes registered surprise.

'To be honest, I've no idea.'

Sophie shook her head in agreement.

'When did you last see her?' Joe asked.

They looked at each other, frowning, trying to remember.

'Oh, quite a while,' Sophie said. 'A month? Six weeks? She made a few calls for us, to Romania.'

The concern on their faces was ramping up.

'Are you aware of any relationship between Ana and Ben Churchill?'

Their concern was now growing, their discomfort obvious.

'Well, yes ...' Michael said. 'They're having a thing, obviously. We try not to get involved. It's a free country. We're ...' He paused, looked at his wife, as if for support.

'We're trying to find another volunteer for the Romanian projects,' she said, finally.

'Why's that?'

'Ana has become a bit unreliable. We can't complain. We don't pay her. But Ben is a donor.' She blew out her cheeks. 'It's ... I mean ... we're not absolutely sure about her motives with Ben. It complicates the situation for us, and potentially for this project.'

Again, she ran a hand across the photo of the hospital ward.

Joe watched her.

Now.

'Ana Dobrescu was found dead this morning. I'm investigating her murder.'

Sophie Benedict let out a tiny gasp, and immediately turned, lowered herself into the chair, Michael's arm still on her shoulder. He embraced his wife, leaning over her.

'Was Ana involved in any money transfers?' Joe asked, ignoring their shock.

'No, not at all!' Sophie said, her voice muffled.

'A bit of translating here and there!' Michael said, regaining his composure, standing up, a hand on his wife's neck. 'She was just a volunteer.'

Joe felt a massive rush of hatred within him, hatred for the world, for a life taken away, and knowing that all he could do was find out why. That was his job. Nothing more.

'Well, she's dead. Murdered. Everything you know, please. Everything, now.'

For the next ten minutes there were tears, fumbled attempts to explain how little Ana had really done for them, how they'd barely known her. Did he believe them? Yes he did. And no he didn't. Not now, because now he believed nothing. Those bodies lying dead on the dockside? And dozens more, every day? No one knew them, other than as statistics. Stefan Nicolescu could so easily have been another. There was nothing he could do to change it. But he could find the person who'd done this, see them stand trial for the murder of Ana Dobrescu. You have to know where you fit in, Joe. And now, suddenly, he knew.

'Right,' he said, slipping his notebook away, his pulse racing, his anger at the situation only just under control. 'I'll be in touch.'

He got to the door.

'We'll get whoever did this. Ana? She told me that …' He stopped himself. Took a breath. 'We'll get 'em.'

He sat in the Mondeo, counted to twenty, forcing himself to breathe more slowly. He felt the cold sweat on his forehead, a touch of nausea at the back of his throat. He started the engine and pulled away. And only then did he glance across at the Benedicts' premises. There it was: behind the window, the blind moved fractionally.

# 26

Rita pulled up at a crossroads. The address of the Workout Employment Agency was a couple of streets away. She was on the Roundhay Road, at the point where the fried chicken bars and halal butchers gave way to patisseries and diners boasting twenty-quid burgers and craft beer from Massachusetts. Bit different from Batley.

As she waited for the lights to change she noticed a restaurant on the corner: EL GATO NEGRO. Burnished steel lettering on dark grey signage. No explanation. No translation. What did it mean? Romano would know. He wouldn't have to google it.

'The Black Cat,' she cried. 'Friggin' Spanish!'

Ana had been in a Spanish restaurant last night. She'd read it in Joe's notes.

'It's worth a bloody try!'

The place was about half-full. But the bustle of lunch was dissipating fast. Two waiters idled by the bar, and there was more activity by the cash register than at the tables. The place didn't remind her of Spain. It could have been anywhere.

Bare wooden tabletops, old, distressed metal chairs, and slate boards announcing unpronounceable wines at Leeds prices.

A tall, young woman came across.

'Hi,' she said, downwards intonation, apologizing in advance. 'We're—'

'DS Scannon, Leeds CID. Not here to eat. You've got CCTV in here?'

'Eh, yes. In the back.'

'Let's go.'

They went through into the kitchen area, which was being washed down by a brigade of three young chefs. On the service area was a large stainless-steel platter. Half of a large potato omelette sat there, deformed and messy, its golden juices seeping out.

'What the hell's that?' Rita asked.

The manager seemed taken back by the question.

'Tortilla. Spanish potato omelette. If you like some, we can ...'

'Nah, just had a kebab, love,' she said, grinning.

They made their way into a tiny office.

'The security cameras go directly onto this,' the manager said, patting a laptop that sat opened on top of a filing cabinet.

'Yesterday evening. A young Romanian woman, with someone else?'

She smiled.

'Miriana.'

'Miriana Dalca?'

'Yes. She's a regular.'

'I'm looking for another woman, late twenties, dark hair, slight of build.'

'Miriana was here 'til about nine. There was someone with her. Hold on.'

She let his fingers run over the touchpad. A few seconds later video footage from behind the bar flicked onto the screen.

'They came around seven, I think,' she said, looking at the screen as she fast-forwarded.

'And her friend?'

'Don't know her so well, but yeah, I've seen her here before.'

'Since when?'

'I've been here a year. I remember her from when I started, I *think*. Here they are! Miriana in the corner. Just after seven.'

'Do they often eat together?' she asked, as he watched the footage of two young women leaning into their table, drinking red wine as they discussed the menus. Ana and her friend Miriana.

'Not recently.' She fast-forwarded again, watching the time counter click over. 'They left around nine.'

'Long time for a few tapas, isn't it?'

'We do traditional Spanish cuisine,' she said with a sniff of contempt.

'Beggin' yer pardon! More of a bhuna girl, me. Not in Leeds, though. The curry's shite.'

'You should give us a try sometime. Our food's not shite.'

'Might just do that, love.'

'Anyway, they had a full meal.'

'Wine?'

'Yep.'

'Here. They left at ten past nine.'

She pressed 'play' again. Two women at the till, Ana Dobrescu the smaller of the two, and perhaps a little younger. They were smiling, but there also was a determination about them, something deliberate, a kind of sternness. It didn't look like a girls' night out.

'Right,' she said, pulling a pen drive from her jeans pocket. 'All of that on here, please.'

'It's legal, right?'

'What d'you think!'

They waited for the files to copy.

'When they left,' Rita asked, 'were they acting unusual?'

The manager thought about it.

'Hard to tell. They weren't talking in English.'

'Could it've been business?'

'Yeah, I'd say so. They had two bottles, though.'

She pulled the pen drive out.

'Here you are, officer.'

'Thanks, love. I'll be back. To eat, I mean.'

Why can't all coppers be like that? she asked herself as she watched Rita move quickly across the kitchen, shoulders rolling, HEAD FAIRY twinkling on her back.

# 27

The offices of the Workout Employment Agency were on a winding residential street so lush and leafy that the houses seemed to have been planted in between the trees, rather than the other way around.

'Inter-war semis, spacious family homes, south-facing, gardens front and back. Out of my price range,' Joe said as he parked, wondering how many promotions it would've taken to make it up here. Too late now.

The Land Rover was up ahead, Rita sitting in it.

'Miriana's at home,' she said as he got into the passenger seat. 'Thought I'd better wait for you. Had a bit of a result.'

He listened as she explained about the restaurant.

'Right,' he said. 'Let's see how things sit with her, then bring her in, no?'

'You're the boss!' she said as they got out.

'Jeez, that sounds weird.'

They walked up the neatly maintained garden of number 25, a shrub-lined lawn on either side of the path.

'How was the charity?'

'Ana was just a volunteer. Nothing permanent. They were

shocked at the news, though. Southerners, well-dressed, refined folk. Right up your street.'

'Did they know owt?'

'Didn't seem to. That's what they wanted me to think, anyway,' he said, as he knocked. 'OK. I'll lead.'

The door opened. And there she was. Miriana Dalca, in a red and yellow floral print dress, the kind you might see in one of the local boutiques, simple but expensive. Her hair was dark, short, and perfect.

'Hello. I'm Detective Sergeant Romano, and this is DS Scannon.'

She paused for a fraction of a second, looking at the two warrant cards, then at Joe's face.

'Miriana Dalca,' she said, stepping back. 'Please, come in.'

'We're here about—'

'I know what you're here about.'

She led them into a spacious living room with a bay window and a large fireplace, complete with coal scuttle and a stack of split logs. The fire wasn't lit, but it had been set with a neat pile of new coal, the hearth around it clean and free of dust. Other than that, the room had the appearance of an office. A work desk over by the window, a single filing cabinet, plus a pinewood table in the middle, a few box files on it, not much else. A strange sort of office, although Joe couldn't work out why.

'This is about Stefan, right? The car wash, in Batley? I can make tea,' she said, as she indicated two chairs around the table.

Rita and Joe remained on their feet, and Miriana stood in front of the fireplace. Her expression was serious, but her manner was resigned, a touch irritated, as if she'd been expecting them and wanted to get on with it.

'So,' she said, hands on hips, 'Stefan gets into trouble, and here we are. What's the expression? Usual suspects?'

Her accent was Eastern European, but her diction was clear. A better speaker than Ana, more fluent, the forthright tone of a businesswoman. Had she been British, one might have called her a touch sassy, but the foreign accent lent her a fortitude that bordered on aggression.

'What does that mean?' Joe asked.

'Because I'm Romanian. It's a Romanian company. I get it.'

'Get what?'

'People judge. We're criminals. Beggars. Gypsies. Illegals. We're always the guilty ones.'

'We're not here to judge.'

Her eyes widened. Then she laughed.

'A Romanian employment agency? In England? Judging is all you people do!'

'It's your company, is it?'

'I run it. The director lives in Romania.'

'That would be …' Joe said, leafing through his notebook, 'Omor Balan?'

She nodded.

'Inland Revenue, DWP, I can show you everything,' she said, her arm indicating the entire room. 'But I have a business to run. And Stefan, I don't …' She let out a huff of breath. 'OK. Stefan, yes, he worked for us. Illegal. I admit it. We have a few people like that. Not many. Like I said, out records are—'

'Stefan has disappeared. And I don't think you'll be running your business today,' Joe said.

He let her think about that.

'Right,' she said, moving over to one of the desks and grabbing a phone.

'Miriana Dalca, where were you last night between the hours of seven and nine?'

She stopped, the receiver in her hand.

'I was working here, all evening, alone.'

'When did you last see Ana Maria Dobrescu?'

'Ana? A month. No. More, I think. She doesn't work here anymore.'

Rita was taking notes.

'Nearer two months, then, was it?'

'Yes. Probably.'

She put the phone down.

'Ana Dobrescu is dead,' said Joe.

He let the sentence hang in the air. Miriana said nothing, didn't move.

'She was murdered sometime after leaving El Gato Negro restaurant with you last night at ten past nine. We have the security footage. As of now, you are the last person to be seen with her.' He gestured towards the phone. 'If you were about to ring your solicitor, please go ahead.'

The amazement flooded her face. A withering horror. She shook so visibly that the hem of her dress seemed to tremble independently of her body, the knuckles of her balled fists white.

'We'd like to continue this conversation down at police headquarters. You are not under arrest. We're asking you to come to help us with our inquiries. Is that understood?'

It was only a question in the strictest sense.

They waited as she disappeared to get a coat.

'She seemed shocked,' Joe said.

Rita was unimpressed.

'She's a clever girl. Seemed keener to talk about Stefan.'

He took another look around the room.

'No computers! No screens!'

'Aye, you're right. Paper-based office, eh? Strike a match, the whole thing's gone. Whoosh!'

They waited on the garden path.

'Nice place,' Rita said. 'Posher than yours. Pricey?'

'Yep. A bit high maintenance for me. Gardens front and back. Pruning, weeding, mowing. Sod that.'

'So Stefan worked for the agency. Does it help us, though?'

'Dunno. The only person Stefan wanted me to call was Ana.'

When Miriana emerged from the house, her eyes were wide and vacant and there was a heaviness to her, a slowness. She looked ten years older.

'Do you have a vehicle?' Joe asked her.

'There,' she said, indicating a silver Volvo parked on the street.

'OK. Perhaps it'll be best if DS Scannon takes you. If that's all right.'

A minute later the battered Land Rover disappeared down the road, leaping through a series of abrupt gear changes, Miriana bouncing about on the passenger seat. She wasn't under arrest; no need for two officers.

He took a picture of the Volvo and sent it to Intel: Tracking on this for last two weeks, please. Log it to the Ana Dobrescu case. Thanks, JR.

He got in his car and scrolled down a few messages. Info was coming in steadily now, too much to assimilate here. In any case, he'd be back at HQ in fifteen minutes.

Then a message from Andy: I'm at St Bart's.

'Oh, well,' he said. 'It is on the way, more or less.'

# 28

St Bart's, a massive, brick-built church from the late nineteenth century, stood amid a swathe of old terraced housing on the edge of the city, in sight of the soaring towers and latticework of modern Leeds. The land rose steeply behind the church, back-to-backs, row after row, as tightly packed as old paperbacks that nobody was ever going to read again, rammed close together to save space.

The Romanos always said they were Catholics, but Sunday morning mass was rarely an option, with the previous night invariably spent in a theatre, club or circus ring. He paused on the steps. When had he last taken communion, last felt the host melt in his mouth? He tried to remember what it was like, the fluttering mystery of it, the strange thrill of the Eucharist … But it had gone, only the memory of a memory remained.

The church doors were heavy and overbearing, Old Testament doors, from a time that had all but vanished. It seemed to Joe as if the last remnants of a common faith were now disappearing, slipping through our fingers even as we tried to hold on to them, until places like this felt odd, out of place, almost embarrassing.

'Get behind me, Satan,' he whispered, grabbing one of the great handles, sensing the need to hold on to something.

And there was Andy Mills, in a black anorak, sitting on a pew halfway down the nave, which was otherwise deserted.

'Surprised?' he asked, as Joe slipped into the row behind.

'To see you here? Yeah, a bit.'

'Ever thought about it? God, all that stuff? 'Course you have. Never stop thinking, you.'

Joe said nothing. He inhaled, expecting the faint aroma of candles. But there was only dust and cold air.

'Been coming here a while,' Andy said, his voice low yet echoing around the church, as if he wanted all his secrets out in the open.

'Didn't know they kept churches unlocked these days.'

'They don't. I ring first. Warden were in our regiment. And there's always a tenner in't poor box when I sod off. So, y'know.'

Joe tried inhaling again. He closed his eyes, seeking out any last traces of his own faith. But there was only the sense of dampness, of things left to go cold. He looked at the altar. It was a stage, a place set for an act, complete with the paraphernalia of magicians, illusionists ... He still wanted to believe in the magic, though. You should never stop wanting to believe. Without a degree of blind optimism, what are we? What can we ever hope to aspire to without faith? In something, anything?

'Post-traumatic stress,' he said. 'You've dealt with it before.'

Andy shook his head.

'Been there. Got the jim-jams. This is different.'

'What, then?'

'Dunno. I'm … it's like … nowt's making sense. Just anger. Nasty, physical. It's getting worse, an' all.'

'You sleeping?'

'Sober? Not a chance. Look,' he said, holding up a picture of his daughter on his phone. 'I'm worried sick.'

Joe had known Karen Mills since she was a toddler. Family parties, barbecues, holidays a few times. He'd watched her grow up, seen her go from sweet kid to surly, sarcastic teen, then emerge as a cheerful young woman. There'd been a time when they all thought Sam and her would get together. But then the Romanos had made their momentous, ill-fated decision to move to France.

'That Romanian girl?' Andy said, his voice not even on the low side now. 'When I saw the picture of her, I saw our Karen.'

In the photo Karen was smiling, her hair pulled back, dark lipstick, large circular earrings. Ready for a night out.

'An' them girls in the grooming case? All I see is my own bloody daughter.'

He turned the phone off.

'Get me in a cell with one of them blokes, I'd break his friggin' neck. What kind of copper does that make me?'

'One with a heart?'

'One as can't do his job. How can I lead the troops into battle when I'm crying over mi cornflakes of a morning?'

'Perhaps you need to talk to someone.'

'Counsellor?'

'Perhaps. Or a psychiatrist.'

'That far gone, am I?'

From somewhere at the back of the church came the sound of a door closing. Or it might have been outside. Then nothing.

'You're leading a large, complex grooming inquiry, and overseeing a murder investigation that's just kicked off. And here you are, sitting in a church in your anorak. How far you gonna let it go?'

He waited for Andy outside, looked down the road. There was a Polish convenience store that didn't even bother to announce itself in English. Next to it a Jamaican takeaway. Further off was the dome of a recently built mosque. This was Joe's Leeds, St Bart's included, the whole messy lot of it. Because this is where he came from. Sicilian grandparents who'd pitched up here and made a life for themselves, in a terraced house just like the ones around here.

He found Dr Wallace's number.

'Hi, Joe Romano here. I wonder if I could pick your brains about something? Post-traumatic stress disorder.'

'You can try. I'm no expert.'

'Friend of mine. About my age. Ex-soldier. Active military service, saw some really awful stuff. Now he's in another stressful job. He's had PTSD before. I think it may be about to come back to haunt him.'

'I see … There was a study done on Vietnam veterans in the States. Rapid eye movement therapy. It worked in a lot of cases, I seem to remember. My husband works in psychiatry. I'll send you his details. WhatsApp OK, is it?'

'That'll be fine.'

'Great. I'm writing the character assessment you asked for now. Shall I send that to your WhatsApp as well?'

'Perfect,' he said, wondering how on earth that might even work. 'Eye movement, you said?'

'Yes. Give it a try. Er, your friend, I mean.'

'It's not for me! I wasn't in the Army. I was a schoolteacher before I joined the police. French and Italian at a comp in Chapeltown.'

'Chapeltown? Out of the frying pan, eh! So how do *you* cope with the stress? Murder investigations can't be very pleasant, I imagine.'

'I really don't know.'

But he did. He knew exactly how. He coped by seeking out a shred of hope. There was always something to hold on to, a flicker of light, a point of human goodness. It was what drove him, still, after so many years. He was ashamed to admit it, but the more horrific the crime, the more alive he felt, the deeper and longer he'd go on pushing. And Ana's death was the worst of all. Because he'd let it happen.

He heard the door open behind him.

'Here,' he said, passing the phone to Andy. 'The name of someone who can help.'

Andy stood there in his anorak, arms folded, scowling; a bouncer at the gates to Heaven. Finally he sighed, took the phone and prodded the screen, forwarding the message to himself.

'I'd better call the Duty Inspector, get stuff reassigned. I'm gonna take a few days off.'

'Sciatica? Safe bet.'

'I was thinking piles. But, yeah. Simon Tennant's the Duty DI. Good luck with that!'

'Tennant? I'll manage.'

'This Ana lass. You don't reckon Churchill did it, do you?'

Joe closed his eyes. 'Forget that.'

'Go on, though. You don't, right?'

'No, I don't. But it's got something to do with this Stefan bloke. Another thing.'

He paused. The Romano pause, good and long. It still worked with Andy, sometimes, despite all the years they'd known each other.

'Go on,' Andy said, expecting bad news.

'Any chance you could approve contact with the Romanian authorities before you ring in sick?'

Andy frowned. 'You'll be in contact with 'em anyroad, won't you?'

'No, I mean Interpol.'

'Jesus Christ, Joe!'

# 29

Detective Inspector Simon Tennant: thirty-four, fast-track graduate, athletic, short hair, no sense of humour. Universally respected. No one drank with him. It didn't matter. He'd be away soon enough, up the ladder.

He was at a workstation in the ops room when Joe arrived.

'Just spoke to Andy,' he said. 'I'm picking up for him. Where are we with Ana Maria Dobrescu?'

Joe took a seat.

'We've got someone in for interview. Her friend, ex-boss. Teams are still out. I haven't done the timeline yet. It's—'

'We'll do it now,' Tennant said, returning to the screen and clicking through the reports. 'There's a call from Ana to Ben Churchill at eleven-twenty last night. Two minutes long, call tracked to north Leeds. Roundhay area. After that her phone goes dead. Out of battery, most likely.'

'We have her up in Roundhay 'til at least nine.'

'Looks like she stayed longer.'

'Her picture's being circulated to all the local cab firms.'

'Good. No Uber on her phone. After that call, we've got

nothing. Timeline, timeline … Logic says she comes home, they argue, end up outside.'

'The woods are right out the back door.'

'So, out they go. Churchill strangles her. Comes back in. Drinks. Goes back out later on, carries her into the house.'

'Fits with the time of death.'

'And he makes a total of twenty-eight unanswered calls to her mobile over the course of the night. Last one at dawn, shortly before he drives into a bridge.' He pursed his lips. 'The footprints. You seen the report?'

'I've just got back.'

'Rita's been back half an hour. What took you so long? Whatever, I've called Financial Crimes in. They can look into this employment agency stuff. We don't do dodgy. We do death.'

'Footprints?'

Tennant got the report up on the screen.

'Across the bottom bit of the golf course. They only found one set of prints. His shoe size. The prints from the house are lighter than the ones going back towards it.'

'So he carried her back in?'

'Yeah. Footprints in grass, though? Not great evidence.'

'He might have found her during his morning ritual. He normally has a stroll outside with a cuppa, early doors. We've got a witness for that. Club security guard. He's on my list for an interview. Plus, we're waiting for the prints on the mug found outside. See if they tally with those from Churchill's car.'

'OK, but we've got a lot of manpower on this. And there's already a main suspect.'

'You don't go out for a stroll with a cuppa if there's a dead body waiting.'

Tennant sat back, the nearest he ever came to a smile.

'You might do if you're smart. You might call her phone all night as well, pretend you don't know where she is. Look, Churchill's still the main. He goes back out, carries her in.'

'With a cuppa?'

Tennant was on his feet. 'By the way, Andy's got sciatica.'

'Nasty.'

'Could've been worse. Should've been, shape he's in. Schedule a meeting for tomorrow, first thing. We'll pull it all together.' He straightened his tie. 'Who's doing this interview?'

'It'll have to be me and Rita. There's nobody else around.'

'OK. Let's see what she has to say. But remember, we've got a main.'

# 30

Joe went across to his own desk, logged onto the system.

Rita arrived.

'Has that bell-end gone?' she asked.

'Yes.' Joe looked at the screen. 'That was quick! There's no ANPR tracking on Miriana's Volvo last night. But she's been all over the place recently. Including Batley. Yesterday morning.'

'Pass it on to Financial Crimes, they're—'

'You dragged up anything on Miss Dalca?'

'The house is worth half a mill. It's not hers, though. It's rented by the agency.'

'Let's see what she says about Ana, which way she wriggles.'

Rita rummaged in the front pocket of her jeans. 'These are the videos from the restaurant.'

She plugged the flash drive into his computer and found the video file.

'How long's this gonna take?' he asked.

'Too long.'

She pressed 'play'. They saw two women in the corner table, their faces serious, leaning into the table as they talked.

'I had a call from Ana around seven-thirty last night,' Joe said. He checked his phone. 'Seven-twenty-eight.'

She fast-forwarded to 19.27 on the video.

They watched as Miriana got up from the table and left.

'That's it,' Joe said, his heart sinking. 'That's when she called me.'

'She phoned you when her mate went to the shitter?'

'Said the statement was going to be bigger. Another person. A lot of information ... something good. Very good.'

'So the other person's Miriana?'

'You'd think so. But why ring me when Miriana's not there? Was the meal a way of persuading her to come?'

'Hold on,' Rita said, moving closer to the monitor. 'Is that a folder? On the table?'

'Yes, it is,' Joe said, leaning in until his face almost touched the screen.

He ran the video at double speed: from time to time Ana pointed to the folder, which sat on the edge of the table, in the shadows. But neither of the women touched it. Fast-forward to 21.07: the women stood, prepared to leave. The shot of the table was obscured, a jumble of movement in a busy restaurant. When they left, the folder had gone.

'Right,' said Joe. 'You know what? I think she's a magician.'

He shifted his weight, raising his left arm and nudging Rita with his other shoulder. He clicked his fingers in her face.

'What the f—'

'Misdirection. Here.'

Joe handed back the phone he'd just taken from her jacket pocket.

'Bloody clown!'

'Runs in the family. It's called misdirection.'

'What is?'

But he'd gone.

# 31

Assistant Chief Constable Jerry MacDonald stood with DI Tennant in the observation room.

'Andy Mills'll be off for a while. Sure you're OK to take over from him at such short notice?'

'Yes, Sir. I've had access to the grooming investigation, at his request. I've been following developments. I'm on top of it.'

'Good, good. Meanwhile, the Romano show ...'

They watched the video feed as Joe and Rita got settled across the desk from Miriana Dalca.

'Main suspect's in intensive care,' Tennant said. 'No crime assessment as yet.'

'Why not? It's a domestic, right?'

'You'd've thought so. Her body was found in the house where they both lived. This woman's some sort of associate. Last seen with the victim.'

MacDonald moved in closer to the screen.

'But it's a domestic? That's the main line of inquiry?'

'It's not my case, technically.'

'You're acting DCI, though. How many people have we got on this?'

'Eight in total. Plus Financial Crimes have been called in, relating to this woman's business.'

'It should be quick, though, the murder?'

'I think DS Romano has his doubts.'

'Well, Romano has form when it comes to complicating an investigation.' He turned to leave. 'Keep a tight rein, Inspector! And copy me in on developments. We need officers elsewhere.'

Tennant watched as DS Rita Scannon kicked off the interview, DS Romano at the corner of the interview desk, taking notes in that slow, thoughtful manner of his.

'Redemption, Joe,' he said. 'That's all you want. She was in danger, and now she's dead. A thousand coppers won't change that.'

# 32

'Right,' Rita said, taking the lead. 'We have CCTV footage from El Gato Negro restaurant last night, plus the local area. Can we go through events when you left the restaurant?'

Joe took notes as he listened. He knew there was no footage of the local area, not yet. Cameras on the main road, probably. They'd get it all. Not that it mattered. Miriana didn't have to lie about her movements. She'd have a story worked out. He was pretty sure about that.

'We went back to my house,' Miriana said, her voice steady, serious. 'Had a bit more to drink.'

'Bit more?' asked Rita.

'Another bottle. She left after that. About two hours later.'

'Phoned for a cab?'

'Said she'd get one on the main road. There's a place.'

'So, about eleven?'

'About.'

'OK, Miriana. You and Ana, you have a nice meal. More drinks after. What was the occasion?'

'Catching up.'

'Who suggested it, you or her?'

'Her.'

'Did she mention any kind of trouble, problems? Boyfriends, arguments at home, work?'

'No. Just chatting.'

Joe shifted in his seat.

'We've seen video footage,' he said. 'It was more than chatting, I think.'

Miriana looked around the room, took her time.

'Yes. She was trying to blackmail me. But in a nice way. In an *Ana* way.'

'And what way is that?'

Miriana raised her eyebrows as if to excuse a child's naivety.

'She wanted to save me. She's a … was … a sensitive person. Religious, y'know. *Moral.*' The word sounded odd, invented. 'It's easy to judge when a millionaire's paying your bills.'

'What was she trying to save you from, Miriana?' Rita asked.

'From myself. From the company. Stefan got into trouble. He works at a car wash. There's been some problems.'

'What kind of problems?'

'They take unregistered workers. It's illegal, I know. We send a few people there. There's been threats, fights, violence. Some of the locals don't like it. It's the same everywhere. People hate us.' She shrugged. 'Anyway, that's finished now. We get fined for it. No big deal. The workers have left.'

'We know. You drove to Batley yesterday to make sure they left.'

She looked straight at Joe.

'We had a few illegal workers. I admit it.'

Joe thought about it.

'When I visited Stefan in hospital, Ana was there. I think

189

she mentioned your name to him. Did she ring you about the attack?'

'Yes. I got the workers to leave. You found out anyway. So we get fined. Is all right.'

Rita rubbed her face with both hands as she thought.

'You said Ana was trying to save you? From what?'

'She said I'd end up in prison. For a few illegal workers at a car wash! It wasn't right, she said. Especially us, because we're Romanian.'

'That's not how the law works, love.'

'It's how you all work, *love*. You know why customers come to us? Because we're Romanian. They expect the lowest wages. And the rest. Illegal hours, bad conditions, no complaining.'

'Ana knew this?'

'Yeah. But then she found a better life. So she started to judge other people for their sins, living up there in Bilton like a princess. Said she was going to tell the police. Wanted me to come with her. *Save* myself, before it was too late.'

Joe leant forward, put his pencil and pad on the table.

'Ana phoned me while she was in the restaurant with you.'

'You'd gone for a wee,' Rita added.

'She told me that someone else was coming to make a statement with her. To tell me everything. Ana was offering you a way out.'

Miriana nodded.

'All evening, she tried to persuade me.'

'Is that why you recognized my name at your house today?' he asked. 'Because she told you she was going to make a statement to me? Romano, quite a memorable name.'

'Recognized your name? I don't think I—'

'Because that gives you a motive, Miss Dalca.'

The room fell silent. Shock registered briefly in her eyes. But she rallied quickly.

'I'm sorry she's dead. I am. But what? You think I *killed* her, over a few illegal contracts?'

'Proof,' Joe said. 'What proof of these business practices did she have?'

Miriana remained defiant.

'She'd been taking notes. Like a schoolgirl. Lists of clients that we don't pay tax on, names of a few casual workers we sometimes use. It wasn't much, but she made it sound like some big, important crime!'

'Looked like a folder full of stuff to me.'

'A sheet or two of paper. That's all there was.'

'OK. There'll be in investigation into all that.'

'All agencies do it.'

'We don't care. We're investigating the murder of Ana Dobrescu.' Joe exhaled, tried to make sense of the woman opposite him. 'Do you know what I think, Miriana? I think that last night you had a big roaring fire in your front room. I sensed it when we were there. There'd been a fire burning recently.'

He let the idea hover there between them. Then:

'Ana's folder. Did it end up in that fire? And after that? Then what? Was Ana angry when she left?'

'A lot of wine, you'd had,' Rita added. 'Bit of a row, was there?'

Before Miriana could answer, a message buzzed on Joe's phone. He read it. Then he leant forward, a concerned frown on his face.

'Don't forget,' he said, nice and quiet, 'we're just having a conversation. You can leave any time you want.'

She thought about it. Then she stood up.

'So I leave!'

She was ready to go, bag on her shoulder, making her way to the door.

'One last question,' he said. 'Did Ana talk to you about the danger she was in? How she feared for her life? Are you scared, too?'

She stopped, turned.

He held up a hand before she could answer.

'Miss Dalca. Two officers from the Financial Crimes Unit are waiting to question you. DS Scannon will escort you to Reception.' He allowed himself the briefest of smiles. 'Like I said earlier, I don't think you'll be doing much work today.'

Her hand remained on the door handle.

'You didn't answer the question,' he added. 'Are you scared?'

She said nothing.

By the time Rita got back to the ops room, Joe was at his desk, typing up the interview.

'Financial Crimes happy to see her?'

'Yeah. She wasn't too bothered about the car wash stuff. I guess she's right. Businesses like that are all a bit dodgy.'

'She's a magician. You'll see,' Joe said as he sat back, stretched. 'And what did you think about her performance? She'd got over the shock pretty sharpish. Was she telling the truth?'

Rita huffed, flopped down into a chair.

'Lying through her bloody teeth. But about what? She's copped for the workers in Batley.'

Joe was shaking his head.

'They're not gonna find anything. Who's betting that filing cabinet is empty now, the whole lot burnt?'

'How can you be so sure?'

'Misdirection. All that bullshit about a car wash? It's to deflect attention. She's hiding something.'

'What?'

'No idea. But I'll bet it was in Ana's folder.'

Rita groaned as she got to her feet. 'Christ, Joe! Churchill did it!'

'Little wager on it?'

'Go on, then. What?'

'New suit for your wedding. My father's tailor in Manchester.'

'Marks and Sparks, Leeds.'

'Done.'

# 33

He stood close to the body, trying to ignore the vinegary smell that hung in the air. He stifled a shiver of nausea, wondering where he'd vomit if it came to that. Her eyes were closed, and the skin on her face and neck had taken on a yellowish hue, the bruises themselves now melding into a general stain of red and purple. There were roughly stitched incisions across her neck and down the chest, and more running from each corner of her mouth as far as the ear.

He never knew what to do in the mortuary. Hands clasped together out of reverence? Or in his pockets, feigning normalcy? Perhaps there was no natural way of doing it. In his more contemplative moments he thought of police post-mortems as amateurish, low-rent versions of Purgatory. Mute bodies queuing patiently to have their sins weighed against the ultimate price they'd paid for some absurd, pointless shit: a few hundred quids' worth of drugs, a drunken argument that got out of hand ...

What sins might Ana have committed to deserve this? He had no idea, but it occurred to him that praying for her soul might be his best course of action now. Perhaps he'd be more use lighting a candle in St Bart's, because he definitely wasn't any use to her down here, stifling the urge to puke, brought on not by the sight of a dead body but by the belief that she couldn't possibly have deserved an end like this.

'Are we waiting, then?' the pathologist asked, tapping the toe of her shoe on the floor, a hand resting on each side of the slab, just behind Ana's head.

She was young, younger even than the body she'd recently cut up and explored. Her accent was clipped, Scottish, and her manner was so cold and unconcerned that it had to be an act. Joe hadn't seen her since the double murder case last year, and it didn't appear that she'd acquired large amounts of tact since then.

'You know,' he said, then waited for the tapping to stop, 'soldiers have a saying: *there's no atheists in the bunker*. What about pathologists?'

'Makes you think, does it? Always worse when they're young and fragile.'

'Doesn't matter who it is.'

'No? Would you be getting all philosophical if it was a tattooed street dealer with a record as long as your arm? Or a murderer?'

He looked down at Ana, at the outline of her narrow shoulders, her pale lips. She'd been sliced apart then stitched back together with thick, dark thread, like a child's ham-fisted attempt at mending a torn teddy bear. But it wasn't even that. There was something else. Then it struck him. She wasn't wearing her gold cross. It would be bagged up in the evidence store now. She looked incomplete without it.

'So,' he said, 'you don't feel anything when you see this?'

She moved around to the side, closer to him, until their forearms touched.

'The human body?' she said, running a finger gently down the stitching on the side of Ana's neck. 'It's a sack of meat. Life is the meaning. Without it, it's just the meat.'

'You really believe that? Or is it a way of coping?'

'Fifty-fifty,' she said, and now she was looking at him.

'Fair enough. And, by the way, it's not worse because she's young. I knew her. She told me she was in danger. Now this.'

She held his stare.

'OK,' she whispered.

The door clattered open.

'Fuckin' hell, sorry I'm late, love!'

'Oh, hi, Reet!' she said, snapping back into her normal tone of voice and moving off to get her notes.

Rita ran a hand through her crew cut, scratching her scalp, grimacing, warding off a quick shudder of revulsion. 'I'm ready, Jen.'

The pathologist retook her place at the head of the slab. And it occurred to Joe that he'd never known what the pathologist was called. How come everyone else gets onto first-name terms so quickly?

'Right,' she said. 'Healthy woman, late twenties. No signs of manual work, nutrition good, teeth fine. Quite a lot of alcohol in her blood. Food and red wine still in her stomach. No drugs, no meds. No evidence of recent sexual activity. The initial report on time of death seems about right.'

'Midnight yesterday, then?' Rita said, taking notes.

'Yep.' Jen consulted her clipboard. 'An hour or two either side.' She flicked over the page. 'Right. The science-y bit. Cause of death is hypoxia, plus cardiac arrest resulting from probable bradycardia.'

'English, love?' Rita said.

'Strangulation. See the pinpoint haemorrhaging on the face and neck? The jugular veins are obstructed. Blood continues to flow to the brain but can't flow back out of it. Effectively starves the brain of fresh oxygen. There's also subconjunctival haemorrhaging.'

'The eyes, right?' Rita asked.

Rita was writing as fast as she could. It would all be in the report, but she noted everything down anyway.

Meanwhile, Joe tried to imagine Ana's final moments alive.

'Position of the killer?' he asked.

'Location of the fingerprints suggests the killer was to the right of the victim.'

'Size of the hands?'

'Average,' she said, holding her own hands over Ana's neck. 'Slightly bigger than mine. About your size.'

'A man, then?'

'Hard to say, but on balance, probably. Finger indentations are a decent size. But,' she said, watching as Rita held up a hand, pen still in it, 'could almost have been you, Reet. No nail marks.'

'Nail-biter?'

'Yeah. You might expect some marking, but it's not an exact science. Gloves, perhaps.'

She stopped. DI Tennant was standing in the doorway.

'Carry on, Jen,' he said as he came over to join them.

'Right.' She placed her hands on her own throat as she spoke. 'A tight, two-handed throttling? You don't need a lot of pressure. Anyone could do it.'

'How long would it take?' Joe asked.

'There's haemorrhaging to the soft tissue in the neck and the base of the tongue, partial fracturing of the thyroid cartilage, damage to the carotid arteries.'

'Hard and quick,' Tennant said.

'Exactly. With enough pressure on the carotids, she could've been unconscious in fifteen seconds, ten, even.' She glanced at Joe. 'So, hypoxia and cardiac arrest to follow.'

Tennant was now leaning into the body, examining the legs and arms.

'Not much sign of a struggle,' he said. 'A faint line of bruising here. Legs swung into something?'

'Most likely. A bit of bruising on the arms too. Might not have had time for much else. There's no residue under the nails. Looks like she didn't have time to fight back.'

'Quick and efficient, then?' Joe asked. 'Any sense of there being medical knowledge involved?'

'Not really. The neck is a vulnerable area. With both hands, you can do a lot of damage quickly. Strangulation is very effective. A small, slim victim, alcohol involved, slow to respond? Very, very effective.'

They stood there, not quite sure what to do. Joe wanted to hear more. She deserved more. More what, though? Words?

'Right,' Tennant said, after a decent pause, 'is that about it?'

'I reckon.' She held up her notes. 'The full report's ready, but the takeaway is that it's classic strangulation.'

'Good,' Tennant said.

*Good?*

'Strange thing,' Tennant continued, as he looked at the corpse, 'she knew it was coming, didn't she, Joe?'

Joe inhaled, kept his eyes down.

'Not the way I'd choose to go,' Jen said.

Tennant turned to leave.

'All pretty straightforward, then. Fits with a domestic. We'll reconvene tomorrow.'

'Those fingerprints on the neck?' Joe asked. 'Is there anything we could get from them? Traces, residues?'

Tennant stopped.

'Yes,' Jen said. 'That'd be the next stage. You want me to go ahead and book that in?'

Joe felt Tennant's presence, forced himself not to look.

'Yes. Whatever we can get.'

Now he looked. But the door was already swinging closed.

'Thanks, love!' said Rita, following Tennant out.

Meanwhile, Jen was stooped over the body, her face just inches from the bruises on the neck.

'I hope it was,' she said, a new softness in her voice.

'Was what?'

'The carotids. I hope it was fast. Poor lass.' She thought about it, smiled at Joe. 'OK, sixty-forty. In your favour.'

'I'll take that as a win, Jen.'

# 34

There was a fire door at the end of the main corridor in the mortuary. It was wedged open with a brick, voices coming from outside. Every door on the ground floor of the building had a brick next to it. Elland Road was one of the UK's newest and most sophisticated police HQs, with a security system to match; but smokers, like termites and house mice, will always manage to make themselves feel at home.

Joe followed the smell of tobacco. Rita was outside, deep into a rollie. Leaning on the wall next to her was someone else.

'Alex, what you doing here?' Joe asked.

Alex Ambler was by far the best-educated person in Leeds district, with a PhD in Computational Analytics and a growing reputation for digital investigation. But today, in a Def Leppard T-shirt, tatty old jeans and boots, the Head of Forensic IT looked more like he'd been picked up for selling blow outside the local comp.

'Came to find you. I pulled more stuff off her phone,' he said, with all the enthusiasm of a sulky teenager, as if anybody could've done it. 'Call history, contacts, apps, websites. It's up on the system.'

'Great. Anything stand out?'

'Thought you might want to see this. There was a text message saved to drafts. No contact selected. Here.'

He held up a print-out: Dove le cose sono cresciute.

'What the hell does that mean?' Rita asked, poking her face into the paper.

'Italian,' Joe said. 'It means, "where things are grown".'

'Code?'

'Dunno. It was for me, though.'

'Yeah, right!' she said. 'It's all about you, Joe!'

'I gave her my name yesterday at the hospital. Alex, did she google me?'

'Got the log from her phone here,' said Alex, squinting at the tiny screen as he scrolled through page after page of data. 'Yeah, she googled you. Hold on ... The Romanos Band-dot-com. That's your band, right?'

'Yes.'

'She accessed that site as well.'

'The band webpage,' Joe said. 'There's a biography of me on it. If she read that, she would have known that I speak Italian.'

'But she's Romanian,' Rita said.

'Italian and Romanian,' said Alex, ready to go. 'Very similar languages, I believe.'

'Yes. So she wrote a message in Italian, ready to send to me.'

'Where things are grown?' Rita asked.

'Dunno. You fancy a trip down the farm? Perhaps they can tell us.'

# 35

The Romanos band was formed by brothers Tony and Joe in 1988. Originally managed by their father, the theatrical agent Benito Romano, they enjoyed some early success as a cover band, playing in pubs and working men's clubs throughout the north of England. They also wrote their own material, which the *Yorkshire Post* described as 'lyrical rock with fierce guitar chops: a band to watch'.

The group was offered a recording contract by Manchester-based indie label Corkscrew Records. However, they broke up before the contract was signed. Their sole recording is an early demo tape, which has never been aired.

Twenty-five years later, Tony and Joe re-formed the band, and now play a wide range of music, from Bill Haley to Dire Straits. The Romanos are available for weddings, birthdays, conferences and bar mitzvahs in the Yorkshire area.

from TheRomanosBand.com

Rita huddled down with her phone as Joe pulled into heavy traffic on the M1. Since she'd been seconded to Leeds district, they hadn't worked together much, and when they did, his occasional tetchiness and a tendency to read too much into everything had sometimes got to the point where she wanted to send one of her black Docs towards his arse. She hadn't wanted to spoil his suit, though, since he didn't seem to have many.

He kept to a steady seventy, watchful of the hundreds of cameras all clocking his number plate. Networked cameras on every bridge, on tall yellow poles, at exits and slip roads, service station forecourts, up in the sky for all he knew.

'You off to Triple-A this weekend?' he asked. 'It's on a weekend, right?'

'Sunday evenings.'

'That security guard from the golf club. Is he a regular?'

'Nick? Regular as me.'

'Married? Girlfriend?'

'Single. Don't worry, somebody'll be interviewing him,' she said, hardly listening.

Around them the traffic was manic, unyielding. He cast his mind back to long, sweaty days on French and Italian motorways, how the pure selfishness of continental driving was somehow more tolerable – a little less malevolent, a kind of blithe fatalism to it – compared to the unremitting aggression of British roads. Suddenly Brexit made perfect sense.

'So,' he said, pulling into the third lane to get past another lorry. 'The Workout Agency? It's a paper-based business. No computers.'

A bulky black Volvo was immediately on his bumper, flashing to get past. Joe pulled back in, ahead of the lorry.

'Jesus, don't they know there are cameras everywhere?'

The motor drew level with them and remained there.

Rita looked across, gave the bloke the finger, holding her hand up proudly, like she'd just won it on the tombola.

'This Miriana chick,' she said, ignoring the Volvo, but her finger still in the air, 'she burnt the lot?'

'I'm guessing. Whatever she was really doing, I reckon it all went up the chimney. Financial Crimes'll have a job proving anything worth a prosecution.'

'Clever cow!'

'Not as clever as me, though. Ana took a taxi from the hospital. I got the number. Gwyn chased it up. The driver said he took her south on the M1 to a poultry farm, paid him a hundred and fifty in cash, then begged him to stay, another hundred-odd for the trouble. She went in, a few minutes later she came out. Running. That was it.'

The Volvo accelerated away, disappearing amid the trail of red and white light that wound through the dark contours of Yorkshire like a fat, glowing python.

'By the way,' he asked, 'any progress on making things permanent in Leeds?'

'Yeah, soon as a job comes up. Federation rep thinks I'd be the first outed lesbian sergeant in the local CID. This day an' age, eh?'

'There you go! Ticked that box.'

'Token lezza!'

'Don't knock it. I'm the token awkward bastard. Any box'll do.'

'Token jammy bastard, more like.'

She pushed herself further down into her seat, wished she'd kept her mouth shut.

'Jammy?'

'I've heard folk, y'know, having a dig. You piss off to France. Job at Interpol, all lah-di-dah, ideas above your station and what-not. When that doesn't work out, you're straight back in CID. Then there's the case last year.'

'Ha! Plenty of scope for digging there!'

'You were trending in the canteen for weeks! Getting pissed in a pub with a suspect, dinner together before you arrest her ... You got off lightly, that's what folk were saying. Andy's yer best mate, all that stuff.'

'I don't bloody feel lucky!'

'Not lucky, then. It's just ... no one knows where you're at, Joe. You're hard to make sense of.'

'Yeah, I have that problem too.'

She pulled a packet of Old Holborn from her jeans pocket.

'And you can forget that,' he added, feeling his resolve give way before he'd even finished the sentence. 'Go on, then. Roll us one.'

They drove in silence as they smoked. The hypnotic rumble of the tyres reminded him of being on the road with the band a lifetime ago. Burgers in lay-bys, peeing at the side of the road, buffeted by the wind as lorries raced past. Hauling the speakers into the gig, setting up ... Scruffy pubs, working men's clubs that reeked of beer and toilet cleaner and fags. Didn't matter. While you're on stage you're in a different world. The audience is pretty much irrelevant. You're the audience. You watch yourself playing, and everything's different. You're different. It's the version of you that you always wanted to be. A better you. That's why bands go on forever. Because without it, there's only the real you.

The thrill of performing was less intense these days, and the sense of chasing old dreams hung over them, the what-ifs, the regrets. But now and then it came back, and he was happy. They never signed that contract, though. *Woulda, coulda, shoulda …*

The Mondeo instantly stank of smoke. It'd be there forever, gradually mutating into the smell of grotty bedsits and old cardboard. A smoker's car. That's what he had now.

"Ere,' she said. 'Something to show you.'

She took the shrivelled fag-end from his lips and docked it in the Kleenex that they'd been using as an ashtray.

'That charity bloke's on YouTube. Look. Crunchy Nut cornflakes.'

She held up her phone. Joe did his best to watch as he drove. A younger version of Michael Benedict walked through a sun-drenched orchard towards the camera, sat at a rustic table under a tree, and ate from a bowl.

'He were an actor. I spoke to his old agent.'

'Benedict? Finance, he told me.'

'He started out as an actor. His wife did a bit of modelling. I guess that's how they met. He got a few small parts in musicals, some voice-over work. It never came to much. Then he jacked it in, became a day trader.'

'Made a pile of cash, started a charity?'

'Yeah. Nice house they've got, an' all. I googled "day traders". It's selling stocks and shares.'

'Is their house bought or rented?'

'Dunno.'

'We can find out. And let's have a look at their bank records. See what kind of—'

'Jesus, Joe! It's Churchill! You know the stats. Odds on it's a domestic.'

He ignored her, squinted at the TomTom.

'Right. Here's our turning.'

They headed along a raised dirt track. On both sides of them ploughed earth extended into the black night. The only thing they could make out with any clarity was a collection of low-slung buildings in the mid-distance, and above them a series of grey cylindrical structures, smooth and featureless, like enormous ghosts hanging in the sky.

'Those,' Joe said, 'are grain silos.'

'Silos. That's grand!'

'And I reckon that's gotta be the biggest poultry farm I've ever seen. This is where Ana came, right after talking to me at the hospital.'

They stopped in front of a set of open gates on the farm's perimeter. There were seven or eight wooden sheds visible, so long that they just tapered away into the distance.

'There must be literally thousands of hens in there,' he said.

Rita shuffled in the passenger seat.

'Literally. What's the plan? I'm busting for a slash.'

'Speak to the owner. See what Ana was doing here.'

'Hope he's got a khazi.'

'Wait. What's that?'

About a hundred yards away, at the entrance to the nearest shed, was a white van.

'It's a Transit, Sherlock.'

The van had just turned around in the yard and now came to a stop, its lights still on. People emerged from one of the sheds and began climbing into the van through the back doors. It didn't take long. Then the doors were pulled shut and the van began moving towards the gate, the beam of its headlights bobbing wildly up and down through the darkness.

'That'll be the workforce,' Joe said.

The van drove right past them, flying over potholes as if its suspension needed a good workout. The driver wore a baseball cap, his face thin, young, unshaven. He looked straight ahead as he drove.

'OK,' said Joe. 'I've got a better idea. You can hold it for five, right?'

# 36

Ten minutes later the van came to a stop on a street of old terraced houses. They were small and narrow, their doors giving directly onto the pavement. A couple of them were boarded up, and there weren't many cars about. They'd passed a several shops on the way, all with heavy security grilles, plus a pub on the corner that looked like it'd been closed a good few years.

'Wish parking were this easy in Leeds,' Rita said. 'Old mining village?'

Joe nodded.

Three houses ahead of them the van's lights went out. A dozen people emerged and trooped through the front door of the nearest house, heads down. The last of them was the driver. He locked the van and went in after them, not so much as casting a glance back at the car which had quite clearly been following them all the way from the farm.

'Left to rot,' Joe said, 'like you leave an old wheelbarrow in the garden. The pits closed, and places like this were abandoned. Everybody in 'em, too. Meanwhile, up in Bilton there's folk arriving in Ferraris and helicopters to play golf.'

He opened his door. 'Two worlds. And to think Ana Dobrescu had a foot in both.'

'Yeah, well I'd gladly take a piss in either.'

They knocked on the uPVC door. A crack ran from top to bottom on the hinge side, repaired with several layers of brown duct tape. They waited. Knocked again. It took a while, but finally the door opened an inch or two. A pair of large eyes peered out. Young eyes, but sunken, the skin around them somewhere between olive and a dusty brown.

Joe held up his warrant card, went through the routine.

The door eased open a little more to reveal the face of a young woman. Her complexion was dull, the skin pulled tight over the features of a strange, asymmetrical face. She was nervous, but her expression was edged with curiosity as she looked past Joe.

'I'll tell you what, love,' Rita said, shoving him to one side as delicately as she could, which was a bit like a Leeds Rhinos prop having a go at ballet dancing. 'I really need the toilet. *Toilet?* Can I use your bathroom? Please, love? Busting here!'

They were ushered inside.

'I'm police, too,' she said brandishing her warrant card. 'Rita. My name's Rita. What's your name?'

A pause.

'What's your name, sweetheart?'

'Sabina,' the young woman said, pointing towards the stairs, which were bare wood, half a dozen of them replaced with chipboard, the banister missing many of its uprights.

Rita sprinted upstairs, leaving Joe there in the hall.

'We need to ask a few questions,' he said, shifting on his feet, the carpet close to the doorframe damp and spongy underfoot.

Sabina's head was shaking. She made a vague gesture behind her.

'Through here?' he asked, indicating the first of two doors.

Small terraces like these often had the two ground-floor rooms knocked through, but probably not this one, Joe thought. The other room would be a bedroom. He'd lived in a place just like it in Nottingham years ago, the worst part of town, five students crammed in a house about this size. His room had been tiny, most of the free space taken up with his amp, speakers and guitars. The only place for visitors to sit was the bed, which in fact hadn't worked out too badly.

He opened the door. It was enough to make you gag: bitter and acrid, the smell of shit, and beneath it the savoury whiff of bodily neglect. There were eleven people in the small front room. Mainly young, but dirty, unkempt, their exact ages difficult to guess. They wore tatty jogging suits, old jeans shiny with grime, army-style fatigues. Three of them sat on a small sofa that was about ready to collapse into the floor, and there was also a battered armchair in the far corner. The remainder were on the carpet.

The TV was on, but it had already been muted. They all stared at him with blank faces.

'Detective Sergeant Romano,' he said, holding up his card. 'West Yorkshire Police. We need to ask you some questions.'

He waited. *Police*. There's always a reaction. A giveaway. Sometimes it tells you more than what folk actually say.

Nothing.

He heard the toilet flush up above, then Rita's heavy footsteps as she came down.

'Bloody hell, sardines in here!' she said, giving the room a quick once-over as she squeezed in and stood against the wall behind Joe.

Normally Rita's soft, kind face had an immediate effect on people. There was a natural warmth to her, something in her voice, in her whole being, that was difficult not to respond to, despite the crew cut and the nose stud. That's why she'd been interviewing rapists for Andy, because eventually, without knowing it, they began to open up to her. Everybody did, in the end.

Not today, though.

'This is my colleague, DS Scannon,' Joe said.

Meanwhile, Sabina crept into the room and perched on the arm of the sofa. She let her hand fall on the shoulder of the gaunt woman next to her, who might have been any age, her cheeks hollow, mouth pinched.

'Right,' Joe said. 'Who speaks English?'

As he said it, he looked at the man who was sitting in the armchair. The driver of the van. He was holding a large mug, almost hiding behind it, arms close to his body. Even from where Joe was standing he could see that the mug contained beer. Several others also had mugs. And on the floor, in various parts of the room, were large brown bottles. Two litres? He didn't recognize the brand, but there was plenty to go around.

Again, he was reminded of his student days. But there was no buzz of youth here, no music in the background, not the faintest trace of joy. Instead, there was a numbness, a lethargy. The end of a long shift with the chickens? It certainly smelt like that. But it was more than tiredness.

'Who owns the van?' Joe asked the driver.

The young man's mouth opened, then he shook his head fractionally to indicate that he spoke no English.

'Come on,' Joe added. 'Someone's gotta be in charge. I get the feeling it's you.'

The young man took a long drink of beer, emptying his mug. Then he got a bottle from the floor and refilled it.

'I speak a little English. The rest, no.'

He didn't seem to be lying. Everyone else was listening, but they didn't appear to understand a word.

'Are you from Romania? All of you?'

The driver nodded as he set the bottle back down on the floor. A fat guy with a mop of knotted black hair and rough, weather-beaten skin grabbed the bottle and drank from it.

'You're not in trouble,' Rita said, easing herself a little way further into the room. 'Just some questions.'

The driver opened his mouth again with that apologetic expression, like he hardly understood a word.

'All right,' Joe said, pointing a finger at him. 'Passport, please.'

The young man got up and left the room.

'See what you can get out of this lot,' Joe told Rita.

The driver had gone to the kitchen at the back of the house. Joe followed, but stopped to take a quick look in the other room. There were three stained mattresses on the floor, each of them strewn with clothes. And now he knew why the whole household was crammed into the front room: it was the only place with heating. The cold in the bedroom was intense, over-laid with the stink of unwashed clothes and damp. But there was also something earthy and sour, like rubbish that's been left too long in the bin. The kind of place where mushrooms grow on the windowsill and slug trails criss-cross the carpet. Where you could take a piss in the corner and no one would notice. A doss house. Rank and stale. About the most miserable he'd ever seen. And he'd seen some shitholes.

The kitchen wasn't much better. An old gas cooker was solid brown on top, none of the white enamel visible through the layers of caked-on filth. The floor was so dirty that only a narrow pathway of pale lino was visible in the middle.

'No passports here,' the driver said.

His features were angular, a sparse beard partly concealing pale, acne-scarred skin.

Joe stood in the doorway, trying to ignore the smell. In the far corner, a black bin liner sat on the floor, full to the top, and around its base a series of dark rings where liquids from previous bags had seeped out and congealed.

'Who has them?' he asked, watching as the guy drained his mug and got another bottle from the fridge, which was about as well stocked as one might have imagined: more beer, an enormous tub of margarine, jars of jam, peanut butter, pickles. Not a single brand he recognized.

'Somebody keeps them for us. ID cards too.'

'The Workout Agency, right? Miriana Dalca runs it.'

The young man refilled his mug, ignoring the question. He drank fast, gulping it down.

'Listen,' Joe said, 'you're not in any trouble.'

He looked straight at Joe for the first time, a painfully sad smile on his face.

'We're always in trouble. Is always trouble.'

His intonation was flat and true. And his English had suddenly improved.

'Not with me, you're not.'

The young man snorted, managed to stop himself laughing out loud.

'People hate us. Shout at us in the street, spit at us, accuse us of things. We don't go anywhere. They hate us 'cos we do the jobs nobody wants to do. Twelve hours a day. Now this.'

Joe looked around. There was sliced bread over on the sink, three loaves, large catering tins of baked beans, coffee, powdered milk. And on the floor were dozens of empty beer bottles, but also vodka bottles, plus wine cartons, stacked against the back wall like bricks.

'Now what?' the young man asked, his face passive, eyes down to the floor. 'Is about Ana, right? She is dead. I know it already.'

'Yes. Ana Dobrescu was murdered last night. How do you know?'

The young man got a mobile phone from his pocket.

'Text. I'm supposed to tell them all. Ana is dead, is the message.'

'Who sent it?'

'Dunno. No name. Didn't recognize the number.'

'You don't seem very upset,' Joe said.

'It is sad. Very. I like Ana. Everybody does. But I'm not surprised with many things.'

'How well did you know her?'

He attempted a shrug, as if he was supposed to accept the idea of death as inevitable. His cynicism felt hollow, over-played.

'When did you last see Ana?' Joe asked.

'Three months. I dunno. Four?'

'Before that? When she worked for the agency? How often?'

'Before? Er … a lot. She used to come here. She looked after everybody.'

'Was she the one who paid you all, bought the food for you?'

'Yes.'

'And now? Who looks after you all now?'

'Me. I do it. Miriana drives down, gives me the money. I pay the others, get the food.'

*Minus your cut*, Joe thought. *Leave it. Someone else can sort that out.*

'Have you ever been to a place called Leeds?'

'No.'

'Where were you last night?'

'Here all night. All of us.'

'OK. That'll be checked out. There'll be security cameras nearby. It's the truth, is it?'

'Yes.'

Rita came into the kitchen.

'Ana,' she said. 'That's all I can understand. Ana. Why are they asking about Ana, love?'

'He already knew,' Joe told her.

'It's not the first time,' the young man said, then drained his mug. 'People disappear. Is nothing.' Poured himself more beer. 'Ana came to the farm yesterday.'

Joe shifted.

'You said you hadn't seen her?'

'I didn't see. I heard them talking.'

'Was it Miriana who told you that Ana was dead?'

'I said already. No name. Didn't recognize the number. I got the message this afternoon.'

He took out his phone as he spoke, found the text, and held up the phone.

'The message is in Romanian, right?' Rita asked.

He nodded.

'*Ana is dead. She was causing problems.* Is all it says.'

Rita took the phone, forwarded the message to herself.

'You say people disappear. Why?' Joe asked.

'If they cause problems. Nobody wants problems.'

Rita was listening, noting down as much as she could.

'The people in this house?' she asked. 'Are they causing problems?'

'No. We just work. No trouble. We stay away from people. Nobody here matters. We're invisible. That's the point. Now this.'


They went over the story with him again. It didn't change and he didn't add anything.

'Right,' Joe said, marching back into the front room, 'we need to tell 'em.'

The young man smiled patiently as he followed.

'They don't speak English.'

'I can bloody confirm that,' Rita added.

Joe got his phone and began typing into Google Translate: *Ana Dobrescu is dead. We are investigating her murder. Please help us if you know anything about Ana or a young man called Stefan.*

He placed one of his cards on the mantel above the fireplace, then read the translation out very slowly in his best Italian accent.

The silence that followed was broken by the rasping breath

of a young woman. Her head quivered, jaw hanging open, bottom lip filling with spittle. Others around the room wore expressions of incomprehension. Someone mumbled something. Then someone else, a few whispered words, all heads turning to listen. A series of groans arose, mixed with wheezing and whimpering. There was fear and a childish panic on their faces. The sounds grew, unnatural, flecked with the crackle of bubbling snot as the moaning turned by degrees to hysteria. For a second Joe wondered whether he and Rita were in danger. A room packed with hysterical people?

The driver stood next to him, looking down at his housemates. He let the bedlam escalate, then whistled and waited for them to shut up.

He spoke in Romanian, pointed at the mantel.

'I told them they can use my phone if they want to call.'

# 37

'Come on,' he said as they got into the car. 'Better make it look like we're off.'

'We're phoning this in, right?' she asked.

'Definitely. Human trafficking. We've got the name of the agency, everything.'

'Weird, though. They don't even speak a few words? How do they phone for a pizza?'

'You'd pick up a bit of English, wouldn't you? Unless there's some reason why you didn't.'

They drove to the end of the street, round the corner, parked outside a shop, its windows masked in metal grilles painted bright red.

'You remember that Polish case a few years back?'

'Yeah. Vulnerable people. Illiterate, alcoholics, down-and-outs.'

'The Workout Agency is running something similar, I reckon. Twelve here, another five in Batley.'

'Now disappeared,' she added.

They sat there. The low-slung terraced houses around them were like withered, anaemic versions of Joe's place.

Half the size and a tenth of the price. The rents would be next to nothing. Perfect for a modern slave slum. Especially with the biggest poultry farm in Christendom nearby, in constant need of docile workers to shovel shit. First sign of trouble, everyone's carted off to another house in another dead town. Untraceable. Their passports nice and safe somewhere else.

'Stefan begged me. "No police," he said. Is this what he wanted? To go back to a place like this?'

'Who's that coming?' asked Rita, watching in the rear-view mirror as a young woman approached.

She wore a brown Parka and walked slowly, close to the wall, a shopping bag hanging from her hand. Her eyes were puffed up, glossy, until her strangely misshapen face looked like something from a horror movie.

'Sabina?' Rita said, opening her window.

She got into the back without any encouragement. She might have been twenty or thirty. It was impossible to tell. A child-woman, frail and nervous, unable to meet their stare.

'I …' she said, fumbling in the pocket of her coat, 'the radio. I can … some English.'

She showed them a small transistor radio, a pair of head-phones wrapped around it. She grinned.

'Zoë Ball. Ken Bruce!'

'Christ, you're learning English from Ken Bruce!' said Joe. 'That's …'

'Good,' Rita said. 'Good girl. Can you understand me?'

'A little,' she said.

Rita leant back and squeezed her hand.

'This is private. Just us. No one else. OK, love? Tell us about Ana.'

She did. In slow, painfully broken English, little more than a series of isolated words which they managed to piece together as they listened, straining to understand her heavy accent. Ana used to come and see them, to look after them.

'Ana,' she said, more resolute, 'is good person. I love Ana. Everybody love …'

'The young man who drives the van?' Rita asked. 'He's not good?'

Sabina shook her head, a mixture of fear and excitement in her eyes as she continued to explain. Ana showed up at the farm yesterday, gave Sabina a phone.

As she spoke, she pulled a cheap phone from her pocket.

'Ana say today she will ring, and we all go in taxis to new house. Better life.'

From another pocket she took out a clump of twenty-pound notes.

'Is the money from Ana as well?' Rita asked.

Sabina nodded. 'But Ana not call, and …'

She stopped, the fear in her eyes escalating.

'Where is your passport?' Joe asked.

'When we come here in ferry, they take.'

'Who? Who took the passports?'

She was beginning to panic now. She clasped her hands together to stop them from shaking, her head twisting from side to side.

'You don't know, love?' Rita asked, holding Sabina's hand again. 'It's OK. Don't worry. It's all right now.'

Sabina began to cry. She rubbed her face, leaving pale smudges where the tears had been. Joe realized that her complexion wasn't dark; her skin was simply unwashed.

'OK,' he said. 'South Yorks can deal with this. God, some duty DI's gonna be pleased! Let's get some uniforms here to start with.'

He turned to Sabina, who was now holding Rita's hand as if she'd never let it go.

'Sabina, you go and do the shopping. Then go back to the house. Wait there. More police will come.'

For a second it looked like they'd have to physically restrain her, such was the convulsion of terror in her body. She flailed about on the seat, rocking backwards and forwards, yet never letting go of Rita's hand.

'Plan B,' he said, getting out of the car. 'She stays with you. Tell 'em we need help, soon as.'

He nipped into the shop, filled a basket with bars of chocolate, crisps, and fizzy drinks, all the crap his mum would never buy him.

Back in the house, Joe went through to the kitchen and was immediately surrounded. Adults they may have been, but they were out of control, like kids, crying Ana's name as they ate, dribbling and wailing right into each other's faces.

'They all knew Ana, right?' Joe asked, above the noise.

The driver stood next to him, nodded, unsure what to do.

'I saw Sabina in the shop,' Joe added. 'She'll be back in a minute.'

'Bring all the chocolate you want. They won't talk to you. They know what'll happen if they do. That's how we live.'

Before Joe could reply, his phone pinged. A text from Rita: Uniforms outside.

The doorbell rang.

'That'll be Sabina now,' Joe said. 'Why don't you go and let her in?'

As the young man went, Joe moved to the back door, made sure it was locked, and positioned himself square in front of it.

# 38

He looked down at the thin chips in front of him, phone pressed to his ear. Tennant had been twatting on for ages and the chips were cold. The gist: the South Yorkshire Force would be heading up the human trafficking case. But it took him forever to say so.

'What a pain,' Joe said as the call finally came to an end.

He had a sip of coffee. It was tepid, but tasted good.

'Takes over from Andy, and the first thing he does is grumble that we've driven down here, then he tells me to make sure this doesn't slow down the Dobrescu investigation. Stick with Churchill, he says. Then, finally, he manages to squeeze out a tiny word of congratulations.'

'Aye. I bet he'll get his name on the case, though. Acting DCI? Kudos for him if there's a big trafficking conviction.' She ran an index finger across the wrapper of her double cheeseburger, trying to scrape the last smears of melted cheese. 'Owt else?'

'He's still at HQ. Sounds like he's taking over from Andy good and proper.'

'Well he's got his next promotion to think about. Married?'

'Tennant? Yeah. He can't see much of his family, though. Always working.'

'When's Andy due back?'

'No idea,' he said.

And it was the truth. He hadn't had time to ring.

'So,' she said, screwing up the wrapper to stop herself licking it, 'we better find Mr Stefan What's-His-Face.'

'Nicolescu.'

'Got anything to go on?'

'Nope. I'm assuming he won't be registered with tax or social security.'

'New suspect?'

'He was a friend of Ana's. She comes to see him in the hospital, then he does a runner. She's dead the same day. He's a person of interest, at least. Oh, we've also got Miriana Dalca. See what the brains trust has to say tomorrow morning.' He glanced down at his phone. 'Hold on. A message from Mihal.'

'Who?'

Joe looked at the screen.

'Mihal Bogdan. Romanian National Organized Crime Unit. Worked with him at Interpol. I kind of roped him into the case, see if he could help. He wants to talk on WhatsApp. How do I do that?'

'Another guy working late ...'

'That's Mihal for you.'

Rita pressed the video button for him.

'Really? It's that easy?'

The call was answered immediately.

'Joe! *Bon soir, mon ami!*'

225

'*Salut, Mihal!*' said Joe, staring at the phone as if it were magic. 'Good to see you! Video phones, eh? Science fiction!'

Mihal Bogdan was in an office, and he was grinning. Dark hair, short but not soldier-short, and a large, well-worn face which might have hidden something kinder beneath, but you were never absolutely sure.

'Welcome to the modern world, Joe! You never liked tech much, did you?'

'No. And I still don't. You're back in Romania, I heard.'

'Yes and no. The perfect bureaucrat's answer! Interpol coordination. I'm in Bucharest. You?'

'Leeds. My old job in serious crime.'

'Joe Romano, the most talented officer that Interpol ever lost!'

'Lost? I resigned. Out of boredom.'

'You rubbed some people up the wrong way. What's the expression? *Têtu comme un mule.*'

'Stubborn as a mule!'

'That's what they said.'

'With a huge sigh of relief, I expect.'

Mihal shrugged.

'Not really. Anyway, the Romanian girl? Tell me.'

Neither man enjoyed idle chat. It's what had drawn them together in Lyon, an irritation with the niceties of the organization, Interpol's endless procedures and shared lines of action. Plus the interminable lunches. From the moment they'd both arrived in France, their conversation had mostly focused on how they could back to real criminal work.

'The girl told me she might be in danger,' Joe said. 'That she might be killed. Then she was. Strange, though. Everybody we've spoken to loved her.'

'Got a main suspect?'

'Got a few. It might be related to a human trafficking operation. Romanian.'

'One of my country's specialities. The girl?'

'She used to work for 'em. The operation's fronted by an employment agency. Two people in charge, both Romanians.'

'Names.'

'Miriana Dalca, manager. Omor Balan, registered owner.'

'Say that one again.'

'Omor Balan.'

'Any details?'

'We have his passport number. Hold on.'

Rita was already on her phone to HQ, hoping Tennant wouldn't pick up. Half a minute later she was writing the number down, courtesy of a data clerk on nights.

'OK,' Mihal said as Joe read out the number. 'Balan's a common surname. I'll run a check on the passport. But *Silviu* Balan is well known to us. That's why I asked.'

'What does this Silviu guy do?'

'He kills people.'

'OK ...'

'And we can never prove it. Drugs, prostitution, the usual.'

'Big?'

'Big-ish. And clever. Under-the-radar type. Ex-military, special ops. He loves your country, too. He had a loan company in London, back when Romania joined the European Union. Ah, here we are. Omor Balan. Clean record. Currently the director of an orphanage. I'll run a check for a family connection, hold on.'

'Where's the orphanage?' Joe asked.

'Near Bucharest, place called Luica.'

'Spell?'

'Lu-ee-ca. Like it sounds. With a "c". Hold on.'

Mihal's face spun out of shot as he put the phone down. For a minute they watched a static image of an office ceiling, the sound of typing in the background. Then Mihal's face appeared again. And he wasn't smiling.

'Joe? They're cousins.' He sat back, puffed out his cheeks. 'Let me know what you need. Anything at all, OK? I'll get things moving here.'

'You should speak to my immediate superior. DI Tennant. Acting DCI, actually. Be warned, he likes the sound of his own voice.'

'Ha! Still hating authority, Joe?'

'I just work better without it. I'll send you his number. He's in his office now.'

'Man after my own heart!'

'Thanks for this, Mihal. There's a case meeting tomorrow morning. I'll ring you straight after that.'

'Good, good.'

'Ah, one last thing,' Joe said. 'Stefan Nicolescu. About thirty years old, we think. He's a suspect. We've got nothing to go on. But he was one of the agency's workers, and a friend of the victim from back home.'

'That name? It's like John Smith for a Romanian!'

'You're a genius with databases. I've seen you in action.'

Mihal unleashed a massive roar.

'Leave it with me. Oh,' he said, his voice dropping in tone, 'Joe? Balan and his people? They're not amateurs. Be careful.'

Joe texted Mihal with Tennant's number. Then he found the

photo of Ana on his phone, stared at it as he replayed recent events in his mind, everything she'd said to him, everything he could have done …

Then the phone was gently taken from him.

Rita set it down on the table between them.

'It's not your fault she's dead, Joe. We'll do everything we can.' She paused, the tiniest of smiles on her soft, round face. 'Anyroad, got a bit of a favour to ask.'

He grunted.

'Last time a girl asked me for a favour, she ended up—'

'The wedding? We were wondering, I mean, it was Ruth's idea, whether your band would play at the reception?'

He felt a smile pull at his cheeks, as if it were a completely new experience.

'Fantastic! 'Course we will!'

'And for the venue, we're thinking about somewhere really gorgeous. You know it, actually.'

'Do I?'

'Bilton Golf Club.'

'Jesus wept! I've seen enough of that place to last me a lifetime!'

She sat back, proud as punch, loving it.

'Well, your dad wanted to be a member.'

'I'll wear that new suit you're gonna buy me.'

# 39

Miriana ordered another wine at the bar. Fifth? Sixth? She took it and sat in the window seat where she'd been for most of the evening, counting down the hours, watching planes as they rose steadily in the evening sky, their taillights disappearing into the distance. Occasionally, she'd place her phone to her ear and pretend to call somebody, making it look like she was on a business trip, alone in a hotel bar all night.

But now the planes had stopped. And there was still nobody to call. No family, no familiar voice at the end of the line. There never had been any family. Friends? Ana was dead. There was no one. Everything was finished. But she was smart. Smart enough to have got this far.

The first thing she'd done when she began working for the agency was to go through all the passports, find one with a photo that looked like her. There were a lot to choose from, and she'd found a pretty good match. Nobody had missed it. So tomorrow she'd walk onto the first flight available – Turkey perhaps, or somewhere a bit further away – with a new identity, plus twenty thousand in cash. She'd start again. It was the best she could do.

Then her phone rang. She saw the caller's name, let it ring, unsure. It was late. Almost time for bed. Tomorrow morning she'd be gone. New life. New name. Yet the desperate loneliness of the past few hours had been too much to bear, the sense of not knowing, of not being able to speak to anyone, after all this.

It rang and rang. Finally, she grabbed it.

'Hello.'

Ten minutes she was standing on the main road outside the hotel. A car approached, pulled up to the kerb. The window wound down.

'Come on. Get in.'

'I'm …' Miriana began, feeling lightheaded, her heart fluttering, an ache within her, growing stronger.

'Come on. You shouldn't be alone. Not now.'

Miriana stared at the road ahead as they drove, seeing the street in duplicate, the traffic little more than shards of light scraping against her eyes. She'd necked that last glass of wine. Hadn't eaten anything all day. It was too much. Everything.

'We'll have a chat, get a coffee somewhere, or a drink. OK?'

Miriana agreed. But it felt wrong. Her head was heavy. She could hardly keep it up. Should've stuck to the plan, stayed where she was. A few more hours alone and she'd've been on a flight.

They were on a country lane, no traffic. In front of them an expanse of black, the odd smudge of pale yellow far in the distance. The car jolted as it hit potholes. Then down another lane, narrower. The hedges rushed past, close enough to touch.

'You hear that? I think it's a flat tyre. Better take a look.'

The car came to a halt and the driver's door opened. Miriana's eyes were almost closed now. She brought a hand up, pressed it to her face. She wanted the night to be over. To walk onto a plane, any plane. Away from here, from everything she'd done.

The door slammed shut again.

'Tyre's fine.'

Miriana opened her eyes.

*Gloves?*

# 40

When he got home, Andy's car was outside.

'Ah, Jesus, I forgot to call.'

He got his phone, checked for messages. His fingers moved slowly now, his eyes almost too tired to follow. Not that many years ago he'd pull an all-nighter, then get into a fresh shirt and be out again the next morning, Mars bar for brekkie, back to it. Not anymore. It was barely midnight and he was done for.

There was a *ring me* from DI Tennant, exactly the kind of scrupulous person who would not call a mobile when an officer was likely to be driving. He probably did a risk assessment before he went to the bog.

'Joe?' Tennant said, picking up on the first ring. 'I've been speaking to Mihal Bogdan. Romanian National Organized Crime Unit. He has a very high opinion of you.'

His tone wasn't complimentary. It was like Bogdan's high opinion came as an unwelcome distraction. Joe half-listened to Tennant's clipped instructions as he got out of the car.

'Oh,' Tennant added, 'I'll have to reduce your team. I've just gone over the case. Once you track down this Stefan guy you'll have three main suspects. And I need a case assessment by morning.'

'Can I keep Rita?'

A long sigh. Joe felt a modicum of pity for Tennant. He'd be at his desk all night, perhaps an hour of shut-eye in his chair as the sun came up. You've got to admire that kind of dedication. Or wonder why.

'OK. And if you speak to DCI Mills, could you politely remind him that we'll need a sick note at some point, plus a timeframe. He's not picking up.'

'Yes, I will. And thanks, Sir.'

He never knew whether *Sir* sounded a touch sarcastic coming from him. Back when he was a teacher the kids could load the word with incredible derision. He wondered where he'd have been now, if he'd stayed. Battling through *Le Petit Prince* with kids who couldn't conjugate être without forgetting what it was? No, he'd made the right choice. He was police. Ana Dobrescu had slipped through his fingers, but her killer wouldn't. If it was Stefan, he'd be behind bars this time tomorrow. It would be Find Stefan Day, going at it hard, no paperwork, all instinct.

He walked slowly up his slightly neglected front garden, too tired to feel guilty about it. He had a crime assessment report to write, then a cold, lonely bed to climb into.

He pushed the door open. Voices. He couldn't hear what was being said, but the patterns of speech were familiar enough: pissed people. It was mainly the voice of Andy Mills, who never slurred much when he was drunk. He did, though, become gradually firmer in his convictions, increasingly confident of his own erudition, like Winston Churchill at the dispatch box, but talking absolute shit.

He moved closer to the living-room door, then leant against the wall and rested his eyes, overcome by a sudden wave of exhaustion.

'Sam,' he heard, 'your dad's an Inspector. You know that, right? Passed the exams, sat the Board, the whole thing. Then you lot pissed off to France. I don't think he even wants promotion.'

'I remember that last exam he did,' Sam said, his voice low and lazy, the words barely crawling out. 'We had a pizza when he passed. Bloody clever bloke. Cleverer than his son!'

'Nah, nah! Don't slag yersen off, mate. You screwed up a few exams, so what?'

'All of 'em, nearly.'

'You don't like medicine? Don't friggin' do it! Simple as. You're young. Do summat else.'

Joe opened his eyes, realized he'd ignored Sam all day. He gathered what little strength he had left and pushed open the living-room door. Andy was sitting on the floor, slumped against the sofa, his long legs out in front of him. Sam was also on the floor, in front of the armchair by the window in a kind of semi-huddle, a can of lager in his hand.

'Dad?'

'Yeah, it's me,' Joe said, smelling whisky. 'The owner-occupier.'

A bottle of Jura single malt – Joe's – was on the coffee table close to Andy's legs. Little more than half the scotch remained, and appearances suggested that the rest was now inside the big man, whose body moved with the involuntary listing of someone who'd sent himself way beyond drunk.

'What's this, then?'

Sam shifted, tried to sit up.

'I failed. I'm a failure.'

'I've been … Sorry, son. I'm sorry. It's been a mad day. Uncle Andy been giving you the benefit of his wisdom?'

He turned to Andy.

'Ring that number, did you? Or is this your therapy?'

DCI Andy Mills' head fell onto his large, fat chest, his mouth hanging open.

'Be so bad, would it?' he mumbled.

'What?'

Andy looked up, tried to focus on Joe, but his head was rolling, his breathing laboured.

'Copper.'

'So it's serious, then?'

Stupid question. None of this was serious. He'd got drunk with Andy often enough to know what happens. Once, they'd drunk a bottle of Stolichnaya between 'em and planned the robbery of a Securicor van. The staff they'd have to bribe, the threats of violence they'd have to make, the kind of yacht they were gonna live on in Honduras … The next morning they were both embarrassed, thinking that perhaps the other one might still have wanted to go through with it.

'What about your student loan?' Joe asked, feeling the inadequacy of his words even as he said them.

A moment later Andy let out a long, guttural moan. He twisted around, arms on the sofa behind him as he struggled to pull himself up to a kneeling position, shirt untucked, big slabs of hairy back fat wobbling. He took a breath, then managed to get to his feet.

'Can I …'

'Spare room.'

'Right,' he said, wiping both hands across his face and neck.

'You OK?' Joe asked.

'I'll live,' he said, staggering out of the room.

Joe stayed where he was. He heard the footsteps upstairs. A door closing. Then nothing.

Sam stirred, tried to stand, his legs loose and disobedient beneath him.

'Come on, soldier, up you get.'

They stood there, a couple of feet apart, Sam too ashamed to raise his head.

Half a minute. Perhaps more.

Then it was too late.

He was gone.


Joe made himself a coffee then went back into the living room. The scotch was over by the sofa. He grabbed it, poured some into his coffee, right up to the brim, then put the bottle back on the shelf, out of harm's way.

He sat down, inhaled the fumes, took a long drink. It raced down into his stomach, warm and strong, waking him up just enough.

'A copper?' he said to himself.

Reluctantly, he grabbed his laptop from the floor and made a start on the crime assessment. He went through as much of the Dobrescu case as he could remember. Something was missing. He'd had the same feeling all evening. Something about Churchill, who was still officially the main suspect.

'The doctor!' he said, struggling to his feet and trying to find his jacket.

Then he realized he was still wearing it. He searched his pockets, found his phone. Sure enough, there was a WhatsApp message from Jill Wallace. It had a file attached, the background information on Ben Churchill that she'd promised to write. For a while he tried to work out how to send it to his computer, then finally gave up and read it on the screen of his phone, straining to keep his eyes open.

The patient is highly intelligent, with a very practical mind. He sees any problem in his life as a challenge. He's thoughtful, confident, a natural achiever; he's thorough and meticulous, a list-writer, a planner. With medical issues, he has always sought to understand the biology behind any condition, and is keen to interpret things like test results himself.

His bearing changed about a year ago when he met his partner. He referred to her as his 'soulmate', and told me that they saw life in exactly the same way. They had 'found' each other, a chance in a million, he said. She came with him to consults sometimes. There was a very natural sense of love and togetherness between them. Absolute trust, they called it.

He also became increasingly philosophical, and told me he wanted to leave the world a better place, to help as many people as he could as quickly as he could. He said he was grateful for what life had given him, that he had been 'blessed'. I got the feeling that he meant meeting his new partner, that she had been the blessing. He mentioned the grace of God, in ways which were difficult to understand, because previously he had not expressed any interest in religion.

Several weeks ago he asked me if there was a medical charity that I was particularly close to. I suggested the Leeds Hospice Foundation (I'm a board member). A very large donation was made the following day, anonymously, in cash.

The patient has no registered family or next of kin.


Joe tried to imagine Ana Dobrescu when he'd spoken to her outside the hospital. Scared and nervous, but also firm, decided, planning something. Something dangerous. Where did Ben Churchill fit into this? She was his soulmate. Absolute trust. They both wanted to help people. Then he'd killed her?

'No,' Joe told himself as he pulled the laptop onto his knees. 'Not Churchill.'

He had a better idea, and no one was going to like it.

# FRIDAY

# 41

He ran his hand across the surface of his new Ikea kitchen table with buyer's remorse. Should've taken his time, found something more solid, more homely. How many kitchen tables does a man buy in his life? Ditto the sofa in the front room. He'd spent two hundred quid less than he'd budgeted for. Never could resist the thrifty option. Now he was stuck with a load of Swedish tat 'til he was drawing his pension. An image for life. His life.

In front of him were two bacon butties and a mug of black coffee, plenty of sugar. A long day in the offing, and he'd need all the energy he could muster. Also, bacon was about all there was.

Sam and Andy's binge last night must have been a longish one, because they'd ransacked the fridge. All that was left now were the remains of a twenty-four-pack of Stella, plus a sliced white loaf, some brown sauce, and three large packets of streaky bacon, all from the corner shop up the road, judging by the brands. That would have been Andy's scran-raid: getting in tomorrow's breakfast along with the evening's beers, like a soldier on manoeuvres, always thinking ahead.

He heard movement on the stairs. It was five past seven. Someone coming down already. Sam? How much would he remember about last night?

'Right on time!' Andy said, striding into the kitchen and reaching towards Joe's plate.

'You can sod off and make your own.'

'Thought you were more of a hot croissant man.'

'Aye, well, today I'm tracking down a new suspect.'

'Really?'

Joe explained about last night, the trafficked workers, how Stefan might fit into it all. Andy poured himself a coffee as he listened, then got two slices of bread, folded them into a wedge, and wiped it around the frying pan. He sat down to eat, apparently none the worse for wear.

'And,' Joe added, 'there's a detail you might be able to help me with. I don't think Tennant'll give me access to the grooming inquiry.'

'Well, no, it's—'

'A detail, nothing else.'

'Try me.'

'Bilton Woods. You said they sometimes took the girls there.'

Andy put his bread down, fished for his phone.

'Dirty raping bastards,' he said, thumbing through a Google map. 'This is off the record, right? Look, there's a back road that runs along the edge of the woods. A track goes off it. It's just a gap in the trees. I reckon it used to go all the way to the big house. Now it stops in the woods. That's where some of 'em used to go.'

Joe took the phone, expanded the map.

'That's the edge of the bloody golf course!'

'No activity there for a few months.'

'Churchill's house can't be more than a hundred yards away!'

Andy sat back, squeezed his lips together. It wasn't a pretty sight, like a massive, constipated baby.

'Aye, I know. I saw it yesterday. Couldn't say anything to you. It'll be flagged up and the grooming case'll contact you. There's gotta be an info-sharing assessment first.'

'Jesus Christ!'

Joe grabbed a bacon butty. Sank his teeth in.

'We had a camera up there in a tree!' Andy added.

Joe froze.

'Is it—?'

'Sorry, mate. Taken down. They must've got wind of us. They're organized.' He crammed more greasy bread into his mouth. 'No networked cameras anywhere on that back road, either. If they drove up there to dump the body, they could've got in an' out without being seen. You'd have to spread the net pretty wide.'

'Will I get the OK on that?'

'You will if I say so.'

'You're off sick. I'll have to grovel to Tennant.'

Joe sat back. Annoyed. Deflated. And the day hadn't even started.

'You didn't phone, did you?' he asked.

'The psychiatrist? I bloody did. Phoned, went. Had my first session yesterday. Straight-talker, he is, none of that airy-fairy crap. Fifty minutes I were in there. Told him everything. Right back to the army. I talked non-stop, got my money's worth. Hundred friggin' quid.'

245

'Post-traumatic stress again?'

'It's not. He reckoned it wasn't. It's depression. Straightforward. I'm carrying too much emotion. Frustration, anxiety, *hate*. I've let missen get too close to it all. Them blokes? I told him, I wanna hurt 'em. I mean, really hurt 'em.'

Joe wasn't sure whether to be impressed or not.

'So, what's the plan?'

'Me? I get away from the case.'

'Agreed. How?'

'To the endex, Joe! Bring it to court, then it's gone. I start knocking some heads together, acting like a copper. *Then* I have mi nervous breakdown. When they're all behind bars.'

'You're full of surprises, Detective Mills.'

'Detective my arse. I've been a paper shuffler, like the rest of 'em.' He stood up, downed his coffee in one. 'I'm off home to get changed. See you down Elland Road.'

Joe sat on the bottom step and listened for sounds coming from Sam's room.

He got his notebook, ripped a page out, wrote:

Sam: I'm literally chasing down murderers today. I'll ring. Or you message me. Relax, and we'll talk. Do it proper. Sort things out. Do or do not; there is no try! Dad.

He considered the note. Screwed it up. Wrote another, minus the last sentence.

# 42

He got to his desk and made a half-hearted attempt to tidy the clutter as his terminal booted up. In front of him were print-outs of almost everything from the Dobrescu case file. All the information was online, but he preferred the disorder of paper copies. When someone is killed, there's always an element of chaos. The key is how you bring it all together, see the patterns.

He picked up a forensic report and read. The mug found outside had Churchill's prints on it, and they tallied with prints from Churchill's car and house. As Joe put the report down, Alex Ambler appeared. He was in the same clothes as yesterday, and his gait was slow and heavy as he made his way across the ops room.

'You all right?' Joe asked. 'You look like shit.'

'None taken. Long night,' he said. 'Competitive *Dungeons and Dragons*. Didn't get home 'til gone five. Hardly worth going to bed. So I had a look at Ben Churchill's emails. Thousands of 'em. I did some analysis, semantic webs, lexical collocations, y'know?'

'Nope.'

Alex sighed, slumped down into a chair.

'Poor bloke. Not often this job gets to me. I've put a summary on the system.'

'It always gets to me. Every time. It wears you down.'

Alex and Joe had got on well since they first met, although they had little in common. It was the best kind of working friendship, the kind that ends when you walk out of the building. No pints after work, no awkward barbecues in someone's back garden, trying not to cuff their annoying kids, drawing out the chit-chat with their neighbours and brothers-in-law. Just respect. Two people trying to do their jobs well.

'He's been giving sackloads of money away. He's ordered, methodical, like a scientist. He's got it all in files. And he's interested in killing himself.'

'Interested?'

'Assisted suicide. He's been researching Pentobarbital. It's a strong barbiturate. You wanna take yourself out, that's the cat's gonads.'

'He was considering suicide before the crash?'

'He could've written a bloody thesis about it! He knew his religion, too.'

'I'm not following.'

Alex breathed in slowly, forcing the exhaustion away.

'I'm not a detective, just a tech grunt …'

'Yeah, one with a doctorate.'

'… it's a sin. Suicide. He'd been reading up on that, an' all. It's like he was weighing up the pros and cons, charting his own road to death. Also, he was looking at the legal aspects, y'know, if somebody helped him.'

'This barbiturate, did he order any?'

'Not as far as I can see. But he'd done the research. He knew the best way of ending it.' He paused, shook his head. 'So, after all the research, all the end-of-life planning, he strangles his girlfriend, rips the airbag out of his motor, and drives into a bridge. That's how he checks out? *That's* his suicide?'

Joe knew there was more. He waited.

'Then there's the obvious thing, the money,' Alex added.

Joe sat back, smiled. 'Go on, Dr Ambler.'

'I read most of the stuff on the system last night. The crime assessment?'

'There isn't one yet.'

'I know. 'Cos you don't think it was him, right?'

'Get to the point, Alex.'

'There's still three hundred and fifty grand sitting in his bank account. Funny time to kill your girlfriend then top yourself, right?'

'Fancy saying that to Tennant?'

'Nope. Like I said, I'm just tech.'

He hauled himself up out of the chair, raised an arm, too tired to say goodbye.

'Thanks, Alex.'

As he walked to the door he narrowly avoided colliding with Mark Francis, fresh for a new shift. He was in his normal dark-blue suit, and as usual it looked like he'd struggled into it for a wedding he didn't want to go to. He was a big, imposing man, but he spoke softly, with precision.

'This just came in from the Romanian authorities,' he said, handing Joe a few printed papers.

'Good. Get it all on the system. By the way, the door-to-door yesterday?'

'No one saw Churchill leave on Wednesday afternoon or evening. And his car wasn't tracked anywhere.'

'So he stayed in waiting for Ana. Did anyone see her come home?'

'Nobody. We've spoken to 'em all, every house.'

'OK, thanks.'

Other people were now wandering into the ops room, among them DI Tennant. But only he had the markings of a man who'd just woken up in his office chair. He went over to the posterboard and stared at the two images of Ana Dobrescu, which were now surrounded with Post-its and other bits of paper. Then he turned, saw Joe, and beckoned him across.

'South Yorks,' he said as Joe approached, his voice a little hoarse. 'They've made a start on the human trafficking stuff. Social Services are involved.'

'Based down there, then?'

'Yes. I'm liaising this end …'

*I bet you are.*

'… most of 'em are vulnerable people. Low IQ, alcoholics, what-have-you. Easy to recruit. They bring 'em over, passports and ID taken away, and they work fifty-, sixty-hour weeks.'

'For less than minimum wage, I assume?'

'Way less. The workers seem to be getting forty quid a week plus board. The agency takes the rest.'

'Jesus.'

Tennant's skin was off-white, rings of red around the eyes, not the least hint of an expression on his face. He looked straight at Joe.

'The squalor of the human soul, eh, Sergeant?'

'Sickening. Comes with the job, I guess.'

'Forget it. Our job is to match a person to a crime. Nothing more.'

Joe had heard it all before. Every copper had. Keep your emotions out of it. Focus on the facts. Tennant's love for the dry, clinical approach to serious crime was well known, and very effective. But Joe had a reputation for letting himself get involved, a tendency to follow his instincts, plus a stubborn disdain for authority. Since last year he'd also become known for wining and dining murderers before he arrested 'em. That didn't help.

Yet he didn't hate authority, and he wasn't deliberately stubborn. He simply hated people who lacked passion and imagination, despised their unwillingness to countenance their own human frailty. His whole police career had been one long exercise in hiding his contempt for folk like Tennant. But he'd never been particularly good at deception, as the DS in front of his name well illustrated.

He counted his breaths, taking them slowly, knowing that today would be worse than normal.

'All this emotional involvement of yours,' Tennant said, looking around as monitors flicked into life and people settled down with mugs of tea, a few minutes of peace before they got stuck in. 'It doesn't help, y'know. Who are you really feeling sorry for?'

Joe said nothing. *One long breath in, then out …*

'And those long dramatic pauses, the bleeding heart? It grates.' He stretched, rotating his neck slowly as he opened and closed his eyes, trying to blink himself awake. 'It's a domestic.'

Joe didn't even bother to argue. *Long breath.*

'Unless,' Tennant continued, 'this Stefan character's done it.

Jealousy? Old lovers? Find him. Also, Financial Crimes raided Miriana's house an hour ago. It's been cleaned out. No files. And no Miriana.'

'She's disappeared?'

'Yep. You put the frighteners on her. Now she's done a runner. Perhaps you'd like to find her as well? Whatever, Ben Churchill's still our main. You know the rules.'

Joe knew: *identify the main suspect, go at 'em hard*. He gathered all his strength for a stab at civility.

'Ana worked for the employment agency, and they're running the human trafficking thing. The bloke in charge last night? He already knew she was dead. Someone texted him. That'll need following up.'

'It will be. Rita already logged the message.'

'There's a connection.'

Tennant tugged at the bridge of his nose, grimacing, until it looked like he was trying to do himself some sort of harm.

'So find it. I read your crime assessment. Drinking on the job, were you? *Again?*'

'I mailed you it. I didn't upload it to the system. It's provisional.'

'It's a fantasy.'

Tennant began to walk away.

'She trusted me,' Joe said. 'Let me go with this.'

Tennant turned.

'Which bit? Not every crime's a bloody—'

'I need more time.'

'Progress today. Meeting at four.'

*Breathe in. Breathe out …*

# 43

Thirty seconds later he was legging it down to the main entrance, taking the stairs two at a time, fag in his mouth. He was flicking his lighter even as he pulled open the heavy doors and threw himself out into the cold morning, a man desperately coming up for air.

Somehow a packet of Marlboro Gold and a lighter had found their way into his possession last night. He couldn't remember where or how, but now he was a smoker again. Cupping his hands against the wind, he took a long, hard pull, the vile nicotine shudder of the first drag immediately flushing Tennant from his mind.

The wind tore into his open jacket, working its way around his body until even the flanks of his back were cold. He thought about Ana. At the hospital, she'd been keen to get off. She said she was going to tell him everything, that she was in danger. A handful of hours later the second part had come true. He was sickened at her death, and sickened at himself, that he had no idea why she'd died, how on earth he'd let it happen. The Romanian police would be knocking on someone's door with the news soon enough. What would they say to her parents?

That the British police have no idea who did it. That the guy in charge had held her hand, had known that there was a problem; then he'd let her go, done nothing …

He took the loose papers from his pocket, scanned the first page. His mouth fell open, fag hanging from his bottom lip, smoke stinging his eyes. Ana Dobrescu: Orphan. No next of kin. Grew up in Luica Orphanage and Children's Hospital.

'Jesus Christ!' Joe said, running back towards the building, spitting the cigarette out as he went.


'Right, gather round,' he shouted, standing with his back to the posterboard.

The team was there, Rita and Gwyn, most of the others, all talking, ready for the day's assignments.

'You've heard about events last night? Human trafficking. The employment agency that Ana Dobrescu worked for is involved. Also, she was an orphan. She—'

'We know,' Rita said. 'It's just gone on the system. Miriana Dalca an' all. Same orphanage. Place called Luica. They're both orphans.'

'The slave workers stuff?' he said. 'It's run from that orphanage.'

'We *know*.'

Tennant's voice was flat and patient, perhaps a bit irritated. Nobody had seen him come in.

'It's the connection,' Joe said.

'Good. I'll share the info with South Yorkshire. How does it help you find Ana Dobrescu's killer? That's today's question, I feel.'

He left the room before Joe could muster a response. There

was a rumble of conversation from outside in the corridor. Raised voices? Not quite, but they all strained to hear, watching the back of Tennant's jacket in the glass panel of the door.

'Is that Andy out there?' asked Rita. 'On a sicky, in't he?'

Joe shrugged, blew out his cheeks.

A moment later DCI Andy Mills yanked the door open.

'Morning, campers!' he said, bounding over to them with the energy of a far younger man, beer belly notwithstanding. 'DI Tennant's been saying great things about the investigation!'

No one knew whether to laugh. He rode the silence for a second or two.

'Right. Joe? Tell us about your new person of interest.'

'Stefan Nicolescu. Ana visited him at the hospital, then he disappeared. The other workers from the car wash where he worked have also vanished. Miriana Dalca organized that.' He stopped, looked around. 'By the way. Have you all seen Alex's stuff about Ben Churchill?'

Everyone nodded.

'Researching his own suicide. More than three hundred grand still in his account. That suggests the thing with his car was spontaneous. It wasn't—'

'Right,' Andy said, rubbing his hands together. 'Find this Stefan bloke. Keep going on all other lines of inquiry, see where it all leads. Joe, your fella at Interpol?'

'Ringing him after this.'

'Good. And them charity folk? Smelling owt there, are we?'

Joe wavered, wasn't sure.

'Yes or no?' Andy asked, carried along by his own momentum.

'I dunno. It's worth a dig.'

'Rita,' Andy said, 'do some digging.'

'I'm think I'm gonna be trying to find Stefan.'

'Heard of multi-tasking, yer lazy cow? Just see if owt dun't look right. And somebody keep going on Churchill. He's giving money away. Where there's money, there's mischief. CCTV'll be coming in by now. Who's on that?'

Gemma raised a hand.

'Right. Ana leaves Miriana's house Wednesday night. Where did she go? Why didn't she get a cab, young lass on her own, that time of night?' Andy said, taking a massive breath, his face lighting up, eyes bright and clear, as if yesterday's half-bottle of scotch had been a bowlful of Viagra.

Gemma sniffed, loud enough to bring the big man to a halt.

'Something else, Sir,' she said. 'Ana worked at the orphanage before she came to the UK. Luica orphanage. And … hold on …' She rifled through a stack of papers that she was holding, her face twisted in concentration. 'Border Service has got her taking a flight to Bucharest a month ago.'

'Bloody hell! You lot've been busy,' Andy said. 'See what it all means. Get this Stefan bloke found. Ana's flat in Chapeltown? Why not start there?'

Joe was going to start there anyway, but why piss on Andy's little comeback parade?

'And this Mariah Carey or whatever she's called?' Andy continued. 'She's done a runner, emptied her office an' all. I'll send her details out, make sure she doesn't leave the country.'

When he'd finished, people sagged a little, taking a moment to recover their strength after the wave of raw energy that had just crashed over them.

'Go on, then, sod off! Back here at four, boys and girls.'

# 44

He was parked in a lay-by, a paper mug of coffee in the cup holder, Classic FM on low, the two things together representing a small but symbolic rejection of teamwork. For Joe, the best way to work in a group was to do stuff on your own then tell everyone else what you'd done.

He dialled, knowing that Mihal Bogdan had an equally low opinion of teams.

'Joe! Good morning! Your boy Stefan!'

The ebullience was a little forced.

'Hi, Mihal. You been at it all night again?'

'Just got home. I've had a busy time with that trafficking case. Your Mr Tennant never stops!'

'That's true. Got anything for me?'

'Does a data genius shit in the forest?'

Mihal was a great fan of English idioms. He didn't always get them right, but they were guaranteed creative misses.

'I went backwards from the data we had. Ana Dobrescu, you've seen the info about the orphanage? Her and the other girl?'

'Miriana. Yes. Both orphans.'

'Stefan Nicolescu too. He's an orphan. Same age as Ana. They grew up there together. The orphanage in Luica.'

'So Ana knew Stefan from way back? That makes sense. The employment agency probably recruited more workers from the same place.'

'Almost certainly. We have people at the orphanage now.'

'Ana went down to the farm. She was organizing them, gave them money for taxis. She was going to get them out.'

'I know. I have access to your case system. Once a mother, eh!'

'Mother?'

'Ana was the mother. Gotta be.'

'Mihal, I'm not following you.'

'Human trafficking, Joe. Modern-day slave rings. How much do you know?'

'Not much, I'll admit.'

'You got a handful of minutes?'

A handful of minutes later, Joe knew all about slave rings. He knew enough to run one himself. And he certainly knew enough to investigate the death of a slave ring's mother.

'You OK with that?' Mihal asked, when the brief lesson was finished.

'Yes.'

'Sit down, Joe.'

'I'm sitting down.'

'Good. The Balans. Silviu and his cousin Omor. They set up a loan company in London back in 2007. Omor worked there, so he's got a British social security number. That's why he's fronting the employment agency in Leeds. We're working on the assumption that both men are involved, recruiting workers here in Romania to be trafficked to the UK. We're coordinating with the team in South Yorkshire, plus Tennant in Leeds.'

'The Balans? They're being questioned?'

'Omor Balan, the orphanage boss? He's disappeared.'

'So they must've heard about Ana's murder. It's connected?'

'Looks that way.'

'And Silviu?'

A pause.

'Joe? Listen. He took a flight yesterday, before we could get to him. He's in the UK.'

'Interesting.'

'Not the word I'd be using. Be careful, Joe.'

# 45

Chapeltown. The word sat strangely with him. For his mum's generation it was a byword for racial tension, a place of street riots, of exotic danger, somewhere to avoid at all costs. For Joe it was different. He'd got his first job here, straight out of teacher training college.

As they drove down Chapeltown Road he remembered most of the larger buildings, their faded Victorian elegance, age-withered and often shabby, but undaunted, oddly defiant. There was a sense that the district had been left to its own devices for a century and a half, and had done a pretty good job of holding on to its humanity.

He'd taught French at a comprehensive school here, given teaching a decent stab. He'd wanted to do something positive with his life. So he'd come to the very place his mother had warned him about. He'd enjoyed it, too, but had finally come to the conclusion that he wanted to help people, and struggling through *Le Petit Prince* wasn't the way. The West Yorkshire Police had provided him with an alternative.

'You know what I did the other day?' Rita said, as they

passed a Polish corner shop, its windows covered in bright red grilles.

'No ...'

'I was in Batley, and I went into one of them Polish places for some baccy. Nine quid.'

'And?'

'Double that normally. Packet wasn't even in English.'

'Illegal? Did you whip out your ID?'

'I friggin' didn't! Saved me a tenner. Funny, though, innit? It's like a different world. They're not even hiding it. That car wash where Stefan worked? Illegals is all they use. Half the cleaners in Britain are illegal foreigners, they reckon.'

He looked around as he drove. This part of Leeds had seen the arrival of plenty of foreigners. He tried to recount them in rough historical order as he drove: Irish, Russians, Poles, Chinese, Lithuanians, Latvians, Serbians, Hungarians, Italians, Pakistanis ... from the Caribbean, Hong Kong, Vietnam ... More recently there'd been Iraqis and Kurds, Syrians, plus a huge wave of Europeans.

This single square mile, as he used to enjoy telling his pupils, had boasted over a dozen synagogues, one of which was now a mosque, an Anglican church that was now a Sikh temple, a Methodist chapel that was now a bingo hall ... A ragbag of change and adaptation. It made him proud of his own city, of what it had done for the people of the world. His mum's obsession with Chapeltown had always seemed strange to him; the family she'd married into had turned up in 1936 from Sicily, with a couple of suitcases and the promise of work at a circus.

The Romanos had done all right. Immigrants mostly do.

They graft and battle for the things that everyone else already has. But now the drawbridge has been pulled up. Still they come, across the sea in inflatable dinghies, clinging to the axles of lorries, boxed up in containers. They come to Britain, like they've always come. But they're not welcome anymore. Apart from Ana Dobrescu. There'd been a warm welcome for her. A job from the day she arrived. Someone had really wanted her here.

'You bought in the end, then?' the estate agent asked.

He had a faint accent from somewhere Joe couldn't place, and thin, wispy hair that had once been red and was now a chestnut-grey. They'd got to know each other last year when Joe was trying to find a place to buy.

'Yes. Three bedrooms, out past the cricket ground.'

'Good. You don't want to be renting forever.'

The man was now stooping, his face almost touching the lock as he struggled to get the key in. Finally, the door opened.

'Here we are!'

Joe and Rita followed him into a large Victorian house with a common hall area and a polished wooden staircase that hinted at the comforts of a former family home. A series of numbered doors, all with Yale locks, all glossed magnolia, said the rest.

'It's upstairs,' the man said, leading the way.

On the first-floor landing Joe counted four doors. The landing itself was several times larger than the front room last night, crammed full of Romanian workers. He tried to imagine the array of people who might have lived here over the years since the house had been divided into flats: the smells of their cooking, the rhythms of their languages, the crying of their babies …

'You want to knock first?'

Rita knocked, good and hard.

No one answered. She knocked again.

'We're all right to … just go in?' the estate agent asked.

'Yep,' she said, waiting impatiently for him to find the right key.

There'd been officers around here yesterday. A cleaner had let them in. They'd reported a tidy flat. Not much in it.

Inside, it was larger than Joe had imagined, with a broad bay window, decent curtains, a sofa with an Indian throw over it. The smell was vague, distant: floral, plus a note of incense, or sandalwood perhaps.

'She came to see you?' Joe said, noting the modern cushions, a large glass vase full of paper flowers, the poster of a very odd white building with ugly, lumpen towers, which turned out to be a Romanian cathedral.

'Two days ago.'

Joe moved into a tiny bedroom, which was well ordered but bare of personal effects. Some women's jumpers in the drawers. T-shirts, size S.

'Her and a young man,' the estate agent said from the doorway, watching Joe.

'Tall?'

'Very. They called in the office, in the afternoon. Rented two houses. Paid a year in advance.'

'Cash?'

'Yes. The receipt's at the shop.'

'Who paid?' Rita asked.

'The girl.'

'Total bedrooms?'

'Six in each house. Student places, y'know.'

Joe was poking his nose in empty cupboards, behind the curtains, flicking through a pocket Romanian–English dictionary on an otherwise empty shelf. It was like his little French and Italian Collins Gems, the colour on their plastic covers worn away with use, the white showing through.

He went over to the kitchen area in the far corner. Four mugs hanging from a line of hooks mounted on the wall, all pointing the same way. Plates stacked neatly in the cupboard. In a drawer the random utensils of rented accommodation. All spick and span, but there was a thin film of dust on everything. A single carton of orange juice sat at the back of the fridge. Three months out of date. The officers yesterday hadn't included it in their report. A murdered immigrant girl and a main suspect in intensive care? They were just waiting for Churchill to croak for it. Or just to croak; if he died it'd be easier all round.

'Right,' Joe said, as they shut the door behind them. 'She clearly hasn't been living here recently. Are these two houses local? We better take a look.'

'Couple of miles away.'

'Stefan Nicolescu's living in one of them, right?' Joe asked. 'Whose name's on the rental?'

He dithered.

'Out with it, love,' she said. 'It's not gonna be a secret for long.'

'Stefan Nicolescu,' the estate agent finally said, a little

awkwardly. 'He's ... I mean, they said I'd have all his full ID tomorrow. I have a photocopy of his passport. He's applying for a work permit. He's got some sort of job, actually. Place called Churchill Cladding ...'

Joe looked at Rita.

'... and they said I'd get to see all the passports and IDs. I mean ...'

'Aye, well there'll be no passports now, love. They're all in custody.'

He nodded, didn't mention the rental money.

'OK,' Joe said, as they stood outside and waited for the big front door to be closed, 'we'll be back to see the other houses later, if needed. Out of interest, how did Ana Dobrescu find this place last year? Did she come to your office, flat hunting?'

He inhaled, pursed his lips, weak and defensive.

'I'd never met her before Wednesday. The flat was rented for her, by a company. Still is.'

'Name?'

'Workout Employment Agency.'

'Right, we're off,' Rita said, with a smile. 'All that cash she paid you? Keep it safe, love. Somebody'll be coming for it.'

# 46

He tried to keep the speed under control as he drove across town, easing past traffic as best he could, all of which was going slightly too slow. He only ever drove too fast when he was confused, as if the traffic itself was an obstacle to his understanding. And today nothing much was making sense. Ana had a perfectly good flat, empty, but Stefan had moved into one of the houses they'd rented. Why?

They got down onto the ring road.

'Just enough time.'

'For what?' she asked, her face buried in her phone.

'Spot of immigrant nostalgia. It's on the way.'

His grandparents' old house hadn't changed. An end terrace in Wortley, the first in a line that stretched up the hill, into the sky, it had seemed when he was a boy, magical castles with their big old attics and cellars like cold, damp dungeons. The red bricks were darkened with age, but still in good condition, all these years later. Gustavo Romano and his wife Maria Grazia came to Leeds from Sicily, and Gustavo would go on to do eighteen summer seasons at Blackpool Tower Circus before founding the Romano Theatrical Agency. Yet he based the family here, not across the Pennines. Blackpool was a frivolous place, he always said, with its revolting vinegary cockles and that rock-sugar with words running through it. ('For why? For why the words in a sugar-stick? *Che fatuo!*') This from a man who fell on his arse for a living. A man who had arrived as an immigrant and built a life here.

Joe pulled over.

'So, Ana has a copy of Stefan's passport. She sets him up in a house rented in his name, not in her flat in Chapeltown.' He drummed his fingers on the steering wheel. 'Promises to get the real IDs, for all of 'em. She's using Churchill's money, renting houses, planning to get another dozen people out ... Then what?'

'Something goes wrong,' Rita said.

He took one last look at the house as they drove off.

'Meanwhile, a Mr Silviu Balan arrives in the country.'

'And somebody puts the word out that Ana's dead.'

They picked up lunch on the way. A McDonald's Quarter Pounder for her, a black coffee for him. They parked at the back of a communal car park that served half a dozen large industrial units and warehouses.

Inside the Mondeo, the smell of fried food was now heavy on the air, and there was a massive strawberry milkshake sitting on the dash. Rita was on her phone, thumbing down the screen, the last of the burger in her other hand.

She called Gwyn.

'The blog? Owt sticking out?' she asked, then took a bite as she listened. 'Worth a try, innit? Metadata? Do what you can. I'll tell Joe. Cheers, mate.'

'Tell me what?' he asked, knowing that if it was anything technical he'd have to ask for a second explanation in plain English.

'We're just double-checking that charity blog. Gwyn can't see owt dodgy. Here.'

She showed him her phone, flicked through the Rebuild website. He'd already seen it. A blog detailing several building projects in Romania. Many of the photos featured Sophie and Michael Benedict.

'That chick's got some pricey clobber,' Rita said.

'Really?'

'See her jeans in them photos? J Brand skinnies. Two hundred quid a pop.'

'Since when did you know so much about high fashion?'

'Since I got a friggin' joint bank account with my fiancée.'

'The jeans do fit her quite nicely.'

'Genetics, innit? She's got the arse for it.'

He looked at the foot-high cup of milkshake, at the empty McDonald's carton on the floor of his Mondeo.

'What?' she said. 'Piss off!'

'Talking about clothes, you remember our bet? You'll be spending two hundred on a suit for me when I find the killer.'

She laughed.

'How about Stefan for it?'

'Why not?' he said. 'All we know is that he's got a job here. Churchill and Ana must've sorted that out for him.'

'So he's Ana's boyfriend, is he? She sets him up like this, house, job, everything. Then he kills her?'

'Or he's her ex-boyfriend? Ana finds someone better, richer.'

'Stef gets the boot and can't handle it?'

'That's plausible. Time for a word. How's your Romanian?'

'Shit. But I can smell guilt at twenty paces.'

'Right,' Joe said, opening the door. 'Stefan Nicolescu. He's gonna be jumpy when two coppers show up.'

'Especially if he killed her.'

He let himself sink back into the seat.

'It's called a mother,' he said, as a wave of sadness hit him, a physical disgust, enough to make his whole body heavy. Perhaps Tennant had a point.

'Mother?'

'They get brought over here. Vulnerable people, homeless, alkies, low IQ … Foreign country, they don't speak the lingo, passports taken off 'em. They need mothering. A bit of a hug, a kindly word, someone to tell 'em it's all right. Make sure they're eating. Watered and fed. Then back to work.'

'Like cattle.'

'Yep. Ana was working at the orphanage. Then they offered her a job over here.'

'Chance for a new life?'

'When she gets here, that's the new life. Making sure the cattle get watered. That's what she came to Britain for?'

Rita screwed up her face.

'She might not've known.'

'Everybody seems to have loved her. She must have done the best she could. But she knew what it was, must have.'

'So what? It's not always black and white. You'd do it, wouldn't you, in her shoes?'

Joe thought about it. Would he?

'I know I would,' she said. 'Get out of Romania? New life? I'd tell myself it were all right. It's what people do, Joe.'

269

'Tell themselves it's all right?'

'Folk get dragged into stuff. Turn a blind eye. Pretend they're not seein' it, that things aren't that bad. She was trapped, just like the rest of 'em.'

'Remember what Miriana said? Easy to judge when you're living with a millionaire. I think Ana was different.'

Rita rolled a cigarette, made a start on a second.

'It's OK, I've got my own.'

She chuckled. 'Two days into a murder investigation, 'course you have!'

'How about this?' he said as they both lit up. 'A few months ago, she leaves the agency. Regrets what she's got herself into. Decides to do something about it.'

'Tries to persuade Miriana to join the crusade?'

'She rang me while they were in the restaurant together. Something good, she said. She was gonna tell me everything. She sounded excited.'

'And Stefan?'

'They grew up at the orphanage together. Two kids with no one else? Whatever, she rescues him first, after the attack. Sets him up with a job, a phone, a house.'

'Aye, somewhere the agency can't find him.'

'Right. Tells the rest of 'em to wait. Gives 'em money, another phone. She was planning to have 'em all rescued. And she wanted me to help her do it.'

Rita stared ahead as she smoked.

'Wanted or needed? Why didn't she just report it all to the police, have done with it?'

'Why indeed. It's Miriana we should be chasing up.'

'One orphan at a time, partner,' she said, as she looked at the building opposite them.

Its walls were clad in a uniform grey material, only a couple of windows and a door at one end, plus a few bins and a skip at the other, partly out of sight. Joe was looking too. Checking out the visible access points. There'd be a fire door at the back, by the bins.

'Churchill's old place,' he said. 'Doesn't look much, does it? Made himself a lot of money here. Now he's contemplating suicide.'

Rita scanned the building, end to end.

'Beatles, innit. Can't buy me love.'

# 47

Inside the unit they were met by a loud wailing noise and the sweet, nauseating smell of plastic. The air was thick with dust, which was lit up from above by fluorescent tubes that ran the length of the ceiling. There was steel shelving on both sides, twenty feet high and half as wide, stacked with thick plastic sheeting. In the middle, between the shelves, was a long worktable, shrouded in clouds of white.

The noise dropped and the dust began to disperse, revealing two men in blue overalls and full-face masks. They stood at either side of the worktable, between them a circular saw, now slowing down.

For a while no one moved.

'Shoot-out at the old cladding corral,' Rita whispered. 'They're not budging.'

Joe stepped forward, his warrant card held up like a sheriff's badge.

'Morning, gents. Police. A word, please.'

The two men looked at each other, then removed their masks. They were both in their middle years, and were curious rather than concerned.

'Not guilty, officer!' one of them said.

'We're looking for Stefan Nicolescu,' said Joe. 'Just started here, we believe.'

'Yesterday. He's helping out a bit. Waiting for a work permit. Good lad, he is. Hard to talk to, like.'

'You the gaffer?' Rita asked.

'For now.'

'For now?'

'New owners. I'm keeping things going 'til we get a new manager.'

'This is Ben Churchill's place, right?' Rita asked.

'Was. He sold up a few weeks ago.'

'What, the whole business? You know why?'

The man shrugged.

''Cos he's rich? Dun't need the hassle? Dunno. Here one day, gone the next.'

His colleague nodded.

'Gave us all a couple of grand, mind. In the pocket, y'know … Didn't want a party. Decent bloke.'

Joe and Rita assimilated the information as they looked around.

'How many people work here?' Rita asked.

'Couple a dozen. Rest of 'em's out on jobs.'

'Stefan?'

'In't back somewhere. Not done owt wrong, has he?' He glanced over his shoulder. 'Here he is. Stef? Police are 'ere!'

A tall, thickset young man in white overalls walked towards them down the middle of the building, a large white patch over one eye. Stefan saw Joe. Froze. His arms went out behind him, hands grappling for anything to hold on to. There was a shuffle in his step as he turned one way then the other.

'Stef? They just wanna ask you … Hardly understands owt… Stef! Come ed, yer barm cake!'

But Stefan now spun on his heels, throwing himself into a lunging, arm-flaying attempt at a sprint. Rita turned and was off out of the front door, head down, shoulders rolling, like a winger who's just copped the ball fifteen yards out. A second later Joe was running towards Stefan, jarring his ankle on the concrete floor as he tripped over in haste.

'Shit!'

He staggered forward, managing to keep upright.

Stefan wasn't moving fast. There was something lumbering and confused about his progress. Yet on he went, towards the fire doors at the back, unsure of whether to continue, it seemed, but determined not to stop. When he got there he slammed into the exit.

A sudden blast of bright light blinded Joe as he ran. Rita was already outside, barking orders, loud. Very loud. He didn't fancy Stefan's chances.

When Joe got to the doorway, he saw Rita with an arm around Stefan's waist, the palm of her other hand flat against his shoulder. She was about a foot shorter than him, but one push and he'd've been on his back. They were walking in a circle, breathless, like athletes warming down after a race. And she was bawling at him.

'Just a chat! No need for all that, pal! A *chat* is all!'

Stefan, despite his size, was cowering, overcome by fear, as if a mother was exactly who he needed.

Too late for that, though. She was dead.

Then he looked up, confused, squinting through his good eye.

'Stefan?' Joe said. 'It's me. Sorry. I lied. I'm police.'

# 48

'Interpreter?'

'Have you heard him trying to speak English?' asked Joe.

'Aye, well, South Yorkshire want to talk to him.'

'After we're done. *If* we're done. He's my suspect.'

Andy rubbed his face, pushing the flab around, rearranging his double chins.

'You better clear the cost with Tennant. I've decided to let him carry on overseeing the case. You working well with him?'

'We'll manage.'

'This Stefan? Got him down for the murder?'

Joe sighed. 'Too early to say. Gotta be a possible, though.'

'Motive?'

'He was involved. Whatever Ana was doing, Stef was part of it. Perhaps something went wrong. It's got something to do with Churchill, as well.'

'His money?'

'There's always that, yes.'

He stood there, in front of Andy's desk, hands thrust into his pockets, ready for an argument. There was nothing to argue about, but he wanted one anyway. Stefan Nicolescu was a victim, brought over to work like an animal. Ana had tried to help him. Now she was dead, and Stefan was in a cell waiting to be questioned about her murder. He was angry because he knew it might be true, that crimes happen exactly like this, in the wake of human suffering, and despite human kindness.

He allowed his temper to subside.

'You all right, then?' he asked.

'Got a prescription,' Andy said, eyes down. 'It takes a while to kick in. I'm gonna sweat a lot, apparently.'

'You always sweat a lot. Whatever you need. Y'know, what, ehm ...'

'Aye, right. Good. I'm ... Aye, all right.'

'Good ... Good ... The interview with Stefan? Me and Rita.'

Andy was already shaking his head.

'She's been interviewing victims of abuse for bloody weeks. It takes it out of you. She's supposed to be having a break.'

'Should be straightforward.'

Andy shifted in his seat, looked past Joe towards the door. 'Simon. Come in.'

Simon Tennant took a step sideways as he entered, as if there was an exclusion area around Joe.

'We just got the formal statement from the cab driver,' he said. 'Ana paid two hundred and seventy pounds in cash for a round trip to a poultry farm in South Yorkshire.'

'That was straight after she spoke to me,' Joe said. 'She'd been to see Stefan in hospital. And she was in a rush.'

'She paid with handfuls of twenties, the cab driver said. Didn't even count it.'

Andy inhaled, drawing half the room's oxygen into his formidable lungs.

'Right. This Stefan. Go at him hard.'

'By the way,' Tenant added as they turned to leave. 'Nothing on Silviu Balan's whereabouts yet.'

'Who the frig's he? Forget it, tell me later. While we're at it, gents, where's Miriana Dalca?'

Not really a question. The two men were at the door.

'Nice going, Sergeant Romano!' Andy called after them. 'Three suspects. One's in a coma, one's been glassed, an' one's pissed off. Your name's all over this case, Joe!'

'I'll do the interview,' said Joe, as he and Tennant made their way back to the ops room, 'then I'll find Gwyn, see what he's got.'

'OK. Miriana's still AWOL. Odds-on she sent that text to the workers' house, telling them Ana was dead. It was in Romanian, sent from Leeds. She used an unregistered number, though. Not her own phone.'

'A warning? Right, we'll find her.'

'Her car's still outside her house. She's done a runner, and she's smart enough not to take the motor.'

'What's her motive?'

'Money,' Tennant said, stifling a yawn. 'Your friend Mihal says it might not be a dozen trafficked workers. Could be a lot more of 'em. A lot more motive.'

'Do South Yorks know about Balan being in the country?'

'Are you joking? The NCA's been called in. They're going ballistic.'

'Well, you can't get far in modern Britain with the National Crime Agency on your tail,' Joe said.

Tennant thought about it, hardly the energy for an opinion.

He took his time leaving, so tired now that even turning to go was an effort. He had the bearing of a man who wanted a bed more than his next breath. Sleepless, and immersed in the human capacity for casual, everyday evil. It was enough to bring any man close to eternal sorrow. Even him.

# 49

Stef sat at the desk in the interview room, doing a bad job of holding his nerves in check. A duty solicitor on one side of him, a young female interpreter on the other. With his good eye he stared down at the desk. He hadn't raised his head to look at Joe and Rita since the interview began.

He was a big, big man. Latent power in his shoulders, enough to take down anyone in the room, in any room. Not the kind of bloke you'd naturally choose to glass outside a pub. Unless you were a racist nutter. But he didn't seem so powerful now. He looked like a frightened boy in the wrong body.

Joe had gone through the basics. Got his name. Confirmed that he'd left the hospital two days ago, met up with Ana later the same day in Leeds. He didn't know the address he was now living at. Ana had organized the new house. He answered carefully, each word slow, separate, his voice a shaky growl. But nothing he said contradicted what they already knew.

Joe and Rita both sat back and shuddered silently to themselves. The next bit was her job. The worst job. Always.

'Stefan?' she said, her voice soft but firm. 'Ana Dobrescu was found dead yesterday morning.'

They waited for the interpreter to deliver the message.

Stefan stared at Rita, his mouth open, like the whole thing was a joke.

He turned to the interpreter, waited for her to repeat what she'd said.

The room fell silent. His face was blank, mouth still open, his breathing steady. Then he slowly extended his forearms onto the desk in front of him, and lowered his head until his face rested on them. There he remained.

His breaths became heavier, faster. Yet still he made no other sound. On it went. A minute, perhaps. Joe shifted in his seat, ready to say something. But Rita held up a hand, made him wait.

Then it came. A groan of anguish so intense, so horrifically loud that Joe felt it in the sinews of his body. Then another. And another. When there was no force left in Stefan's body, he emitted a high-pitched cry of fear. He screamed, squealed, gasping for air, the sweat already visible through the short-cropped hair on his scalp, his head twisting in his arms.

Finally, he drew himself up, face glistening, his good eye swollen, unfocused, the patch on his other eye sodden with tears, his mouth awash with saliva. And now, for the first time, he stared at Joe.

But it wasn't Joe who spoke. It was Rita.

'Stefan Nicolescu,' she said, calm and clear, 'where were you on Wednesday night?'

Not an ounce of compassion in her voice. She raised her head a fraction, waited for the interpreter to repeat the question. Then, as the incredulity spread across Stefan's face, she leant forward across the desk, until there was less than a foot between them.

'Stefan? Wednesday evening? Where were you? And I think you understand the question just fine.'

'In the house,' he said.

'The house? The one you can't remember the address of?'

But he wasn't listening now. He stood up. His body filled the room, the physical threat not even remotely disguised.

'I not kill Ana,' he said, towering over her, flecks of spittle landing on her face as he spat the phrase out. 'Say that, an' I kill you!'

Rita never so much as blinked.

Immediately, Stefan's whole body deflated. There were tears rolling down one side of his face as he dropped back into his chair. With trembling hands he pulled a wallet from his pocket. He was crying in a steady stream now, his body shaking as he sobbed.

'Here,' he said, rocking backwards and forwards, fumbling to open the wallet.

He took out a thin wad of photos and laid them out on the table.

'Ana and me. Kids.'

'In the orphanage? Luica?'

'Orph …?'

He waited for a translation.

'Yes. From baby. She is' – he tapped his head – 'intelligent. Me? No.'

'You're intelligent enough to understand me, right?' Rita said.

'Is Ana! She teach me English! Teach us all!'

The photos were old and creased, their corners rounded with age.

'Here. Ana and me.'

He pointed to the photos one at a time, as if each one was a precious relic. There were groups of children on a bright, sunny day, acting the fool, posing for the camera. And in another, Ana Dobrescu as a teenager, short hair, stern face, as if she didn't want to be photographed. In another she was with Stefan, who was young but already tall, standing proud in front of a fountain, Ana at his side, about half his size; she'd glanced up at him as the photo was taken, a look of maternal concern on her face.

'What happened?' Joe asked. 'Later on, when you were adults?'

'Ana has job. Working at the *orfano* … eh, eh … the …'

'Orphanage,' Joe said.

'Yes. Is clever girl. Me? No job. A lot of us. No work. Very bad life.'

He came to the final photo of Ana, a young woman in formal-looking clothes standing outside a church. Stefan looked at it with childlike affection.

'She help us. Always. With papers. Things …'

'Then here. A job in England. Did Ana help to organize that?'

Stef listened to the interpreter, nodding.

'But is very hard job. Bad. Is not so good. She has house for me now. New job. Clever girl. Helps me! Look!'

He opened his wallet and showed them a clump of bank-notes.

'Money from Ana?'

Stefan nodded again.

'And I help her!'

Joe thought about it.

'How do you help Ana?'

'Names. I tell her names.'

'Other people she was going to help?'

Stefan breathed out, shook his head. He reached out, grabbed Joe's arm with both hands, pulled him close.

'Who kill Ana? When I go from here I kill him. You tell me. I can do. No problem. I kill them. No problem.'

Joe eased his arm away, stood up. Rita followed, cast Joe a quick glance, a nod.

'Stefan Nicolescu,' she said, 'I am arresting you on suspicion of the murder ...'

# 50

A short stay in the cells often clarifies things, he told himself as he made his way to the top of the hospital building. Rita was sensing something with Stefan, but Joe wasn't so sure. Whatever, they had their suspect for thirty-six hours.

He paused for a moment before knocking, felt the unnerving quiet of the Oncology Department, the absence of urgency.

'Oh, hello,' Jill Wallace said, waving him in with the muted brio of someone who doesn't have all day to waste on pleasantries. 'You tracked me down!'

He took a seat, felt like a patient awaiting bad news. In fact, he realized now that he always felt a bit like that, in a permanent state of negative expectation.

'I saw the official announcement on Twitter,' she said, as she finished typing something then gave him her full attention. 'It was definitely the girl who was coming to consults with Ben.'

'OK, right. Thanks very much for your notes, by the way.'

'I hope they helped.'

'Absolutely,' he lied. He didn't know if anything was helping at the moment. 'I'm …' he searched for the right words, 'I'm still trying to get a handle on Churchill's state of mind. Seems such a violent way to try and end it.'

She waited, made sure he'd finished.

'So,' she said, 'as you've probably worked out, I'm Mr Churchill's oncologist.'

She let the word sink in.

'And his … *condition*?' Joe ventured, wondering whether it sounded medical enough.

'We have no consent to divulge his condition. I have to make sure that any disclosure is justifiable.'

'I think in the circumstances …'

She exhaled, took her time.

'Cancer,' she said, finally. 'I can't give details.'

'Terminal?'

'He'd already entered the stage of palliative care, I mean, before the accident. He has morphine drips at home. Tablets. He wanted to remain independent for as long as possible. It's very brave, soldiering on like that.'

'Timeframe? Before the crash?'

'A couple of months, perhaps.'

'And now?'

'It's not looking good. Although, I think he's better prepared than most. Over the last eighteen months I've talked to him a lot. About life. Death. Suicide.'

'Suicide?'

'Dignitas has a lot to answer for. People naturally think about assisted dying at this stage. It's a way of keeping control. But it can confuse the end-of-life process. Ben's palliative care would have been excellent. His death would have been ordered, painless. Sad to say, but we really are very good at death.'

'He would have died here?'

'Yes, probably.'

'Did he ever ask you about a substance called Pentobarbital?'

'Oh, God! Nembutal. That's the commercial name. No, he didn't.'

'Would you have been worried if he had?'

'Worried? No. Saddened. Has he …?'

'We don't think he's tried to buy any. But just to confirm, the meds he has at home are not enough to end it?'

'No. They're controlled, for that reason.'

'And he would have known that?'

'It's the kind of thing he would definitely have known. Down to the last milligram.'

She smiled. It was a watery, well-practised expression of professional kindness, as if she were about to deliver bad news.

'Ben isn't capable of strangling anyone,' she said.

'You mean physically?'

'Temperamentally.'

'How can you be so sure?'

She took her time, chose her words with care.

'He's a very clever man. And practical. But there's also a gentleness to him. You can see it in his intelligence. I mean, his thoughtfulness is almost physical. Does that make sense?'

'His bearing? The way he moves?'

'Exactly. He's very deliberate, never wants to get anything wrong. It's like he actively enjoys getting things exactly right, every last detail.'

'How about his physical strength?'

'Strangulation? I'd have to see the injuries. Even then, I'm not a pathologist. But it's not that.' She paused, gathered her

286

thoughts. 'If he *had* intended to kill someone, I think he would have done his homework. It wouldn't have been strangulation.'

'Not his style?'

'I'm sorry,' she said. 'It sounds like I'm trying to do your job for you. But I know Ben pretty well. He would have been cleverer than that.'

'Spur of the moment? We can all do strange things.'

'Spur of the moment. Not a phrase I associate with Ben Churchill at all!'

Joe let the information sit in his mind for a moment.

'His own stab at suicide wasn't very clever, was it? Morphine and booze, then straight into a concrete pillar at high speed? Without an airbag?'

'Completely out of character.'

'People can do almost anything, if pushed, provoked.'

'Murder? Not Ben. I really don't think so.' She looked at her watch. 'Sorry, I have a meeting, and I'm already late.'

'OK. I appreciate your help.'

She stood, looked down at the desk in front of her.

'Ben was in love,' she said, almost against her will, ashamed of herself. 'The happiest I've ever seen him. Please tell me he didn't do this.'

# 51

Quarter of an hour later he was in Greggs, eyeing up pasties with Gwyn Merchant.

'We arrested Stefan,' Joe said as they stood in the queue. 'Meanwhile, Ben Churchill's dying of cancer. He only had a couple of months to live. I've just spoken to his doctor. She's convinced he didn't kill Ana. Go figure.'

'Interesting,' said Gwyn, his face close to the glass. He didn't seem interested in figuring anything, other than what to have for a late lunch.

'You read my stuff about the charity folk?'

'Yes,' said Joe. 'It was a bit sketchy, though. Run it by me again. The Benedicts don't change their trousers?'

'Aye. They've got this charity blog. Insta an' all. Children's hospitals, good works, all that stuff.'

'I've seen it.'

'So, they go over to Romania, post stuff on the blog, six, seven days in a row, like they're on trips to see the work they're funding. Day one a new hospital ward ... next day the plans for this ... for that ... There's photos of 'em with poorly kids, on building sites, all that shit. But the dirty bitch doesn't change her kecks.'

'A bit gendered of you, isn't it?' Joe said, noticing that several people in the queue were now casting glances at them. 'Anyway, she wears fancy jeans. Expensive.'

'Yer not jokin'! Tight-fitting. Ex-model, right? But him? Have you seen him? How does he pull someone like her?'

'Ah, the vagaries of the human heart, DC Merchant …'

'Dunno about hearts. But he doesn't get changed much either. A week in the same strides? Filthy buggers! Not that I've met 'em.'

'You haven't spoken to them yet?'

'Can't find 'em! An' they don't answer the friggin' phone. I'm off up to their house again after this. Just north of Bilton. Nice place. Posh.'

'A week? I mean, I often wear trousers a week.'

'Nah,' Gwyn said, eyes still on the pasties. 'It's the metadata on the digital photos that's not right, y'know, time, geolocation. The snaps from their last visit to Luica were all taken the same day. Same *hour*. They changed jackets and shirts, to make it look like seven days. Didn't change their kecks, though.'

'Just on this one trip?'

'No. We checked the last three. Always the same. Whatever they're up to over there, it's not visiting hospitals.'

'Get back to HQ, dig a bit more.'

'Aye, right,' said Gwyn, turning to the woman behind the counter. 'Bacon and cheese pasty and a steak bake, love. Chuck a couple of yum-yums in an' all. I'm a growin' lad.'

He said it with a boyish grin, managing to make it sound like he was propositioning her as a favour. She tried not to smile back, didn't do a very good job.

Joe ordered two vegan sausage rolls, gave her his best grin, got nothing for his trouble.

# 52

*You drive in a bit.* He stood and looked back the way he'd come. It was little more than a space where trees had been cleared years ago, now thick with undergrowth. He'd left his car just off the road and walked in about fifty yards, following the track into the woods that Andy had shown him on the map. Where would Stefan've got a motor? Could he even drive?

*Not too far, though. Don't wanna get stuck.* He considered his vegan sausage rolls. Hadn't really fancied vegan. It was like clicking on the *Guardian* website when all you really want is the *Mail*'s sidebar of shame. Shoving them back in his pocket, he walked on.

*Out of sight of the road.* The ground underfoot was springy, thick with dark green creepers and dead leaves. No clear signs as to whether a car had been here recently. *Park up, carry her from here. Carry or drag?* He stopped again, put himself in a killer's shoes.

*Carry. Your blood's up. You're full of adrenalin.* Pitch dark. A dead body on your shoulders, the body of a girl you've just strangled. She wasn't heavy. *Anyone could do it.* You're stumbling over fallen branches, heart feels like it's going to punch its way out of your chest. Shitting yourself.

Before long he saw the edge of the golf course through the trees. He veered right until he came to the place where Ana's body had been found. There was no indication of where she'd been dumped, the crime scene now packed up and gone.

He crouched down by the base of the tree, pressed his fingers into the damp earth. *Anyone could do it*. He thought about it. *Could he? Could he kill someone?* He'd never truly answered that question, after all these years in serious crime. He'd asked himself a thousand times, though. Every copper in CID had.

Beyond the trees Churchill's house was in darkness. Only a line of tomato plants at the edge of the patio gave any hint that life continued there, and even they were wilting. He tried to imagine Ben and Ana living together. A last, desperate stab at togetherness for Ben, as he walked towards death? And for her? A second, fleeting childhood, perhaps. Whatever, somebody had put an end to it. Within days she'd be forgotten. Paperwork back to Romania. No one there to mourn her death. Case closed.

Romania. He cast his mind back, three decades ago. The empty expressions of Romanian orphans on the news. It had been the first time he'd felt sorry for other children, the first time he'd sensed how privileged he was, in the band with Tony, playing in smoky clubs, burger and chips on the way home, money in his pocket … Then the scrawny kids on the telly, the silent horror in their huge eyes, their faces dusty, old, vacant.

*Could he?* He looked across the fairway. The grass was so neatly cut that if you squinted it was like velvet. Is this the happiness that people seek? A pointless sport in a safe, manicured version of nature? A playground for grown-ups? Is this why people strive for riches, to be a child again? To be safe?

It came to him in a cold flush of realization. *He could.* If he found Ana's killer, he could do it.

By the time he got back to his car, Rita was leaning on it, smoking.

'You found it all right, then?'

'Your car's here, dick.' She looked past him into the woods. 'That grooming stuff? They used to bring 'em up here.'

'Yeah, I know. It's starting to get to people, that case.'

She signed, big shake of the head.

'The bigger the case, the more it drags. And the victims are adults. Bringing charges is a bloody nightmare.'

'Andy's worried about you. All the interviews. It's gotta be a strain, week after week. You needed a break.'

'I'll interview rapists all day if there's a conviction at the end of it. Yorkshire Regiment my arse. He's a wuss.'

Joe smiled.

'I wouldn't say that.'

She drew heavily on her rollie.

'Aye, well, them girls need someone. When I were their age I had our kid. Big lad, our Carl. Him and his rugby mates. No one messed with me. The whole estate knew what'd happen if they did. Whole of Batley. What if I'd had nobody, eh? 'Cos them lasses've got nobody.'

'You can't let personal feelings get in the way. Jesus, listen to me! I sound like Tennant! Do what you want, but take a break.'

He watched her as she smoked. He'd heard the gossip about Carl Scannon. Everyone had. Promising rugby player, got caught up in something dodgy, fell to his death during a police raid on a disused building in Batley. Rita had never mentioned it. She'd never even mentioned Carl's name before.

She sniffed, looked around at the woods.

'So? You got Mr Stefan down for it?'

'Dunno,' he said. 'There was a lot of emotion in the interview. And he's definitely scared of something. Or someone. Let him stew a while.' He also glanced at the woods. 'Nothing to see in there, but it's not far from here to where her body was dumped. Whoever did it knew Ana was living with Churchill. You ever read *Hamlet*?'

'Did it for my GCSEs. Got a B, as it happens.'

'He commits suicide.'

'Sea of troubles? He shits it. Takes the easy way out. Your point?'

'Ben Churchill was considering the same thing. Suicide. He has terminal cancer. I just spoke to his doctor.'

She sucked in air.

'Jeez, that's a bit of a spanner! Explains why he put her in the guestroom, though. Carrying her upstairs would've been too much for him.'

'Yep. So, what do we have? Mr Ben Churchill. He's dying, and he knows it. Then he meets a Romanian orphan. You remember those orphanages, after the fall of communism?'

'Before my time.'

'Bloody awful. Must have been a loveless world to grow up in. Horrible. Worse than we can imagine. She had no family.'

'Came over 'ere for a better life.'

'Yeah, mothering slaves in a foreign country.'

'Then she bags a millionaire,' she said, but softly.

'A millionaire who's dying. You said they'd looked comfortable together the other day. Homely. Tender.'

'Something special, for sure.'

'His oncologist said Churchill was in love. Love and suicide. How are we squaring that?'

'Question, *mon brave*, is whether Ana were in love with him. Come on.'

They got into the Land Rover.

'Right,' he said. 'You dump her. Then what?'

Rita pointed to her left. 'Main road's half a mile that way. If you know the area, you go right. Snakes around a bit, then there's a couple of old lanes. You go down either of them, you're away. Not a camera in sight.'

'Let's go.'

She never changed out of first gear, however much the engine seemed to beg for it, whining like a whipped dog that for some reason remains loyal to its owner. The road was old, only the distant reminder of white lines down the middle, and its edges crumbling away on both sides, melding into the undergrowth. They had their windows open, scanning the area.

'You dump her,' he said. 'And … and what?'

'You're shittin' yersen. If you've got owt, you get rid quick.'

'Got what, though?' Joe asked. 'What're we looking for?'

'A coat? Something that fell from her pocket? Or what they brought her in?'

'Bag, sheet?'

'Dunno,' she said, driving up onto the dirt at the side of the

294

road and coming to a stop. 'This is about it. Round that bend there's a few houses. You got owt to chuck, you do it now.'

So they got out and looked, one of them on each side. He walked slowly through the undergrowth and around the closest trees, starting from the bend in the road and moving back the way they'd come. Meanwhile, across the road Rita barrelled her way through the undergrowth, booting away leaves and dead wood, dredging the undergrowth with her Docs.

Joe tried to imagine being here at midnight, alone. The sound of blood in your ears, trying to keep it together, knowing you'd just killed a small, vulnerable woman. *With both hands, you can do a lot of damage very quickly.* You dump the body where you know Churchill will find it on his morning stroll; Churchill, her partner, who is conveniently dying. *You don't need a lot of pressure. Anyone could do it.*

A fleck of colour to his right. Green? Light green. No bigger than a thumbnail. About ten feet from the edge of the road, behind the nearest tree. Behind a tree?

He moved closer. A milky glow of colour in the half-light, beneath a pile of leaves. He knelt down, carefully removing each leaf.

'Over here!' he shouted, his voice echoing off the tree trunks around him and quickly dissipating.

By the time Rita had run across the road, he'd cleared the leaves away. A pair of green gardening gloves lay in a slight indentation in the ground.

'They've been pushed down. But they're clean and dry. Haven't been here long.'

'Driver gets out,' she said. 'Leaves the car running. Shoves 'em behind the tree. Job done. You remember the PM? No nail marks on the neck?'

'Can you get these back to HQ?'

'Where are you off?'

'Following the money.'

# 53

Charles Malthouse was sitting in a cushion-lined wicker armchair on the veranda behind the clubhouse. The stone-paved floor was littered with cables, boxes and bubble-wrap. Several people in overalls were up ladders, installing small white spheres high on the wall, as if to see how many security cameras a golf club could sustain, strung up like Christmas baubles beneath the eaves.

He still had a hint of superciliousness, a tendency to hold his head a little higher than necessary. But his body was depleted, and it was only with some effort that he managed to maintain the pose. Also, there was a cigarette in his hand.

'Bad habit,' Joe said.

Malthouse stared at it.

'I try to limit myself,' he said. 'Strange, though. I was in the petrol station this morning, saw the packets lined up behind the counter. And I said to myself, why shouldn't I? People do all kinds of things. Really, they do whatever they like.' He fumbled in his jacket pocket. 'Sorry. How rude of me! Please, have a seat.'

He held out a packet of Silk Cut as Joe sat down.

'A murder inquiry,' he said, taking one and leaning into Malthouse's lighter as it was flicked into action. 'Pressure, long shifts, what-have-you. A lot of officers smoke the odd one.'

Malthouse looked at the flame.

'Must be a constant strain, a job like yours, year after year,' he said. 'Whereas I've spent my life making sure members don't trail mud onto the carpets, checking there's enough chilled Chablis for their wives.'

Joe smiled. 'I believe that's what they call a gendered comment.'

'Ha! We have female members, of course. No sexism here. All the same, I'd be surprised if one glass of white wine in a hundred is served to a man. Apart from champagne.'

He waved a hand towards a bottle of Dom Pérignon on the table in front of him.

'Can I tempt you?'

Joe smiled, shook his head.

'There are dozens of cases of the stuff inside,' Malthouse said. 'All for *one* man!'

'Lucky chap! Mr Rajvansh, I assume?'

Malthouse either ignored him, or wasn't listening.

Joe took a draw on his cigarette, realizing that there was no nausea now, just the comforting reassurance that tobacco provides once you're back in its thrall. He watched Malthouse, who was gazing out across the pristine grass. *People do all kinds of things.*

'Ceremony's at noon tomorrow,' said Malthouse. 'Mr Raj Rajvansh is formally taking over as the new owner of the club.' He flicked a hand towards the clubhouse behind him. 'Some sort of charity announcement with the Benedicts, too.' He thought for a moment. 'You're too young for early retirement, aren't you?'

'Afraid so,' Joe said. 'Why do you ask?'

'They're recruiting a new security team for the club. An ex-police officer to be in charge. *Very* good salary. Your Assistant Chief Constable's helping to find the right man.'

'Or woman,' Joe added, just for devilment.

'Has to be a man, apparently. He who pays the piper ...'

Joe made a note to speak to Rita about the remuneration of pipers.

The bottle on the table was about half-full. Had there been another bottle earlier in the day? How early does a man in quiet torment start drinking, a man who's lost his job, his life, turfed out by some jumped-up money god?

'I haven't seen anything in the news,' Malthouse said, holding the glass close to his face as he spoke. 'About the girl.'

'Could I ask,' Joe said, 'was she complicating things? With the sale of Churchill's house? Or here at the club, perhaps?'

Malthouse seemed not to hear.

'How old was she?' he asked.

'Twenty-nine.'

'Fragile. Slip of a girl. Very slight.'

'How well did you know her?'

'She may have had lunch here. I can't recall. A few times. I can't—'

'You can't recall if she had lunch, or you can't recall how many times?'

Malthouse was unconcerned by the question. He took a drink, then leant forwards and refilled his glass.

'You don't mind if I drown my sorrows? If you buy this in

299

the bar, the mark-up's four hundred per cent! I'm … well, I'm taking advantage, I suppose. Like everyone else.'

'Did Ana come to the clubhouse? Did she ever meet other people here?'

Malthouse frowned, pushed out his lips. He was further gone than Joe had realized, his gestures slow and a little exaggerated, his bearing almost petulant.

'Churchill seemed happy with her. Easily led, perhaps, a man of his age.'

'Did you see her here with anyone else?'

Another drink. There was plenty left in his glass, but he refilled it once more.

'The Benedicts. I believe that she, er, what was her name …?'

'Ana. Ana Dobrescu.'

'Ah, yes. Ana. She used to volunteer at the Benedicts' charity. I'm sure she must have met Michael here. He's always around, talking to everybody, networking, buttering donors up.' He turned, a kind of grimace on his face, pointing with his thumb towards the large French windows behind them. 'Lots of butter for this one!'

'Why do you say that?'

'A billionaire flies into town? Everybody sees an opportunity. They're all excited, on the make.'

'Apart from the man he sacked? Sorry. That came out wrong. No offence.'

'None taken. My grandfather was on the first committee here. All amateurs in those days. I'm the first Malthouse to be paid for my services. And the last.'

'Worked here long?'

'Me? Since I was eighteen, one way or another. I was

a decent golfer. Didn't quite make the pro ranks. So I went into management.'

'It must have been quite a shock, to be relieved of your duties.'

Malthouse drank once more, the slightest tremble in his hand. He ignored the question.

'Got any plans now?' Joe asked.

'I suppose I'll come here. Hit a ball around, less and less proficiently, for as long as I'm able.' He smiled. 'My severance includes life membership.'

'The new owner's generous that way, is he?'

'Two billion dollars? That buys him all the generosity in the world. These people can do absolutely anything they want. The other day, when he bought the remaining share of the club, he just got his phone out and made a call. Couldn't have been more than a minute. When the club lawyer contacted our bank, the money had already been wired. Nine million pounds. Simple as that.'

Joe was on his feet.

'Will you be around tomorrow for the function?'

Malthouse had the glass to his mouth.

'I suppose I will.' He paused, confused, close to sleep. 'He was black-balled as well.'

'Who?'

Malthouse had slipped down in his seat, legs stretched out.

'Michael Benedict. His application was rejected.'

'On what grounds?'

'Said he'd been a partner at an investment bank. Something like that. I can't remember. One of the committee members thought it was odd. Asked around. He'd never worked there.'

'What about his wife? Did she apply as well?'

'Doesn't seem interested in golf. Or in the club. We hardly ever see her.'

'Was Benedict told about his membership being rejected?'

'No. It's all very discreet here. Always has been. The application was put on hold, some excuse given. Nobody wanted to make a fuss.' He drained his glass. 'It's all an act. The expensive clothes. The cars. The civility of gentlemen. All an act.'

He closed his eyes, the empty glass resting on his stomach.

One of the French windows was ajar. Joe slipped inside, to find himself in a large, high-ceilinged ballroom, now being prepared for tomorrow's event. Young men in white shirts came and went, carrying small gold chairs with red velvet cushions. Down the opposite side of the room ran a long table, silver champagne buckets and large cardboard boxes of wine glasses at regular intervals. And at the far end there was a stage, just a low platform with a table and three chairs on it, all shrouded in white. THE RAJVANSH FOUNDATION, it said in modest gold lettering.

Michael Benedict was at the other end of the room, between the windows and the stage. He was setting up a series of posterboards, his silver-tinged hair catching the light from the windows. Joe did a quick comparison as he went over. Him: old, scuffed Oxfords; Benedict: pristine brown suede slip-ons. Him: a Burton's suit, last dry-cleaned about six months ago; Benedict: neat, faded jeans and a powder yellow polo shirt. Him: average height, average everything; Benedict: dressed like a well-seasoned film star.

Sensing somebody behind him, Benedict turned. In his hand

was a poster-sized photo of a child lying on a hospital bed, the sheets old and stained. She had sallow skin and dark, impossibly large eyes, so painfully endearing that Joe had to look away.

'Hello. DS Romano again.'

He took the opportunity, grabbed Benedict's hand and shook it. Soft, pliable, fair size.

'Yes, yes. I assumed you'd want to … Ana. I didn't know whether to contact you … or …' He exhaled hard. 'Is there any news?'

'I'm afraid not. But I'm going to have to ask you where you were on Wednesday evening.'

'Absolutely. Shall I come to the station for an interview?'

Joe looked at the posters on display. The images were familiar, the same ones he'd seen in the charity's office, plus others from the website: the Benedicts outside a hospital, surrounded by kids, the Benedicts on a building site … the same trousers.

'Here's fine for the minute. We need to know what you were doing on Wednesday evening.'

'Right, yes. Absolutely. I dropped Sophie off in town. She had dinner with some potential donors. Clerk's Restaurant?'

Joe knew it. The kind of place detective sergeants couldn't afford to go too often.

'Well-off clients, then?'

'Yes. With a certain kind of donor, the more lavish the entertaining, the more they give.'

'And you? Wednesday?'

'I came up here at about eight. It's a constant battle to keep the money coming in, so we often find ourselves entertaining people separately. I was here quite late, actually, until just before they closed. Then I went straight home.'

'There's security footage of the car park. Did you leave in your car?'

'Yes. A black Range Rover.'

He recited the registration as Joe noted it down.

'And your wife? What time did she get home?'

'Not long after me, as I recall. Sometime after midnight, I suppose.'

'OK. I'll need to talk to her as well. Is she here?'

'She's gone hill walking, down near Buxton. She loves the open air and she fancied a bit of time off before the big day tomorrow.'

'OK, could you give me her mobile number? Big day, you said?'

Benedict held out his phone. As Joe wrote down the number, Benedict explained: Raj Rajvansh had not only bought the golf club, he was planning to base his charitable foundation there as well.

'In fact, we're moving Rebuild up here. We're becoming a branch of the Rajvansh Foundation, a rather larger organization than ours.'

'He made you an offer you couldn't refuse?'

Benedict held up the photo in his hand.

'Why would we refuse? He's making a substantial investment in our projects. We'll be able to finish the hospital.'

'Must be a wrench, though? You two built the charity up on your own. All the hard work, the kids?'

'Yes, yes.'

Joe put his notebook away.

'Romanian children's hospitals?' he asked. 'Why those places in particular?'

Benedict's smile faded a little. He tilted his head.

'You know, I can't quite remember. There were other institutions we considered. But they seemed to be where our help was needed the most.'

'I'm sure you're doing a lot of good.'

He shook Benedict's hand again.

Back in the car park he saw a black Range Rover. He checked his notebook. It was Benedict's. He made a note to find out what motor Sophie Benedict drove.

Then he glanced at the time. Meeting in an hour.

Just time to call home on the way back to Elland Road.

# 54

He stopped at the traffic lights. Saw the El Gato Negro restaurant on the corner. He wondered whether it was worth organizing another search of Miriana Dalca's house. Probably not. Financial Crimes hadn't found anything. And what about Miriana herself? She couldn't leave the country, not by conventional means. Then again, she hadn't struck him as a conventional woman. Smart, tough, pretty.

Pretty? What the hell did that have to do with it? She was a bloody suspect. He closed his eyes, pressed his fingers into them. Ben Churchill was still the main suspect, officially. But Miriana had disappeared in a rush, and Stefan was shaky at best … The case was slipping from him. The momentum would fall away by degrees as priorities changed and people were needed elsewhere. There'd be no grieving relatives ringing for updates, and press interest would fizzle out in no time. Dead immigrants on a dockside? In a wood? Yesterday's news.

Behind him a horn sounded, long and loud. In the mirror he saw a white SUV bearing down on him, the sound of its engine throaty and guttural. The woman behind the wheel was alone, yet she was speaking. She looked insane, on her own, talking.

As he pulled away, she raced past, not even a sideways glance, still talking. Jackie had been the same, on the phone for ages, wherever she was, talking to people she'd been with the same day, a handful of hours earlier. God knows what they said. His own conversations weren't like that. In a pub with colleagues there'd be few short blasts of gossip, something about work, the inevitable football bullshit. But mainly it'd be him staring vacantly at his pint as other people chatted; eager glances across the room to see if anyone else was coming; relief when he could dash off to the bar for another round … It wasn't a Mars and Venus thing. Sometimes he thought the whole of humanity was from a different planet.

No sign of Sam when he got home. His phone rang. He'd ignored two messages already. Someone needed to speak.

It was Tennant. The conversation didn't take long. There weren't many details yet. But Miriana Dalca had been found. Strangled.

He went into the kitchen, fighting the urge to vomit. He got a glass of water, drank it down in one. And there was Sam, out in the back garden. It was more of a deluxe yard, a patch of grass the size of a couple of bedsheets, rose bushes down the sides, a little shed at the bottom. Sam was lying on his stomach on the grass, surrounded by beer cans, head down into his phone.

Joe opened the back door, stepped out, watched him for a while. Sam was playing some sort of driving game, the tinny sound of gunfire, the screech of tyres.

Then he looked up.

'This your alternative to a medical degree?' Joe asked.

He felt a huge knot of emotion in his chest, knew he'd got it wrong, the very first sentence. How much had he got wrong, over the years?

For a while neither of them spoke. There was birdsong from somewhere or other, and the rumble of a plane way off in the pale-blue sky. Folk off on holiday from Leeds and Bradford Airport, a week or two in the sun.

'So you want to be a copper? This is how you go about it?'

'I've been on the police website …'

'How many beers is that you've had? I just got a call about a young woman, lived not far from here. I interviewed her yesterday. A strong woman, gutsy, impressive. An immigrant. Now she's in a skip, dead. You wanna come help me pull her out? Tell her parents?'

Lies. There was no skip. No parents. It didn't matter.

'You can get her justice.'

Joe repeated it to himself, stunned at how hollow the words sounded, how innocent, stupid. Yet exactly what he always told himself. They were his words, in his son's mouth.

'Two young women, now. Immigrants. They came over here to make something of themselves. Just like our family did. Now they're dead. You want this? Really? 'Cos I don't.'

Sam mumbled an answer. Joe saw the boy in him, the same boy he'd scooped up off the ground whenever he fell, who he'd hugged endlessly, tried to keep on hugging 'til the kid was in his teens, 'til it became too embarrassing.

'Doctors keep folk alive, Sam. Coppers clean up after they're dead. You want to be a cleaner? Be a bloody doctor, for Christ's sake!'

'You changed careers. Why can't I?'

'Changing careers? Is that what you call it? Playing on your bloody phone!'

'But—'

'Two young women who had *nothing*. Grew up in a shithole. Got involved with the wrong people. Dead. Go on, have another beer! I've got to go.'

He sat in the Mondeo, slammed the door shut, and threw the balls of both hands onto the steering wheel, pummelling it until pain jarred his arms.

'Shit! Shit! Shit!'

# 55

Friday evening. But there was no end-of-week lethargy now. The conference room was filling up. Even out in the ops room those getting ready to clock off were craning their necks. Some of the eager ones were wondering whether they'd be roped in; a few of the more seasoned constables had made themselves scarce, keen not to be dragged into anything at all with the weekend coming up.

Gwyn was sitting on Joe's desk, so smug he was just asking for a slap.

'Photos on the charity blog,' he said, that know-it-all voice of his. 'All taken in one place. A kids' hospital and orphanage. Luica.'

'Luica? Jesus, you're joking?'

Tennant walked past.

'Simon?' Joe said, following him as he walked briskly across the room. 'You heard this?'

'Yes,' Tennant said, as he made his way into the conference room. 'We need to speak to the Benedicts.'

They both sat at the large table, waiting for it to fill up. His diction was slow, and he forced his eyes wide open each time they threatened to close.

'I just spoke to Michael Benedict. He was up at the golf club,' Joe said. 'His wife's climbing mountains in the Peak District, apparently. Here, I've got her mobile number.'

'They live north of Bilton,' Tennant said. 'It's not far. She can come in for a chat soon as she's back. I'll sort that out now.'

He got up and left the room, crossing paths with Andy Mills in the doorway. The two men had a quick word, a nod.

Andy was already speaking as he took the seat next to Joe.

'Right, another body. I'll give you the basics. But everybody here stays on Ana Dobrescu. There's another team on this new one. Compare notes tomorrow.'

He stopped, waited for the last of the stragglers to file in. Then he stared at a printed page in his hand, glowering with concentration.

There wasn't a sound. Joe imagined the British Army twenty years ago, sergeant Andy Mills with a load of young lads under his wing, all pumped up, all shitting themselves. They'd've done anything for him, marched anywhere, fought anyone. And here he was, leading the troops into battle again, despite being so screwed up in the head he'd been sobbing his heart out in the toilets.

'Miriana Dalca,' Andy said. 'Thirty-four, Romanian national. Friend of Ana Dobrescu's. Living here legally for three years, running a dodgy employment agency now under investigation for human trafficking, the same agency that Ana used to work for. Miriana was strangled, left in Rawdon, near the airport. Put up a bit of a fight, this 'un. So, somebody's in control of events, and it's not bloody us. But, like I say, separate team to start off. Joe?'

Tennant slipped back into the room. A young DC vacated a chair for him. He flopped down, too tired to say thank you.

'She's staying in Buxton overnight,' he said, catching Joe's eye. 'Then she has an important do in the morning. Earliest she can make is tomorrow afternoon.'

'That's Sophie Benedict,' Joe said. 'We have a line of inquiry on the charity she runs, Rebuild, and it just got complicated. But first, Ben Churchill is still in intensive care. Meanwhile, Andy's statement just went live, and it'll be on *Look North* this evening. We've got people manning the phones. Right. Gloves!'

'Smoking gun!' Gwyn shouted, wafting a sheet of paper in the air, about as cocky as a bloke could be without jumping on the table and pulling a moony. 'Strangle wounds on Ana's neck showed minute traces of a green substance, the same material as the gloves found near Bilton Woods. The gloves are on their way to Wakefield.'

He sat back, Cock o' the North.

Joe could only admire the cheek. *He'd* found the gloves, Rita had brought 'em in, but Gwyn was mopping up the glory.

'How long for the DNA?' Andy asked, forestalling any ovation for DC Merchant.

'Tomorrow morning, if we fast-track it,' said Gwyn.

'Do it. Get over to Wakefield first thing, give 'em a kick up the arse, make sure they prioritize it.'

'Also,' Joe said, 'we'll need swabs from all POIs tomorrow. We'll be bringing everybody in for formal statements anyway. Moving on. Stefan Nicolescu. We've arrested him. He's thirty. Been working here a few years. Can't remember where. Shunted around farms and factories, shovelling chicken shit, washing cars, living in overcrowded slums for next to no money. Slave worker.'

'And when you told him about Ana?'

'Cried like a baby. When DS Scannon implied that he did it, he threatened to kill her.'

Rita nodded with pride.

'His timeline's solid for the night of Ana's death, though,' she said. 'Ana bought him a phone. He was on it all night. YouTube, porn, all the normal stuff, 'til late. Looks like he stayed in the house all evening. He also called Ana's mobile five times that night. No reply. He's called her a lot of times since. Dozens. Oh, and when they took him back down to the cells, he kept saying that she was like a sister to him, an angel. And that he was gonna kill whoever did it. He's making no secret of that.'

'Right. We'll have another go at him in the morning. Moving on. The night Ana died. Any idea where she went late on? Who's been on CCTV?'

'Me,' said Gemma. 'I got this, if it helps.' She handed around print-outs of a map. 'Ana came out of Miriana's house and disappeared. No cameras picked her up. So I've marked all the stretches of roads that don't have networked cameras on 'em. She might have gone cross-country. Plenty of open land going away from town. Close to midnight, though, young woman on her own?'

'Pissed young woman,' Gwyn Merchant added, holding the map close up to his face. 'Leafy streets, posh semis, Mercs outside … Not a camera in sight. Then a bit further out and it turns into the bloody countryside. Pokey little villages, narrow lanes and shit. Funny old place, innit?'

'Never fell in love with Leeds, did you, Gwyn?' Andy said, sitting back, hands behind his head.

'Aye, well it's not exactly Batley, is it?'

A few sniggers. Gwyn surveyed the table, doing a good impression of being offended, until no one knew whether he was serious or not. And it wasn't as if anybody was gonna pick a fight with him. Other than Andy Mills, who'd pick a fight with the time of the day if he fancied a bit.

'Anyroad,' Gwyn continued, 'you could drive round up there all night long an' never see a camera. If you knew where you were goin'. What if she were killed at the golf club?'

'No,' Gemma said. 'Footage from the club for Wednesday. No sign of Ana.'

'Doesn't mean she didn't go,' Tennant said. 'Who was there that night?'

'I went through everything twice. Only POIs there were a security guard, plus Michael Benedict and the president, Malthouse.'

'Soon to be ex-president,' Joe said.

'All three left in their own vehicles.'

'The security guard,' Rita asked. 'Is that Nick Evans?'

'Yes. Someone's spoken to him,' Joe said. 'He'll be in tomorrow for a formal statement and a swab. Anyway, returning to cartographical renderings of the city ...'

'English!' Gwyn shouted.

'Maps. Let's broaden it out. Three-mile radius, all routes not covered by cameras. Stick folks' houses on the map as well, plus the dump sites. See if that helps. One last thing. The young bloke in charge of those trafficked workers from the poultry farm yesterday? He'd already heard about Ana's death.'

'A warning?' asked Gemma.

'A text. It was in Romanian, and it was sent from Leeds.'

People prepared to go, shaking their heads.

'We haven't done yet!' Andy shouted. 'Simon?'

Tennant took a moment, gathered his strength.

'Thanks to DS Romano's unparalleled network of international espionage operatives …' he waited for the chuckles to subside, 'we now know that the Workout Agency, where Ana Dobrescu used to work, and which is implicated in the human trafficking investigation, is owned by a certain Omor Balan. The NCA and the Romanian National Crime Agency are now involved. Joe?'

'Omor Balan is the cousin of Silviu Balan, suspected of at least nine organized killings on mainland Europe. Nasty. Dangerous. He'll kill anyone who gets in his way. Used to run a loan company in London with his cousin, so he knows the UK. And that's the thing. Silviu Balan landed in Heathrow yesterday afternoon.'

The room exploded, everyone jabbering, hunched over their phones, googling the name …

'There's more!' Joe said, shouting. 'Balan's cousin, who has disappeared, is the director of an orphanage in the town of Luica, where both Ana Dobrescu and Miriana Dalca grew up, as well as several of the trafficked workers from yesterday.' The chatter subsided. He waited until there was absolute silence. 'That orphanage is the institution funded by Rebuild, the charity run by the Benedicts.'

'You've gotta be shitting me,' Mark Francis said.

Andy rose from his chair. 'No, DC Francis. No shitting involved. So, ladies and gents, if you've got hot dates, tell 'em you just got a better offer. Them that's married, tell 'em they're on their own with Netflix tonight. Back to it, soldiers! Meeting at eleven.'

Joe and Tennant were the last to leave the room.

'Stefan Nicolescu,' Joe said. 'I reckon the cells might be the best place for him tonight.'

Tennant nodded.

'It's not him, is it?'

'Don't think so,' said Joe. 'But we can't let him go now, not yet …'

'I know. Last thing we want's another dead body. We go three down, it's a whole new game.'

'I'm popping over to the hospital. You could get yourself off, I reckon. I'll be here all night after that.'

'Nah,' Tennant said, drawing himself up slowly, like he had sandbags in every pocket. 'You go home, have a shower, change. I'll keep everything together 'til you get back. Can't promise I'll be awake when you arrive, though. And, sorry if I've been a bit, y'know. Haven't slept.'

'Don't worry about it. I'm always a bit, y'know.'

'Shall we say eight?'

'OK. You got a hot date, as the DCI likes to say?'

'Going purple!' Tennant said, dragging himself towards the door.

# 56

Nothing had changed in the Intensive Care wing, the same feeling of unhurried control, a chemical precision in the air. Ben Churchill was lying in the same bed, hooked up to God knows what, all so that his body might drag itself back into sentient life. And for what?

Joe stood well back. The young doctor was at his side, his voice low, almost a whisper.

'He's deteriorated quickly. Pretty lucid, though. It's not uncommon at this point. You can speak to him.'

Joe nodded, waited for the doctor to move away. Then, with a heaviness that threatened to crush him entirely, he approached, pulled up a seat, and sat as close as he dared. Churchill's eyes opened and closed in response to the sound, and his breathing was light and fast.

'Ben? Mr Churchill?'

His eyes opened wide. They were focused, alert, surprisingly so.

'Yes, that's me.'

His speech was laboured, but he was not delirious.

'I'm DS Romano, West Yorkshire Police. CID. Joe

Romano.' He paused, wondering what Churchill knew, how he should proceed. 'I'm investigating the murder of Ana Dobrescu. She was found dead outside your house on Thursday morning.'

Ana's name made Churchill smile. It didn't seem right. Joe looked around, to ask whether Churchill was in fact fit to speak. But there was no one there.

'I know. I found her,' Churchill said, his voice faint and breathy, but determined. 'And now I'm dying too. It doesn't matter, any of it. Not now. But you have your job to do.'

'When did you last see her alive?'

Churchill twisted a little, moved his head.

'She went to have dinner with Miriana, from that agency. Never came home. I found her outside the next morning, brought her in the house.' His face was suddenly flushed, his eyes red. 'Nothing else matters now.'

'How long had you known her?' Joe asked.

'Eleven months.'

'Friends?'

He took a long, unsteady breath, seemed to forget that Joe was there.

'Much more than that. Partners. Difficult to explain.'

'Try me.'

Churchill appeared to weigh up what to say. Or, perhaps, whether it was worth saying it at all.

'We met at Rebuild, the charity. I was a donor. We just found each other. We saw the world in exactly the same way. I don't know whether you believe in fate, Sergeant ...'

'Joe. Call me Joe.'

Churchill's eyes fluttered, and his speech became slower.

'I had a business. Did well. But eventually you've got to ask yourself why, haven't you?'

'Sudden awakening?'

'What's my purpose in life?' The idea seemed to give him strength. 'You've gotta strike quick, Joe. Nothing lasts forever. Nothing.'

'And Ana felt the same way?'

'Exactly the same. Soulmates. Complete trust.'

'Sharing?'

'I sold the business. We were using the money to do good. Spending what wasn't needed.'

'Your money.'

'Ours. What's it for, other than to do good? I loved her, and respected her, the goodness that I saw. Isn't that enough?'

'Was Ana in some sort of trouble?'

Churchill was straining to stay awake, his words becoming more difficult to make out.

'She'd had a tough life, and she got into trouble. Made some mistakes. Who doesn't? Then she found me.'

'What trouble?'

'She came over here to help people. That's not how it turned out. She decided to put it right. She was brave. She …' He struggled to find the strength to continue. 'She saw life clearly. We both did. Together 'til the end.'

'A promise?'

'Of love. Of life. Of everything. My guardian angel. Not just mine, either.'

Churchill was fading fast, his voice now little more than a croak, his eyes hardly open.

'What kind of colleagues do you have?' he asked. 'In the police?'

'Decent folk. On the whole.'

'It's not like that for everyone. Life … it's not like that. Really it isn't. Not for everybody.' His eyes finally closed. 'We found that out together. A plan … she had …'

And then he was asleep.

Out in the waiting room, Joe scrolled down his messages. A new entry from forensics: the airbag in Ben Churchill's car had been gouged out with a screwdriver, which had been found on the back seat. Both the airbag and the screwdriver had Churchill's prints on them, and no one else's.

Then there was a message from Sam: Rita and Ruth are here for curry. What time yer cumin? He brought the phone closer to his face, struggling to make out the tiny letters. Rita and Ruth?

'Need an eye test?'

He turned. Jill Wallace was at the door.

'Oh, hi,' he said, fumbling with his phone.

'We've become a nation of squinters,' she said. 'How's the case going?'

'Complicatedly, if that's even a word.'

He waited for her to sit down. She was wearing a cream shirt and black trousers. He couldn't work out if they were silk or leather.

'Finished for the night?'

'I've just knocked off,' she said.

The trousers? Who did they remind him of? Years ago, who was it?

'Sorry,' he said, realizing he was staring at her thighs. 'It's been a long day. Long night ahead. All night.'

'One of the benefits of oncology,' she said. 'You don't do nights. Dermatology's another one.'

'I'll tell my son. He's just dropped out of medical school. Thinking of joining the police.'

'And would that make him happy?'

The question hit him hard.

'Is it that simple?'

She ran her palms down her thighs. He forced himself not to look.

'It's quite simple, isn't it? And he's got a police officer and a doctor at his disposal. Chance to compare and contrast. Let me know if you want to meet up with him and talk it through, give him the benefit of our combined wisdom. It's a big decision.'

She glanced at her watch.

'I just spoke to Ben,' Joe said. 'He was quite clear-headed.'

'Terminal lucidity, I'm afraid. He's nearing the end. His body is in the process of shutting down.'

She paused, looked around the waiting room. Then, abruptly, she stood up.

'He didn't kill anyone, did he?' she asked, something almost childlike about her now, a sudden insistence, a desperation.

'No, I don't think so.'

It was all she needed to hear. She seemed to shiver with relief.

'Right. I better be off. Let me know about your son.'

Leather, he decided, as he watched her go. Then he realized: she reminded him of Suzi Quatro, humanity's greatest ever filler of leather trousers.

His phone rang. Andy.

'Joe? Listen, a bloke just called from St Makarios. You know it? Romanian Orthodox church up in Farnley?'

'Vaguely …'

'He saw Ana's face on Twitter. Recognized her. Apparently, she went to mass there most days. And they were gonna get married.'

'Who?'

'Ben Churchill and Ana Dobrescu. At St Makarios.'

'Bloody hell, when?'

'Next month.'

'Right, right … Jeez, I don't even know what to think about—'

'Oh, sorry for getting Sam pissed. I thought he needed a blow-out. Kid's suffering a bit there, I reckon.'

'And you? Seeing that therapist again?'

'Twice a week from now on. Another thing. Try and steer me away from the booze.'

'It'll be a pleasure. I'm … glad you're, y'know, that you're …'

'Aye, it's … yeah, right. Cheers.'

'By the way, what does the expression "going purple" mean? After work, someone's "going purple"?'

'You never gone purple? Bloody hell, Joe! Premier Inn! It's where you go when your wife kicks you out!'

# 57

'Thought we better get cracking,' Rita shouted from the kitchen.

'What're you doing here?' he asked, as he dropped his jacket on the sofa.

'Pleased to see you too,' she said, coming through with an armful of foil cartons. 'We need to talk, so I kind of invited us around.'

A woman appeared in the kitchen doorway.

'This is Ruth,' Rita said.

Ruth smiled, seemed a little awkward, there in a stranger's house.

'Hi,' Joe said, shaking her hand. 'Congratulations, by the way!'

She was a few years older than Rita, perhaps, and her attire was more muted, though modern, a whole generation ahead of Joe's collar and tie.

There were four settings at the dining table, a bottle of fizzy water, Fleetwood Mac low in the background. It was like he'd been asked around to someone else's place for supper.

Sam was in the armchair by the window. He shuffled forward, but didn't get up.

'Oh, hi,' Joe said. 'Didn't see you there. Sorry, y'know, about earlier. I've been a bit …'

''S allright.'

There was a can of lager on the floor near Sam's foot. He took it, thought better, put it back down.

'I should do a bit more listening sometimes,' Joe said. 'It was just so sudden.'

'I know. A bloody waste.'

'Not a waste. Look, I met a woman.'

'You? That's great.'

'What? No, no. At the hospital. She's an oncologist.'

'Excellent!'

'No, I meant for you. *Her*.'

'You pimping me out?'

'What I mean is, why don't we sit down, all three of us, talk it through? Before you make any career decisions. A copper and a doctor? Compare and contrast.'

'It's not just your way of getting a date, is it?'

'No!'

'Food!' Rita shouted, parking herself at the table.

'When are we meeting this oncologist, then?' Sam said, as he got up.

'As soon as I find the person who killed two young women. And that,' Joe said, as he sat down, 'is the life of a police detective. Am I right, Rita?'

'What? Oh, yes,' she said, spooning curry onto her plate. 'Anyway, listen. Ruth does pro bono work for a few charities.'

'I'm an employment lawyer,' Ruth explained. 'I've been asking around, about Romanian nationals in the area.'

'OK …'

'A young woman has been making enquiries about work permits, and modern slavery legislation, applications for residence.'

'It was Ana,' Rita said. 'They've confirmed it from the photo.'

'I see,' he said, slowly. 'She also rented a couple of terraced houses. We think she planned to get a dozen of 'em out.'

Ruth shook her head.

'My information is that she was talking about a lot more than that.'

'What kind of numbers?'

'She was very careful on details, apparently. Kept things vague. Talked a lot about timing. But there was money available. She had funds ready for legal fees.'

'And then,' Joe said, feeling the weight of the news as it sank in, 'she went and got herself killed.'

'*Look North*!' Rita shrieked.

Joe switched the TV on.

'You're on the news?' Sam asked his dad.

'Me? No, Andy.'

'Back leading the troops quick, eh?' Rita asked.

Joe wondered what she knew, what Sam knew …

'Those two,' he said, pointing at Sam, 'got pissed last night while we were out liberating farm workers. Jesus, was that only last night. Seems like—'

'He was going on about the Army,' said Sam. 'How you get shot at, and you shoot back. Balance of good and bad. All that stuff. Made it sound kind of philosophical.'

'Half a bottle of scotch'll do that.'

'No,' Sam said. 'He was talking about the truth. It's always there, in front of you. Just act. React. Use your instincts. It was quite inspiring, actually.'

'Talk of the devil!'

Joe turned the sound up and they watched the report on Ana Dobrescu, which was first up on the news bulletin. There was some footage of the golf club, plus her passport photo. But mainly it was Andy outside Elland Road, his considerable upper body squeezed into a dark jacket, sombre tie. He looked jowly, drained. But it gave him a concerned air. There was a weariness in his eyes, a man ground down by the murder of a young woman.

When it finished, Joe switched the TV off.

'Right,' he said to Ruth. 'The stuff about the legal enquiries fits the picture we have of Ana. She had a rich boyfriend. She was using his money. Something went wrong, though. She told me it was "all too soon". Reet, your mate up at the golf club? Security guard. Know him well?'

'We see him up the Triple-A.'

Ruth cocked her head. 'Nick Evans? I know him.'

'What's he like?' asked Joe.

'He's thoughtful, quiet, bit of a loner, I'd say.'

'Triple-A?' Sam asked.

'Agnostics and Atheists Assembly,' Joe said. 'He's been working at the club a month or so. Long enough to spark up a relationship with a young woman? Y'see, Sam? The murderer could be a friend. Gotta think the worst of everybody. Ask yourself what a person's capable of.'

Rita was having none of Joe's wistfulness.

'We'll see. Tuck in.'

There was a lot of food. Joe wasn't hungry.

'Thanks for coming, by the way,' he said to Ruth. 'That information really helps. Her boyfriend was providing the funds. But there's more to it. Some sort of pact. They'd planned everything together, Ben and Ana. He's got terminal cancer. He's considered suicide, researched it, knew the best way to do it, exactly what to buy … Now I've just found out they were planning to get married up at St Makarios. I don't know what to think!'

He pushed a fork through his lamb bhuna.

'St Makarios?' Ruth asked.

'Yes. Ana was very devout by the look of it. Romanian Orthodox.'

'Not gonna be suicide, then, is it?' she said, tearing herself some naan. 'Not if she's involved. That'd be a sin. Orthodox? They're worse than the Cathos!'

Joe stopped, fork in hand. Then he stood up, grabbed his plate, shovelled curry into his mouth. He took a drink of fizzy water, then realized his mouth was too full. He tipped his head back, tried to chew, but watery bhuna sauce ran down his chin.

'I'm off,' he said, after swallowing.

'Something we said?' Rita asked.

'Yes.' He pointed at Sam again. 'Try and talk him out of being a copper. See this? Off to work on a Friday night!'

'Doctors do that all the time,' Sam said.

'Not dermatologists!'

# 58

The ops room stank of grease. There were burger cartons on desks, cans of this and that, people eating as they stared at screens, food held up, ready for another bite.

Andy and Simon Tennant were both there.

'Good news, bad news. Which?' Andy asked as Joe walked in. 'Didn't get a change, then?' he added, noticing the brown stains on Joe's collar.

'What? Oh, curry. Bad news first.'

'The National Crime Agency's here. In the building now,' he said, as if announcing an infestation.

'And the good news?'

'Financial Crimes want to see you. They're waiting.'

Joe took it all in.

'Right, I think I've got something. Does everybody know about the marriage planned up at St Makarios?'

'Yep,' said Andy. 'It's on the system.'

'Good. Two things.'

He logged onto a terminal, found the image of Ana lying on the bed. Everyone crowded around.

'Here. Around her neck. A crucifix. She was fiddling with

it when I spoke to her at the hospital. And she was wearing it when she died. She was religious. A devout Romanian Orthodox Christian. And this.' He held up his phone, showed them a website. 'From a few years ago. News report about a Romanian singer that committed suicide. There was a CD of hers in Churchill's house. Mădălina Manole. She killed herself, and the Romanian Church refused to give her a burial. Suicide is a sin in the Orthodox church.' He paused, looked around. 'How are we doing on background into Churchill? Religious affiliations?'

'He's a Catholic,' Mark Francis said. 'There are donations to the Holy Cross on his bank statements. I rang the church. It's in Middleton. Doesn't attend regularly, but he was baptized there. He's a generous donor, goes to the odd mass.'

'Right,' Joe said. 'I think Ana may have persuaded Ben not to take his own life. She didn't want him to die a sinner. And he probably didn't want Ana to be found guilty of assisting him. They had a deal instead. She'd stay with him 'til the end.'

'Sort of a non-suicide pact?' Gemma asked.

'Yes. He only had a couple of months left. I'm thinking her plan was to care for Ben first, then deal with the slavery stuff, using the money he was going to leave her.'

'But Stefan got into trouble,' she said.

'Right. He gave his name to the hospital. The agency pulled the other workers out of Batley. But Ana knew it wouldn't stop there. You mess with Balan, you're gonna be in trouble. I think that's why she was killed.'

'It happened too soon, then?' Tennant asked. 'She was planning to come to the police eventually, get the trafficked

329

workers out. But then the stuff with Stefan forced her to act sooner.'

'That's the other thing. My information is that it wasn't a dozen workers. She was planning to help a lot more than that. She needed more time, though.'

Tennant ran a hand around his neck, squeezing out the last cogent thoughts of the day.

'We've looked at every aspect of Churchill. Nothing contradicts any of this. He's giving his money away. He's dying, researching palliative care, assisted suicide. Life revolves around Ana. Their romance blossomed almost a year ago. There's a constant back and forth on their phones, especially the last four months, since she moved in with him. Happy messages, tender, quite moving. Bottom line, they were in love. They'd found happiness, just as the poor bloke was dying.'

'She was all he had,' Joe said. 'All he wanted. They were soulmates, that's what he said.'

'God almighty!' Andy said.

He took a large bottle of Dr Pepper from a Tesco's bag on the floor. The hiss of gas filled the otherwise silent room. He brought the bottle to his lips and drank, saw that everyone was watching him, and put the bottle down.

There was a sniff. Mark Francis was blowing his nose on a bit of tissue.

'Sorry,' he said, shaking his head, surprised at himself. 'It just hit me. He said they were soulmates. What about Ana? A bloody orphan. She finds the one person, her soulmate, and he's dying. How sad is that!'

Joe blew out his cheeks.

'Sad enough for her to try something reckless? Simon, ideas from here?'

Tennant inhaled long and hard. On it went, until people started to count, wondering where all the air was going. The exhaustion on his face was so pronounced that it looked like he was staying awake for a bet and he'd got down to the last few minutes.

'That text to the workers' house?'

'Ana's death was an example. A warning. Word was supposed to get around.'

Tennant nodded.

'It was in Romanian. We haven't identified the sender yet.' He paused, did his best to think. 'We go with this. Discount Churchill. The body was dumped near his house, so the killer wanted to set him up. Re-focus. Timelines, routes in and out.'

'Right,' Joe said. 'Let's get back to it.'

The room moved into action, although at a slightly more subdued pace, mutterings of incredulity, flat and muted, as the real tragedy sank in: Ana hadn't managed to stay with Churchill to the end. Even that had been denied her.

'*Look North*, anything?' Joe asked, as he prepared to leave. 'Who's on the phones?'

'Me,' said Mark, still in shock, no attempt to hide it. 'Not a single call. No one.'

'We'll get her justice. All we can do now. For both of 'em.'

# 59

'On your own?' Joe said, unnecessarily.

The lone officer still at his desk in the Financial Crimes Department was in his mid thirties, crew cut, and had the air of someone who's into martial arts and wants you to know.

'Friday night. I've been waiting for you.'

Joe considered a quip about dermatologists, decided against it.

'Let's get to it, then.'

'Right. Take a seat. Human trafficking. We're assuming the Workout Agency is running a pretty big operation, channelling the profits back to Romania. But there's no evidence. They've only ever declared enough income to cover two salaries. Those of Ana Dobrescu and Miriana Dalca.'

'Both dead,' said Joe.

'It's a paper-based business, but the paper has all disappeared. No evidence. Then this.'

His finger touched the screen: a column on a spreadsheet.

'Ben Churchill. He's been making large payments to various charities, including one called Rebuild.'

'It's where Ana Dobrescu volunteered as a translator. Where she met Ben.'

'Yep. That's the connection. Rebuild: a lot of money being sent to Romania.'

'It's a project they've—'

'You spoken to the NCA yet?'

'Next on my to-do list.'

'Look,' he said, opening another spreadsheet. 'Rebuild's current account. Electronic transfers from Ben Churchill, more than a hundred grand in total. Some other donors, smaller amounts, but steady. Then these.'

Joe strained to read the numbers on the screen.

'Lots of small donations, in cash,' the officer explained. 'Over half a million last year alone. It's bullshit. You might get the odd person giving cash, but not all these. No way. So, they're running a charity, plus they're laundering money out of the country for someone. Although,' he said, closing down the files and logging out, 'not all of it. Mr and Mrs Benedict live a very comfortable life, judging by their private spending. We'll be speaking to 'em as soon as we can.'

'Soon? I think I'll bring 'em in now.'

The guy smiled as he turned the computer off, then rose from his seat, grabbed his coat.

'I think you'll find there's a queue. Talk to the NCA.'

Joe was already out the door.


'Joe, come in,' said Assistant Chief Constable Jerry MacDonald from his desk. 'I had a call from Michael Benedict earlier. He's a bit concerned about all the police activity.'

'A lot going on at the golf club, Sir. I believe you're a member.'

'Yes. I know Michael Benedict, met him at the club. He

asked if I could make sure there'll be no problem with their presentation tomorrow. Big day for his charity.'

'Don't know whether I can guarantee that. Two people dead, and—'

'Please, sit down.'

Joe did as he was told. He felt his face heating up, his pulse quickening. But he kept his mouth shut. He heard the confident tones of senior officers on the corridor outside, high spirits, verbal back-slapping.

'Ah,' MacDonald said as a woman and a man appeared at the door and walked straight in. 'This is DS Joe Romano.'

Joe stood, shook their hands. Hard grips, hard stares, the usual crap. Both were younger than him. The woman he didn't recognize, the bloke he most certainly did.

'Sergeant Romano?' said DCI Paul Grunhill, who'd headed up the review of the double murder case last year.

Grunhill: wire-framed glasses, tight-fitting mid-blue suit, skinny, no hair to talk of. Late thirties. More like a snooker player than a high-flying DCI at the National Crime Agency.

'Sir,' Joe said. 'We met last year.'

'Yes. This is DI Sykes,' he said. 'Also from the NCA.'

They all sat down, Grunhill looking about as pleased with himself as a copper could. The review last year? The whole thing had been a waste of time.

'The double murder? You got a result at the trial, I hear,' he said. 'Well done on that.'

'Thank you.'

'Anyway, not to beat about … Feast yer eyes.'

DI Sykes passed Joe a tablet. The screen showed a poor-quality video image.

'Ah, he's not there at the minute,' she said, her voice hard, clipped. 'But coming in and out of shot is one Silviu Balan. He's at a hotel, place called Saxford. This is a live feed from the bar area.'

'Up near York?' Joe asked, looking at the tablet in his hands. 'How did you find him?'

She ignored the question.

'We're patched into the hotel's security system. He's being kept under observation. Tell us what you've got on the Romania connection.'

It wasn't much, not yet. Joe explained what he'd just been told in Financial Crimes, how money was being channelled back to Romania. Also about Ana's plan, how it was probably a lot more than a dozen workers. Grunhill and Sykes seemed impressed, like teachers moderately pleased with a child's homework. Grunhill raised his eyebrows when Mihal's name was mentioned.

'Mihal Bogdan, yes. He's helping out. Very useful. Thanks for that, by the way. Gave us a head start.'

Grunhill sat forward, manspread, stern eyes.

'Listen to this,' he said, handing over to his colleague again.

'Five years ago,' she said, 'Michael Benedict was working as an actor. Getting nowhere. Then his mother died, leaving him a house in Sussex. He sold it, used the money to become a day trader. You know what that is?'

'Stock market.'

'Right. Quick trades. Single day, hence the name. Big money to be made. But very risky. Especially,' she leant across and clicked through to a spreadsheet on the tablet in Joe's lap, 'if you're using your inheritance. And you're a dick.'

Joe hardly wanted to look. Two young women in the mortuary, and here they were, doing maths.

'See?' she said. 'This is his account the year *before* they set up their charity. Benedict had blown most of the money. He was making ridiculous bets, crazy stock. Then this.' She tapped through to another page. 'Transfer of half a million pounds from a company called Alibi. Registered owner, Silviu Balan.'

'Jesus Christ ... Balan?'

'There's more. Benedict doubled down on his losses. Another loan. Ends up owing Balan nearly a million. And that's where the trail goes cold. Balan's loan company was wound up.'

Joe took a breath, tried to assimilate the information.

'What's the connection?' he asked. 'Why does Benedict go to a Romanian money lender?'

'We don't know, yet,' said Grunhill. 'Bad choice, though, getting himself caught up with someone like Balan.'

'Right,' said Joe, handing Sykes the tablet. 'I'm bringing Benedict in.'

'No, no,' Grunhill said. 'We're gonna let this play out. There's a presentation up at Bilton tomorrow. The Rajvansh Foundation is going to donate a million quid to the Rebuild charity. By our calculations Benedict still owes Balan at least that. There'll be a lot of interest to pay on those loans. The donation'll clear his debts.'

Joe took his time.

'His debts? The orphanage in Luica? Has it been seeing any money at all?'

'Crumbs,' Sykes said. 'Enough for a bit of building work, photo ops, nothing more. The charity's a front. Most of the donations to Rebuild have gone into Balan's pocket, through his cousin.'

Grunhill sat back, exhaled, waited for everyone's attention.

'Plus, Benedict has been laundering Workout's illegal earnings out of the country.'

'Yes, I know, it's—'

'One way or another, the debt to Balan is being repaid. The donation from Rajvansh tomorrow will end up in Balan's hands. That's why he's in the UK, we think. To make sure everything goes to plan.'

'Right, Joe,' said MacDonald from behind his desk, 'we need to make sure your investigation doesn't jeopardize all this.'

But Joe wasn't listening.

'Why Saxford?'

'Just somewhere discreet, perhaps?' Grunhill suggested. 'He'll be here tomorrow to monitor things. You can bet on that.'

Joe wasn't so sure.

'Balan didn't come over to kill Miriana Dalca, then?' he asked.

'Talk to your friend at Interpol,' Grunhill said. 'He doesn't think so. Neither do we.'

'Balan's a suspect in a double murder investigation. One of those investigations is mine. I need to speak to Balan and Benedict. We can bring 'em both in now. We've got all night.'

Grunhill shook his head.

But Joe wasn't done.

'I've got DNA evidence coming. Could be the key. I need to get cracking.'

'DNA? When?'

'Tomorrow morning.'

'So? You can wait a few hours, right?' Grunhill sighed. 'Look, Balan's trafficking operation could be big. Huge.'

'I've got two dead women. That's pretty huge.'

'All we need you to do is join the dots on the Dobrescu murder. It'll all fall into place. But this is good to go. And we go tomorrow, after Rajvansh pays Benedict. Conspiracy to defraud, on top of everything else. Get 'em in custody. Job done.'

Joe was done as well. He got to the door, no handshakes.

'Oh, Joe?' MacDonald said. 'We'll be needing your team up in Bilton tomorrow. Suits and ties, please. You could do with a clean shirt yourself, actually.'

Activity in the ops room came to a halt as Joe appeared.

'We can all go home,' he said, sinking down onto the nearest chair as people left what they were doing and gathered around. He explained, reducing his last two meetings to a handful of bare sentences.

Meanwhile, Gwyn was staring at an image on his phone, shaking his head.

'Michael Benedict's a bloody bankrupt? What's a woman like Sophie doing with a loser like him?'

'What d'you mean?' asked Joe.

Gwyn shrugged.

'He owes a million. On the hook to some Romanian gangster. Running a laundering operation … If you were her, would you stick around, playing along with that piece of shit, risking serious jailtime? She could walk away, have any bloke she wanted.'

'Listen to yourself, knobhead!' said Gemma. 'You just walked out the Sweeney, or what? Never heard of love, devotion, 'til friggin' death us do part? Happen she sticks by him 'cos she loves him?'

Gwyn chuckled, still admiring the image of Sophie Benedict.

'You're shittin' me. For love, all his? She's well out of his league. An' she's gonna do time for him?'

'Jesus ...!'

'*So*,' said Joe, cutting them off, 'Sunday best. We'll meet up at the golf club at eleven. Gemma and Mark, not you two. I've got something else. Could you lose the suit tomorrow, Mark?'

'Oh, the gloves,' Gwyn said. 'They're saying it's the same kind of residue on Miriana's neck.'

Joe leant back in his chair. 'Two dead. One murderer. And all we can do is wait.'

Mark exhaled hard, his body convulsed with exasperation. 'One murderer ... *One?*'

'Say what you see, Markie!' said Gwyn.

Mark marshalled his thoughts, looked around for support, found none.

'So we're counting Churchill out for the murder of Ana,' he said, slowly. 'Same MO for Miriana, so she didn't do Ana either. Meanwhile, Balan wasn't in the country 'til yesterday, which puts him out of the frame for Ana ...'

'If!' Joe said. 'What do we count Miriana *in* for? Did she tell Balan about Ana's murder? Is that why he got a flight?'

'Nah,' said Gwyn. 'He bought his flight first thing yesterday morning. Transaction details are on the system. Miriana didn't know until the afternoon when you told her.'

'What if Miriana killed Ana and phoned him the same night?'

'She didn't, though, kill Ana. She didn't know …'

'Unless she were lying,' Gwyn said.

'The gloves!' Mark cried. 'It's the same MO. It's not her!'

'Round in circles are we going!' Joe said, doing his best Master Yoda impression. 'I was right about the misdirection, though.'

They all looked at him, confused.

'The agency admitting to those workers in Batley? It was to deflect attention. The agency had planned for a situation like this. They get charged for a few illegal workers, and they burn all their files. Job done. No digital records. But there's a lot more workers. Gotta be. All currently untraceable.'

'Ana Dobrescu flew to Bucharest a month ago,' Gwyn said. 'Who did she meet?'

'Perhaps she went home,' Joe said. 'To the orphanage. Found out what was going on, decided to do something about it.'

'Where things are grown,' said Gemma. 'The text she never got around to sending you? Could it be like "where people grow up". The orphanage?'

Joe saw the nods of agreement.

'Things?' he asked. 'As in slaves. Not people, things?'

'Could be owt, though,' Gwyn said. 'Trees, grass, plants?'

'Enough! My head's spinning. There's nothing more we can do tonight. DNA and golf tomorrow. Get some sleep, folks!'

# 60

A couple of hours later Joe was still there. On the next desk there was a bit of a cheeseburger in a polystyrene carton, a layer of congealed orange cheese running along the edge of the exposed meat. He leant over and grabbed it. Took a bite. It tasted fine.

He got a pencil, started estimating the profits on trafficked workers as he chewed. About five grand a year profit from each one, he reckoned. Tax-free. If there's a hundred, that's half a million a year in Balan's pocket. Every year. Then Ana Dobrescu threatens to screw it all up. Ana … Ana … She grew up in the orphanage. She'd known Stefan since they were little kids, perhaps some of the others. Then a new job, a new life in England. She'd tried to do her best for the workers that she found here, to mother them, do whatever she could to help. A pact with the devil, perhaps, but one with a purpose, a kind of sad, desperate logic. Then she went back to Romania, saw what was really going on, where Ben's donations were going …

Joe mumbled to himself as he scribbled his thoughts down, putting names in boxes, connecting them with lines and arrows, trying to see a definite link.

The agency has no digital records. Ana would've had to write it all down by hand. Was everything in that folder? She confronts Miriana, shows her the evidence. Is that what she had with her the night she died? Written proof. And how did Miriana react? Was she going to come in with Ana to speak to him? Is that why she was dead, why they were both dead?

He got onto the system, found Gemma's new map. Routes away from Miriana's house. The homes of all the POIs were flagged, plus the golf club, the two dump sites. Again and again he traced possible routes out. She could've gone to any of these places. Late at night, alone, drunk. Angry?

His phone buzzed. Took him a while to find WhatsApp. Too tired to think now.

'Joe! At last, your Crime Agency has traced Mr Balan!' Mihal said, narrowing his eyes in mock-intrigue. 'I'm feeding you this info in case somebody over there forgot to tell you. Balan arrived in London, met up with an old associate. They drove to a place called Saxford, North Yorkshire. Their car was flagged up on your Big Brother camera system!'

'That's how they found him? And I'm getting this info from Romania!'

'Joe, you know how it works with national agencies. Anyway, have you seen the Interpol internal website?'

'I don't have access anymore.'

'I'll send you a screenshot. Silviu Balan is a big deal. If they convict him, they get a medal, or a kiss from the Prime Minister or whatever you Brits give each other.'

'I know. It's all about the glory. Two dead women? Not so much.'

'Joe? Don't bother with Balan, for the murders.'

'Why not?'

'We have him implicated in nine kills in Romania alone. It won't have been him, not directly. Do you know where he was when they all died? Sitting in the lobby of a small hotel in Bucharest. He owns it. The Hotel Alibi.'

'Is that a joke?'

'Yes, Joe! It's his little joke to us! When Miriana was killed, Balan was sitting somewhere or other, right in front of a security camera. I guarantee it.'

'But he ordered it?'

'Of course! Anyone who threatens his business, that's how it ends. You won't prove it, though, not straight away. Your National Agency is correct. Get him on conspiracy to defraud first.'

'The murders? We're close, just a bit hampered, a bit …'

'So find the connection. Force the issue.'

'OK, can you help me out? Michael and Sophie Benedict. They make trips to Luica, but it's all for publicity. Any chance you can find out what they do when they're in Romania, who they're meeting? I've got flight histories, passport numbers. Do you have clearance for that?'

'Clearance? I've got more clearance than you've got warm dinners.'

'Well, that's good to know. I'll email you the details. Thanks, Mihal. See you later.'

'Hot potato!'

He checked his messages. Mihal had sent a screenshot of Balan. He was a large man, slim but muscular, not bad-looking. A hundred and ninety-five centimetres, the profile said. Ex-soldier, with a thin, confident smile. The hands? Big. Way too big.

He looked around for more food. Nothing left. Eleven o'clock. The case was grinding him down, and now the NCA was poised to take over. Go home, wait until tomorrow.

He stood up. *Go home. Wait until tomorrow.* It's what Ana should have done: gone home and waited. And the text message? *Where things are grown.* It was on her phone, ready to send. You don't save text messages for long, not short ones, the kind you can type in a few seconds. Her phone went dead, though, out of battery. Did she know she was walking into danger that night? Was the message supposed to be a back-up? Where was she going?

He grabbed his jacket.

Down the ring road, past the showrooms for Lexus, Mercedes, Jaguar. Over the river, the train station ahead, a flash new apartment block to the left, where the Post Office building used to be. Flash apartment blocks wherever you looked. The old Leeds was still there, a handful of ancient pubs down winding alleyways if you knew where to find 'em. But most of it had gone. The old, lopsided Victorian buildings on Boar Lane, pawn shops and tattoo parlours on the ground floor, cut-price solicitors on the second floor announced in gold lettering on the windows. All gone. The purple sign of a Premier Inn caught his attention as he pulled up at a turning. The lights in the bar were still on, people drinking, away from home.

He crossed Wellington Street. Clerk's Restaurant was on a row of converted town houses that had been hideouts for the city's well-heeled lawyers long before the rest of Leeds caught up. Their red brickwork was immaculate, as if each brick had been cleaned with a toothbrush, the sandstone lintels smooth and spotless.

Service was winding down, the last of its diners lingering over their coffees. He went straight through to the kitchen, no time for pleasantries, found the only member of staff not in whites.

A few minutes later he was back in his car, a tiny pen drive in his pocket.

# 61

When he got home, Sam was fast asleep in the armchair, and
Rita was slumped on the sofa with her phone.

'You still here?'

'No, I've already gone.'

He smiled, watched her struggle to her feet.

'You look knackered,' she said. 'Sit yersen down. Drink?'

'Small one. Where's Ruth?'

She got two glasses from the kitchen, half an inch of Jura in
each, tiny dribble of tap water.

'She went home. Needed an early night. Here,' she said,
sitting on the floor in the middle of the room.

'Two lives gone,' he said, 'and they're nothing more than
pieces in the Silviu Balan story. Ana wanted to be with
Churchill to the end. She didn't even get that.'

'You can only do your job, Joe.'

'To protect Balan's investment! To keep the money coming
in, keep the slaves working. That's all the deaths meant.' He
looked across at Sam. 'Is this the kind of world he wants to
see?'

'What does Tennant say?'

'He's in a hotel. Sounds like his marriage is, y'know … Anyway, big day tomorrow. They're gonna pull folk in on conspiracy charges. Sod the murders. The NCA way!'

'Talking of which, Nick Evans rang me. He's worried sick. Said he'd never even met her, doesn't know why you want another statement.'

'He's a person of interest.'

'That's what I told him. Routine.' She paused. 'Is it?'

'He's not a big fella. Medium-sized hands, you'd think, no?'

'Just do your job, officer. By the way, I've got a suggestion. For Sam.'

'Oh yes?'

'It was Ruth's idea, actually. He's already got some course credits. So he switches to criminology, psychology, whatever. Gets himself a degree. Then if he still fancies the police, there's graduate entry, fast-track.'

'You told him that?'

'Yeah. Plus, it gives you time to get him to change his mind. Right. I'm off.' She took a while pulling herself up. 'And you go to bed!' She put her untouched whisky on the coffee table, then turned to Sam, nudged one of his legs with the toe of her Docs. 'You an' all!'

'Eh?' Sam said, his body twisting as his eyes opened.

He dragged himself up out of the armchair, blinked, stretched.

'How's your Italian these days?' his dad asked.

'It's all right. Why?'

'*Dove le cose sono cresciute*. Thoughts, officer?'

'Code?' Sam said, confused.

'Dunno. Where things grow. The message was for me, but it was never sent. The person who sent it's dead. You wanna be a copper? What does it mean?'

Joe waited, looked at his son. He was like a seven-year-old, the forlorn expression of tiredness, the soft, limp body ready to be picked up and carried off to bed … the delight of carrying a child, your own child, knowing that you have him in your arms, that you can feel his heartbeat, his warmth, that he's yours …

'It's where things *are* grown,' Sam said. 'Not where they grow.'

'Same difference, innit?' Rita said as she got her bag.

'No. It's …' Sam said, rubbing his face, '… it's like, to cultivate stuff. It's where you *grow* things. Can I go now?'

They watched him leave.

'Don't stay up all night, Sergeant,' she said. 'Golf club tomorrow.'

'I'd dress up this time, if I were you.'

'Hetero-chic?'

'To the max. Eleven. See you there.'

'Sleep!'


Silence. He didn't like it. It felt wrong to be at home now, waiting. Waiting for Ana Dobrescu's death to mean even less than it did now.

He swirled the whisky in his glass. Didn't really want it. He waited for the amber liquid to settle. A calm had descended. But someone was about to shatter it. He could sense it. A job left undone. A clue he'd missed.

Balan was in his hotel. Stefan in a cell. Churchill in a hospital bed. The Benedicts, Charles Malthouse and Nick Evans all at home …

No one was moving.

Two dead.

Who was left?

# SATURDAY

# 62

At six-thirty he found himself on the sofa, still in his jacket, shivering. He got up, shuffled into the kitchen, switched on the kettle.

He'd spent the night somewhere on the edges of consciousness, thinking about his single meeting with Ana Dobrescu, replaying it over and again in his mind, what he could have told her, how he might have stopped her walking away from him. Yet by what right could he have stopped her? She'd put herself in danger, but she'd done so consciously. She'd found a kinship with someone, and he was dying. Was risking her own life such a crazy notion? There was a horrible grace to it, a dignity that was hard to refute: she'd decided to bring down a trafficker of human beings, whatever the risk to herself.

Miriana was also dead. He was sickened by the thought of it, that death can mean so little. Neither Ana nor Miriana had any family. And now they were gone, no one to inform, nothing. He leant against the table to steady himself, closed his eyes. And there it was. Something hard in his pocket. Bloody idiot. The memory stick. He'd been so tired yesterday that he'd forgotten all about it.

He took his coffee through to the living room, sat at the dining table, pushed the pen drive into his laptop: the week's security footage from Clerk's Restaurant. Clicked on Wednesday evening. The quality was good, a camera high up, taking in the whole dining area. The image on screen whirred forwards at four times the normal speed, waiters like Charlie Chaplin on the sprint, diners gobbling their food down as if they hadn't eaten in weeks. Even at this speed there was an affectation to the place; the pretentious flicks of hair were swifter, the savouring of wine comically short, the flamboyant laughter of men like fleeting heart spasms.

He fast-forwarded, peering hard at the screen. Leapfrogged half an hour, then again, right the way to the end of the file. Michael Benedict had lied. His wife had not been there. He sat back, had a mouthful of tepid coffee. Why would Benedict lie? He closed the file. There were ten videos in total, lunch and dinner, Monday to Friday.

He clicked on Thursday evening. Different actors, but the same script. Quadruple speed. Hair-flicking, heart spasms, Chaplinesque waiters. Then Sophie Benedict appeared. He dropped his mug as he leant forward, pressed normal 'play', felt the liquid seeping into his trousers. She was shown to a table in the centre of the room. She sat down, alone. No flicking of the hair, and she didn't look pleased to be there. Her face was still wildly attractive, but her movements were careful, studied, like a teenager, unsure of herself.

A bottle of champagne arrived in a chill bucket. Two flutes were set down on the table, but the bottle was not opened. Dinner with a donor, her husband had said. But that was the previous day. Or was it? There was a lie somewhere in all this.

As he watched her idle the time away, he considered popping into the restaurant, getting the price list and pinning it to one of the notice boards up at the charity presentation today. This is how they spend your donations! Apart from paying Michael Benedict's massive debts ...

Then her dining partner arrived. It wasn't her husband. Bigger, taller, very tall, pale jacket, handsome.

'Shit ...'

# 63

They crowded around the monitor in the ops room, several flavours of morning breath hanging on the air.

'Silviu Balan?' Andy asked.

'Yeah, he must know the Benedicts,' Simon Tennant said, less impressed. 'It figures. He's connected to the charity.'

Joe grinned.

'He's connected to Sophie Benedict, all right! Flies into Heathrow, up here in a jiffy, and this is who he comes to see? Watch. I'll put it on double speed.'

The champagne was cracked open, a toast, a kiss, long, even at double speed, Balan's hand running through her hair and down her neck. They ordered food, ate, drank toast after toast, a coy smile creeping onto her face, a feminine softness that hadn't been there before.

As they watched, something was niggling Joe, but he didn't know what. Something about Sophie Benedict, her mannerisms, the way she responded to Balan. What was it?

'Where's her husband in all this?' Gemma asked.

'I'm bringing him in today,' said Joe. 'Whatever the bloody

NCA says. He's lying through his teeth, and he owes Balan serious money.'

'Sophie, though,' she said. 'It's a bit weird, isn't it? Having dinner with Balan?'

'They leave at nine-thirty.'

'Balan checked into his hotel in Saxford around ten, alone,' said Tennant. 'He must've got a train up from Heathrow, had dinner with her, then got a cab. Doesn't have any wheels.'

Joe's body tensed. 'No motor? Strange. Any road, look.' He froze the video. 'He's carrying a bag when he leaves. But she brought it.'

'A woman's leather shoulder bag,' Gemma said. 'Full of something. Bulky.'

'Who's betting Romanian passports, ID cards?' Joe said. 'Lots of 'em.'

'Were the Benedicts keeping the passports for him?' Tennant suggested, already on his phone. 'Somebody had to be,' he added, turning to leave. 'Didn't want 'em anywhere near the agency. Joe? I'll need a copy of these videos, asap.'

Tennant moved quickly across the room, phone in hand, dialling.

'Balan goes back to his hotel and waits. He's there now,' Joe said.

He wasn't looking at the screen, though. He was watching the door that Tennant had just scurried through like a waiter on fast-forward.

Gemma and Mark stood there, not knowing what to do. She was in her usual jeans and leather jacket. He was wearing a pair of cream chinos and a Leeds Rhinos top. The short sleeves revealed chunky biceps, which had almost certainly never been on display on police premises before.

'Thanks for dressing down, by the way,' Joe said. 'You play?'

'Yeah, just pub sevens. What are we doing today, then?'

'Get up to Saxford. Bit of a recce. Low profile.' They were already looking at their phones as he spoke. 'The NCA think Balan'll be coming down to Leeds for the big event at the golf club.'

'And you don't?' Andy asked, a trace of resignation in his voice.

Joe took a breath, rubbed his face.

'Dunno. I'm thinking, if I were in Balan's shoes? See where he's staying? Mile and a half east of the hotel?'

Gemma and Mark peered at their Google Maps.

'What are we looking for?' Mark asked.

'Private airfield, hardly ever used. You'd miss it if you didn't know it was there. If he comes down to Leeds, great. We'll get him here. But if he doesn't?'

'He's off with the passports?'

'It's a thought. Happen he reckoned he could keep his trafficking business going. There'll be a lot more illegal workers, and at the moment they're all invisible, untraceable.'

'Balan doesn't know he's under surveillance,' Gemma said.

'Exactly. If I were him, I'd come over here, make sure everything was OK with the Benedicts and the money transfer, get the passports, then disappear.'

'With no passports, there's no evidence back to Balan,' she added.

'None at all. Hold on,' said Joe, fishing in his pocket for his phone, which was buzzing.

'Hi, Mihal,' he said as the WhatsApp video link jumped into life. 'Best behaviour. You have an audience!'

'Understood,' the Romanian said, smiling, pleased with himself. 'The Alibi? Balan's hotel in Bucharest? Sophie Benedict stayed there. Three times in the last six months.'

'Tallies with her flights?'

'Yep.'

'Only Sophie, though. Not *Mr* Benedict. He was at the Holiday Inn, right across town. All three times. Are they married?'

'The Benedicts? As far as I know.'

'Well, they're not consummating anything while they're in Bucharest. Check your email! Right, I'm off. Been a busy night.'

An email message was waiting for Joe when he ended the call.

'Can you all see this?' he said, holding the phone up as he clicked on the first of three video files attached.

'Jesus, I can see that!' said Andy.

Balan and Sophie Benedict burst through the main doors of a hotel lobby, grabbing each other like randy teenagers. They staggered towards the lift together, no pretence of decency, tugging at each other's clothes, her hands down the front of his trousers, and his hands everywhere, pushing her against the wall. They went into the lift, and even as the doors closed, her mouth was running down his chest.

The other two videos were similar, although in the last one Balan was at the bar when she arrived. The same performance, but without even bothering to go to the lift.

'Bloody hell!' Andy said. 'Talk about *One Night in Bucharest*! Come on, let's watch it all!'

'Pervs!' Gemma said, reaching over and pausing the video, inadvertently capturing Balan on a barstool, his trousers unbuckled. 'Jesus, he's pleased to see her!'

Joe held up his phone, the proud epicentre of Balan's manhood frozen on-screen. Then he placed the phone carefully on the desk, like a court exhibit.

'OK. You two get up to Saxford Airfield. Routes in and out. See what you think. I'll be in touch.'

Andy stood there, waited 'til they'd gone.

'What's with you and Tennant?'

'Foot in both investigations,' Joe said. 'He's overseeing my case, and he's working with the NCA.'

'Bloke's got some bloody staying power.'

'They're keeping info back. Stuff I need. That we need.'

'Like what?'

'He just said Balan had no car. That's bollocks. He's got a motor. Drove up from London with an old associate of his. That's how the NCA found him.'

'Can I ask how the hell you came by this information? Forget that. I'd rather not. You're intel's good?'

'Cast iron.'

'So?'

'They want Balan. That's all they want.'

'You've lost me, Joe. We're all on the same bloody side!'

'This isn't about what's right. Two young women get killed? Nah, they want to bring Balan down in a ball of flames. They don't care about justice for Ana Dobrescu. Or Miriana.'

'Same side!'

'Wait,' Joe said, getting out his notebook. 'I need to order tracking on a motor for the night she died.'

'God, you're an annoying twat! Don't you ever bloody stop?'

'Nope.'

He placed the order, then waited until Andy had gone.

'Sorry to disturb you again.'

'Not disturbing,' Mihal said, as he picked up. 'Not in bed. Yet!'

'My turn to send you a video. It's footage of Balan and Sophie Benedict in a restaurant.'

'What am I looking for?'

'You remember that Albanian case at Interpol? They used lip-reading evidence in court?'

'Yes, I remember.'

'Right. You got any lip-readers handy?'

'First thing on a Saturday morning in my Bucharest apartment? Yeah, the place is full of them!'

'Any chance you could find someone?'

'I try, I try!'

'The video. It's Sophie Benedict and Balan. Just tell me what language they're speaking.'

'Ah-ha, Mr Romano! Now you're thinking like an Interpol man again!'

# 64

The car park was filling up when Joe and Andy arrived. The owner of every Italian sports car in Leeds seemed to be there, eager to catch a glimpse of the man who'd just bought the club, a billionaire who could have bought fifty Maseratis with the annual interest that dripped from his great pile of wealth. Or a thousand second-hand Mondeos.

'Right,' Andy said, 'I better get inside, see what's what.'

With that he was off, head down, checking his tie as he went.

Rita was over by the clubhouse steps rolling a fag. Joe walked across to her. There was a pulsating thud in the air, distant but getting louder. It took him a while, but then he recognized the sound of a helicopter.

'Moneybags himself!'

'What?' she said, as he approached.

'The new boss is here.'

She slipped the unlit rollie into the jacket pocket of a navy-blue trouser suit. The nose studs had vanished.

'You know your bum looks big in that, right?' he said, making a half-hearted attempt to bound up the stairs.

'Prick. Anyway, it's my court outfit. Where's Gwyn?'

'Gone for the DNA results on the gloves. Then he's coming.'

'Right. Straighten yourself up. There's brass inside. You haven't changed your shirt? And what's that on yer kecks?'

'Coffee. Brass?'

'Marie Coleman, no less.'

'Who?'

'Jesus, don't tell me you've never heard of her? Regional Commander, National Crime Agency. Orders in five minutes.'

'We're the foot soldiers, are we?'

'Tennant's already here.'

'Oh, I bet.'

She looked up as the noise from the sky intensified.

'Come on,' she said. 'Showtime.'

He took a few deep breaths, got himself focused, then followed her through the doors. Immediately he was stopped by three security operatives in black suits and ridiculous scowls. He stated his name, pulled out his card. One of the men studied it, then examined Joe's face, taking his time.

'The office is over to the right,' he said, as he and his colleagues stepped aside in what Joe now realized had been a physical cordon. 'I'll show you—'

'No need,' Joe said, marching straight ahead.

The ballroom was filling up. Not even midday, but champagne and canapés were being served. Plenty of shiny suits, plus a few guys in saggy linen jackets and scruffy deck shoes. Why did old deck shoes always make a bloke look rich?

Jerry MacDonald was there, over by the French windows with the Benedicts. The three of them were animated, beaming, ready for the big event, sipping Dom Pérignon. Michael

Benedict's arm moved in expansive arcs as he spoke to the Assistant Chief Constable.

'They're being kept busy,' Andy said, coming up behind Joe. 'We let all this play out. That's the order.'

'Two women dead,' Joe muttered as he watched Michael Benedict, 'and we're running a bloody fraud sting!'

Malthouse's office was crowded. It stank of aftershave, and the air was charged with an electric buzz of anticipation, a kind of controlled jumpiness, like you get in a dressing room before a gig, but here there was also a competitive edge.

Joe's constables were over by the windows, Rita, too, all keeping out of the way. Malthouse was with them, banished from his desk in the middle of the room, which was now invisible behind a forest of authority. Tennant was there with a huddle of officers from the NCA, and perched on the desk itself was Commander Marie Coleman, effortlessly yet evidently in charge. Average height, neat pinstripe suit, nothing out of the ordinary. But she was the one. Joe knew it the moment he'd walked in. Eighty per cent rank, he reckoned. The other twenty? Hard to say. Not many have it, though, whatever it is.

Andy went up to Coleman, whispered in her ear. The Commander glanced at Joe, nodded. That was that.

'Ladies and gents,' she began, broad Yorkshire accent, the kind whose owner had never thought to hide it. 'Mr Rajvansh is in the building! You might have heard his vehicle arrive.' Chuckles. 'We've been talking to him since last night. DCI Grunhill?'

Grunhill was towards the back of the room, near the

fireplace. He didn't move, and spoke without notes, his voice sure and unwavering, like a seasoned politician on the stump.

'Today, the charity Rebuild is going to receive a transfer of one million pounds ...'

His voice tailed off as heads turned to the door.

Joe felt himself being pushed from behind. He shuffled forwards with everybody else. A thin man stood in the doorway. Dark suit, white, collarless shirt. Raj Rajvansh. About Joe's age and height, with a close-cropped beard and tinted glasses. Behind him was a taller, thickset man in a dark grey uniform, half-military, half-lounge suit. It must have been the pilot.

On the other side of Rajvansh was Jerry MacDonald, now wearing a beatific smile. And he wasn't the only one. The very sight of a billionaire had sent people weak at the knees. It used to be rock stars. Now it's money. Billionaires: the new gods.

'Mr Rajvansh,' Grunhill continued, 'has agreed to cooperate with the case. Thank you very much, Sir.'

Rajvansh waved a hand, as if it was nothing.

Does money trump power so completely? Joe asked himself. Commanders, Assistant Chief Constables, Superintendents, DCIs ... The royal flush. All wetting themselves. What do they know about this bloke? What if he beats his kids? What if he's a paedo, or a thief, or just a shyster? A billion in the bank and you can walk on water.

'A donation of a million pounds is to be transferred to the Rebuild charity as part of today's ceremony,' Grunhill continued. 'It's supposed to fund work on an orphanage and children's hospital in Romania. Our information is that the funds will be channelled into offshore accounts linked to Silviu Balan. We've had very little time to set things up, and

Mr Rajvansh has very generously offered to let the transfer go ahead, with the inevitable risk that the money might not be recovered. If we use Interpol or Europol to block the accounts involved, we raise the alarm. We can only thank Mr Rajvansh for his most generous cooperation.'

Rajvansh took the slightest of bows, in acknowledgement of the murmurs of approval from around the room.

'I assure you, it is the least I can do.'

Joe did the maths. It was like him offering to stand a round of drinks. Three cheers for the man-god.

Commander Coleman stood a little straighter.

'And it will be duly noted at the very highest level, Sir,' she said.

Joe's stomach almost deposited its contents onto the carpet.

'Could I butt in here?' he said. 'I'm about to make an arrest for two murders. Balan should already be in custody. I think, in the circumstances …'

'How does that affect anything, Joe?'

Everyone looked. The voice was Simon Tennant's.

'*This* way,' Joe said, 'a double murder gets sidelined for a case of fraud. Since when did a million quid trump the life of two young women?'

'What evidence do you have?' Coleman asked.

'Sophie Benedict met Balan on Thursday. They're lovers. We have video footage of them in Bucharest, three times over the past year.'

Coleman took a moment.

'Is any of this confirmed? Dates, authenticity?' she asked Tennent.

'Just come to light, Ma'am.'

'I've got a video of 'em together,' Joe said. 'She's *blowing* him. Christ, two women are dead. Her husband lied. The normal process ...'

'Joe?'

When Joe turned, the Assistant Chief Constable was smiling at him, a hand on his shoulder, their faces no more than a foot apart. Then he exerted some pressure, swivelling Joe gently around until he looked out across the room. MacDonald raised his other hand, the index finger pointing at Coleman, then Grunhill, Sykes, Andy, plus three or four other higher-ranking officers that Joe didn't recognize. The message was lost on no one.

It may have been the worst ever. Cuckolded by his next-door neighbour in France? That had been pretty humiliating. What else? A couple of times when he was a teacher. Kids can be cruel. Then, only a few months in uniform, he's got diarrhoea when he was sorting out some trouble at a club in town. Racing to the bogs, holding his arse, everybody falling about laughing ... *Do it in yer tit-hat!* they'd shouted as he'd locked himself in a cubicle, managing to avoid a dry-cleaning bill by seconds.

But no. This humiliation was the worst. Forty-five years on the planet, and finally Joe Romano knew who he was. The Omega in a room full of Alphas. The most-pecked in the pecking order. The gang of one. He looked around, saw the severity in their faces, the carefully nuanced sense of power, while twenty paces away a murder suspect was sipping champagne and soaking up the adulation.

'Ma'am,' said one of the NCA coterie, phone up to his face, 'Balan's on the move.'

'Got a definite ID on him?'

'Not yet, but the car's heading this way. Lone driver. Male. Right sort of age.'

A murmur of interest arose, Joe's humiliation already forgotten.

'Get somebody close, ID him,' the Commander said. 'Right, I think we're ready. The ceremony begins in …'

'Six minutes precisely, Madam,' said Rajvansh, consulting his Rolex, to a rumble of amusement.

Even that was funny, apparently.

But Joe wasn't interested. He was watching Malthouse, who wore a benign expression as the room burst into activity, his hand playing with the leaves of a large plant, the one in the Victorian plant stand by the window.

Joe went across, easing through the bustle, his presence now irrelevant. Rita was waiting for him. It wasn't often she looked embarrassed, but there was a definite pink tinge to her complexion.

'Talk about fighting your corner, Sergeant!' she said into his ear, nudging him in the ribs.

'See 'em all brown-nosing the money!' he said, not quite at a whisper.

Malthouse raised his eyebrows.

'Is that an aspidistra?' Joe asked.

The president seemed pleased by the question.

'Yes it is. My father grew it from a cutting. Now I suppose it belongs to Mr Rajvansh, like everything else. Funny, isn't it? The smallest things sometimes mean the most.'

He smiled at Joe, his eyes glazed.

'Take it,' Joe said. 'We'll overlook the theft.'

'It doesn't matter. I'm glad you're standing up for that poor girl.' He paused. 'All the money in the world, it shouldn't mean everything. It does, though, doesn't it?'

His hand searched for the plant's densely packed stems, his fingers wrapping around them. With one forceful twisted the whole thing snapped.

'What was it Sam said last night?' Joe asked Rita, as both of them stared at the aspidistra. '"Where things are grown". Wait here. I'm gonna be a few minutes.'

The Men in Black watched as he ran across the reception towards them.

'Coming through!'

He took the steps outside three at a time. Down onto the gravel, arms windmilling as he struggled to stay upright. Across the car park, his breath heavy in his ears as he raced past the lines of cars and out onto the grass. A lot of information, she'd said. Everything.

On the fairway, and sharp arrows of pain were shooting up his thighs. If only she hadn't tried to persuade anyone else to come with her, if only she'd told him ... She knew who she was dealing with. If she screwed up Balan's business, she'd be in danger. The pain got worse, as if his muscles were being sliced open from the inside. He winced, cried out, felt himself being carried along, the turf springy underfoot, blood pumping in his ears. He saw Ana Dobrescu's face, purple neck, eyes closed, the tiny gold cross resting on her neck. Something good, very good. If only she'd told him. If only he hadn't let her go. *Where things are grown.*

His chest was heaving as he got to the house. A stitch in his side. He pushed a palm into his abdomen. At one side of the terrace was a wooden ledge hinged to the wall. Tomato plants, three long plastic sacks. *Dove le cose sono cresciute.*

'Right,' he said, getting both hands under the ledge, panting, his legs unsteady beneath him.

He strained, finally managing to lift the whole ledge up an inch or two. He kicked the wooden supports away, one side then the other. Then he let go. The plants and sacks of soil crashed to the ground, covering his shoes and the bottom of his trousers as he tried to jump out of the way.

And there it was, among the mess, wrapped in a black bin-liner, bound up with tape.

He jogged back up the course, a plastic folder under his arm, full of photocopied pages, lists of names, dates, locations, money, all in neat handwriting, the letters rounded, like a schoolchild's. Ana doing everything she could. Something good.

His phone rang.

'Mihal,' he said, breathing heavily, trying to keep going.

'Joe. They were speaking Romanian.'

'Sophie Benedict? With Balan?'

'Yes. But she's not called Sophie. I have her passport details, remember? I ran a trace. Should've done it before. She changed her name. Marriage of convenience to Benedict, I assume. She's called Sofia Albu. Born in the UK, but her family's from Bucharest. The Albu family. They're ...'

Joe pressed the phone to his ear, ran faster, hardly hearing anything above his own rasping breath.

'Mihal?' he said. 'They're what?'

'Worse than Balan. Bad people, Joe. It's her. Gotta be. Her and Balan, working together.'

He was in the car park now. Gwyn had just arrived. Joe stopped, phone still held to his ear.

'DNA in the gloves!' Gwyn shouted as he got out of his car. 'Didn't you see my messages? The forensics? X chromosome on the gloves? It were a woman!'

'Mihal, I've gotta go.'

'Careful, Joe. This isn't good.'

Joe gulped air, felt his body sway, steadied himself.

'And the tracking's just gone up on the system,' Gwyn added. 'Sophie Benedict's motor was clocked on the Harrogate Road, midnight on Wednesday, going towards Bilton Woods. The night Ana died.'

'Not Sophie. Sofia. Sofia Albu.'

The sound of a single gunshot rang out from within the clubhouse.

'Call armed response,' Joe said as he turned and ran.

No one was manning the main entrance now. Rajvansh's security officers were outside the ballroom, flat against the wall, no idea what to do. As Joe got to the double doors, the screams fell away to nothing.

He stood there. The silence was impressive, surreal. There were people on either side, all cowering into one another, trying to ease themselves behind somebody else but without showing massive cowardice. Then, actually against the wall, and indeed under tables, were more people, the ones who didn't give a toss about cowardice; they huddled down there like frightened mice, curled up, trembling.

Right in front of the doors, however, there was no one other than Joe. And that was because a gun was pointing directly at the exit. At him.

'Detective Romano!'

She stood on the stage at the other end of the room. It was little more than a platform, just a foot high. But it was enough. She looked down on everyone as she spoke, her voice rich and full. Joe took a step forward, his legs beginning to tremble. He kept his eyes on the gun, which she held in both hands. There was a slight smile on her face, whimsical, like someone getting ready to shoot ducks at a fairground.

He stopped. Most of the front line were police officers, his colleagues among them. They'd got themselves well spaced, a semi-circle of sitting targets. The pinstripes? Coleman was the nearest person, no more than three yards from the gun, just to the right of the stage. She had her arms out in an attempt to conduct proceedings. But she was looking at Joe. Everybody was looking at Joe.

Then he sensed someone behind him.

'Loaded.'

It was Andy. He could smell the sweat, the whiff of his best friend's breath.

'You sure?' Joe whispered, feeling Andy's large body push into him.

'Glock. Army issue. There's a magazine in it. Best I can tell you, mate.'

'Right.'

He had no idea what to do. This wasn't right. This wasn't in the plan. But now?

He took another step forward. From the corner of his eye

his saw Commander Coleman over to his right, hands out, palms down, subtly gesturing "no".

The fear coursing through his body was overpowering, ridiculous. He wanted to run, to hide from danger. Fight or flight? There was no question which side he came down on. But Ana hadn't hidden from danger. And she knew who these people were. She knew everything. She'd decided to fight. He owed it to her to do the same.

'I'm going to come a bit closer,' he said, struggling to get the words out. 'Is that all right, Sophie?'

'Is that the police manual talking?' she said.

'Absolutely.' He took another step, pushing down the fear, the urge to wilt. 'I'm supposed to tell you my name. Repeat it. Then repeat yours.' He watched as her chest rose and fell with each breath. But her head was steady. She was in control. 'Where's your husband? Run off with the money, has he?'

'My husband? Ha! He's under a table, shitting himself. Husband in name only, unless you hadn't worked that out.'

Joe didn't know whether he was petrified or delirious. Didn't matter. Here he was. Too far into the room now. Too late to back down. Too exposed to hide.

'The money's been wired, has it?'

She nodded.

'This is plan B, then?'

Nothing.

'If it had all gone through without a hitch, fine. You disappear, meet Balan somewhere, off you go. But a load of coppers have turned up, and it's all getting a bit dodgy. By the way, you can spot us a mile off, can't you? It's the suits, right?'

She smiled. It was like she'd been saving it up for him.

Nobody could have delivered a more seductive smile, and she knew it.

'So, Joe Romano?' she said, the Glock pointing right at him as she glanced around to make sure no one was moving.

'There's an armed response unit on the way,' he said. 'What's it to be?'

She sniffed at the irrelevance of it all.

And in that single gesture she betrayed herself. It took him a while, but then he realized. She had a way out. Joe looked at Coleman. Had the Commander also worked it out?

'Ana came to your house, didn't she?' he asked, staring squarely at the woman who could have killed him at any moment.

She said nothing.

'About midnight, we reckon,' he continued. 'She walked all the way. Drunk, emotional. She wanted the passports, all of them. She was gonna bring the whole thing down. Ana was scheduled to see me the next morning. She had a file. Here, I have a copy. Your name's in it. Silviu Balan's too. Stuff about your charity. Plus the names and locations of over a hundred trafficked workers.'

He glanced at Coleman again. Right beside her was Raj Rajvansh, arms crossed, looking more impatient than afraid. And next to him was his pilot.

'So,' Joe continued, 'Ana marches up to your house, rings the bell, tells you that she knows everything. Embezzlement of charitable donations, trafficked workers, laundering the illegal profits back to Romania … You're the connection. She'd been back to the orphanage, worked out what was going on. It was you. You even kept the passports. In that safe. The one in your unit, right?'

374

'She was a pathetic little hypocrite.'

'Ana decided to put a stop to it. Is that what she told you on Wednesday night? You let her in, did you? Listened to her, told her it was complicated, that she should think things over. Then you drove her home.'

'A hypocrite. Out of her depth.'

'Oh, the gloves you used?' Joe said. 'We found 'em. There's a woman's DNA inside them. And your car was there. You dumped the body—'

'OK!' she said, raising her voice. 'I get it!'

Joe was shaking his head.

'But I don't. You gambled on the chance that there were no copies of this file?'

'Gamble? We knew there'd be copies. It was just a matter of timing.'

'We?'

'Me and Silviu. You think my *legal* husband has a clue about what was going on? He's happy to see his debts paid off, to enjoy his comfortable golf club life. Strange, but in the end he's actually convinced himself that we're running a charity. It's,' she said, searching for the right words, 'it's like he needs the comfort of believing he's doing good.'

Her eyes met Joe's. A moment's understanding.

'Like everyone here today,' he said.

'Exactly. Charity makes people feel so *very* good about themselves!'

'It's the perfect cover. So you killed her, made it look like Ben Churchill did it. What I don't understand is why Miriana Dalca had to go the same way.'

'Miriana wasn't as strong as she seemed. After Ana died, she panicked. She knew I had the passports. She knew too much, how everything worked, where all the money was going.'

'But now we know anyway.'

She smiled.

'Without the passports what have you got? A work of fiction written by Ana Dobrescu and a few illegal immigrants. The rest of 'em'll disappear, you see. They always do. There's no link back to anyone. All you have is the cretin I married. The perfect English gentleman!'

'And your link to Silviu Balan? How do you explain that, Sofia Albu?'

She didn't flinch. But she couldn't hide the shock.

'You!' she said as she swung around and pointed the gun at Rajvansh.

But it wasn't the Indian who moved. It was the man next to him.

The pilot knew immediately. He said something to his employer before walking towards the stage, where the waving gun sent him over to the French windows on the other side of the room. By which time everyone else had worked it out.

Logic said that fifteen well-placed police officers could manage to detain one person with a handgun, that she had only the slimmest chances of making it as far as the helicopter. But fourteen officers were now putting instinct on hold and doing a swift risk assessment, making sure they'd got every last detail right.

Thirteen.

Andy was by Joe's side.

'We rush her,' he whispered, staring at the gun, almost as if he wanted her to know what he was saying. 'She's not fuckin' walkin' out of here.'

'How?'

'When she steps down. See if we can get a bit closer first. Go on, do summat.'

'So,' Joe said to her, as the pilot walked stiffly across to the windows, 'off somewhere nice? Another night in the Alibi Hotel?'

He edged forward as he spoke, Andy right next him. Sophie's eyes went from the pilot to the rest of the room, then back, all residue of calm having now drained away.

'How many outside?' Joe asked Andy.

'None.'

Sophie moved forward until she stood at the front edge of the stage. She stopped, took one long breath. Joe recognized it: the breath before you walk out to perform, the flutter of nerves replaced for an instant by flat dread, when you'd rather be anywhere else in the world.

She lowered a foot, dropped down onto the ballroom floor.

Andy charged, mouth wide open, bawling a massive war cry, his arms waving as he shifted from one foot to the other, causing as much confusion as he could, a moving target.

A second. Less. She focused, seemed to flinch, her arms frozen before her.

She looked as shocked as anybody else when the sound of the gun filled the room.

# 65

People were screaming, running, falling over each other. Joe was on his knees, deaf, ears ringing, hands pressed into Andy's chest, feeling the heat of the blood, watching as it spread across his white shirt. Rita was beside them, keeping Andy's head still.

For perhaps ten seconds Sophie was only partly the centre of attention. Officers crowded around Andy, Commander Coleman standing close by, barking orders ... Others were getting people out of the room, all of 'em keeping an eye on the gun, wary now, but nobody assessing the risk. Joe pressed his hand down hard on the right pectoral, a big flabby chest, but solid, bulky.

'Harder,' Andy croaked, in no apparent pain, but his breathing agitated, wheezy, his eyes wide open but beginning to lose focus.

Sophie stood over by the windows.

With a single finger she pointed at Joe, beckoning him.

He had no idea what she meant.

But then he did.

So did Rita, who slid her palm under his and took over, as he got to his feet.

He emerged into the bright morning light, just the faintest brushstrokes of cirrus high in a powder-blue sky, the kind of sight that in other circumstances might have lifted his spirits. Next to him on the veranda was the pilot, with Sophie Benedict a good three or four paces behind them.

They heard footsteps. Around the corner of the building came Gwyn, running fast, then pulling up even faster, hands flying in the air as she took aim.

'Whoa!'

'That'll do,' she said. 'We're going on a little trip. No one gets hurt. OK?'

'Who's we?' Gwyn asked.

'Me, the pilot. Sorry, I don't know your name.'

'You don't need to.'

She shrugged.

'Fine. Me, *him*, and Sergeant Romano.'

Then she ushered the two men towards the helipad.

'Andy?' Joe asked as he turned.

Gwyn shook his head, non-committal, arms still in the air.

'Mark and Gemma,' Joe whispered. 'Where *they* are now.'

More officers piled around both corners of the building.

'Keep back!' she shouted as the three of them made their way over to the helicopter.

Joe's legs began to buckle. Yet he walked. Had no choice.

The 'copter was big. What the hell did he know? Never even been near one before. Didn't like flying much. Never been held at gunpoint either. And he'd never been human insurance. He was ticking off one hell of a bucket list today.

A wave of nausea hit him, so intense that he had to stop, hands on knees, sucking in the cold air.

'Come on,' Sophie said. 'You're up front.'

The seat was ridiculously comfortable. It didn't feel real, the seat, the 'copter … His body was shaking. There was still a buzz in his ears. And he was going to vomit. The helmet slipped on effortlessly over his perspiring head. There were headphones in it. She was speaking to the pilot. He couldn't hear what. Only the buzz.

He looked around for something to puke into. His body was cold. But his face was scalding hot, the flesh trembling. He forced himself to breathe, cowering against fear, hands balled up tight, fingers terracotta, sticky with Andy's blood, more of it on his sleeves, his shirt.

The pilot was calm, no discernible expression on his face, only the slightest tremor in his hand as he flicked switches and punched coordinates into a navigator. Its multicoloured screen lit up, incomprehensible to Joe as he leant forwards, twisting, ready to throw up.

'Here,' the pilot said, grabbing a paper envelope from a pocket in the side of Joe's seat and giving it to him.

Joe closed his eyes, pressed the bag against his forehead to absorb the sweat, which was running down into his eyes. The paper was hard, unyielding. He put the bag to his mouth and breathed. His sickness worsened as the thunder of the engine began to drown out his thoughts. The vibrations got stronger, the engine throbbing until its vibrations seemed to pummel his whole body.

Then they were up. The world tilted. Sam? That rollercoaster at Euro Disney. The slow, clanking journey to the top, scarily high, both of them laughing, not sure how nervous they were …

He opened his eyes. They were still rising. His body moved, seemed to swirl and spin, stomach twisting until it felt like it had come loose inside him. The noise was deafening, even with the helmet on. He held on to both armrests. There was a screaming in his head, but he had no idea whether it was real or if his nerves were exploding.

More talk in his earphones. North. They were going north, Sophie giving instructions from her seat behind them. His body fell forwards, then jerked back upright as the helicopter levelled out and took its course. The acceleration through the air was even worse. A massive push of speed, more frightening than at Euro Disney, when Sam had laughed all the way down, and Joe had nearly had a bloody heart attack.

For perhaps a minute he held tight on to his seat, forcing himself to breathe. He willed Andy to live, for those around him to do their jobs … He tried not to look out of the windows. But it was impossible. They were surrounded by glass. Below them was a miniature version of Yorkshire, God's own county, the land an impossibly bright shade of green, neat and ordered in its beauty, like the set for a model railway. Even the brownish mottling of towns was clear and precise. Is this what Ana had seen when she arrived? A model country, somewhere to start a new life? To do good? A company with links to the orphanage where she'd grown up?

The idea hit him so hard that his fear vanished instantly. Sophie wasn't the connection. She was the instigator. Her and Balan. She'd found Ana, seen her value, her goodness, and nurtured her. She'd organized for Ana to come to England, to work for the employment agency. Eventually Ana had seen through it, though. And by that time she had Ben.

Joe turned in his seat, struggling against the safety belt. Sophie was on her phone, texting with one hand, the gun in her other hand. It had been her. She'd sent that text to the slave house. She'd got the word out that you don't mess with the operation. A warning for the other trafficked workers. It had been her. It had all been her. Her and Balan. Right down to the Benedicts' marriage of convenience and their bogus charity.

Her face was now white, the lines deeper, her mouth strained. Yet there was a defiance, a fire in the eyes. Madness? Disbelief? The hard bit was over. They were up in the sky. Life or death. All or nothing.

What she didn't realize, as they ploughed through the air, was that Joe knew exactly where they were going.

Officers everywhere, sealing off the crime scene, marshalling members of the public into empty rooms. Rita was in the ambulance with Andy, and Michael Benedict was in a car ready to be taken to Elland Road, incapable, pathetic. The armed response unit had already arrived.

Gwyn Merchant was in the reception area, finger in his ear, bawling into his phone, slamming his foot into the wall with rage.

'She's fuckin' shot Andy … Dunno, mate … looks bad … What? Stop it flyin'. Just stop it. Balan an' all. Get 'im. And when the 'copter shows up, it'll be Sophie Benedict, the pilot, and Joe gettin' out. She's got a gun. Do your best, mate.'

He ended the call, saw Simon Tennant making his way towards the office. Gwyn collared him, explained as they went in, his body shaking with rage, eyes bloodshot, wide open.

The office was less busy now. Only the senior officers, plus Raj Rajvansh.

'The man in the car is not Balan,' Coleman said as everyone settled. 'The vehicle's been stopped. It's not him. He's slipped away somehow. We don't know where he is.'

'The 'copter's heading north,' Grunhill said, turning to Rajvansh.

The Indian was monitoring the progress of his helicopter using an app on his phone.

'Almost exactly north,' he said.

'It's gonna go east,' Merchant said.

They were all surprised that a DC was there, and that he was looking ready to tear the head off anybody who cared to ask why.

'It's possible,' Tennant said, as if to excuse his junior colleague. 'We've got two officers at an airfield in Saxford, not far from Balan's hotel.'

'There's a plane there,' Gwyn added, holding up his phone. 'They just told me. Came in an hour ago. Pilot's sittin' there waitin'.'

'Speaking of pilots,' Coleman said, 'how's your man in a crisis, Sir?'

Rajvansh seemed taken aback by the question.

'Ex-British Army. I think he'll be all right.'

'Timing,' Tennant said. 'She said it's all about timing. They only need a minute. She lands, gets in the plane with Balan, and off they go. He'll be somewhere close to the plane.'

Coleman took a second.

'Is there air traffic control?'

'None, Ma'am. Private airfield. Nothing.'

'Right. Let's get bodies up there now.'

The rush was ordered but urgent as they all crowded out through the single doorway.

'Saxford?' she asked Tennant as they went. 'Why've you got officers there?'

Tennant looked at Gwyn for suggestions.

'Joe Romano, Ma'am,' Gwyn said. 'He had a hunch.'

He forced himself to watch the ground far below, stifling the spasms in his throat. Villages he'd probably never visited, hills he'd never walked, rivers ... The whole bloody county, beautiful and majestic. His county. They were heading north. But not to the Dales. He was pretty sure there'd be another order soon. A quick dash east to Saxford, where Balan would be waiting. At least, he hoped that was the script. Because if not, he was screwed. Three down, and he was next.

Mark and Gemma were sitting in a police Astra, parked up on the verge of a narrow road that ran along the perimeter of Saxford Airfield. There were a few other vehicles there. On the other side of the road was a wooded area, complete with a picnic area. Prime dog-walking territory, right down to the red plastic shit bins.

Mark was looking into the distance, at the furthest table.

'Definitely him?'

Gemma had zoomed in as close as she could with the camera on her phone.

'Right age, size. Brown leather bag. And he's on his own. Gotta be.' She drummed her fist on the steering wheel. 'What yer wanna do, partner?'

'Gwyn said arrest him.'

'And if he does a runner? We're gonna look like a couple of prize dildos. Lose him now, *we'll* be on Interpol's most wanted list.'

She stared at her phone, considered the grainy image of the man sitting a hundred yards from them, tried to compare it to the vision of Balan that was stuck in her mind.

Then her phone rang.

'This is Commander Marie Coleman, NCA. DC Pearson?'

Coleman was in the passenger seat of her unmarked Jag, speakerphone on, her voice loud and authoritative. Her driver was pushing a hundred up the A64, the first in a line of vehicles, most of them marked, enough sirens and blue lights to empty the fast lane.

On the back seat of the Jag were Simon Tennant and Gwyn Merchant.

'Yes, Ma'am,' came Gemma's voice. 'I am with DC Francis.'

'We're on our way to Saxford. What's your location?'

'Parked next to the airfield. There's a plane, came in an hour ago, pilot hasn't got out. A man fitting Balan's description is sitting across from the airfield. We're watching him. Request orders, Ma'am.'

'Stay put. We're on the way. ETA ten minutes.'

She ended the call, shaking her head.

'Something doesn't add up here, gents,' Coleman said.

Joe listened through his headphones as Sophie read out the new coordinates. They were turning east. Her voice was strained now. Adrenalin only gets you so far. She was petrified, pushing the fear away with aggression. Either she landed and got in the plane with Balan, or she went down for two murders. Perhaps three.

The new coordinates were punched into the navigator, and the helicopter changed course. They banked to the right, the sun's rays angling down onto Joe through the glass door, warming his thighs, yet making him shiver.

Gemma and Mark? Had it been a mistake to send his youngest pair out there? Or were they his best bet, the savvy ones, the fittest? No idea. Not now. No idea what Balan was planning, or even if he was there.

Breathe. Wait.

'They've changed course,' Tennant said, phone pressed to his ear. 'How far away are we?'

'About seven, eight minutes,' the driver said as they raced serenely past a line of lorries, going so fast that you couldn't read the massive lettering on their sides.

'We're not gonna make it,' Tennant said. 'They can't be more than a couple of minutes away by now. Arrest Balan, Ma'am? We have two fit young officers there.'

'We don't know whether he's armed,' Coleman said, staring at the road ahead. 'No, no …'

'Sophie's definitely armed. Take Balan out now? Before she gets there and they both fly off.'

Coleman was shaking her head, hardly listening.

'This isn't right. The money's been sent. Balan's got the passports. Why's he still there? Something's up with all this.'

'She's his lover, Ma'am.'

She snorted. 'Men like him don't have lovers. Not the kind you risk being arrested for. And can everybody stop fuckin' calling me Ma'am?'

'Happen it's both,' Gwyn said.

Coleman and Tennant looked at him.

'Balan doesn't know he's being watched. You see?'

He waited, as if he was down the pub telling a joke, and the punchline was obvious.

'See what?' Coleman asked.

'If I were him, I'd be waitin' an' all. She's got a gun. He's got a plane. But she wouldn't be comin' with me.'

A second.

'Jesus, he's right. She's the only connection. He's gonna kill her and fly off. There'll be no evidence. Nothing to link him. Absolutely nothing.'

'They've gotta arrest him!' Gwyn said.

'He might be armed,' said Coleman as she dialled. 'Let's wait 'til we're sure …'

Gemma picked up immediately.

'No sign of the 'copter yet,' she said, her voice strong and clear through the car's speakers. 'Bloke we're watching hasn't moved.'

'OK. We won't be long. Plenty of manpower on the way,' Coleman said, seeing the white armed response unit van in the mirror.

'Hold on,' said Gemma. 'I can hear … Yep, helicopter coming in from the west.'

As she spoke, Mark began to shout.

'He's running! Balan. He's legging it to the plane!'

'Just get 'im!' Gwyn shouted, throwing himself forwards

between the front seats and screaming into Coleman's phone.

'We're off,' Gemma shouted.

The phone went dead.

Gwyn hung there, red-faced, gasping.

# 66

The noise from above reduced, and Joe's stomach tightened as they took a series of sudden downwards steps through the air, changing direction as they went. He was delirious, not from being in the air, but because he knew they'd be landing soon. The sky now felt like the safest place to be; once they were down, there'd be a killer to deal with, a killer with a gun and nothing to lose.

They lurched towards the airfield. Sitting at one end of a narrow concrete runway was a small white aircraft, its wings and bodywork iridescent in the sunlight.

'Close to the plane,' came the instructions, Sophie's voice hoarse, her throat seizing up, breathless. But there was a cackling levity to it as well, until she sounded ready to disintegrate in a ball of contradictory emotions. 'Closer!'

Then they saw the tall frame of Silviu Balan. He was jogging towards the plane from the edge of the field, moving at a steady pace, a large leather bag in his hand.

The helicopter's descent slowed as it neared the ground and hung there. The air filled with dust. Then they touched down with a heavy thump. Immediately the pilot began closing things down.

As the dust settled, Joe saw that Balan was still running towards them, but now he was glancing over his shoulder. Behind him, at the edge of the field, was a car. And it was driving straight at him.

Sophie began to shriek, desperate to be out, slamming her shoulder into the glass door. Her helmet was gone, and her hair was damp, stuck to her head in patches, like the hair of an old, time-ravaged doll. The pilot held up a finger, indicating the rotating blades above as he continued to switching things off.

The car? It was bouncing towards them on the uneven ground, Balan running ahead of it, but the motor gaining quickly.

Sophie continued to scream, her eyes slaked with madness as she smashed her hand into the glass, wielding the gun, loose-armed, making sure they didn't forget she had it.

The noise level fell and fell.

'Right,' Joe heard in his helmet, the pilot's voice clear and measured. 'I'll follow her down. You straight after.'

The pilot turned to Sophie, his hand still in the air, and gave her the thumbs up as the sound of the engines faded away to nothing. Even as she struggled to open the door, he was easing out of his seatbelt, his movements smooth and practised, almost imperceptible, like a magician's sleight of hand. Joe did the same, but his hands shook so hard that he couldn't get a grip on the buckle with his sweaty, bloodstained fingers.

Outside, the car swerved in front of Balan and stopped. Mark Francis got out and the car drove off again. Balan had changed tack, but Mark was after him, arms pumping, knees high in a disciplined sprint. Within seconds he was right behind Balan, who looked confused, unsure of what to do, although he kept moving.

The 'copter's door opened. Sophie was watching the two men run as she swung a leg out. She grappled with the gun, waving it behind her as she climbed from the cockpit and down onto the footrest, which had folded out.

Mark lowered his shoulders. With an explosive burst of speed he ploughed into Balan, so hard that the Romanian buckled at the waist, his torso and arms thrown backwards before both men crashed onto the turf.

Sophie had both feet out, still watchful of the two men behind her in the 'copter. She took a step down, teetered, cast out a hand for support, grabbing the edge of the door. Another step.

The pilot sprang from his seat and went straight after her, head-first, barrelling horizontally out of the door. They both fell, disappearing down to the ground in perfect silence.

Joe scrambled across the pilot's seat and got out as best he could. He saw Balan and Mark in a scrimmage. And the car? It circled around and came to a stop on the runway just ahead of the plane. Gemma got out, bolted over to Balan and Mark, and threw herself on the Romanian's legs.

Joe stood on the ground, his head loose, swirling. Beside him the pilot was kneeling there, holding Sophie in a neck lock. She was sitting on her backside, wailing and thrashing about, legs kicking as she twisted around, unable to break free. A little further off was the gun. It must have been knocked out of her hand when they fell.

Twenty or so yards away Balan was also on the ground, two officers on top of him, struggling to keep hold of his squirming body, a three-way brawl on the grass.

The gun? It was a few paces to his right.

No one noticed him. Two separate struggles, and he wasn't needed in either of them.

He picked it up.

A touch heavier than he'd imagined. Warm. Innocuous.

He felt his fingers close around the handle.

It felt about right.

Balan was face down on the ground, two officers sitting on him, Mark shouting into his ear. The pilot still had Sophie in a neck lock. She was losing strength, flopping about as she struggled, a moan of desperation from deep within her, a haggard strain on her face.

He stood facing her, held the gun up, waited.

She stopped moving. Her expression told him that the gun was still loaded.

'You OK there?' he shouted over his shoulder.

'No cuffs!' Gemma cried. 'Cavalry's on the way, though.'

'Sit on him. Tell him I've got a gun.'

'This one?' the pilot asked, although he seemed quite comfortable keeping hold of her.

Sirens in the distance now.

Joe looked at Sophie.

'Here they come,' he said. 'Piling up from Leeds. That fat bloke you shot? Andy Mills. Two tours of Afghanistan. Bravest man you'll ever meet. My best mate. If he's dead …'

He set his feet a little further apart, raised his other arm, held the Glock with both hands, forcing himself not to shake.

There were tears in his eyes, enough to blur his vision.

'If he's dead …'

# 67

He heard his name. Someone patted his shoulder as they passed. No idea who it was.

There was almost no sound in the ops room. But it was busy. People came and went, walking fast, voices low. A million things to do. Brass were all in the building somewhere or other. NCA too. Comms people were going apeshit, press room downstairs full, reporters desperate for news on Andy.

Everybody was desperate. But there was no news. He was in Jimmy's. Still nothing.

Joe sat at his desk. Looked across at the windows. Dark outside. What time was it? Felt like hours ago. Everything did.

Up in Saxford they'd had to ease the gun from his hand, finger by finger. So many officers there, an armed unit, all crowding around the plane, the helicopter, everywhere. They took the gun, ushered him into a car, then an ambulance. He managed to hold it together. Then, when the doors of the ambulance closed, he vomited. They gave him little cardboard trays. He filled two, three. It went over the back of his hands, down his trousers. Slimy. Stank like rot. The silver sheet he was wrapped in crinkled when he moved. And in his ears the drumming sound of the helicopter wouldn't stop. He asked about Andy. The paramedics didn't know. Just breathe, they kept telling him. Breathe.

There'd been a medical check-up somewhere or other. When was that? Where? Didn't remember. Then back to Elland Road. He'd made a statement. Bare bones. Tennant had done it. Clear, straightforward, no fuss. Take your time, Joe, he'd said. Then a psych assessment. That hadn't gone too well. Like a zombie. He'd done his best. Home and get some rest, they said. Is there someone there for you?

He looked down at his desk. Big mug full of pencils, photo of Sam. The monitor was off. It was like staring into a mirror, but he couldn't see himself.

Gemma approached. No colour in her lips, cheeks.

'They're waiting for you outside, Joe. Shall I go down with you?'

He got up. His legs trembled. Had to lock them at the knee to stop it. Been sitting too long.

Off he went. Silence as he walked, all eyes on him. As he got to the doors someone clapped. Then someone else. Slow, sombre applause. The whole room.

No idea what to do. Didn't want this.

He held up a thumb. Tried to look grateful. Grateful he wasn't dead.


'You found the spare keys?' he said, easing himself into the passenger seat of the Mondeo.

'Copper at the golf club wouldn't let me take it. Had to show him some ID!'

Sam was smiling. Eyes glazed. He'd always been a happy kid.

'Dad? Are you … ah, bollocks!'

He threw himself on Joe, hugging him, pinning him back in his seat.

'It's all right, son. I'm fine. Shaken, that's all.'

Sam pulled himself away, got settled behind the wheel.

'You're in the news again!' he said, half-laughing, half-crying, his whole body jumpy with relief, ignoring the tears that streamed down his face.

'You heard about Andy?' asked Joe.

Sam's smile disappeared.

'He's still in theatre. Bullet's clipped his heart. Some other stuff. Quite a bit of damage.'

'Heart?'

'Bullets can bounce around inside. Incredible, but true.'

Joe was confused.

'Was this on the news?'

'No. That doctor friend of yours? She's keeping me updated. You sent me her number, remember?'

'No. When?'

'Today.'

'Don't remember.'

'Shock'll do that to you. You had anything to eat?'

# 68

He talked non-stop, words pouring out of him unchecked. He hardly heard them, hardly needed to. A lifetime's paternal love spilled onto the table between them like a vein of gold that had been tapped. Out trickled the nuggets, fully formed, one after the other, the kind of warm, glowing truth that normally remains unspoken. Especially by men. By Joe.

He didn't care. Half of it sounded probably like unhinged shit. Pure and honest and not really appropriate for a McDonald's on the ring road, full of teenagers and families stopping off there after a day's shopping. He didn't care, because he knew it would never happen again. He told Sam how deep and debilitating the love for a child can be, but how the delight is greater than anything, that you've given the world a person, someone who can add to the common good, make a difference, who can do something meaningful with their life.

He stopped talking. The table was littered with empty burger cartons and endless ketchup sachets. He didn't recall having eaten, but he must have done. The coffee cups were also empty, a dusting of sugar across the table and little plastic pots of milk everywhere, loads of them.

'I wanted to help her,' he said, his hands flat on the table, as if to hold him steady. 'But the police? It's like the opposite sometimes. We don't help. We just clear up afterwards. I didn't help her.'

'Dad, don't ...'

'Road to Jericho? You stay on that road, Sam, whatever you do. Be the Good Samaritan. Do something good. I can't promise you it'll be worth it. But what's the option? What else is life for?'

And then he was done. He looked around, kids spilling from the tables, hanging on to their parents, everyone noisy and tired and ready for home.

'Mum's coming,' said Sam. 'She managed to get a flight. Getting the last train up from King's Cross.'

'She'll need picking up from the station.'

'I'll do that. She can have the spare room, right?'

Joe nodded.

'Will you drop me off at the hospital?'

'You should be resting.'

'I know. I will.'

Sam didn't argue.

'Come on then, fella.'

# 69

There was a police presence outside Jimmy's, a few uniforms inside the main entrance too. Joe asked one of them to take him up, knowing he'd never find his way through the maze of corridors alone.

Neither of them said a word, all the way to the surgery unit. The silence between them was ghostly, a nervousness in the stomach. Around them the noises of the hospital were amplified, somebody shouting in the distance, doors clattering shut, a sudden burst of laughter.

They got to the waiting room. The young officer turned to Joe, but his eyes were down to the floor.

'Here it is. Well done, Sir.'

'Thanks, I appreciate that,' Joe said as he pushed open the door.

Inside, five vacant faces looked up. Faces with nothing written on them. Not a scrap of emotion.

No one moved.

Rita was sitting in the corner with Gwyn, their heads close. She had a hand on his knee, and Gwyn's face was like a Munch sketch done in greys, a face made of shadows.

The Assistant Chief Constable was there, standing with Simon Tennant over by the window, plus Commander Marie Coleman. But it was Rita who finally got up and came across.

'His heart stopped in the ambulance,' she said. 'They managed to get it going. Stable when he got here. Straight into surgery. They patched him up. But then he had another attack. He's back in now.'

'Latest?'

'It's been touch and go for an hour or two. Last we heard, he's fighting.'

'Oh, he'll fight.'

'Why don't you get off home? I can keep you up to date?'

'Aye, I will. I will.' He gave Gwyn a nod. Got one back. 'Arrests all went OK? Charges coming soon?'

'It's all fine, Joe.'

'Stefan still in the cells?'

'No. He's out. Ruth's offered to take his case. We'll see what we can do for him.'

'Good. That's good. Right. Better speak to the boss. Bosses. Whatever.'

The three senior officers by the window watched as he walked towards them.

'How are you, Joe?' Marie Coleman asked.

'I'm fine, Ma'am.'

'Without these two,' MacDonald said, indicating Joe and Tennant, 'Balan and Sophie Benedict would be somewhere in Europe by now.'

'It was all Joe's doing,' Tennant added.

She nodded.

'Well, you'll be glad to hear that most of Balan's trafficked workers have been taken into protective custody over the course of the afternoon and evening.'

'How many?' Joe asked.

'Just shy of a hundred. One raid still pending.'

Joe imagined the paperwork. It was all he could bring himself to think about now. Some poor buggers'd be on it for months. There'd be meeting after meeting, joint ops, high-ranking egos buzzing around like flies on shit.

'Charges on Balan and the Benedicts are looking rock solid,' MacDonald said. 'The case was impeccably handled. You couldn't have done any more, Joe.'

He nodded. They were still dead, though. Ana and Miriana.

'OK. I just wanted to check on Andy. I'll be getting home now,' he said, wondering how long he'd be out of the room before MacDonald ordered an internal inquiry.

Tennant followed him to the door.

'Joe,' he said, 'this might not be a good time, but that Indian bloke's been ringing all afternoon, wants to speak to you, to thank you personally. You up to it?'

Joe shrugged. 'Why not?'

Tennant dialled and handed him the phone.

Rajvansh's voice was unhurried, well-mannered, courtly. The gratitude was sincere and thoughtful, the words of a man who is accustomed to getting the best of everything, but who knows how to be gracious when he does.

'I hope you managed to get your money back!' Joe said, not knowing what else to say.

'The money was always very safe,' Rajvansh said. 'I have some excellent lawyers in Bucharest. They acted quickly. The bank, too, once they understood the situation.'

'That's good.'

'If there is anything I can do for you,' he said, 'please, don't hesitate to ask.'

A day's interest on two billion? A Maserati? He felt the twist of a smile on his cheeks.

'There is something, actually. The club president, Charles Malthouse? Our fathers knew each other. I wonder if you might reconsider your decision to replace him? He's a very good president, highly respected, the heart of the club, really.'

'I found him a bit old-fashioned.'

'He's traditional, yes. Not always a bad thing.'

A pause.

'Consider it done, Sir.'

'I appreciate that.'

He didn't add 'Sir'. You had to earn that. It wasn't for sale.

Out in the corridor he pushed the palms of his hands into his eyes, then blinked. He fumbled with his phone, found a picture of Ana Dobrescu. He tried to think of something to say to himself, but he had no idea what to feel.

'Oh, hello.'

Jill Wallace emerged from a door with PRIVATE: NO ACCESS on it. She smiled, but her voice belied a sadness. The contrast was striking, almost absurd.

'I've sent a message to your son. The surgery's gone well,' she explained, gesturing towards the door behind her. 'They're closing him up. I just spoke to one of the team. They've got him back.'

'For definite?'

She let the smile fall away. Her expression was still kind, generous.

'As far as anyone can say.'

'You gonna tell that lot in the waiting room?'

'No. That'll come when the lead surgeon's ready.'

'OK, thanks. I'd like to check up on Ben Churchill. Any news?'

'He's going. Slowly.'

'Can I see him?'

'Of course.'

He looked around, sighed. The thought of finding the way to another ward was too much.

'Come on,' she said.

'Are they taking good care of you?'

Churchill stirred. Just the slightest movement of his head, a twitch of the lips.

Joe pulled up a seat, as close as he could.

'I want to tell you that the person who killed Ana has been arrested.'

The news had little effect on Churchill. Yet he appeared to be thinking. His body shifted fractionally.

'Is there anything I can …?' Joe began.

'I'm OK,' he croaked, his eyes hardly open. 'She didn't deserve … not this.'

'She did something good, Ben. Something extraordinary.'

'We found each other,' he whispered.

'You did. And together you made the world a better place. That's how you've left things. Both of you. A better place. Better than you might know. For a lot of people.'

'Where?' he said, his voice losing what little force it had. 'Ana?'

'She'll be buried at the Romanian church in Farnley. There'll be a mass for her. I'll be there. We'll all be there.'

A single tear ran down Churchill's cheek.

'With Ana … next to me …' he began. Joe had to lean close in to hear. 'It wasn't death I feared … it was dying without her … We found each other. Found ourselves. Forever.'

His breathing was shallow, slow.

Joe got his phone, sent Sam a message: Might be late. Switching phone off for a while. Look after Mum.

He placed his hand on top of Churchill's, gave it the faintest of squeezes.

'I'm not going anywhere.'

He slipped the phone into his jacket pocket, settled in his chair, and prepared for a long night.

# Acknowledgements

For expert information and suggestions of various kinds, thanks to Dr Chris Burke, Amalendu Misra, Nazim Wissam, Adrian Tudor, Neil Lancaster, Sam Fuentes and Fernando Domènech. To Avram, Florin and Mihal, thank you all for very valuable and honest conversations about your difficult lives. I also continue to be indebted to the real Joe Romano for lending me his name, although I still won't pay him royalties. Enormous thanks to everyone at HQ, not only for producing such consistently great books, and for promoting them with flair and imagination, but for making writers feel respected and valued throughout the process. In particular, thanks to Jon Appleton for improving the text so much, and above all to my editor Cicely Aspinall for fabulous editorial notes on every draft, full of subtlety, intelligence, and a sharp appreciation of how to improve a text. She also doesn't complain when I beg another few weeks for a quick thirty-seventh read through... I'd also like to express my sincere gratitude to my agent Nicola Barr, for drawing on a seemingly limitless supply of forbearance over the course of what has been quite a challenging book, written in challenging times. People have struggled through the pandemic in a variety of ways, and she faced the added burden of having to struggle through it with me. So, thank you Nicola for everything. Finally, to Susana, Nico and Stef for being a constant source of happiness, pride, pleasure, frustration, anxiety… and everything else that makes life worthwhile.

ONE PLACE. MANY STORIES

Bold, innovative and
empowering publishing.

FOLLOW US ON:

@HQStories